Summoning all of his courage, he asked, "Is it okay if I ask you a few more quick questions?"

The naked overhead bulb shined down on Cecelia, brilliantly illuminating her face.

"Sure, of course," she replied. "Ask anything you like."

"I've only got a few more days left. Do you mind if I come calling on you again?"

She smiled. "I'd like that."

"And do you mind...what I mean is, would you allow me to write to you while I'm away? A large army base is an awfully lonely place."

"Sure, Michael, you can write to me if you like."

And, finally, he voiced what he had been working up to. "And one last question. It's been ages since I kissed a pretty girl. Would you mind if...if I–"

"I wouldn't mind at all," she said, helping him and flashing a smile that would win any man's heart.

It was the sweetest first kiss he had ever experienced, and he knew at that very moment, it was a kiss that he would take back to Nebraska with him–one that would sustain him no matter where this man's army sent him, even if it was to the front lines.

HERE'S WHAT READERS HAVE TO SAY ABOUT GARY SCARPA'S WRITING:

"This was a lovely read with characters who have stayed with me."

"His characters are relatable, their stories indelible, and his references memorable!"

"Loved the historical perspective and the easy flow of dialogue. Worth the read!"

"Thoughtful and well written."

"Amazing, riveting, fast paced, couldn't put it down."

"The author brought the characters to life, feeling as if you knew each one."

"It's a fast paced narrative that draws you in quickly and locks in your attention right until the end."

"A deep and moving novel that also provides several lighthearted laugh-out-loud moments. Highly recommended."

"I took my time reading this engaging novel because I just did not want it to end. This book made me laugh, cry and think of years gone by."

"What made it even more special for me was that I grew up in the area that the book takes place in, but the story could have been set anywhere and would have been just as enjoyable."

"Filled with nostalgia in the form of music and culture, detailed descriptions of people and places, and a thought-provoking story."

WHAT
are the
CHANCES?

A Novel

GARY SCARPA

NEXT
CHAPTER
PRESS

Book cover design by Mario Lampic

Printed in the United States of America
Names: Scarpa, Gary, author
Title: a novel / What are the Chances?
Description: First edition / Next Chapter Press
Identifiers: ISBN: 978-1-7365146-2-7 (print) | ISBN: 978-1-7365146-3-4 (ebook)
Classification: Historical fiction

For more information about books by Gary Scarpa, visit www.garyscarpa.com

For Mom and Dad

---

*L*eaning against a pillar on the outskirts of the dance floor, one loafer-encased foot casually crossed over the other, Michael DeMarco stood, calmly viewing the festivities. There was something deep within him, something introspective, that compelled Michael to hang back–a penchant for observing. It was as if he were a scientist and the world around him merely phenomena to be analyzed. This world, at the moment, was composed of a large gathering of young men and women who were dancing to the melodious sounds of the Glenn Miller Orchestra. Dozens of couples moved in rhythm to the beat of one of the biggest acts in the country, unbelievably here in the little town of Derby. He had been going to dances at the Lakeview Casino Ballroom on the river ever since he was seventeen, and Friday nights were always a welcome escape from the boredom of everyday life. Although he liked dancing, he wasn't a numbers guy. Rather, he fancied himself as being selective. With a contented smile, he strolled toward the bandstand at the far end of the room, watching the many couples dancing, considering which girl he'd like to ask to dance. Near the stage, his focus changed. There stood the famous Glenn Miller, leading eighteen musicians decked out in shiny silver jackets and charcoal gray trousers, their golden horns raised skyward in glorious harmony. How Michael loved music. How he wished he himself possessed some shred of musical talent. Knowing he didn't, he chuckled, sighed, and shook his head.

His best pal, Scooter, approached him. "Hey, Mikey, whattaya hear, whattaya say?"

"I don't hear nothin', and I don't say nothin'," Michael replied, his pat response to Scooter's greeting.

"Mikey, c'mon, man. Yer in a daze. It's 'Tuxedo Junction.' Grab one of these babes and ask her ta dance."

The spell now broken by Scooter's interruption, Michael muttered, "What I wouldn't give to be one of those guys."

"One of the guys dancin'?" Scooter asked.

"No, not them," Michael said, his eyes still focused on the bandstand.

"Who then?"

"The musicians. What I wouldn't give to be one of them."

"Oh, them guys. Well, I got a flash for ya," Scooter said. "You don't play no instruments."

"Yeah, that's for damn sure. And that's only one of my problems. Scooter, just look at the bass player and the drummer. They're flying high right now, man—at an altitude a couple of poor saps like you and me will never reach. I'd give anything to soar with them in their world."

"Well, listen, go take some tuba lessons if ya want, but do it tomorrow. Tonight you should be dancin'."

"Not ready to dance yet. Maybe a little later...but wait! Will ya look at that trombone section? Look at the choreography those guys are doing with their mutes. What a thing of beauty."

"Mikey, yer an oddball if I ever seen one. Didn't nobody ever tell ya that before? Because if not, they shoulda. My opinion is we came here ta dance, so let's–"

Michael placed his palm over Scooter's mouth. "Wait! Shut up and pay attention for once in your pathetic life, will ya?"

As he paused, the trombone section that Michael was so enamored with was now on their feet. A second later, the saxophones stood, followed by the trumpets.

"All that gold, pointing at the heavens! Especially those slides on the trombones, sending a musical telegram directly to God."

"I swear, yer gettin' weirder all the time. Whattaya talkin' about, Mikey?"

"What I'm talking about is that if there's a God, he's listening to this music right now."

"Yer sayin' God is up in Heaven, listenin' to the Glenn Miller Orchestra playin' 'Tuxedo Junction'?"

Michael chuckled. "Yeah sure, Scooter. That's exactly what I'm saying."

The end of "Tuxedo Junction" was greeted by a raucous round of applause from the appreciative dancers.

Glenn Miller, his trombone slung around his wrist like a precious jewel, stepped up to the microphone. "Thank you, music lovers. For our next tune, we've got 'In the Mood'." Then, turning to the band, his voice could be heard counting them in, "A-one, and a-two, and a…"

"Okay, Mikey, ya made me miss 'Tuxedo Junction,' ya ain't makin' me miss 'In the Mood.' Have a good life."

As Scooter disappeared into the crowd, Michael resumed his stroll along the perimeter of the dance floor as if he were window shopping, taking in all of the animated couples. He wasn't quite sure what he was shopping for.

He noticed the number of guys in uniform was growing from week to week, ever since the bombing at Pearl Harbor nine months ago. Back from boot camp or home on leave, the G.I.s seemed to be the main attraction at the weekend dances. Michael felt envious, realizing that girls liked a man in uniform. Why wouldn't they? He himself had been as outraged as anyone by the attack, so what stopped him from signing up? He had learned that G.I. stood for "government issue" and he also knew that lots of guys were using the term sardonically to suggest that they, as soldiers, were being mass-produced. Maybe that was it. *Maybe I don't want to be a mass-produced commodity*, he thought to himself as he scanned the room of khaki, starched uniforms and Navy dress-whites topped with tilted round caps dotting the dance floor.

It was inevitable, though, he knew. If he didn't sign up, he'd be drafted soon enough. Standing at 5'11" and sporting a powerful, v-shaped frame, Michael was as able-bodied as the next guy. He wouldn't be able to hold out much longer, but some magnetic force kept him at home. Some inexplicable inertia. He had been rationalizing that Mom and Pop needed the income that he brought home, but maybe putting off the inevitable wasn't a good idea. Maybe, in fact, joining the military would be an exciting adventure that would take him away from the tedium of his job at the shipping yard, and maybe then his earnings could be his own. So many maybes!

As thoughts of joining the Army washed out of his mind, a soldier spinning a girl across the floor captured his attention. Wearing stockings with crisp vertical seams and bronze heels, she followed her partner perfectly, every movement mirroring the beat and the tempo of the song. A white gardenia contrasted her raven hair like the North Star in the black sky, beckoning and inspiring Michael. His eyes remained fixated on her.

"Mikey, how can ya *still* not be dancin'?" Would Scooter ever give him any peace? "Whatsa matter? Yer not still thinkin' about God listenin' to the band because–"

"No, Scoot, I'm not thinking about that. I have my mind on something else."

Observing the direction of Michael's gaze, Scooter said, "Oh, I think I see what yer thinkin' about. The white gardenia! There's the Mikey I've knowed my whole life."

"Yeah, Scoot. You ever see anything like her?"

"I seen some good lookers in my day, but she's in another class. Go ask her ta dance. Make hay while the sun shines."

"I may do just that."

"Whattaya mean, *may*? Just do it, but ya gotta get in position before some other guy jumps in."

Michael knew Scooter was right. With no time to waste, he moved closer to the girl as "In the Mood" drew to its conclusion.

On the last note, Michael moved in and addressed the G.I. instead of the beautiful girl.

"If you don't mind, soldier, I'd like to have the next dance with the young lady."

As the miffed G.I. withdrew, the girl turned to see Michael's piercing brown eyes and his dark, curly hair.

"May I?" Michael asked.

She smiled. "Yes, you may."

It was Michael's good fortune that the next number was "The Nearness of You," a fox trot.

As the clarinets, accompanied by saxophones and muted brass, began the romantic introduction, Michael placed his right hand firmly on the small of the girl's back and took her right hand in his left. Leading her in a box step, he wasn't surprised at how effortlessly she followed him, having just witnessed her in action.

"And what might your name be?" Michael asked, mustering up as much charm as possible.

"My name might be Cecelia. What might your name be?"

"My name might be Michael," he replied, liking the game they were playing.

"Michael. Nice name," she said. "Well, why don't I call you Michael, and why don't you call me Cecelia, even if those are only what our names *might* be?"

Cecelia's sharp wit wasn't lost on Michael. "Very cute!"

"I try."

With undeniable confidence, she pursed her painted red lips and flashed a flawless white smile at him, and he knew he was a goner.

Suddenly, Michael felt a tap on his shoulder. Glancing to his left, he saw a sailor standing there with a dumb look on his face.

"Mind if I cut in, pal?"

"Yeah, I do mind," Michael replied. "This isn't the senior prom, so get lost."

"Don't worry, sweetie," Cecelia interjected. "I'll dance with you next."

As the sailor backed off, Cecelia remarked, "Wow! You're rather possessive of girls you dance with, aren't you, Michael?"

"Sorry. It's just...just that when I focus on something, I don't like being distracted."

"Well, in case you haven't noticed, Michael, I'm not a something, I'm a *somebody*."

"Yes...yes, you are," he said, welcoming the repartee. "Believe me, it's the first thing I noticed about you. Me, myself? Let's just say I'm *hoping* to be a somebody."

Cecelia smiled and looked directly into his eyes, where she saw intelligence and veracity. Looking back into hers, Michael was hopelessly blinded by her beauty.

When the song ended, the sailor wasted no time in moving in, propelling Michael back into the outer margins of the dance space, once again a spectator. For the rest of the night, he couldn't seem to get near the girl who "might be Cecelia," who danced with an unbroken chain of men, her talent and versatility obvious whether dancing a jitterbug or a rhumba. In each case, she made her partner look good, as Michael knew she had made him look good.

At 10:50, Glenn Miller stood at the microphone and said, "On behalf of the Glenn Miller Orchestra, I want to thank all of you kids from the Lower Naugatuck Valley for a great night. Remember our soldiers fighting in Europe and in the Pacific, and keep dancing, everybody. Now, boys, take your favorite girl in your arms and let's end the night with 'Moonlight Serenade'!"

Realizing he had lost track of time, Michael made a beeline for Cecelia, but before he was within ten feet of her, a lanky G.I. had beaten him to the punch. Sulkily, he retreated and watched her one last time in the evening's waning moments.

When the song ended and the crowd headed for the exits, he lost sight of her.

A sea of people washed him out the door as he heard Scooter's voice. "Ya ready ta go home, Professor?"

"Yeah…I guess so."

"I saw ya dance with that pretty little number once, but you didn't dance again, did ya? What gives, Mikey?"

Sullen, Michael didn't respond to Scooter, nor did he feel like talking as they crossed the road and jumped into Scooter's pickup. Scooter primed the truck, turned the key, and punched the stick shift into first gear before pulling the old heap out of the parking lot and turning onto the Derby Turnpike.

"I don't know if you were payin' attention to me, but I danced all night long. Hardly missed a beat. I fancied one babe the most. She was wearin' a striped dress and saddle shoes. Did ya see the one I mean?"

All but oblivious to Scooter's chatter, Michael sat, staring right through the dusty windshield, his mind on a distant planet.

"Mikey," Scooter repeated, "What are ya, deaf? I asked a question. Did ya see who I'm talkin' about? She got a big gap between her front teeth, but otherwise, she's a cutie, so who cares if she got a gap–and I just kinda…"

"Scooter. Slow down."

"Whattaya mean, slow down, Mikey? Am I talkin' too fast for ya or somethin'?"

"Not your mouth, you knucklehead, slow down the truck…and pull toward the shoulder of the road."

Scooter did as instructed as Michael rolled down his window, cranking the squeaky handle on the door.

"Hey there!" Michael called. "Where might you be walking so late at night?"

Cecelia recognized him right away and smiled. "We *might* be walking home."

"We would offer you a ride, but there's no room except in the bed of my buddy's truck, but it's awful dirty back there. We'd hate to have you ruin those pretty dresses."

"That's fine," Cecelia said. "My mother told me never to take a ride from a stranger."

"But I'm not a stranger, I hope," Michael called out over the rattle of the engine.

Cecelia liked his energetic sincerity. "Well, you're *practically* a stranger."

"Who is this guy?" her sister Connie asked.

"Just some guy I danced with," Cecelia whispered. "Don't worry. Just keep walking."

Michael turned to Scooter. "Listen, Scoot, I'm jumping out. See if you can get the two sidekicks in a conversation while I see if I can get to know more about the white gardenia."

The truck was still moving as he hopped out and slammed the door shut.

"Three girls shouldn't walk alone in the dark," Michael offered. "I'll walk alongside you to keep you safe."

"It's nice to know chivalry isn't dead," said Cecelia, "but, for the record, we can handle ourselves."

"Who are your friends?" Michael asked.

"This is my sister, Connie, and our friend, Connie, who lives with us. Girls, meet Michael."

Michael flashed a charming smile and shook each girl's hand. "What an incredible coincidence. My buddy Scooter's sister's name is Connie too." Then he called, "Hey, Scoot, get a load of this. Meet Connie and Connie. My friend has two Connies. What are the chances?"

As the truck slowly putted alongside the walking group, Scooter followed his orders.

"Holy cow! You two ladies got the same name as my kid sister. Scooter O'Brian at your service—son of Sally and Patrick O'Brian and brother of Constance Colleen O'Brian. Hey, how about you two Connies come duckpin bowling wid me sometime? I'll spot tall Connie ten pins, and I'll spot little Connie twenty."

"I don't need a spot," Cecelia's sister argued. "I could beat you blindfolded."

"Oh, yeah?" Scooter replied. "How much ya wanna bet?"

Connie smirked. "I can tell by looking at this dump truck of yours that you don't have two nickels to rub together."

"Hey, Mikey," Scooter shouted. "The tall one's spunky! Listen, maybe I don't have two nickels ta rub together, but if yer so rich, how come yer walkin'...."

And before he knew it, Michael was almost ten yards ahead of the truck, walking side by side with Cecelia in the luminous glow of the truck's round headlights.

"Will ya look at that, Cecelia? Your sister is arguing with my pal Scooter. I think she's already sweet on him."

"Scooter? Where did he ever get that moniker?" Cecelia asked.

"It's a family nickname. Everyone's called him that since he was a baby, or so he tells me. You know nicknames. They stick."

"Well, my sister isn't going to go sweet on your buddy, I can assure you of that. He's like a character out of a *Dead End Kids* movie," she said with amusement.

"Aw, lay off Scooter."

"It appears to me that he needs elocution lessons."

"Look, Scooter's a good kid! He can't help it if he hasn't had much of an education. The kid had to drop out of school at eleven and go to work to help his family."

"Okay, I'll lay off, but I feel compelled to warn you that if he gets fresh with my sister, she'll give him a good punch in the kisser. Connie's no one to play around with."

"And would you give me a punch in the kisser if I got fresh with you, Cecelia?" Michael asked, a playful smile on his lips.

"No, I wouldn't. But Connie would."

Michael reacted with an amiable laugh. "A tough cookie, that Connie. Well, you'll never have to worry because I'd never get fresh with you. Scout's honor! Let me ask you another question. Do you have other brothers and sisters?"

"Yes, I do. I have three older brothers and, besides Connie, three more older sisters. I'm the baby."

"Wow! If my math is right, your family has three boys and five girls."

"That's right."

"Well, I'll be darned. The same for my family. What are the chances, do you suppose? About a thousand to one?"

"At least," Cecelia answered with a laugh.

"Only, I'm not the baby. I'm fourth in line. My three older sisters were born in Italy. My father came here first, but it took him seven years to earn enough to send for Mom and the girls. They were thirteen, eleven, and eight when they arrived. I was the first one born here, so you know what that makes me?"

"What does that make you, Michael?"

"A true American. The first to be born on American soil."

Cecelia could tell that he was proud of it. "Well congratulations, Michael, true American citizen. Of course, I'm Italian too, and I think one or two of my older brothers were born over there. Being the baby, the two eldest were married before I was even born. A few of my nieces are practically the same age as me."

"That's interesting to hear. Are you from Derby? Because while I was in school, I never saw you."

"Nope. I just started my senior year at Shelton High School. Did you graduate?"

"Sure thing. I'm the only one so far. My older sisters didn't make it past the fifth grade because my parents needed them to work, the Depression and all. They let me go all the way, though. I guess I'm the smart one in the family. Not that I applied myself."

"I'm hoping to graduate too, but it's hard because my family is pretty poor too."

"I know how that is. Where does your father work?"

"He doesn't work. He died...a long time ago. It's one of the reasons we're poor."

"Aw...jeepers, Cecelia. I'm sorry about that, I–"

"You don't need to be sorry. Like I said, it was a long time ago."

"Yeah...well I mean...it must have been rough growing up without a father, especially during these hard times. I'm sorry for asking."

"You couldn't have known."

They continued on wordlessly now, just breathing, gazing at the starry sky, and taking in the silence of the night, if you could call the banter of Scooter and the two Connies silence.

"I don't know why you two Connies won't jump in the truck. There's enough room on the seat for all three of us."

"Thank you, but we are perfectly content walking," Cecelia's sister replied.

"Aw, c'mon! I don't bite!"

But despite the chatter of the others, Michael and Cecelia now experienced a mutual, personal silence, borne out of attraction and awkwardness and melancholy. He took a deep breath and gazed upwards, studying the countless stars in the late September sky twinkling above the placid surface of the river, not fifty yards to their right as they walked.

Cecelia finally spoke. "It was a heart attack."

Puzzled, Michael asked, "What was?"

"Papa. He died of a heart attack."

Cecelia surprised herself in sharing this detail, and Michael wasn't sure how to reply.

"He had a fish wagon. He pedaled fresh fish."

"A fish wagon...pedaled fish," Michael echoed pensively.

"Yes. If he had lived, Papa would have sent me to college. That's not possible now, though."

"But how would your father have paid for college from pedaling fish?"

Michael immediately regretted having allowed his skepticism to get the better of him.

"Because he would have! He wasn't like most greenhorns who come here from Italy." Her use of the word *greenhorn*, her bluntness, took Michael by surprise, but he liked her passion and her spark. "My father was kind and generous and modern thinking. He took Connie and me to carnivals and even bought us cotton candy and let us ride the merry-go-round. And pedaling fish wasn't the only way he earned income. Besides our house, he owned a three-family house with tenants. I know he would have made it possible for me to go to college if, well, if things worked out differently."

Cecelia's emotion was palpable, and Michael's gut told him to shut up and not question her again. As they approached the intersection of Main and Bridge Street, the two fell back again into silence, accompanied by the rambling give-and-take of Scooter's conversation with the two Connies.

As they reached the corner, Cecelia spoke. "Thank you for walking with me, Michael. It was a gallant gesture!"

"I'm happy to walk you across the bridge right to your doorstep," Michael replied.

"We'll be fine the rest of the way. I'm always safe with my sister at my side."

"It was swell talking to you, Cecelia. Might I ask your last name and your address?"

"You *might* ask," Cecelia replied with a wink, "but my dear old mother told me never to give my name and address to strangers."

"You're not playing very fair," Michael complained, his prominent eyebrows raised plaintively.

"Sometimes the game of life isn't very fair, unfortunately," Cecelia said with a playful grin. "But who knows? Maybe one day we'll be more than strangers. Only time will tell."

The two Connies now caught up to them, and Michael stood on the corner as the three walked across the bridge and over the Housatonic River, which separated the two neighboring towns. Transfixed, he couldn't take his eyes off the backs of the trio as their image grew smaller and smaller in the distance and finally disappeared at the other end of the bridge.

Finally, he was startled by the loud honk of the truck's horn. "Mikey, for Christ's sake, c'mon. Let's go! Didn't nobody ever tell ya how odd you are?"

2

Cecelia – 1932

*T*he impact of their little feet causes the two girls to keep redrawing the grid in the dirt with a twig from the peach tree, but they don't mind. Despite the usual challenge of not having a concrete surface, they persevere, tossing the gray stone into the next square and hopping on one foot across the grid.

Spotting the milk wagon, Cecelia leaps out of her square and lands on both feet before running to greet the milkman. Stella follows in hot pursuit.

"Hello, Mr. DeAngelis!" Cecelia calls out excitedly.

"Ah, my little-a principessa," Mr. DeAngelis replies. "You gawna take-a the milk-a bottles to you mama for Mr. DeAngelis?"

"We sure are. Right, Stella?"

"Right, we sure are," Stella echoes.

"That's-a good-a girls."

The old mare pulling his cart neighs as DeAngelis removes four cold glass bottles from the ice-box compartment of his wagon, wipes the dripping condensation from the bottles with a towel, and hands Cecelia and Stella two bottles each.

"Now don't-a drop them or you gawna make a big-a mess, and then you no have-a no milk-a to drink," he admonishes, wiping his hands on his long apron.

As if she hasn't heard this admonishment, Cecelia announces proudly, "My birthday was last Sunday, Mr. DeAngelis!"

"No keeding. How old a-you now?"

"Seven years old!"

"Ah! Nice! Buon compleanno, Cecelia! Where's-a you papa?"

"He's down in the back yard digging a well with my brother, Dominic. Hey, Mr. DeAngelis, guess what! I bet you can't guess. My sister Phyllis is getting married in two weeks."

"Si, you papa tol-a me. Phyllis, she a nice-a girl. I hope-a she has a happy life. Okay, basta. Mr. DeAngelis has-a the milk-a to deliver. Lotsa customers. Tell-a you papa I say hello."

"Okay, bye, Mr. DeAngelis! C'mon, Stella."

The girls run up the steps with their cargo and burst through the screen door.

"Mama...Mama...here's the milk from Mr. DeAngelis!" Cecelia hollers.

No sooner have the girls returned from the house to resume their game of hopscotch when eighteen-year-old Dominic comes sprinting around the side of the house.

"Mama...Mama...somebody! Papa...it's Papa! He...he...he just collapsed. Get a doctor. Somebody, run for a doctor, quick! Mama! Help!"

Mama appears at the door. "Cecelia," she calls, "Va a prendere un dottore! Subito!"

As Mama moves through the house to the back door, Cecelia runs down Hillside Avenue, en route to Howe Avenue with Stella close at her heels. By the time the girls arrive at Doctor Manzi's office, by the time he is able to decipher their excited gibberish, and by the time he is able to drive to the house, it is too late. Gennaro Alberino has suffered a massive coronary at the age of sixty-one while digging a well.

The next morning, Cecelia stands at the foot of the bed while her sister Valentina helps her get dressed.

"Why are you pinning a black ribbon around my neck?" Cecelia asks.

"Because black is the color we wear at funerals," Valentina

replies.

At fourteen years old, Valentina has many responsibilities, not the least of which is taking care of the two younger girls, Cecelia and Connie.

"Why don't I have a black dress like you?" Cecelia asks.

"Because this dark green one is the only good dress you own. It's going to have to be good enough. Mama can't afford to buy you a black dress, and even if she could, there's no time. So, a black ribbon will have to do."

"But why black?"

Cecelia's unending questions make Valentina feel impatient. "I don't know, Celia. It's just the color of mourning. Death is sad, and black is a sad color."

"Oh, I think I understand," says Cecelia, but she isn't sure she does.

"Is Connie going to wear a black ribbon too? She doesn't have a black dress either. She only has a blue one."

"Yes, Cecelia, she is."

"Where did you get a black dress?"

"I bought it! That's where I got it. I have a job."

"Is your job the reason you don't go to school anymore?"

"That's right."

"Are you happy that you don't go to school?"

"No, Celia, school is much nicer than work is." Valentina ties the cloth sash in a bow around Cecelia's waist, perhaps a little more tightly than she needs to. "Now, stop asking so many questions. We need to go downstairs. You're going to see Papa in the living room in the casket. You understand that he died?" Cecelia solemnly nods. "It'll make us feel sad seeing him like that...but try not to ask any questions. Try not to say anything, please."

It is already 10:00, and a line of neighbors stand outside the door on the sparse front lawn. Their dusty shoes have erased the hopscotch grid.

The Alberinos' neighborhood is a little different from some inhabited by immigrants, where it seems Italians have created their own small insulated communities. Hillside Avenue has a more eclectic combination of ethnicities, not only Italians, but Ukrainians, Poles, Czechs, and more.

Valentina leads the way down the narrow stairs as Connie and Cecelia timidly follow. When Cecelia enters the living room, the first thing she sees is the simple wooden casket in the middle of the room. She sees her father in the coffin, as though asleep, in a brown suit with a white shirt and bow tie, his complexion a pale contrast to his dark handlebar mustache and hair.

Mama, Robert, and Ernie are seated on the couch; Dominic, Phyllis, and Betty sit in kitchen chairs. Astute, Cecelia realizes her siblings are seated according to age next to Mama. Three empty chairs await Valentina, Connie, and her. It makes Cecelia sad to see Mama crying.

Valentina leads her by the hand to the casket, and Connie follows. Valentina whispers to both of them, "Kneel down, close your eyes, and say a prayer, girls."

All three kneel on the threadbare area rug before the casket. Cecelia can hear her own breathing. She shuts her eyes so tightly that they almost hurt, and in her mind she says, *Dear God...Dear God...Dear God...*

Opening her eyes, she tugs on the hem of Valentina's dress and whispers, "I don't know what to pray."

"Say the Hail Mary."

Cecelia nods and closes her eyes again. *Hail Mary, full of grace, the Lord is with thee, blessed art thou among women, and blessed is the fruit of thy womb, Jesus. Holy Mary, mother of God, pray for us sinners now and at the hour of our death, Amen.*

When she opens her eyes, she gazes once more upon her father's face. His lips look purple and too tightly shut. Cecelia looks back down at the floor.

Valentina takes Cecelia by the hand and the three take their places. Cecelia's feet don't touch the floor and her legs, two spindles, begin swinging back and forth. Valentina reaches across Connie and squeezes Cecelia's thigh in an effort to settle her down.

The line of people enters, grim and silent, each one stopping at the casket to offer a prayer and then making their way, in order, to offer each family member their condolences.

Thinking about the Hail Mary, little Cecelia wonders, *Why didn't Mary pray for Papa as he was digging the well and as his heart was about to stop? And if she did pray for him, why did he die anyway?*

People gaze down at her, their eyes filled with pity. Neighbor after neighbor takes her dainty hands in theirs, attempting to offer comfort. "We're so sorry about-a you papa"..."It's very sad to lose your papa"..."Your papa, he was a good man." Cecelia feels uncomfortable, and, not knowing how to respond, she just smiles at each neighbor. Many have tears in their eyes, and some murmur in languages she doesn't understand. Others offer a doleful shake of their heads and look at her without uttering a word, but Cecelia doesn't understand.

After two hours, only Stella's parents and her decrepit babusya who lives with her remain, offering their regrets in Ukrainian.

The entire family then squeezes into Robert's and Ernie's cars and heads to St. Joseph's Church for the funeral Mass. The cars follow a shiny black hearse, which looks like an enclosed truck to Cecelia, down Hillside Avenue and onto Howe Avenue en route to the brick church on Coram.

The Mass seems just like every Sunday Mass except, of course, for the coffin sitting in the middle of the aisle, and Cecelia has never experienced sitting in the very first pew of the church. She had once asked Papa why they always sat so far back. "It's a-becawz the front-a pews are reserved-a for people who give-a the most-a money to the church," he replied. She realizes that the richest donors aren't at her father's funeral.

She listens closely when the priest delivers a brief homily and explains that her papa is now in heaven because he has been baptized in the Holy Ghost. Cecelia has heard of hell in Catechism class with its burning fire, and she feels relieved to hear that Papa isn't going there.

At the cemetery, she notices that neither she nor her three brothers shed any tears. The three young men stand stoically next to their mother, three sentinels towering over her. Cecelia wonders why she's not crying like all of the girls. When it is time for the casket to be lowered into the ground, Cecelia is startled when Mama wraps her arms around the flower-laden box and embraces it as if she is hugging Papa himself. Feeling pain in her heart, she watches Mama's body heave in spasms as she sobs. She sees Robert and Ernie gently peel Mama's hands from the casket and lead her back to the car. Unable to look at Mama's pain, Cecelia closes her eyes and imagines it beginning to snow. In her mind, peaceful white flakes cascade down on the gravesite, covering the coffin, the grass, the trees–until Mama and all the crying people in their black dresses and suits, until everything and everyone is covered in a soft mantle of whiteness.

Later that night, once all the food brought by the neighbors has been eaten or put in the icebox and after everyone has departed, the Alberinos can rest at last. With Phyllis' impending marriage, it is the last summer that the five sisters will share the small second bedroom at the top of the stairs. The attic serves as Dominic's bedroom where he sleeps on an old army cot under the naked rafters.

It is late, and the girls' bedroom is uncharacteristically quiet, like a convent dormitory after vespers. Phyllis and Betty, who share one of the twin beds, are already asleep. Cecelia changes into her cream colored, cotton nightgown and climbs into the other twin bed between Valentina and Connie as she does every night. It has been a long and confusing day, and she feels sleepy. She lays still in the dark room, listening to the mournful sound of the chirping crickets. Finally, their pulsing rhythm lulls her to sleep.

She isn't sure how long she has been asleep when she hears Valentina's tired voice.

"What is it, Mama?" Valentina asks. "Is everything alright?"

"Si," her mother answers. "Valentina, dammi la bambina."

In a state of half-sleep, she feels Valentina cradle her in her two arms and hand her to Mama. Then Mama carries her into the darkness of her room and lays her down on the soft bed. Mama wraps her arms around Cecelia and begins to hum the melody of an ancient lullaby. No words. Just a soothing humming. Cecelia opens her sleepy eyes and sees Mama's tear-stained face very close to hers. With her index fingers and thumbs, Cecelia wipes away droplets of tears from her mother's eyes and cheeks and wipes her moist fingers on the sleeve of her nightgown, repeating the process several more times. Then, in the safety of Mama's arms and the warmth of her song, Cecelia drifts back off to sleep.

3

*W*ithout saying a word, the girls walked across the bridge. As they side-eyed each other, Cecelia knew they were all holding it in, almost like playing that game where you inhale and see who can hold their breath the longest. As soon as they passed over the crest of the convex bridge, they broke out into a flurry of laughs.

Cecelia shoved the two Connies and shushed them. "Stop it, God dammit! He'll hear us."

"Oh, get lost, you worry wart. We're too far away–he can't even see us," her sister said.

"That horse laugh of yours can be heard in Timbuktu, Connie," Cecelia complained, which only made little Connie shriek with more laughter.

For the remaining fifteen minutes of their walk home, the two girls teased the life out of Cecelia, asking what the boy with the curly hair and the muscular build said and what Cecelia said back.

"Did he ask you where you live?" her sister asked.

"Did he ask you on a date?" little Connie added.

"Yes and no," Cecelia replied. "He did ask what my last name was, *and* he also asked me where I live, but I took the fifth on both."

"Awww," little Connie moaned. "Party pooper."

"Besides, boys like a challenge. A hint of intrigue. I'm sure I haven't seen or heard the last of him."

"But how about that guy, Scooter, or whatever his name is?" little Connie said. "What a corker!"

The two Connies imitated Scooter's fractured speech and then howled.

"Please don't be unkind, girls," Cecelia scolded. "He can't help it if he isn't educated. Michael told me Scooter had to drop out of school years ago."

"So did our sisters and brothers, and for that matter, so did I," her sister argued, "but we don't talk like thugs."

"I'll say it again. Don't be unkind." After five seconds of contrite silence, all three helplessly broke into laughter again.

Arriving home, they found Mama sitting in her cushioned rocker, reading her Italian Bible. No matter how late they stayed out, Mama never retired until she knew that they were home safe and sound. Before the girls knew it, Mama was serving them milk and buttered toast at the kitchen table. That was Mama—always feeding them. It was one of the million and one things Cecelia loved about her.

Within seconds of sitting down in the kitchen, Cecelia kicked off her heels, and the two Connies followed suit.

"Oh my God," she said. "My feet are killing me."

"Mine too," her sister said.

"Walking all that way in heels is sheer torture," little Connie giggled.

Cecelia, massaging her right foot, added, "The things we do for fashion."

Of course, the two Connies couldn't wait to tell Mama about the handsome stranger who walked Cecelia home and about his hilarious sidekick.

With a devilish grin, Connie, her bare feet on the edge of her chair and her arms wrapped around her knees, did what she did after every Friday night dance.

"Mama, I don't know about you, but I don't think it's very seemly for Cecelia to be kissing boys she hardly even knows." Not that Mama knew the word *seemly*, but she got the gist of it.

"Stop it, you!" Cecelia warned. "Mama, I did *not* kiss anyone. A boy I danced with walked me to the bridge. He was a perfect gentleman the entire time."

"Don't believe her, Mama!"

"You stop it, you b-i-t-c-h! That's my final warning," Cecelia vehemently whispered, as if she could, in fact, do anything about it, considering Connie had beaten up just about every boy in the neighborhood while they were growing up. Cecelia knew she was no match for her sister, and Connie knew it better.

Finally, their friend came to the rescue through her laughter and tears. "No, Cecelia is telling the truth, Mrs. Alberino. She didn't kiss anyone tonight. At least I didn't see her kiss anyone."

Connie Radecki had been living with the Alberino family for almost a year now. When her mother cried to Mama that little Connie's father was a mean drunk and that he was abusive, Mama took poor Connie in. Unable to bear to see a stray cat out in the cold, Mama's door was always open to those in need. Connie was the third hard luck case that Mama had provided food and shelter for since Papa had died.

Persisting, Cecelia's sister said, "Just because you didn't see her kiss anyone, Connie, doesn't mean that she didn't. Cecelia is often hiding behind a column kissing one boy or another."

"C-o-o-o-nnie-e-e!" Cecelia shouted.

Of course, her dismay caused the two girls to nearly fall out of their chairs.

Mama just kept nodding her head before muttering, "Ridi? Ma queste sono cose che dovrebbero farti piangere."

"Wait…wait," little Connie said. "What did she say? What did she say?"

Through tears, Connie translated. "She said, 'Laugh? These are things you should cry about'!"

To Cecelia's horror, the two Connies exploded into an even greater clap of thunderous hysterics.

Then Mama waved a threatening hand at Cecelia. "You-a better not-a kiss-a the boys, or I gawna give-a you a good-a *schiaffo!*"

Knowing Mama had never hit her, even Cecelia couldn't resist laughing now.

"Hmph…Smetti di ridere!"

"Okay, Mama, I'll stop!"

Mama's command of the English language was less than perfect, to say the least. When the two sisters were little ones, they had learned to converse in Italian, but as Connie and Cecelia grew into their teen years, they now spoke in English to Mama, while she responded mostly in Italian. Mama understood that they wanted to be American girls now, and Cecelia knew her Italian was getting more and more rusty with each passing year.

"But Mama, didn't you kiss Papa before you met him?" Cecelia asked.

Mama just smirked and shook her head in the negative.

"But how did you know if you loved him if you didn't kiss him?"

"Baciarlo? Nemmeno l'ho conosciuto," she said with another smirk.

"What do you mean you didn't even know him?" Connie asked in stunned surprise. "How could you marry someone you didn't even know?"

"Becawz-a...becawz-a...my papa tell-a me to."

At that moment, Cecelia realized her parents must have had an arranged marriage. What she also understood was that somehow her parents had grown to love each other even though they married hardly knowing each other. Over the years, they had conceived and given birth to eight children. *No,* she thought to herself, *more than eight because there were also several miscarriages.* And the image of Mama hugging Papa's coffin and weeping was imprinted in her memory. If that wasn't love, Cecelia felt there was no such thing.

As the clock in the parlor struck 12:30, the girls realized it was time to go to sleep. They were all exhausted. The two Connies retired to the bedroom they shared, and Cecelia slipped into a nightgown and climbed into bed with Mama. She wasn't sure how it was that, at seventeen, she was still sleeping with her mother, but ever since the day of her father's funeral, that's the way it was.

As she rested beneath the crocheted afghan which had warmed her for as long as she could recall, Cecelia thought of her life as having two chapters–the chapter before Papa's death and the chapter after. Lying there, she contemplated what life might have been like if Papa had lived.

Mama lay down next to her and rubbed her shoulder as Cecelia's eyelids grew heavy. Then, as had been the case for more than ten years, Cecelia heard Mama's soft voice humming the ancient lullaby.

As Cecelia reached the precipice of sleep, Mama whispered, "Ragazzina?"

"Yes, Mama?" she mumbled in a sleepy whisper.

"Non baciare i ragazzi, figlia mia."

"Uh-huh, ok, Mama...I won't kiss them," she murmured as she drifted off to the sound of Mama's soothing song.

The morning after the dance, Michael headed over to his sister Lucia's house. The two had a standing lunch date every Saturday. If he stayed home, Michael knew he'd be stuck doing chores for Mom and Pop. Mom could sure be a tyrant. It was bad enough turning over his entire paycheck to her with nothing to show but a modest allowance for his labor, but Michael didn't want to spend Saturdays and Sundays working around the house.

Anyway, he had exciting news to share with his big sister. Calling her his big sister was ironic since she was not an inch taller than five feet.

He hoped his brother-in-law, Marcello, would be at home. Marcello sometimes worked on Saturdays. Not at a regular job like most people, but at one or another of the many handyman jobs he took on. Marcello had become connected with a few rich Derbyites, like Mrs. Barber, the owner of the department store on Main Street, and he took care of their yards or whatever needed fixing.

Marcello (everyone called him *Buzz* because he also kept bees, jarring the best honey Michael had ever tasted) had created a life for himself where he seemed a little freer than most poor suckers. Michael saw him as a true individualist and admired him for it.

Pulling off of the Derby Turnpike, Michael arrived at their small bungalow on the outskirts of town. He had recently bought a 1933 Ford Coupe from Scooter's uncle for thirty-five bucks. The junker had lost its sheen, and flaky orange body rot decorated the bottom of the car on the inside rims of the fenders and underneath the doors. It wasn't much of a car, but it drove. Usually. It was working out fine, anyway, because Buzz was teaching Michael how to work on the engine.

He found Buzz tinkering around a slightly used truck that he'd purchased a week before.

Hopping out of the car, he said, "Hi. What are you up to?"

"What am I up to? I'm up to exactly what it looks like I'm up to."

Buzz grinned at Michael and then went back to work. With a flat screwdriver and a small ball peen hammer, he pried the chrome Dodge insignia off the back of the truck.

Puzzled, Michael asked, "Why're you doing that?"

"I'm doing that," Buzz grunted, "because you can bet your ass that Dodge doesn't pay me to advertise their vehicles."

"I see what you mean," Michael said.

Buzz looked right through him. "Do you?"

When the silver insignia fell at his feet, Buzz attacked the insignia on the hood of the engine.

"Lucia inside?"

"Where the hell else would she be?" The second insignia popped and fell on the pavement.

"Right. There's something I want to tell her. I'll see ya in a bit."

"Maybe."

Buzz isn't going to win any personality contests, Michael thought, but he liked how direct he always was. Michael pondered, *Prying the insignias off his truck...there's only one Buzz!*

Michael didn't knock but just walked in. That's how it was with the DeMarcos. Michael didn't remember anyone ever agreeing on it—walking in without knocking was just kind of an unspoken rule.

He found Lucia in the kitchen. Where else? She was either going to be in the kitchen or the garden. On tiptoes, he snuck up behind her.

"Hey, Lu," he said, wrapping her compact torso up in a generous embrace.

She placed her hands over Michael's and said, "Ooh, Michael, you startled me. I was wonderin' if you were comin'."

She sat Michael down at her kitchen table and made him a delicious sandwich, salami and gabagool with roasted red peppers on the best Italian bread on earth, a product of her own baking. To top it off, she drizzled just the right amount of olive oil over the top and added a hot stuffed pepper that would be too much for most mere mortals.

"So, I have something important to tell you," Michael said, his teeth ripping into the sandwich. "I met a girl last night."

"You meet lotsa girls," Lucia replied.

His mouth now full, he continued. "No...but this one's different. She's Italian like us, and there are eight kids in her family too, just like us. And I don't even know how to describe her, Lu. She's...she's just swell."

"What's her name?" Lucia asked.

He chewed faster and tried to swallow before continuing.

"Slow down," his sister said.

"Damn, this is good. I was starved. Yeah...that's the problem. I only know her first name. It's Cecelia. Nice name, right? She's a good kid and a real beauty to boot. An angel from Heaven above, believe me. And, jeepers, can she dance!"

"But can she cook?"

"Well, she's Italian, so she must be able to cook, right?"

"That's not always true, Michael. Some young girls today are useless in the kitchen. It's a sin!"

"Anyway, I'm going to figure out who she is and where she lives. I've just got to, Lu."

Lucia let a skeptical laugh escape. "It sounds like you're gettin' carried away."

"I know. I am getting carried away. Isn't that amazing? But she's worth it."

At that moment, Buzz entered the kitchen, his big hand clasping a stack of Dodge insignias.

"Did Michael tell you he's sweet on a new girl?" Lucia asked.

Buzz plopped himself in a kitchen chair. "No, he didn't say a word about it. He's afraid I'll say somethin' he don't wanna hear."

"I'm not afraid," Michael protested. "Say anything you like. I can take it."

"Tell me about her then," Buzz challenged.

"Well...let's see. She's got a gorgeous smile and just about the prettiest face I've ever seen. Uhm, she's got beautiful dark hair, and she wore a white flower, a gardenia, in it. Just incredible. And I was just telling Lucia that she's a great dancer–"

"And that's all ya can say about her?" Buzz said, unimpressed.

"Well, I...I only just met her last night."

"Don't be so defensive. I'm just teasin' ya, that's all. But here's a little wisdom for ya. Just make sure she's the one before getting yourself in too deep. You know what I mean by *the one*, right?"

Michael felt confused.

"I mean she's gotta be your friend first. And she's gotta be someone who's in your corner no matter what. And I mean no matter what. Capice?"

As he drove home after lunch, it hit Michael that Buzz was always full of pearls of wisdom. The problem was that Michael didn't exactly know how he was going to find out if she would be in his corner "no matter what," not even knowing her last name or address. What he did know was that he had found her immensely attractive. He also knew they had plenty in common, and that was a good thing.

Ten minutes after leaving Lucia and Buzz, Michael motored into downtown Shelton, wondering if he might see her walking on Howe Avenue. *It's a long shot*, he thought, *but a guy can hope*!

4

Cecelia – 1938

*T*he walk to Lafayette School is a short, downhill trip. The two girls live, after all, only across Howe Avenue and up the hill. On this last day of their years at Lafayette School, the two best friends make their way down steep Hillside Avenue, a short distance along Howe, and then across and onto Grove Street where the brick school building stands solidly waiting for them as it has for eight years.

Both Cecelia and Stella are brimming with mixed emotions–a nostalgia for their grade school years coupled with an anticipation of their high school future which lies ahead, just two and a half months away.

"Can you believe it, Celia? When September gets here, we'll be high school freshmen."

Cecelia just shrugs and shakes her head. "Heavens, no. It seems like yesterday we were in first grade."

"Gosh, it's crazy, isn't it? I'm scared of going to high school, aren't you?"

"I'm looking forward to it. I'm going to study hard and try to go to college like Papa always told me I would. I don't know how it'll happen because Mama certainly doesn't have any money to pay for it, but I'm hoping for the best, anyway."

"My mother obviously can't afford college either," Stella replies. "I'm just going to take the business course and try to become a secretary. Like the principal said last week when he came to talk to our class. They teach you how to type and take shorthand and file and all that kind of stuff. A secretary is a good job."

"I suppose." Cecelia just looks ahead, a dreamy expression on her face. "I just want to be an English teacher. To read and talk about novels and poetry with students would be, I don't know—just perfect."

With a laugh, Stella says, "If you become a teacher, you're not going to be able to get married. You'll end up an old maid like Miss Collins or Miss Ott."

"Not all teachers are old maids, Stella," Cecelia replies with a smirk. "Teachers not being able to marry is becoming an antiquated custom. Think about our sixth grade teacher, Mrs. Oglethorpe—young, married, and pretty. Times are changing."

"Don't forget, smarty pants, when Mrs. Oglethorpe got married, it was the talk of the town."

"I suppose," Cecelia reluctantly concedes.

"Name another."

"Another what?"

"Another married female teacher."

"Well, she can't be the only one," Cecelia pouts. "And since Mrs. Oglethorpe is married, it mustn't be a rule that teachers being married is forbidden, so there. And besides, don't forget that Mr. Larson is married too. If a male teacher can get married, so can a female teacher."

"Have it your way," Stella says.

Being the last day of school, the day is more fun and games than anything else. Their eighth grade teacher, Mr. Larson, begins the morning with a spelling bee, "just for the fun of it," he says. Stella is eliminated early on the word *schism*, but Cecelia remains standing; she and Dorothea Willoughby are the final two left. The contest goes back and forth between the two girls for the better part of a half hour before Cecelia is eliminated on the word *vacillate*, which she unfortunately spells: *vascillate*. Dorothea gets the win when she correctly spells the word, *ubiquitous*. Dorothea comes from the most well-to-do family in the neighborhood, and Cecelia has harbored jealousy in her heart against her ever since they started school.

Mr. Larson then informs the class that, before lunch, they will read an abridged version of a new play by Thornton Wilder, *Our Town*, in which he will assign parts and then have the students act out the play. Cecelia is assigned the role of Emily Webb, and Stella suppresses a giggle when Mr. Larson tells her she will be playing Emily's mother, Mrs. Webb.

In his most dignified voice, Mr. Larson gives the students a little background about the play—how it had played in New York on Broadway, winning the Pulitzer Prize for Drama.

Cecelia feels he almost sounds like he is British, and while he isn't English, he speaks with perfect diction and elocution. She imagines speaking with the same polish as Mr. Larson.

Continuing, Mr. Larson explains, "The Stage Manager is a kind of narrator who both begins and ends the play. He coordinates it throughout all three acts, dwelling both within the setting, Grover's Corners, and yet transcending it, at one moment, acting as a resident of the town, and at the next moment, breaking 'the fourth wall,' addressing his remarks directly to the audience."

The class feels a tad confused as he further clarifies, "Because of the complexity of this particular role, I feel it is best if I play the Stage Manager."

The students nod to each other, indicating that they agree that their teacher is the man for the job.

"It will help you appreciate the play more," he adds, "if you will imagine Grover's Corners to be our own town of Shelton."

Cecelia and Stella both have major crushes on Mr. Larson. All the girls do. At thirty-two years old, he is tall with broad shoulders and hair and eyebrows the color of wheat. He has a strong, handsome face, and he wears wire-rimmed spectacles which, when he stands close to a student, magnify eyes that are as blue as the summer sky.

In Cecelia's mind, Mr. Larson's acting is unparalleled, even compared to the occasional movies she has seen. She finds herself remembering the middle of the year when they had read *Romeo and*

Juliet, and she and Mr. Larson had played the star-crossed lovers. Even though in that case, they simply read the play from their seats, she could feel her heart pounding when they read scenes together, despite the fact that he is an adult and a married man. But sometimes a girl can't help having the feelings she has.

As mid-morning journeys dramatically toward noon, the eager students and their teacher bring the various characters of Grover's Corners to life, leading up to the marriage of Emily and George and then, eventually, to Emily's untimely death as a young married woman.

When Emily, as a disembodied spirit, asks the Stage Manager to visit Grover's Corners one more time, Cecelia can hardly contain her tears as she realizes an important theme of the play–that human beings don't enjoy the simple beauty of life as it's happening to them.

With raw emotion in her voice, Cecelia delivers Emily's final monologue as she takes one last glimpse at her beloved Grover's Corners: "Wait! One more look. Goodbye, goodbye, world. Goodbye, Grover's Corners. Mama and Papa. Goodbye to clocks ticking. And Mama's sunflowers. And food and coffee. And new-ironed dresses and hot baths. And sleeping and waking up. Oh, earth, you're too wonderful for anybody to realize you."

When she asks Emily's last burning question of the omniscient narrator, a single tear streams down Cecelia's cheek.

"Do any human beings ever realize life while they live it?–every, every minute?"

With compassion and sensitivity, Mr. Larson's eyes meet Cecelia's as he replies: "No. The saints and poets, maybe they do some."

As the play reaches its conclusion, Mr. Larson as the Stage Manager delivers the last lines of the play. "Eleven o'clock in Grover's Corners. Everyone's resting in Grover's Corners. Tomorrow's going to be another day. You get a good night's rest too."

After a moment's pause, the eighth graders erupt into a heartfelt round of applause. Mr. Larson takes a humble bow from the waist and motions the other actors to do so as well. Cecelia and Stella hesitate, smile at each other, and then each bows from the waist the way their teacher had. Lost in the moment, Cecelia can't remember ever feeling happier.

At lunch, the two friends unwrap the wax paper from the sandwiches they had brought in brown paper bags from home.

"You were incredible," Stella gushes. "You could be a movie star."

"Get out," Cecelia replies, biting into her salami and provolone sandwich.

"I kid you not. You really could."

"And how could I? You have to go to Hollywood to act in films."

"Well, maybe you could go to New York first and act in plays. Don't forget what Mr. Larson said about the play. About how it played on Broadway."

"Oh sure, Stella. You bet. I'll just move to New York and star in Broadway plays."

Taking a sip of milk, Stella argues, "Why not? Besides your acting, with your singing voice, you could star in musicals as well."

Although flattered, Cecelia has grown up to be a pragmatist. "I don't know about you, Stell, but I'm not prone to invest in pipe dreams. It's not my style."

After lunch, the entire student body assembles in the gymnasium for an awards ceremony. The students sit according to grades, with the first graders in the front rows to the eighth graders in the back so that all students can see the festivities. To begin, the students stand to sing "My Country, 'Tis of Thee" and to recite the Pledge of Allegiance. Then the distinguished, white-haired principal, Miss Whitworth, approaches the podium where she addresses the eighth graders, her resonant voice filling the vast space.

"As we wish you success and good fortune in the next phase of your education, we know you will represent Lafayette School well at Shelton High School. What a wonderful group you've been. We send you off with pride in our hearts, and we hope, next year, you will come by and visit us. Remember, your school day will end an hour before ours!"

Her comment elicits a warm wave of laughter from the back rows.

"And now, boys and girls, I turn the program over to Mr. Larson, who will announce the award winners. When your name is called, please approach the stage, where I will present you with a certificate for your achievement."

Mr. Larson, now at the podium, begins: "Mr. Walter Daigle for the highest average in mathematics; Miss Jane Pawlowski for the highest average in social studies; Miss Dorothea Willoughby for the highest average in language arts and, again Miss Dorothea Willoughby for the highest average in science; Miss Susan Jaroszewski for the best work in art; Mr. David D'Ambroso wins the physical fitness award, and once again, Miss Dorothea Willoughby for the most likely to succeed."

The packed gymnasium resounds with applause as each student receives an award. From the first to the seventh grade, all of the students anticipate the day when, just maybe, their name will be called.

Although it seems all of the awards have been given, Mr. Larson speaks once more. "Boys and girls, we have a new award today. We are calling it the Creative Writing Award. It isn't often that we have a talented writer here at Lafayette. Before I announce the recipient of the award, I'd like to read one of her many fine poems to you:

On a wintry day in old England,
While snow is beginning to fall,
Trudge two hapless children together
A boy and his sister, quite small."

Realizing it is her poem, Cecelia feels her face begin to warm, her cheeks as hot as the cast-iron stove in the Alberino kitchen. Mr. Larson continues:

"While lamplighters snuff out the gas flames,
They hear the dogs guarding the mill,
Alone in the world these two orphans,
She feels the hunger while he feels the chill.

He whispers, 'Don't worry, my sister,'
She looks up with fear in her heart,
They walk on together in silence,
Their wish is to ne'er be apart.

Not a morsel of food for these children,
Not a kind word nor nary a smile.
Their parents now taken by sickness,
Alone in their heartbreak, alone in their trial.

The Londoners scurry right past them,
Ignoring their ill-fated plight.
They wander all day in exhaustion,
As, by and by, day turns to night.

Her brother, for her, is a fortress,
To his sister, he feels entwined.
His goal is to love and protect her,
In a world rendered cold and unkind.

Dark night falls once more on the city,
They plod through the black streets afraid.
Two children with no one to turn to,
Lost and alone and betrayed.

On a corner illumined by street lamps.
Church steps now come into view.
The boy says, 'Come, sis, let me help you,
Let me help you, my dear little Sue.'

In weakness they climb the stone staircase,
Traipsing through tall drifts of snow.
They hear the steeple bell tolling,
Their movement is labored and slow.

Two orphans alone in a city.
On church steps, in snow icy and deep.
Two orphans alone and uncared for.
On church steps, forever asleep."

Upon hearing her name, Cecelia walks down the center aisle to the applause of her fellow students, feeling dizzy and unsteady on her feet. She and Mr. Larson smile at one another as the principal hands her a gold embossed certificate with her name and the words, *The Creative Writing Award*, in a shiny black type font.

When the school day reaches its conclusion at 3:00, Mr. Larson conveys his best wishes once again right before the bell rings.

At the sound of the bell, he calls to Cecelia, "May I speak to you for a moment, Miss Alberino?"

Stella leaves to wait out in the hall while Cecelia approaches her beloved teacher.

"You know I'm very proud of you," he offers.

"Yes, thank you, Mr. Larson. I feel so honored."

"You have a gift with words, and not only words, but also with rhyme scheme and meter."

Blushing, Cecelia replies, "Thank you, sir."

"I've noticed your poems are always about death, though."

"Yes, sir. I have a little joke with Stella and with my sisters."

"Oh?"

"I always say, 'no one gets out of one of my poems alive.' "

Mr. Larson feels the ironic humor of the remark but suppresses his laughter.

"You lost your father when you were very young, isn't that correct, Miss Alberino?"

Cecelia somberly replies, "Yes, sir."

"I've been thinking a lot about this. I believe you are a young person who feels very deeply, and I have something for you."

Opening his drawer, Mr. Larson takes out a leather-bound book with a small matching strap that closes around the front, adorned with a tiny gold lock and key.

"It's a diary," Mr. Larson continues.

Almost speechless, Cecelia whispers, "Yes, I...I know."

"I think it would be a good place for you to store all of those feelings that you have bottled up inside of you. Write in it every night–thoughts, feelings, poems, stories, anything you like–then just lock it. Let it become a private place you can escape to."

Cecelia, again fighting back tears, smiles and says. "Thank you, sir. It's the most beautiful thing I have ever seen. I shall treasure it."

"I'm happy you like it, Cecelia. We will miss you!"

That night, Cecelia lays in bed while Mama washes some dishes downstairs. Unlocking the diary, she begins her first entry:

June 14, 1938

Dear Diary,

> *Today was the most wonderful day of my life. It was the last day of eighth grade, and I almost won a spelling bee, I got to play a beautiful girl in a play called Our Town, and I received a Creative Writing award. I was given an official certificate and everything.*
>
> *In one week, Diary, I will turn thirteen years old. I am a young woman now, and I have a great many hopes and dreams. You have no idea. I'm going to tell you each and every one of them, but no one else may ever know. The words I write to you will be my biggest secrets, but for my eyes only, Diary, and yours, just the two of us...*

5

*T*he sun was streaming through the edges of the window shades, causing Cecelia to squint as she opened her eyes. Mama was already out of bed, no doubt preparing breakfast. Lazily, Cecelia stole a few precious moments to think about the week ahead. It seemed like things were always changing. Valentina had married a few years before at twenty-one, which left Connie and her. Well, and Connie Radecki. There were also the times when Cecelia's sister Betty was mad at her husband and would come live at home for a day or a week before going back to him. Betty, now pregnant with her second child, had suggested that she might be moving in with her husband and their three-year-old son again (it wouldn't be the first time). Cecelia couldn't imagine where everybody would sleep.

Life never got any simpler. A lot more was being expected of her now—more household chores, some of which, at the moment, she tried to block out of her mind. And there was the expectation that she would get a part-time job. Connie had dropped out of school after her sophomore year to work at the Sponge Rubber plant downtown, along with Valentina and Betty. It seemed like everyone worked there. She found the idea of factory work revolting, but what else was she to do? Even though Cecelia had begun her senior year, she lay beneath the bed linens, ruminating about school. *What's the point of staying in school, anyway? There's no future in it. Not for me.* What a life. If her older sisters were any indication, there weren't any options besides dropping out of school, toiling away in a factory, and then marrying, which was something Cecelia couldn't even imagine.

An hour later, the three girls soaked up a hearty breakfast of eggs and toast, "birds in the nest," that Mama had fried up in the heavy black skillet, and then needed to bathe. Since it was Saturday, they decided to indulge in more than a sponge bath with the old ceramic pitcher and basin. The two Connies dragged the oval tub from the pantry into the small kitchen as Cecelia began lugging buckets of water from the pump outside. Some of the water would be heated up in the big kettle on the stove in order to make the bath at least tepid. Little Connie draped a bedsheet from one wall to the other in order to give each bather a modicum of privacy.

"I have first dibs," Cecelia called out.

"The hell you do," Connie argued. "There's no dibs here. We'll do it fair and square. We'll draw straws. Well, spaghetti. I'll get some."

Little Connie chimed in, "You two can draw since it's your house. I volunteer to go last."

"Unacceptable," said Connie. "You're like one of the family, and besides, you've gone last three times in a row now. Fair and square from now on."

Cecelia hated how fair her sister always was. Connie emerged from the pantry with three lengths of dry spaghetti sticking out of her hand.

"Whoever draws the longest piece goes first. Whoever draws the shortest goes last. You first, Connie."

"No really. I'll go last."

"You first, I said," Connie ordered.

Little Connie drew a short strand.

Connie frowned. "Now you, princess."

Cecelia drew a longer piece. Little Connie shrugged weakly, as if to say, "I told you so."

"Now me," Connie said. She opened her palm, grimacing as she revealed the middle piece.

"Ha-ha," Cecelia jibed. "I told you I was going first!"

Unable to hide her annoyance, Connie said, "Well, that takes the cake."

Cecelia speedily disappeared behind the sheet, removed her nightgown and stepped into the lukewarm water, which reached to her lower calves. She then leaned over, soaped up a washcloth, and started by scrubbing her shoulders and arms.

"Don't take all day," Connie complained from the other side of the sheet. "The water'll get cold."

"It's practically cold already."

"Then snap it up!"

Once all three girls were bathed and wrapped in their towels, they washed and rinsed each other's hair, using the pitcher and basin.

"Are we ever going to have indoor plumbing?" Cecelia whined.

"You *are* a princess, aren't you? We can't afford it," Connie replied.

"We're probably the only family in Shelton that doesn't have it," Cecelia said.

"You know that's not true."

Little Connie offered, "My parents don't have indoor plumbing. My father is always too drunk to work. How would they afford it?"

"Speaking of plumbing," Connie said. "You've been procrastinating, Cecelia, about painting the bacous. You promised Mama you would, and it needs to get done before the winter."

"Yuck! I know. I know, I know, I know!"

Disgruntled, she helped little Connie lift the big basin and dump it over the grass outside the back door.

Cecelia found it depressing to even have a bacous, never mind to have to paint it. And it was no small task either. It would need to be painted inside and out.

"Get going on it. There better be some paint slapped on the bacous when I get home from work on Monday," Connie ordered.

"Oh, for the love of Christ! Stop using that word. I hate it! You sound like a goddamn greenhorn."

"I know that's what you call it, but where does the word even come from?" little Connie asked.

"It's bastardized Italian," Cecelia practically shouted, exaggerating the pronunciation, "Bac-HOWZ–like back house–the toilet shack in the back yard!"

It's bad enough we have to use the damn thing, Cecelia thought to herself, *but why can't we call it an "outhouse" or a "privy" like normal people?* Sometimes she wished she wasn't Italian.

She knew her bossy sister was right. Since she didn't have a job, she needed to do her part at home, and she had been shirking her responsibilities. But how she hated it, especially having to leave her warm bed on chilly mornings to use it. And sharing bath water was so uncouth. She was sick of being poor. Was it asking too much to be able to afford the clothing styles, the movies, and the music she loved? And an indoor bathroom to boot?

She decided to take Monday off from school to get the odious job done. *For God's sake,* she thought, *I'm not going to do it after school when all the kids in the neighborhood will see me and make fun of me.*

She had to make do with a couple of partial cans of paint that her brother Ernie gave her. She was embarrassed to have to lug the cans across town from Ernie's house. Cecelia hated scraping the old peeled paint off the planks, and she especially loathed having to paint the fetid interior of the shack. While slapping on the paint, she closed her nasal passages and breathed through her mouth.

Before the school day ended on Monday, Cecelia packed up the paint supplies lest the neighborhood kids see what she was doing. Monday turned into Tuesday and Tuesday into Wednesday before she finished. A combination of daydreaming, singing songs, and writing in her diary prolonged the culmination of the task. Although Mama watched her from the kitchen window, she didn't say a word. Mama knew it was a struggle for Cecelia, and being a gentle soul, she left her youngest alone.

When Cecelia walked into her homeroom class that Thursday morning at 7:30, her teacher, Mrs. Burke, informed her that the principal wanted to see her.

"You've missed three consecutive days of school, Miss Alberino," Mr. Cox said. "Were you ill?"

"No, I wasn't ill," Cecelia replied flatly.

"Well then, I'm curious to hear your story. What is your excuse, pray tell?"

Cecelia felt her throat constrict. Mortified, she sat in silence.

"Miss Alberino, perhaps you didn't hear my question. I expect an answer."

Cecelia stoically looked down at her saddle shoes, maintaining her silence.

"I am going to ask you one more time, Miss Alberino. If you don't answer me, I'm afraid I'm going to have to give you a week's detention."

Giving Mr. Cox a stone cold glare, she said, "Thank you very much, sir, but that won't be necessary. I've decided to quit school."

Puzzled, Mr. Cox leaned back in his chair and squinted. "I don't think that's a very wise choice. You're a senior and so close to graduation. Why would you do that?"

"I have to, Mr. Cox. My mother needs me to go to work."

The principal's voice grew softer and somehow more sympathetic. "But, Miss Alberino, I'm very troubled to hear this. You have such potential. I sincerely urge you to stay in school and complete your education."

Cecelia stood up. "I don't see any point in doing that, Mr. Cox. Thank you for your time, but I need to be going now."

Without another word, Cecelia marched herself out of the Main Office and pushed through the double doors of the building onto Hill Street. Involuntarily trotting now, she headed downtown, rushed across Howe Avenue, and then toward the Star Pin Factory on Canal Street where her brother Dominic worked. She needed to talk to him.

Arriving on the factory floor, she headed straight for his machine.

"What're you doing here, sis?" Dominic asked. "You know you ain't supposed to be here."

"I need to talk to you, Dom!"

"Whattaya talkin' about—ya need to talk to me? Can't ya see I'm workin'? And, besides, why ain't you in school? It ain't even 8:00 yet."

"I know. That's why I need to talk to you."

Dominic could hear the emotion in her voice. Befuddled, he shook his head, flicked off the big red switch on his machine, and headed along the shiny varnished wooden floor, approaching a man who appeared to be his supervisor.

As Cecelia listened to the machine stammer and chug to a stop, she felt guilty for bothering Dominic. The thing was, though, that not only was Dominic accessible to her, he was also the least authoritative of her brothers. He was uncomplicated and understanding.

He walked back to where she was waiting and waved a dirty, calloused hand at her. She followed him as he trotted down the cement stairway and through an exit that led outside.

"Alright, what is it, sis? I only got five minutes, so let's have it."

"Gimme a cigarette, okay, Dom?"

"Look, I ain't givin' you a cigarette. Yer just a kid. And I hope ya didn't make me ask my boss to take a break, which, by the way, I ain't supposed to be takin', to bum a cigarette off me."

"C'mon," Cecelia begged. "Just one, Dom. I could sure use a cigarette right now."

"Celia, don't get me mad. How many times have I tol' ya that I don't like gettin' mad at you? I ain't givin' you a cigarette, and that's that! Now what is it?"

"Well…" Cecelia began tentatively. "I need a job. Do you think you can get me a job here at the Star Pin? Because I really need one."

"Whattaya talkin' about? Ya can't go to school and work in a factory. Yer smart enough to know that. Speaking of, lemme ask again. Why ain't you in school, Celia?"

"Yeah, well, see, that's just the thing…" Cecelia could feel a tremor in her voice.

"That's just *what* thing?"

"It's just that I…I just quit school. I told Mr. Cox I'm not coming back."

"What? You did wha…why would you do that? Yer the smart one, sis! You read books and write poetry. You could be somebody, don't you see that? You could be an English teacher or a writer or somethin'. Don't you under–"

Cecelia's hardened shell cracked. "No I can't, Dom," she yelled. "I can't be a teacher or a writer! I can't…"

Tears began running down the sides of her face, this way and that, in crooked, wet streams.

"Whattaya mean, ya can't? Didn't Papa always tell ya that

someday you was gonna–"

"Don't say that to me," she shouted angrily. "Don't you dare tell me what Papa always told me. And don't tell me I can be a some-body when all I am is a big nobody!"

Dominic looked over both of his shoulders, afraid that someone might have heard the outburst. The two stood in silence as Cecelia wiped away the wet tears with the soft palms of her hands.

Finally, Dominic broke the silence. "But why, Celia? Why?"

She shrugged and then spoke in an almost inaudible volume. "Why? Because we don't have the money to send me to college, that's why, and because we have a bacous and I have to paint it, and because I feel so…just so humiliated…and because I need to go to work, just like everybody else. That's why."

Dominic couldn't think. He hated seeing her so emotional.

Attempting to collect herself, Cecelia continued, "Just see if you can get me a job here, okay, Dom? Because I'm not tellin' Mama about this until I have a job…so I need one fast, okay?"

"Okay."

Cecelia left Dominic outside the big factory door, scratching his head. Heading back to Howe Avenue, she couldn't recall the last time she had cried like this. She was grateful, upon arriving home, to find that Mama wasn't there. *She must be visiting a neighbor,* Cecelia thought. She would have pretended not to be feeling well if it had been otherwise. In the noiseless house, the only sound to be heard was the creaking of the stairs as she made her way to the bedroom. Picking up the diary, her solace in such an uncertain world, Cecelia flopped on her bed, opened the volume, and began to write:

September 21, 1942

Dear Diary,

    Today, I mourn the death of dreams. Today, the wings of hope took flight, and I am rendered heartbroken. Today, I dwell in a desolate place, despondent and alone with my thoughts. We are, after all, alone in this cruel world, aren't we, Diary? If only Papa hadn't died; if only he had lived. Let me give you the unhappy details, though. It all began when I was called from homeroom this morning by the principal…

6

Michael – 1930

*I*t is a bitter January morning. Frigid air seeps through the drafty windows of the school building; crumbs of rotting caulk lie on the sill. The overworked cast-iron coal furnace in the building's basement sputters and spits in its inefficiency.

Michael, bored as usual, whispers to Jimmy Polaski, distracting him from copying his times tables.

"Do I see you whispering to your neighbor, Mr. DeMarco?" his teacher asks.

Startled, Michael looks up. "Yes, Miss McVay."

Miss McVay is very strict. Her dour expression suggests perpetual anger to Michael.

"Come to the front of the room this minute," the stern teacher commands.

She seems extraordinarily tall to Michael as he surveys her thin, sinewy body.

"Palms facing the floor," she orders.

Miss McVay picks up a yardstick and, in view of the entire class, delivers six swift, sharp blows against the knuckles of his small hands. Hot tears begin to roll down Michael's cheeks, but he isn't sure if they are the result of the sting or the embarrassment of being made an example of in front of his classmates.

"Do you suppose you'll be whispering again anytime soon, Mr. DeMarco?"

Breathing through his nose, Michaels stares down at the floor and shakes his head.

"I didn't hear you. *Do you suppose you'll be whispering anytime soon?*"

"No, ma'am," he mutters, knowing fully well that he isn't being truthful.

Michael's young heart burns with an overwhelming sense of resentment for Miss McVay.

Setting the yardstick back down on the blackboard's dusty white ledge, the teacher sits at her desk and takes pen and paper in hand. Michael, eyes still cast downward at his scuffed shoes, hears the scratchy sound of the fountain pen as Miss McVay scrawls her note. Then, folding the cream-colored stationery in two severe creases, she tucks it into an envelope which she licks, seals, and hands to Michael.

"This probably won't do any good because you people will never learn to behave, but bring this note back tomorrow signed by your mother or you will receive twice the number of raps with the yardstick."

Michael understands that by *you people*, she means Italians.

Leaving the school building at the end of the day, Michael spots the group of fourth graders lined up against the stone wall, their lips twisted in sardonic smiles. He knows what's in store. It's been going on since the beginning of the school year.

"Hey, everybody, here comes Michael, the *wop*," one yells. Another echoes the slur–then, down the line, one after the other mocks him.

But on this day, as usual, Michael can't contain himself. "I'm not a wop!" he yells back, understanding the invective is somehow related to his being Italian. "I'm an American!"

The chubby leader jumps off the wall and motions for the group to follow. Michael counts five of them. The boys encircle him and then begin pushing him back and forth from one to the other in a cruel little game of their own invention.

"Okay...even worse! An American wop! The biggest wop on Smith Street."

"Wop, wop, wop, wop, wop..." the boys yell as they push Michael back and forth, tossing him like a ball around the circle. The thin soles of his shoes slide on the icy pavement, causing him to slip and fall over and over again. In the process, his textbooks and the teacher's note are scattered onto the snow-covered pavement.

When the bullies finally release him, bored with their own cruelty, Michael grabs his books and the dirty wet envelope and scurries home.

Waiting until an hour before dinner to give the notepaper a chance to dry, he finally hands the note to his mother.

Her face is lined with a deep level of concern, and she pushes the note back into his hands and commands, "Leggilo!"

Michael knows that his mother can't read English. She barely reads Italian, for that matter. He begins to read the script slowly since it is challenging to translate the written English into her Italian dialect:

"Salute, Signora DeMarco,"
(Dear Mrs. DeMarco,)
"Il comportamento inaccettabile di Michael a scuola mi ha indotto a disciplinarlo oggi."
(Michael's unacceptable behavior at school caused me to discipline him today.)
"È facilmente distratto e non si concentra molto."
(He is easily distractible and completely unfocused.)
"Mi aspetto che i miei studenti prestino attenzione in ogni momento."
(I expect my students to pay attention at all times.)
"Ulteriori comportamenti negativi da parte sua saranno affrontati con una disciplina più severa."
(Further bad behavior on his part will be met with harsher discipline.)
"Cordiali saluti,"
(Sincerely,)
Miss Susan A. McVay

Upon hearing the final words: "Cordiali saluti, Miss Susan A. McVay," Michael's mother frowns and then, amidst a torrential storm of energy, unleashes a barrage of short slaps to Michael's shoulders and raps to the back of his head, admonishing him in a stream of Italian dialect that Michael himself can barely understand.

After being sent to his room for the remainder of the afternoon, Michael buries his face in his pillow and contemplates the events of the day. He hates the way his teacher disciplined him and despises being bullied even more. It is a way of being treated that Michael knows, innately, he will never get used to. A way of being treated that causes resentment to boil inside of him. He makes a decision that, from then on, he will act, in all ways, like an American, even down to the smallest detail, like how he addresses his parents. They will no longer be *Mama* and *Papa*, but rather *Mom* and *Pop*. That'll be a start.

At dinnertime, Michael notices that his white bowl is piled high with spaghetti and broccoli, cooked in oil and garlic, a favorite meal.

Everyone is eating and speaking in Italian–the older sisters at one end gabbing about their workday at the local factories, and the younger ones at the other end blabbering about school and friends.

A man of few words, Pop sits at the end of the table, chewing slowly and sipping his homemade wine, the tall water tumbler filled with purple liquid. Michael knows that Pop sacrifices by working long hours at the factory. In fact, a year earlier, Pop had sacrificed half a finger to a machine when he lost his concentration at work.

Michael is cognizant that his mother's concerned eyes are on him as she sits, not touching the meager portion of food in her shallow bowl.

"Mom," he says, "take some of my food. It's too much."

She blinks at being addressed in this new way and then replies, "Va bene. Non ho fame."

Michael shrugs, not understanding why his mother would say she isn't hungry when she had worked in the gardens all day.

After dinner, he sees that it is Lucia's turn to wash the dishes, and he lingers nearby and helps wipe them with a dishtowel.

"Lu, can I ask you a question?"

"Sure, honey. Anything you like."

"What does *wop* mean?"

"Who called you that?"

"Some boys. Fourth graders. Every day now for weeks."

"It means 'without papers,' " she answers.

"What kind of papers?"

"Oh, I don't know. Official papers. It means that you're in this country illegally."

"But I'm not here illegally, am I?"

"No, honey, you were born here. I told you before. Anyone born here is American. Don' listen to boys who say that word."

The two siblings continue washing and drying the dishes in silence until Michael asks, "Can I ask another question, Lu?"

"A' course."

"Why are we so poor?"

"Because a' the Depression."

"I've heard of that before, but what does it mean?"

"I don't know, Michael. We were already poor, but the Stock Market crashed las' year, and now it's worse."

"But why?" If nothing else, he is persistent.

"Like I'm tryin' to say. We don' understand the Stock Market. It's just hard to find jobs—even Papa. And the bosses don' wanna pay us too much."

This isn't the first time Michael has noticed that she pronounces the consonants at the ends of her words in a lazy way, the slightest trace of a lingering accent.

"Do you think Mom works too hard in the gardens, Lu? All she does is work, from sunrise to sundown. And then she hardly even eats!"

"She gotta, honey. It's our food. She wantsa make sure we all eat. But why are you callin' her *Mom* instead of *Mama*?"

"Because *Mom* sounds more American."

As always, Lucia understands and continues. "Yeah, so we all pitch in to try to make ends meet. Tha's how we do."

"Is that why you and Vincenza and Josie quit school so young?"

"Yeah, Michael, tha's right," Lucia answers. "Mama and Papa didn't have too much school in Italy neither. Hardly any. They were just poor peasants, so they don' believe in education. You know what I mean? They don' understand that it's important in America."

"Will I have to quit school soon?"

"I don't know. Maybe. We'll see."

"But I don't wanna quit," he says. "I like school, even though I got hit with the yardstick today."

Lucia smiles sadly. "Yeah, Mama tol' me. Then you try to behave and listen good to your teacher, okay?"

"I'll try," Michael says.

When they are finished, Michael goes to his room and lies on his bed. He remembers being a toddler and watching Mom work like a man to help Pop clear the land behind their house, cutting down trees and leveling the hillside into a half dozen terraces where they would grow vegetables and fruit to sustain the family through the hardest of times. Michael can picture Mom holding a chisel steadily on boulders as his father swung a sledgehammer, splitting the mammoth silver and white rocks with a loud clang into manageable pieces to be moved by his three older sisters and stacked into neat stone walls separating one terrace from another. Mom's stoic expression, her eyes focused on the iron chisel, trusted that Pop wouldn't miss his target, and he never did.

Michael's thoughts shift back to the classroom and he hears the slap of the yardstick–back to the street and he feels the taunting insults of the bullies. In this ocean of resentment, he understands that the only people he can count on are his family, especially his mother. Mom is his role model; she is his rock. An observant child, he can see, plain as day, that she puts her family and children first– that she has sacrificed for her family time and time again.

At this moment, Michael makes another decision. He will do his best to never again give his mother reason to hit him. The teacher hitting him is one thing, but he knows his mother hitting him means that he has disappointed her. He'll try harder to behave in school, and when he falters, he'll do anything to hide it from her, even forge her signature if necessary.

For the rest of his life, Michael will see his mother as the strongest person he has ever known. To him, she is a towering giant, but a good giant who takes care of the little people around her. He knows that he is one of those little people. He also knows that he won't always be little.

7

*W*ith the weekend come and gone, Michael was preoccupied with thoughts of the lovely girl he had met as he labored at his latest job at the Farrell-Birmingham plant in Ansonia. Loading trucks with boxes of metal gears to be delivered to Navy ship yards wasn't his idea of a dream job. The crates were cumbersome and heavy, and the work was an exercise in regimented tedium.

It was the third lousy job he had taken since graduating high school. The first was working on an assembly line at the American Brass Company where Pop worked, repeating the same ho-hum maneuver eight hours a day. He couldn't stand it, and Pop was disappointed when Michael told him so. The second was laying down asphalt on public roadways, a job he also loathed.

And now this–loading trailer trucks. He hated menial labor and big-mouthed, two-bit foremen. He detested taking orders.

This job was no better than the others, but work was hard to come by, and he needed to be employed in order to pull his weight in the family. What he wanted to do with his future, Michael didn't quite know, nor did he feel he had many options.

As the day began, he and his crew hauled heavy boxes from the factory's loading dock, then walked up the metal ramp into the trailer and loaded them efficiently, making economical use of space. The trailer had two ramps, one for entering and one for exiting. The crew moved up and down in a single-file line, allowing proper distance for an efficient routine. To Michael, it felt like being on a chain gang.

On this day, at least, he had the distraction of picturing the beautiful, witty girl with the gardenia in her hair.

Doyle, the foreman, stalked the line of men and barked orders. "Let's move it, losers. We ain't payin' yous to dog it, that's for fuckin' sure."

Momentarily distracted from his daydream, Michael thought to himself, *I hate that asshole.*

Doyle, in his button down cap, ragged flannel shirt, and baggy overalls, was a sloppy looking sight. Unshaven and overweight, he had an inflated concept of his station in life. *He probably only makes five or ten cents more an hour than we do,* Michael mused, *and for the measly thirty cents an hour that I'm making, it doesn't seem worth it to put up with the jerk.*

But Doyle's hounding, like a needle on a scratched record, continued relentlessly.

"I said, move it, ya deadbeats. This ain't a country club. Move it, I said, goddammit!"

"How about that guy?" Kowalski muttered to Michael as they passed each other on the ramp. "Who the hell does he think he is?"

"Damned if I know," Michael replied.

At noon, Michael took his lunch in the corner of the factory yard, preferring solitude over the small talk of his fellow workers. Eating his sandwich and gulping down mouthfuls of steaming black coffee from his thermos, he planned and plotted how he would learn Cecelia's last name and address. *I need to think like a private detective,* he mused.

He lit a cigarette, one of the few things that gave him any relief. Inhaling the first drag, Michael felt a hungry ache deep in his belly. He wondered why a classy girl like Cecelia would ever choose him, a guy stuck in a job he despised, a job without a future. Somehow he knew a better life awaited him, but he just couldn't figure out how the hell to make it happen. It was a puzzle that he just didn't know how to put together. And what did he get for all of his hard work, anyway? All he had to show for a full week of work was the lousy three dollars Mom let him keep after he turned his sealed pay envelope over to her each Friday. With resentment in his heart, he knew she sent a portion of his earnings to her relatives in the old country. *I don't even know them. Where in hell do they get off benefiting from my hard work?* he often thought to himself.

Three lousy bucks didn't go far when it came to his own entertainment and spending money. Christ, he couldn't even afford to take a girl out on a decent date. It would have been swell to have invited Cecelia and the two Connies for a nice *abeetz* at River Restaurant, but he couldn't afford it.

His gut told him that he would be better off in the military. He still couldn't put his finger on what made him hesitate when others had joined. But if he signed up, he could bust out of this crummy, small town and meet new people and have new experiences. Maybe they'd train him in something useful. And if he ended up on the front lines and got his head blown off, wasn't that better than putting up with the likes of a shithead like Doyle? On the other hand, if he joined, how would he solve the mystery of Cecelia?

Lost in thought, Michael puffed on his cigarette, not realizing that he had gone over the allotted fifteen minute lunch time. Doyle's bluster roused Michael from his daydreaming.

"What the fuck, DeMarco? Don't you know that the lunch break is fuckin' over, ya lazy sonofabitch?"

Michael squinted at Doyle with contempt, screwed the aluminum cap back onto his thermos, and pulled himself up to his feet. Struggling to control his temper, he headed in the direction of the loading dock to resume his work.

"The boss shoulda knowed better than to hire a lazy, fuckin' wop like you!"

Wop! The sound of the word grabbed Michael by the collar and changed his direction. In the flash of an eye, he stood nose to nose with Doyle, the toes of Michael's shoes not three inches from Doyle's shoes, Michael's face not an inch from Doyle's.

"What did you just say to me?"

"You heard me," Doyle growled.

"Yeah, I heard all right. But I wanna hear it again. Go ahead. Let me hear it again!" Michael's volume was low but calculated and menacing.

"You hard a' hearin'? I said, the boss shoulda knowed better than

WHAT ARE THE CHANCES?

to hire a lazy, fuckin' wop like you." Doyle took his meaty hands and gave Michael an unexpected shove, sending Michael reeling onto his backside.

Like a cat, Michael sprung back to his feet in an instant, ready to attack. Grabbing Doyle by the shirt, he came around with a wild right-handed roundhouse that Doyle barely managed to block with both forearms. Michael followed with a hard left, hammering the side of the foreman's head, and then, in a flash, right back with his right fist, viciously pummeling Doyle between the eyes. The bludgeoned foreman went down hard, blood squirting from his nose. Before Doyle knew it, Michael's hard knee was pinned against his chest and his fist cocked next to Doyle's head.

"Go on!" Michael yelled. "Lemme hear it one more time. Please! Give me a reason to put you out of your fuckin' misery for good!"

Doyle cried out like a small child. "Somebody get this animal off me! D'yas hear? Get 'im off me or I'll fire the whole fuckin' lot of ya!"

Michael felt two pairs of hands grab his arms and pull him up to his feet. Blinded by the attack, Doyle clumsily dragged himself to his knees. "Yer fired! I should call the cops on you, you piece of shit. I should have 'em lock ya up, I tell ya! You're fired!"

Then, shaking himself free, Michael replied in muted, measured tones, "Fuck you, asshole. I quit!"

Making a beeline for his car, Michael tore out of the parking lot with a jarring squeal. The back tires of the Ford sprayed gravel as he floored the accelerator. Weaving in and out of traffic, Michael couldn't halt the tears that spilled from the corners of his eyes.

Lost, his mind was spinning in a tempestuous storm of thought. *What have I done? How will I explain this to Mom?* He had no idea what to do or where to go. The old Ford seemed to be driving itself now. Moments later, he found himself in front of a building he had passed numerous times before, a building he had been avoiding. Shifting the car into neutral, he turned off the key, pulled hard on the emergency brake lever, and rubbed the tears on the sleeves of his denim shirt.

Michael DeMarco stepped out of the car, wiped his nose, and looked up at the red, white, and blue painted sign over the door: U.S. Army Recruiting Station.

he next Friday, Michael decided he would drive to the dance at the Lakeview Casino on the river. Scooter had driven that beat up old truck of his the week before, and Michael regretted not being able to offer Cecelia and the two Connies a ride because it didn't have a back seat. Michael wasn't about to make the same mistake twice.

Pulling to the curb, he gave the horn two good honks. Scooter came dashing out of his house, his shirttails flying and his sleeves unbuttoned. *The guy is never ready for anything,* Michael pondered, *but he knows he better come running when I beep or I'll leave him the hell behind.*

Michael hated picking on the guy, though, considering their history together, having grown up in the old neighborhood. And even though he wasn't Italian, Scooter O'Brian never acted towards Michael the way many of the Irish he'd known. Who the hell the Irish thought they were, Michael had no idea, because their people immigrated to this country just the same as the Italians did, except that maybe many of them had come a decade or two earlier. In the case of the O'Brians, Michael felt they were just as nice to him as if he were one of the family.

Scooter jumped in the car and said, "Whattaya hear, whattaya say?"

"I don't hear nothin', and I don't say nothin'," Michael shot back with a chuckle.

If anything, Scooter was predictable. "Whattaya hear, whattaya say?" was how Scooter greeted everyone, which Michael knew he had picked up from a favorite movie, *Angels with Dirty Faces*.

"Don't you ever get tired of that expression?"

"What expression? 'Whattaya hear, whattaya say?' That one?"

"Yeah, that one."

"Why would I get tired of it? It's from our favorite movie."

"Yeah, but–"

"And our favorite actor was the lead character."

"True, but–"

"Don't tell me you don't like Cagney no more!"

"Stop interrupting me, for Christ's sake!" Michael yelled. "All I'm trying to say is we saw that movie four years ago. What were we? Maybe tenth graders?"

"You were in tenth grade," Scooter replied. "I quit school a long time before and went ta work on the docks, remember?"

"Of course I remember. What I mean is, we saw it years ago, back when it played in the movie theaters."

"What's the point? You don' like me sayin' it or somethin'?"

"No, it doesn't bother me. I'm just wondering if you're ever going to come up with something new."

"Why would I come up wid somethin' new? Rocky Sullivan said it all the time, and I loved Cagney as Rocky Sullivan. That's what. If somethin' works for me, I stick to it!"

"Hooray for you! I got bad news for you, pal. Rocky Sullivan ended up getting fried in the electric chair at the end of that movie, so a lotta good saying it did him."

Scooter shot a wounded look at Michael. "Are you tryin' ta say that I'm gonna end up gettin' electrocutionized?"

"Okay, let's change the subject, Scoot. I've got some news for you. Guess what I did this week."

"I'm lousy at guessin'."

"Okay, I'll tell ya then. First, I quit my job."

"Get outta town! Why'd ya quit, Mikey?"

"Because that asshole foreman pissed me off, so I slugged him."

"Get lost! You slugged the guy, huh? Whattaya gonna do now with no job?"

"That's the big news. After I left Farrell's, I went to Ansonia and joined the Army."

"Get the hell outta town! You joined up, huh?"

"I sure did. Because there's no friggin' opportunities in these hick towns, so I didn't know what else to do. And besides, we're sure to get drafted any time now. So what's the difference?"

"Do you think I'll get drafted soon, Mikey?"

"Almost definitely. There's no getting around it."

"Geez! When do you go in?"

"I'm on my way to Massachusetts the first of the month. Fort Devens. I won't be there long, though. That's where they decide where they're sending me for boot camp."

"Jesus. That's not even two weeks away."

"That's right. Before I go, though, I'm hopin' to catch up with that girl Cecelia we met last week. I wanna see her again."

"I'll bet," Scooter said. "And I don' blame ya...a beautiful dish like her."

"Don't call her a dish, Scoot."

"Why not?"

"Because I'm gonna marry that girl!"

As soon as they entered the ballroom, Michael scanned the room, looking for Cecelia. Like a periscope on a submarine, his whole body rotated in a three hundred and sixty degree motion, but he spotted no Cecelia in the sea of dancers. Undeterred, he knew it was still early. If she had to walk there from Shelton, she might be late, although he hadn't seen her as they drove along the Derby Turnpike.

Michael could see that Scooter was off and running, asking girl after girl to dance. Scooter was a numbers guy, relentlessly asking until someone said yes. The guy loved to dance, and he didn't care who it was with. As the hour wore on, Michael saw his pal dancing with all kinds of dames from short numbers who he twirled around like they were gyrating wooden tops to tall drinks of water whose elongated arms stretched with each and every spin, like rubber bands ready to snap. Michael marveled and shook his head.

Fifteen minutes in, Scooter came over and urged him to ask someone to dance, but Michael had no interest. For him, it was Cecelia or nobody. He was more interested in watching the band than in dancing. Like always, he imagined playing one of the solid gold horns. Michael couldn't conceive of life with no music in it.

When he looked down at his wristwatch and saw that it was 9:30, he felt prickles of discouragement. Where had the time gone? Was he going to go off to basic training without getting to see her again? Without talking to her? Without asking her on a date?

Maybe I've made a mistake by joining up, he thought. It had been an impulsive thing to do, he knew. Not his most sterling quality, but he considered, *I can't help that I am who I am.*

At 10:00, he whistled to Scooter who was talking to a little number with tight blonde pin curls. Scooter appeared to excuse himself from the girl, and he trotted over to his buddy.

"What gives, Mikey? Didn't ya see I was makin' time with that little blonde?"

"Yeah, yeah...I see everything. I just wanted to tell you that I'm shovin' off."

"Shovin' off? Whattaya mean, shovin' off? The dance ain't over yet."

"Yeah, well that's big news, but I'm bored and tired, so like I just said, I'm takin' off."

"Wha's this all about, Mikey? About that dish you're pinin' over?"

"I told you not to call her a dish, Scooter."

"Okay...okay. I got it. Yer gonna marry her."

"That's right."

"Okay, well if it's all the same to you, I'm gonna stay till the end because I'm makin' some headway with Miss Pin Curls over there. I'll hitch a ride home if I hafta. That's why God gave me a thumb, right?"

"Yeah, that's right."

As Michael walked out into the night, he heard the fading sound of the band playing a great tune from a few years back, "It's Only a Paper Moon." Peering up at the clear sky, he knew that the moon wasn't paper and the sky wasn't cardboard, but they may as well have been for all the good they were doing him. All he could think of at this moment was, more than anything, he needed someone to believe in him.

"But it isn't going to be Cecelia Whatever-Her-Name-Is," he mumbled to himself. It might be a long time before he'd get to see her again...or worse, maybe never.

When Cecelia and company walked into the Ritz Ballroom at the Pleasure Beach Amusement Park in Bridgeport, the three of them were all agog with excitement. It was hard to get a ride out of the Valley, and when an opportunity came along, they seized it.

"Those guys who drove us here are classics," Cecelia said. "Where did you find them?"

"I told you," her sister Connie replied, "the guy who drove, Barney–he works with me at the Sponge Rubber."

"Oh, right," little Connie tittered. "He looks like a monk with that bald spot in the back of his head."

"Aww! He's kind of cute," Cecelia said.

"Well cuter than the one who stutters," little Connie replied, suppressing her laughter.

With a tight smile, Cecelia cautioned, "Now don't make fun of the poor guy, Connie. He can't help it."

But the three girls could no longer maintain control as tears rolled down their cheeks, and they were awash with laughter.

"And how about that third one?" little Connie asked. "Did he say a single word the whole way here? Talk about shy!"

"Well, don't forget, girls. In order to get Barney to bring us both ways, I promised him that all of us would dance with all of them."

"I haven't forgotten," Cecelia replied. "But I'm going to be far too busy to dance with any of them more than once."

Cecelia had felt a little torn about coming to Bridgeport. From the moment the girls found out they could get a ride, Cecelia began to think about the boy she had met a week before. Something about him intrigued her. But what was it? It wasn't just that he was good looking or that he was also built the way a man ought to be built.

There was something else. Something intangible. She bet he was at the dance on the river in Derby again. She knew she had to let it go, though. Finding decent guys who would drive you to Bridgeport or New Haven didn't happen every day. *Barney and his pals are such good eggs while many guys are such jerks,* she thought, *and who wants to wrestle with some slob in the back seat of a car?*

No sooner were the girls in the Ritz when Cecelia sized up the room, anticipating how much fun it was going to be to dance with new guys. The big city boys were snazzier dressers and were usually better dancers than the boys from the Valley. And dancing was what Cecelia was all about.

When a soldier took her by the hand and said, "C'mon, doll face, let's dance," she was off and running without a chance to catch her breath for the rest of the evening. She adored the variety of dance numbers–a jitterbug followed by a rhumba followed by a fox trot. At one point, the band even treated the crowd to a little nostalgia as they all danced the Charleston.

The band was Danny DePaolo and the All-Stars out of New Haven, and even though they weren't famous, for Cecelia's money, they were just as good as the more renowned bands. Danny himself was confined to a wheelchair, the result of polio, and he played a mean clarinet. A rosy-cheeked, affable fellow, Danny radiated a paternal warmth that made Cecelia like him. She wondered, *How does a Benny Goodman get to be a Benny Goodman while a Danny DePaolo stays, well, just a Danny DePaolo?*

The All-Stars also had a vocalist, Claire Fontaine, whose singing Cecelia had always enjoyed. Claire's voice reminded Cecelia of a favorite, Jo Stafford, whom she had heard with Tommy Dorsey's band on the radio. When Danny took the mic and said, "We're going to slow things down with 'I'm in the Mood for Love,'" Cecelia had a string of a half dozen guys waiting to dance with her, but when the next batter stepped up to the plate, she said, "If you don't mind, handsome, I'm going to sit this one out. I need a little breather. But I'll be ready to cut the rug with you on the next song."

What Cecelia didn't say was that when Claire Fontaine, or any female vocalist, sang with a band, she just wanted to listen and imagine what it might be like to be in her shoes. Listening to the sweet, warbling sound of Claire's voice, Cecelia was able to forget that it was hard for her family to make ends meet, that she had recently quit school, and that she now spent her days in a state of boredom at the Star Pin Factory.

What must it be like to be Claire Fontaine? she wondered.

When the band hit the final harmonious chord, the grateful crowd showered Claire Fontaine with an enthusiastic round of applause. It reminded Cecelia of how good the applause had felt when she had sung years before at competitions at the local movie theaters.

Danny DePaolo now took a microphone in hand once again. "Isn't she straight from Heaven?" The audience answered with an even greater ovation.

"But I've got some sad news for you, music lovers. Claire is going to be leaving the All-Stars."

The crowd emitted a collective moan.

"But the good news is Claire has a good reason. She's having a baby!"

The happy news delighted the crowd.

Danny continued, "Now, I want you all to know that the All-Stars will be holding auditions at our rehearsal studio in New Haven tomorrow from 12 to 5 p.m. So, all you talented signorinas out there, why not pay us a visit tomorrow? Just head to New Haven and swing by 158 Chapel Street, Suite 7. Maybe you'll be the next Claire Fontaine!"

The All-Stars picked things up with "Stompin' at the Savoy," and when Danny soared into orbit with the classic clarinet solo, Cecelia found herself in a universe of her own making, dancing to the swinging tune and picturing herself auditioning in New Haven the next day.

At the end of the night, she was able to head to Barney's car with a clear conscience because she knew that she had danced with their three hosts, and she assumed the two Connies had done the same. Cecelia even danced with Barney himself twice because he was such a sweet guy.

On the ride home, everyone talked incessantly except for the shy one and Cecelia, who was lost in thought. She didn't hear a word anyone said but just a droning of chatter as the car raced along Bridgeport Avenue back to Shelton.

Later, after the girls had their cup of tea with Mama, Cecelia stepped out onto the porch and looked up at the cloudy sky, wondering about all kinds of things. She couldn't help thinking about that boy, Michael. *Had he gone to the dance on the river? Did he look for me? Been disappointed I wasn't there?*

Cecelia also wondered if she could muster up the courage to go to the audition. *What would they want me to sing? If I go, will I be nervous?* Brimming with hope, she contemplated what the world had in store for her now, when the screen door creaked open. "Do you mind if I join you?" little Connie asked.

"No, I don't mind. Please do."

"Or, if you'd rather be alone, I can just go to bed."

"Don't be silly. It's always nice to have company, especially your company."

"Oh, because all the way home you seemed distracted."

"Yes," Cecelia said. "I suppose I am."

Connie looked at her with sincere eyes. "What are you thinking about?"

"Oh, I don't know…about nothing…and everything. I guess I'm just worried where my life is going."

Connie sat on the step next to Cecelia. "I see. Maybe it would help if I read your palm."

Cecelia was more than a little surprised by the offer. "Read my palm? I never knew you read palms. Who taught you how to do that?"

"Nobody. It's just something I've always been fascinated with, so I got some books on the subject from the library. Actually, the correct terms for palm reading are 'palmistry' or 'chiromancy' although personally I prefer 'palmistry' because the word *palm* is right there in it. Anyway, it's a very ancient practice. Even Aristotle wrote about it."

"He did?"

"He sure did. And you know what he said? He said, 'Lines are not written into the human hand without reason.' Can you believe that? Aristotle!"

"That's amazing."

"Let me see your hands."

Cecelia offered her two hands, palms up, allowing little Connie to cup them in hers. "Lucky for the porch light," Connie said, "or I wouldn't be able to see them so good."

A half dozen moths, white and tan and gray, swarmed around the bare light bulb in the heat of the warm September night.

"You're a righty?" she asked.

"Sort of," Cecelia responded. "I think I was born left-handed, but my teachers in grade school made me do everything with my right hand. You know how they were. So I do everything with my right hand, but I'm not very good with either one. They ruined me. I describe myself as *non-dextrous!*"

Connie giggled and said, "That shouldn't matter. At least I hope not. I have to look at both hands, because the non-dominant hand reveals your natural personality and character, while the dominant hand shows how these traits have been actualized in real life. See, looking at both hands together will give me an idea of how you are utilizing your potential."

"Okay," Cecelia said, feeling a surge of excitement.

"Okay," Connie echoed, deep in thought. "First off, I need to figure out what kind of hands you have. I'd say these are...I'd say we have *water hands* here. Your palms and fingers have a tall, slender appearance."

"Is that good?"

"Oh, what kind of hands you've got isn't good or bad. It's just *what is*. See, there are four types—earth, fire, air, and water. Yours are definitely water from what I'm seeing."

In a way, Connie's explanation was driving Cecelia crazy. "But what does that mean?"

"Well," Connie continued, "it means that you are in tune with your emotions and your intuition and your, uhm, psychic ability. It means you're compassionate and imaginative. Let's see...also that you're creative, which is true of you. I mean, you're always writing poems. But..."

"But what?" Cecelia asked, worried.

"It also means you're extremely sensitive and that your feelings are easily hurt. I don't know if that's true of you, but maybe. Maybe you just don't show it all the time."

"Yeah, maybe that's true of me. So, what else? What else do you see?"

"Well, let me see. I need to examine your prominent mounts. Those are fleshy parts of your palms that correspond to planets on the astrological chart."

"This is quite sophisticated, isn't it?"

"Oh, yes, for sure," Connie agreed, and then both girls giggled. "Okay, then. Your elevated mounts reveal areas that you're nicely balanced in, and sunken mounts show where your blind spots are."

"I can't wait to hear. Tell me!"

"I see...I see...oh, yes, I see the Mount of Apollo, a nice fleshy part right below your ring finger. That shows that artistic side of you, and it indicates that you have a lot of potential for happiness and success."

"Oh God, really? That's good, right?"

"That's very good," Connie almost whispered, still studying her friend's hands.

"What else? What else? Tell me more!"

"Okay, let...me...see." It was clear that little Connie was concentrating very hard. "Oh, here's what might be a blind spot. See, right under your thumb, it's not that fleshy. It's almost, sort of, sunken in. That part of your palm is called the Mount of Venus. That might be a blind spot."

"Jesus Christ, Connie! Blind spot to what?"

She looked into Cecelia's eyes with great seriousness. "The Mount of Venus is about just what you'd think it's about. It's about romance and passion and...and *sex*."

At the sound of the word *sex*, neither of the girls could keep a straight face, and they both let out a guilty laugh.

"Oh great," Cecelia said, trying to suppress more raucous laughter. "What a place to have a blind spot!"

At that very moment, the screen door rudely swung open and Cecelia's sister Connie interrupted them.

"What the hell are you two up to out here?" she asked.

"Oh, just some palm reading," Cecelia said.

"You don't believe in that nonsense, I hope," her sister said.

"But it's not nonsense," Cecelia argued. "Even Aristotle believed in it."

"Aristotle, my ass!"

"Oh, we were just having a little fun," little Connie pleaded in a mousy voice.

"More like waking up the whole damned neighborhood with your bullshit. You two are a couple of lulus. Do you realize what time it is? It's after midnight."

"Oh, I'm so sorry," little Connie said, "We didn't mean to be so loud. I'll just…go up to bed. Goodnight, girls."

"And what about you?" Cecelia's sister asked. "Don't you think you should go to bed too?"

"I think I'll just sit out here for a few more minutes."

"For what purpose?"

"Just to think," Cecelia answered.

"About what?"

"Oh…not about anything, really. Not about anything important, anyway."

Connie shook her head and went back into the house, letting the screen door slap shut behind her.

Alone now, Cecelia sat examining her palms like she was seeing them for the first time. With the tip of the index finger of her right hand, she massaged the skin below the ring finger of her left. "The Mount of Apollo," she muttered, "which means I have a lot of potential for happiness and success." Taking a deep breath, she decided to audition for the All-Stars the next day. Maybe dreams weren't as elusive as she sometimes thought. Maybe they were written in the palms of her hands.

9

Cecelia – 1936

*A*s they walk across the Shelton-Derby Bridge, Cecelia realizes that she is just about as tall as Valentina, even though Valentina is almost six years her senior. To the casual observer, Valentina is a doll-like wisp of a thing. But Cecelia knows that, despite her sister's diminutive size, Valentina is strict, assertive and strong.

On this blustery afternoon, Valentina has agreed to take Cecelia to a singing competition at the Commodore Hull Movie Theater in Derby. A stubborn wind creates resistance, blowing their hair and their dresses as they cross over the bridge. In her heart of hearts, Valentina thinks it is a waste of time, but Cecelia has pestered her and a promise is, after all, a promise. It isn't Cecelia's first competition. The last time, Betty had taken her. Cecelia is crafty and knows not to ask one or the other too often.

Fighting their way across the bridge, the two sisters hurry around the corner on Main Street. As they pass the Howard and Barber Department Store, Cecelia slows to a stop. She can't resist admiring the finery in the large, beveled windows–cut glass knick knacks, women's fashions adorning three elegant mannequins, and gleaming jewelry exquisitely displayed on dark green satin.

"Celia," Valentina calls. "You really try my patience sometimes. Let's move it. We'll be late!"

"But these things are so pretty, Val. Don't you like looking?"

"We'll never have the money to even walk through those doors, Celia, so what's the point in looking?"

Cecelia nods, reluctantly tearing herself from daydreams of owning such finery. They continue to the intersection where Cecelia is once again distracted by the smaller window dressing at Vonette's Palace of Sweets.

"Cecelia Louise Alberino," Valentina calls again, "do you want to go to this singing competition or not?"

"Yes...yes, but, Val, can we get an ice cream sundae after the competition?"

"No, we cannot get an ice cream sundae! Do you think that I'm made of money?"

Disappointed, Cecelia simply follows Valentina across to Elizabeth Street in the direction of the movie theater.

"Let's not pout, Cecelia. I'm taking you to the singing competition, am I not?"

"Yes," Cecelia sighs.

As they cross over from Main to Elizabeth Street toward the theater, a thoroughly irritated Valentina pulls her distractible sister across the intersection but finds herself thinking about their older brother Ernie and his darned mandolin. Valentina can't help but blame Ernie for Cecelia's obsession with singing.

It was true. It all started with Ernie and his mandolin, his most prized possession. The eight-stringed instrument, lavishly crafted out of rosewood, tortoiseshell, and mother-of-pearl, had miraculously survived the sea voyage from Naples to New York in 1908 when Ernie was five years old. It had belonged to his grandfather, long before buried in the hills of Southern Italy. Using a dog-eared manual he bought at a church bazaar for three cents, Ernie had taught himself the chords and the picking style, and before long, he was able to make the mandolin sing with tremolo melodies and harp-like accompaniments. Valentina remembered Ernie then buying their brother Dominic a second-hand guitar and encouraging him to learn to play it. She couldn't have been more than eight and Dominic, perhaps, twelve. Before long, with the eldest, Robert, serving as debonair host, the three boys would invite friends over to "the Club" which was nothing more than an old tool shed in Mama's yard. The boys would sing folk songs and cowboy tunes while their invited guests sang along or danced. And Valentina had been standing on the outskirts of one of those parties the very same summer Papa had died, when Ernie invited little Cecelia to sing a solo for their guests. Cecelia became the main attraction at her brothers' soirées. Strumming rhythmic chords on his mandolin, Ernie would accompany his little sister as she performed a catchy old Tin Pan Alley hit, and the guests would delight as she crooned "By the Light of the Silvery Moon" or roll over in stitches as she belted out "Won't You Come Home, Bill Bailey?" or clap along as she sang "Five Foot Two, Eyes of Blue."

And now Valentina feels, because of age and circumstances, she has ended up being stuck with taking Cecelia to singing competitions and dealing with her silly pipe dreams.

The movie marquee, now in view, flashes the title of the latest film being shown, *Poor Little Rich Girl*, starring Shirley Temple. Cecelia wonders how a rich girl can also be poor. The competition costs ten cents, and it costs another ten cents per person to see the film that follows the competition. Cecelia knows better than to ask Valentina to spend that amount. The rare occasions Cecelia has seen a movie have been cosmic experiences that have launched her imagination into a galaxy she loves visiting.

The competition has thirteen participants, ranging in age from six to seventeen, all girls. At eleven, Cecelia falls into the middle of the age group. Whichever contestant receives the most applause will be named the winner.

With Valentina as her sole supporter, she realizes her disadvantage. Other competitors often come replete with family and friends to cheer them on. Still, Cecelia is content to sing in front of a large audience with a real pianist instead of singing in the kitchen or at a yard party.

Like helium inflating a colorful balloon, Cecelia is filled with excitement when the M.C., bedecked in a straw hat and bow tie, announces, "And now, ladies and gents, boys and girls, I'd like to introduce our seventh talented singer, Cecelia Alberino, from our neighbor across the river, Shelton. Let's all give Cecelia a big round of applause."

Butterflies flutter every which way in her tummy as she saunters down the aisle and climbs the stage steps. As instructed, she marches herself over to the pianist who looks sleepy in his wrinkled vest and Derby hat, a stogie dangling from his lips. She whispers, "I'll be singing, 'When the Red, Red Robin,' do you know that one?"

"I know 'em all, dolly," the rotund musician with the droopy eyes replies.

As the song begins, she likes the bouncy tempo the accompanist opens with. Feeling her voice reverberate throughout the vast theater space, her confidence grows and grows as she sings. Feeling in union with her musician as she reaches the last bars of the tune, Cecelia goes for a big finish, repeating the second to the last line three times, "When the red, red robin goes bob, bob, bobbin'…when the red, red robin goes bob, bob bobbin'…when the red, red robin goes bob, bob, bobbin'," and then the last money note, "a-l-o-o-o-o-ng!"

As she hears the applause begin, she blushes and curtsies gracefully, and then runs down the stairs and to her seat as the M.C. steps into place and says, "What a nice performance by little Cecelia of a song made famous by the great Lillian Roth. Next, ladies and gents, boys and girls, we have…"

"How did I do?" she whispers to Valentina.

"You did great," Valentina says. "You were perfect!" And she gives her little sister a loving squeeze.

"How loud was the applause? I was so excited, I couldn't tell."

"Better than some, not as good as others," Valentina replies realistically. "You know, sweetie, that a lot of folks hold back so that their kid will win."

When the final contestant has sung her song, the M.C. invites all of the candidates back to the stage.

"Now, ladies and gents, boys and girls, when I hold my hand up behind a contestant's head, show them what you thought of their performance. Our judges will be listening closely to determine the winner of today's competition."

Cecelia's heart races, and despite knowing better, she hopes that maybe this time she'll win. But after each contestant has received her round of applause, the M.C. announces that Minnie Walker has won the first prize blue ribbon and that Mary Reagan is the runner-up. Cecelia can't help feeling a twinge of envy as the two girls proudly curtsy and receive their ribbons.

As the crowd is shepherded out of the theater to either buy a ticket to the movie or head back home, Cecelia and Valentina are approached by a young man with a pencil-thin mustache and a fedora.

"You're quite a singer, miss...what was your name again?"

"Her name is none-of-your-business, sir," Valentina says, "But thank you for the compliment."

Yanking Cecelia by the hand, Valentina pulls her down Elizabeth Street.

Following in hot pursuit, the gentleman calls after them, "Hey there, missy, now wait just a minute, will ya? I want to tell you something about the little girl."

Valentina keeps walking.

"Sis, let's hear what he has to say," Cecelia pleads.

"I'm not in the habit of talking to strangers, Celia, and you would do well to follow my example."

"But, sis...please?"

"But here's the thing," he calls from two yards behind. "The kid is a bundle of raw talent, and I'm the guy who can develop that talent into something special."

In the quietest soprano, Cecelia implores her big sister again, almost squeaking, "Please, Val? Please? Please?"

Valentina exhales, comes to a stop, and turns to the stranger.

"Help her how?" Valentina asks.

Eyeing Valentina up and down, the stranger says, "Now I know you can't be the little girl's mother because you're far too young and pretty."

"I'm her big sister," Valentina replies sardonically.

"But not very much bigger," the man says, his attempt at humor falling flat.

"Help her *how?*" Valentina repeats, her patience wearing thinner and thinner.

"It's like I just told you. The little girl is the real McCoy, and with coaching and vocal training, there's no tellin' what heights she can reach."

"What is that supposed to mean?" Valentina asks.

"What it's supposed to mean, missy, is that a talented kid like this could make it big in New York or even in Hollywood with the right coaching."

"And where would we find the right coaching? And how would we pay for it?"

"I'm glad you asked, because I just happen to be a voice teacher, and I feel that if you gave me six months to a year with this kid, I'll have her singing like Shirley Temple or even like Judy Garland."

Puzzled, Valentina replies, "I beg your pardon, mister, but I'm afraid I don't have the slightest idea who you're talking about."

"Oh, you must mean Garland. Haven't you seen the film, *Pigskin Parade?*"

Valentina, growing more infuriated and sarcastic, says, "No we have not, mister. I'm sorry to report that we don't have ten cents a week to spend on movies."

"Well, I'm tellin' ya, sister—Garland is the biggest thing to hit Hollywood since—well, since Shirley Temple herself. You're goin' to be hearin' a lot about her. You can take that to the bank. Of course, Garland's older than Shirley Temple and, I'm guessing, a little older than your kid sister here, but I think your girl's pipes are just as good."

"If my sister is so great," Valentina says, "why didn't she win the competition?"

"Come off it, girlie. You know these things are rigged just the same as I do. The best singers never win. You don't see me chasin' the winner down the street, do you? Why do you s'pose that is? I'll tell ya why. It's because she don't have it."

"Don't have wha—"

"Do you really think I can sing like Shirley Temple or what's the other one's name?"

The tall stranger puts his hands on his knees and bends over. "Her name is Judy Garland, and like I told your big sister here, you'll be hearing a lot about her."

"But you think that I can sing like...like..."

"You betcha, little lady. I don't have the slightest doubt about—"

"Don't you go swallowing a lot of pipe dream talk, baby," Valentina interrupts. "Girls from small towns like ours don't make it big."

"Oh, yeah?" the stranger says. "Maybe you don't know it, but ever since the first talkie came out, Hollywood scouts have been scouring every hick town in the country, looking for talent."

Cecelia looks at Valentina with big doe-eyes. "At least give him a chance to tell you more, sis."

Valentina scrunches up her face and exhales audibly. "Okay, I'm listening."

The man explains that he will come to their house once a week and give Cecelia an hour-long lesson, using proven vocal exercises to improve volume, pitch, and the ability to sustain long notes, and all of that for only four bits per lesson.

"...and if you don't see an immediate improvement, you can quit at any time."

"Fifty cents a lesson is steep," Valentina complains. "Where on earth do you think we're going to get that kind of money?"

"It's an investment in her future, an investment in the future of your family because if she hits it big, everybody wins. Listen, here's how it works. You pay the first month up front to show you're serious about it. That's a mere two bucks. Better yet, though, if you pay five bucks up front, it'll cover the cost of ten lessons and I'll throw in another ten lessons for free. You won't find a deal like that anywhere. Go talk to your family about it, and I'll swing by in a day or two to see what you've decided. Just tell me your address."

Valentina almost can't believe her own ears as she hears herself giving the man their street address in Shelton.

Heading back across the bridge, Cecelia asks, "Do you think we can come up with the five dollars, Val?"

"Don't talk to me right now, Celia. I need to think."

"But, sis, do you think—"

"Shush! I said don't talk to me right now."

Valentina decides that she herself can scrape together seventy-five cents. She asks for help from the next in line, Betty, who throws in another dollar. When Valentina asks her big sister Phyllis, she can contribute only fifty cents because her husband is out of work.

Valentina decides to go to Ernie because he is the most successful. She also knows how much he loves music in general and Cecelia's singing in particular. Ernie is trimming the hedges in front of his house with giant metal shears when Valentina asks him.

"I don't know about this, sis," Ernie says. "Two seventy-five is a lot of dough. It seems like a reckless waste of money. And, besides, what's the guarantee?"

"There are no guarantees in life. Christ, Ernie, you know that as well as—"

"Now, you just hold it right there. I need you to adjust your language, Valentina. I expect you to talk to me with respect."

"I'm sorry, Ernie, but in case you have a short memory, you're responsible for filling her head with dreams."

"Don't blame me. I just love music, and she sings like a little nightingale."

"Yeah, well, you're the one that got her started singing in front of people, aren't you? Maybe—just maybe, she's as good as the man said she is."

"Yes...maybe she is. Well, it's against my better judgment, but okay." He reaches down into his pockets and pulls out a dollar bill along with a handful of quarters, dimes, and nickels and hands the sum to his sister.

When the voice teacher drops by the house on the following Saturday, Valentina pays him the money.

"You've made a very smart decision," the man says. "I can't wait to get started with the little girl. I'll see you next Saturday at 10:00."

Cecelia can't wait. She spends the week driving both sisters mad by announcing, like a scratched record, "five more days"..."four more days"..."I can't wait"..."three more days"...

When Saturday arrives, Cecelia is sitting on the front stoop at 7:30. When Valentina emerges from the house at 8:00, she says, "Celia. The man isn't coming for two more hours!"

With a closed-mouthed smile, Cecelia replies, "I'll wait!"

But when 10:00 comes, and then 11:00, and then 12:00, Cecelia knows.

Valentina, who has been helplessly watching her sister from the window, pushes open the screen door, sits on the top stair beside Cecelia, and wraps both of her arms around her little sister.

"I'm so sorry, baby. I know how heartbroken you must feel...and I feel very disappointed too–"

Cecelia's sadness suddenly erupts into a trembling volcano of defiance. "NO! No, you don't know how I feel," she screams, breaking free of Valentina's embrace. Almost losing her balance, Cecelia stumbles down the two remaining steps, miraculously landing on her feet. "You'll never understand how I feel. Do you hear me? No one will ever understand! EVER!"

As Valentina watches helplessly, Cecelia runs into the house and up the inside stairway. Throwing herself on Mama's bed, she buries her head in the crocheted blanket and cries and cries–her tears purging her heart of its innocent hopes, washing away unrealistic dreams.

10

*C*ecelia waited for the bus at the corner of Howe Avenue and Bridge Street after surreptitiously leaving the house early. This was her secret for the time being. She stopped a block away at Mahoney's Drug Store and enjoyed a buttered hard roll and a cup of coffee at the lunch counter. This wouldn't be her first bus trip to New Haven. She and her gang had often taken the bus to go to dances at the New Haven Armory on Goffe Street, although they told Mama they were going dancing closer to home. A little white lie was only a venial sin, and she'd do anything to go to a dance hall in a bigger city. Dancing was, in its way, Cecelia's great escape. *And now,* she thought, *maybe singing can be an even better escape.* Standing on the corner, she imagined what it would be like to be the new Claire Fontaine–to be the new featured singer of the All-Stars. It was almost unimaginable.

Boarding the bus, Cecelia heard a ding for each of the nickels and pennies she inserted into the glass farebox, and then she took a seat. The bus made its way over the Shelton-Derby Bridge and picked up several more passengers on Main Street in Derby before heading for the Derby Turnpike. The passengers on the bus were older than the usual crowd who rode to the dances. Mostly middle-aged women, probably on their way to enjoy the finer shopping that a city like New Haven offered.

As she stared out the bus window, Cecelia's mind drifted to

thoughts about how life seemed to be unfolding for her. She contemplated her decision to quit school–something that had been haunting her for weeks. It had been an impulsive and unwise decision, she knew. She was so close to the finish line, and everyone in the family had expected her to be the one to complete a high school education. Still, none of her siblings, despite their displeasure with her decision, made her go back. *If Papa were alive, this wouldn't have happened,* she thought. *He wouldn't have allowed it. Papa would have marched me straight to the principal's office, made me apologize, and beg to be re-enrolled.*

Maybe if she could succeed in the audition, it would make things better. She'd still have to work in the factory because what else was she going to do with herself on weekdays? And, besides, Mama needed every cent anyone had to offer. But if she could sing with a big band on weekends, it would supplement her weekly pay and give her dull life the sparkle it needed.

When the bus arrived at her stop, it was 9:55. Danny DePaolo wouldn't start seeing people until noon.

Cecelia used the time to walk across the vast New Haven Green, which sat opposite three majestic churches. Turning at the corner of Temple and Elm Street, she strolled amidst the campus of Yale University. She marveled at the Gothic architecture of the buildings, and she couldn't help but notice the overabundance of males– some in dapper sport coats, some wearing small beanies, others smoking pipes–walking in twos and threes and fours. It hit her then that Yale was a men's college.

Some of the boys smiled and did double takes as they passed by, moving in and out of archways which reminded her of the entrances of churches. Cecelia slowed as she passed by the first archway, rubbed her palm against the open black wrought-iron gate, and peered into the lush green courtyard beyond. The utter grandeur of this port of entry made her feel like a college was somehow a holy place, a sanctuary. Noticing the carved, wooden sign above the gate, Calhoun College, it occurred to Cecelia that not only didn't she understand the difference between the words *college* and *university,* but, in fact, she knew very little about college in general. For her, like religion, college was shrouded in mystery.

What she did know was, if college had been in the cards, her one option would have been the New Haven Normal School where she could have earned a degree in teaching. A teacher had once told her as much. She wondered how far from Yale the New Haven Normal School was and how the two were similar and different.

Cecelia decided to turn back and head once more toward the green. After passing the New Haven Public Library and the Court House, both with towering white columns, she continued on Elm, turning on Orange Street, and then turning again on lower Chapel Street. She marveled at the various shops she passed on her jaunt—jewelers, women's clothing boutiques, furriers, haberdasheries, and more. She wouldn't dare enter any of them, but it sure was fun to admire the finery displayed in the shop windows.

With an hour still to kill, Cecelia made her way back to the Green. She noticed a small crowd gathering together. As she got closer, she saw a mustachioed man with a floppy cap, a tattered vest, and a red scarf around his neck. He reminded her of Papa. The man turned the large crank of his organ machine, playing a tune Cecelia didn't recognize but which sounded like a merry-go-round calliope, badly out of tune. Taking a seat on a nearby park bench, she was amused by an impish monkey sitting on the man's shoulder. The monkey, a long rope attached to a collar around its neck, hopped among the spectators brandishing a small tin cup into which pennies and nickels clinked as they dropped from the hands of a few kind-hearted souls in the crowd.

When the monkey skipped over to Cecelia, she said, "I'm so sorry, Mr. Monkey, but I don't have any money, so I can't help you."

The monkey peered into her eyes for a moment, as if questioning her, and then scooted away. Watching the little rascal, Cecelia thought to herself that she wasn't unlike the monkey, shackled to a proverbial leash around her neck and limited by a tin cup in her hands.

As the organ grinder continued to play his dissonant song, he smiled at the crowd warmly. Feeling very alone, Cecelia wished she could talk to him. She wondered if he spoke English, and she knew that her rusty Italian would make it hard for her to communicate with a native speaker.

The time was nearing noon, and Cecelia wanted to arrive at the audition on time.

As she made her way from the Green to Chapel Street, she noticed a man carrying a big burlap sack. *He must be Chinese or Japanese*, she thought. She realized she had never before met or even seen an Asian person except in movies.

In a strange way, the man, clad in a threadbare suit that was too big for him, reminded her of the organ grinder she had just watched.

Four teenage boys passed by simultaneously, and she heard one say, "Hey, fellas, will ya look at this chink? It's Charlie Chan."

"Aw, he ain't no chink. I think this one's a *Jap*, which is a hundred times worse," another boy fired back, amidst the sniggering of his friends.

Watching the man lug his sack as he continued on his way, Cecelia felt disconcerted by the boys' treatment of the man, to say the least. What had the little man done except to look different from the boys? He had probably come to this country in search of a better life just as her parents had. *I'll bet he has a wife and children at home*, she thought. Her family had also faced ridicule and indignities when people called them *wops*. She knew she needed to put the little man out of her mind, though. What could she do about him?

Looking up, she saw the number 158 on a transom window over a black lacquered door. Her destination. She entered the building and saw that Suite 7 was on the third floor. Climbing up the narrow stairs, she could hear the clicking of her heels echo off the marble surface in rhythm to the rapid beating of her heart. Turning the corner onto the second flight of steps, she could now hear the sounds of the band pour into the stairwell. When she reached her destination, Cecelia grasped the brass doorknob and turned it.

Even though she was right on time, there were already more than a dozen girls in the room sitting in wooden folding chairs. A young man, puffing on a cigarette, sat at a table outside the audition room.

Approaching him, Cecelia asked, "Do I sign up with you?"

"That's right, sister. What's the name?"

"Cecelia Alberino," she almost whispered.

"Alright, Cecelia Alberino. Take a seat and I'll give ya a holler when it's your turn."

She could hear a girl singing "Green Eyes" accompanied by what was unmistakably the All-Stars. The singer was no Helen O'Connell, but she still sounded pretty good, whoever she was. Worried, she wondered if she needed to tell Danny what song she wanted to sing, or if he would pick one for her.

Listening intently to the various girls sing as best she could through the heavy oak door, Cecelia evaluated their talent in her mind while trying to determine how good she herself would need to be. *If there are this many girls here in the first few minutes of the audition,* she thought, *how many will try out by the end of the day?* She tried to push discouragement out of mind. *I'll just do my best and see what happens,* she concluded.

"Okay, next up…uh, let's see." The young man at the table scanned the list on his wooden clipboard. "Oh yeah, next up is Cecelia Alberino."

Walking by him, he said, "Show 'em what ya got, sister," which lifted her spirits. She smiled at the young man and opened the door.

The group of musicians filled up most of the available space in the room, and there before them was Danny DePaolo himself, sitting in his wheelchair.

"Okay…here's number 16. And your name is what, doll?"

"Cecelia…Cecelia Alberino."

"Ce-ce-lia Al-be-ri-no," he said, scrawling her name on a list on his music stand.

"Whattaya gonna sing for us, Cecelia Alberino?" he asked.

"What would you like me to sing?"

"Well, whattaya know, doll?"

Cecelia thought for a second and sighed. "What do I know? Well, I know just about anything, Mr. DePaolo. What songs can you play?"

"Us?" Danny flashed a benevolent smile. "We can play just about anything! How about this? How about we do something upbeat? Can you sing 'Zing! Went the Strings of my Heart'?"

"Gosh, why sure I can," said Cecelia.

"And what key do you sing it in, doll?"

"What key? Well, I don't exactly know…I–"

"Okay, no need to worry. Just sing me a line."

"A line? Sing a line?"

"Yeah, that's the stuff. Sing Danny a line so I know what key is good."

No sooner had Cecelia sung the first four or five words when Danny interrupted. "That's good. We're gonna do it in G, fellas. Let's give the little girl eight bars, okay? A-one, and a-two, and a-three, and a-four..."

Cecelia wasn't sure what he meant by eight bars, but she miraculously came in singing in time after the snappy introduction.

She hadn't even gotten through the first verse when Danny stopped the band.

"Okay, boys, hold up a second...hold up. So, uhm, listen, Cecelia, you sound just swell, but you seem a little nervous. Just loosen up and relax. Think about it like you're singing in your living room to your dear old mom and dad, and trust me, you'll be fine. Can ya trust ol' Danny?"

Something about Danny comforted Cecelia. "Yes, I...I trust you."

"Perfect. Okay, boys, let's take it again from the top. A-one, and a-two, and a-three, and a-four..."

Cecelia came in again, perfectly in time. The full sound of the big band filled her heart and transported her to another world made of harmony and rhythm. Danny looked at her the entire time, squinting and nodding, his brown eyes giving her more and more encouragement with each note and each musical phrase. After she let out the last big note and the band brought the song to its flourishing conclusion, Cecelia inhaled and looked at Danny.

"Well, whattaya think, fellas?" Danny asked.

Cecelia was stunned when the boys in the band gave her an enthusiastic round of applause.

"You're quite a singer, Cecelia Alberino. Anybody ever tell ya that?" Danny asked.

Blushing, Cecelia replied, "Uhm...well...maybe somebody told me that once."

"Well, *I'm* tellin' ya. You've got quite a set of pipes there. And we don't hear intonation like that every day, that's for sure."

Cecelia stood, silent and puzzled.

"What I mean, Cecelia, is...think of it this way. Think of the notes you're supposed to hit like big targets, each one with a nice, red bull's eye right smack in the center. Of course, the bull's eye is the smallest circle in the target. When you hit a note, sweetie, you hit it right in the center of the bull's eye. And I mean, *dead* center."

Danny's remarks left Cecelia speechless. Feeling her eyes fill with tears, she struggled to avoid crying.

"Can any of you mugs venture a guess why else I like this girl?" Danny asked.

A trumpet player in the back row chuckled and called out, "I think it's because she's Italian, Danny."

"Well, see," Danny replied. "That's where you're wrong. I like her because *I'm* Italian!"

The entire group was swept up in a tidal wave of laughter.

"Okay, here's the deal. We got a lot more girls to hear today, Cecelia, but let me ask you this. How do we get in touch with you if we decide you're the one? Because there's a better-than-average shot that's what we're gonna decide. You got a phone we can call?"

"Oh darn, we don't have a phone. We're supposed to get one soon, but..." Cecelia said, and then in a rapid burst of words like machine gun fire, "but my best friend, right next door...my best friend has one. Her name is Stella Kostenko and her mother's name is Irina. Her father's name was John, but he died, you see. Oh, God, I think I'm rambling. But, oh gosh! I think it's a long distance call!"

"Don't worry about that, sweetie–"

"You'll need to tell the operator their number is 4062-W in Shelton. If you call their phone, Stella can run next door and get me. "

His lips upturned in an amused curl, Danny said, "Okay whoa, slow down! That's just fine, Cecelia Alberino. Let's see," and writing the number on a pad on his music stand, he continued, "that was 4-0-6-2-W, right? And we'll call Stel-la Ko-sten-ko if you're our girl."

With wings on her heels, Cecelia flew down the hallway steps. As the bus floated along the Derby Turnpike on its way back to the Valley, Cecelia's heart was brimming with optimism, something she hadn't felt in ages.

Arriving home a little before 3:00, she walked into the house and didn't see anyone. Looking out the kitchen window, she spied Mama out back in the vegetable garden. She wanted to go out and help her, but she needed to eat something. Cecelia went to the icebox and took out some lunch meat and then began slicing some bread at the counter.

She heard someone's feet coming down the stairs, and then Connie entered the kitchen.

"What are you up to?" Connie asked.

Cecelia placed three slices of prosciutto on the bread. "I'm up to making a sandwich. You want one?"

"And where, pray tell, have you been all day?"

"Here, let me make you a nice sandwich."

"You're evading the question."

"What question?"

Connie was losing her patience. "I asked where you were!"

"Oh...nowhere special."

"Don't give me that bull. You've been gone all day. Where were you?"

"I can't say just yet."

"Oh? And why not?"

"Because it'll be bad luck if I do. But eventually, I'll tell you," Cecelia said, a broad smile plastered across her face.

Connie frowned. "Don't smile at me! You look like Cinderella just back from the ball."

"Well...maybe that's just what I am."

---

11

*F*rustrated, Michael couldn't find a parking space on the busy streets of downtown Derby. *Have people already begun Christmas shopping?* he wondered. *It isn't even November yet.* It seemed like every year there were more cars on the streets. He remembered a time when there were more horse-drawn wagons on Main Street than automobiles. Finally finding a vacant space, just below the Howard and Barber Department Store, he squeezed the Ford into the spot.

Famished, Michael could almost taste the BLT that he planned to order at Woolworth's. Next, he would run over to his sister Lucia's, and then motor to New Haven to see his sister, Vincenza. With his first day in the Army two days away, he had goodbyes to say, and with no time to waste, he headed up Main Street on foot. *Maybe I'll get a hot chocolate with my sandwich,* he thought, feeling the chill of late October. *That'll hit the spot.*

He glanced at his wristwatch. It was almost noon. Passing by Vonette's, he took a gander in the window like always to see if any of the gang was in there. There were plenty of friends that didn't know he had enlisted, and he was all too happy to share the news with anyone who would listen. It made him feel good when friends wished him well and told him they'd miss him.

Squinting as he looked through the window, he tried to see if he knew anyone and said to himself, *This place is bustling the same as the rest of downtown*. The stools at the counter were lined with high school kids except for old Mr. Chesney, a permanent fixture, sitting at the end of the counter, his cane hooked over his forearm as he sipped his coffee. It looked like all the small tables in the back of the parlor were full as well. It was then that he spotted her through the glass. With a military life in his immediate future, Michael had given up hope of seeing her any time soon, or maybe ever again. And now, opportunity was staring him in the kisser. *I'll stop in and say hello and casually mention that I'm in the Army now,* he decided.

Making his way through the front door, he could see that Cecelia was sitting alone. *What a lucky break,* he thought. He patted Mr. Chesney on the back and then sidestepped a few kids who were chatting with friends at tables. There were more customers in the store than there were places to sit, but the chair across from Cecelia was vacant, luckily.

"That looks like a tasty sundae ya got there," he said.

Cecelia looked up, and seeing him, smiled and said, "Well, I'll be darned! If it isn't…"

"Michael."

"Yes, Michael. How nice to see you again."

Michael couldn't hide his delight. "I spotted you through the window and thought I'd pop in and say hello."

Cecelia, feeling no less delighted, smiled. "What a small world."

"For sure. I was hoping to run into you again, but what are the chances, do you suppose? About a thousand to one?"

Cecelia remembered this exchange. "At least! Because Derby and Shelton are such big towns," she teased.

With a touch of chagrin, Michael shrugged.

"How's your buddy?"

"Oh, Scooter? He's doing okay. Scooter never changes. He's sure and steady–always ready for a good time. And how about the two Connies?"

"You score two points for remembering their names. They're both good. My sister is still keeping an eye on me, and my friend Connie is still living with us."

"Hey, there's something I'd like to tell you. Mind if I sit down?"

"Oh, well normally I wouldn't mind, but I'm…kind of here with someone. He might not like it. I'm sorry, Michael."

"I...uhm...I don't see anyone," Michael said, looking at the vacant chair across from her.

"He's right over there, two tables away, talking to some friends."

Glancing behind him, Michael saw a mixture of guys and girls and wasn't sure which one she meant. "Oh, yeah. I get it. You're kind of out on a little date."

"Yes," she said. "I kind of am."

"Okay. I better get lost then. But, listen. Maybe I'll see you again sometime."

"Yes, Michael. I hope so."

"Yeah...great. Well, look. It was just grand seeing you, and I hope I run into you again soon, but you never told me your last name because you said I was a stranger. Am I still a stranger?"

"No, Michael. Not anymore. You're a friend now."

"Then maybe you won't mind telling me your last name and–"

"Sorry I was away from the table for so long, Cecelia," a voice interrupted. "I didn't mean to neglect you."

"Oh, I didn't feel neglected," she replied.

"I can see that," the stranger said, giving Michael a skeptical look, "but I guess that's what I get for leaving you alone."

Cecelia, ever gracious, said, "Michael, meet Ralph. Ralph, meet Michael."

"Hello, friend," Ralph said. "Michael what?"

Michael looked Ralph squarely in the eyes. "Just Michael, friend." He could feel his face burning, and he could hear the sarcasm in his tone. He wasn't going to get to tell her about the Army.

"Listen, I have to run, Cecelia. Like I said, it was just swell seeing you again. Give my best to your sister and your friend."

Michael flew past the soda fountain, back toward the front door. He looked up at the nearby Woolworth's sign, its big gold letters the most prominent on Main Street. Holding tightly to his punctured ego, Michael burst through the double doors and grabbed a menu from the silver holder on the counter. The letters on the page were a blur to him.

Floating in a soupy pool of disappointment, his mind raced. *I'm glad to get out of this crummy town. There's nothing for me here and no point in my being here neither. Monday can't come fast enough for me.*

He wished the last ten minutes of his life had been a movie scene that he could rewrite. He wished he hadn't gotten so rattled. He wished he had given her his last name and asked for hers. He wished he had told Cecelia he had enlisted. He wished he hadn't gone into Vonette's in the first place.

The voice inside his head continued to berate him. *I should have known a girl like that wouldn't be sitting alone in Vonette's. Sometimes I'm a goddamn dope.*

"What can I get you today, Mikey?" he heard the waitress ask, snapping him out of it.

Michael placed the menu back in its chrome holder.

"Uhm...yeah, Mabel. I'll have a BLT and...and a hot chocolate."

"Comin' right up," Mabel said, reading Michael's dark mood. "Hey, don't look so glum. A good looker like you should feel like the world is his oyster. Cheer up and start livin'."

As she moved down the counter to the next customer, Michael thought to himself, *Right, the world is my oyster. The problem is the goddamn oyster is empty.*

12

*A*fter rehearsing with the All-Stars every Saturday for four weeks, it was Cecelia's moment of truth. Singing the final verse of her first song of the evening, "Love Me or Leave Me," Cecelia wondered how the crowd would react. As the All-Stars brought the tune to its tender ending, the entwined dancers un-curled from each other's arms and brought their hands together in an enthusiastic round of applause. Their genuine clapping and whistling exhilarated her.

Cecelia heard Danny's voice reverberate through the P.A. system. "Didn't I tell you she was terrific, guys and girls?"

She turned to him and smiled, remembering the day Stella had run across the grass between their houses, yelling that Danny DePaolo was on the phone. What a thrill that had been.

With a broad smile, Danny mouthed, *I told you so,* and then he spoke into the microphone again.

"Now we're going to have the beautiful and talented Cecelia do something a little more upbeat. You're going to love this one, kids. It's the tune that she sang for us at her audition a month ago. She won our hearts with this one, and I think she's about to win yours too. And here we go!"

And before she knew it, there she was belting out "Zing! Went the Strings of My Heart," after which the applause was even greater, with louder whistling and shouting, "Encore! Encore! Encore!"

If Cecelia's thermometer had heated up before, it was now ready to shatter and explode.

"Alright, music lovers. If you want one more from Cecelia, you got it. This is a tune made popular by a hilarious Abbott and Costello film I'll betcha you've all seen, *Buck Privates*. The song was sung in the movie by the Andrews Sisters in three-part harmony, but I've made a special arrangement for our girl. Ready, boys?"

The All-Stars launched into "Boogie Woogie Bugle Boy," and Cecelia sang like she'd never sung before with the same result. Just like the previous two numbers, the crowd was enthralled, this time cheering.

When she ran off-stage, Connie was the first person to greet her. "I'm so proud of you, sis," she gushed. Then, like a silver ball in a pinball machine, Cecelia ricocheted from Connie to Stella to little Connie, and to Valentina and Betty, receiving giant embraces as they showered her with compliments. She was thrilled that her married sisters had come.

"You wowed 'em, honey," Valentina said.

"Oh, baby, I love ya so much," Betty added

Cecelia bubbled, "Pinch me so I know this isn't a dream, girls!"

"What're ya gonna do now? Dance?" Valentina asked.

"Gosh, no, Val," Cecelia replied. "Danny said no dancing when the band has a job. He says I need to save my energy for singing. He also doesn't want me to get too cozy with the fellows in the crowd."

"That's gotta be hard for you," Connie said.

"What's that supposed to mean, Connie?"

"You know what I mean!"

"Oh, damn you, Connie! You're going to ruin my reputation if you don't watch out. Anyway, I've gotta do what Danny says. He's got rules for everything. For instance, the guys in the band aren't allowed to date me."

"That sounds sensible to me," Valentina said.

"And to me, too," Connie added. "Because you don't need to get tangled up with any musicians."

"Aw, come off it, Connie. They're great guys," Cecelia argued.

"Yeah...I'll give ya, 'great guys'!"

The plan was for her to sing two songs in each set, and there were two more sets to go. Cecelia and the girls walked over to the bar and grabbed some Cokes and then strolled over to the towering Christmas tree, which stood in the corner of the hall by the windows. Cecelia took a deep breath and gazed through the glass at the constellations that filled the December sky, millions of stars twinkling down at her, promising better days to come. Life, at last, felt good. What could be better? It was almost Christmas, and she was a featured singer with a big band, a dream come true.

It seemed that previous star gazing had been obscured by the dark clouds of war, and with so many men having enlisted or having been drafted, the male population in the Valley had been dwindling, especially evident at dances. It had become commonplace for two girls to dance with each other in their absence.

Cecelia herself still wasn't dating, but rather, playing the field was more her style. Not having seen that guy Michael in weeks, she wondered if he would turn up at this dance. She hoped so.

She turned to admire the lights on the tree, when Valentina, forever playing the parent, warned, "You better get away from these drafty windows, Celia. You have to take care of your voice now that you're a big celebrity."

Cecelia gave her sister a gentle shove. "Get out, Val! I'm not a celebrity."

"Well, to us you're a celebrity," said Betty, giving her a little squeeze. "And judging by the reaction of the crowd, I'd say we're not alone in feeling that way."

No sooner had they reentered the dance hall when a tipsy G.I. stumbled into them. As his eyes traveled from Cecelia's face to her chest, he said, "My, oh my! It's you! You sure gotta great pair o' lungs! Wha's your name again? Cecelia somethin', right? Come on, baby. Le's dance!"

"Thank you," Cecelia said, trying to be gracious, "I'm awfully sorry, but I'm not allowed to da–"

"C'mon, baby. Don' be a cold fish. Give a guy a break!"

"I'm truly sorry, but I'm really not allowed to–"

"What're ya sayin'? Are you too good for me or somethin'?"

All of a sudden, Connie stepped in between the sailor and Cecelia. "Okay, pal, my kid sister just told ya she isn't allowed to dance, but maybe you don't hear so good. Just get lost before I get mad!"

"Listen, sister…what you need is a…a–"

"You listen to me, Buster Brown! What you need is a hot cup of black coffee," Connie countered, coming on even stronger.

The intruder shook his head and stumbled away. When he was out of ear-shot, the entire group of girls broke into laughter as everyone congratulated Connie on her forcefulness.

"Aw, the poor guy," Cecelia said. "He didn't mean any harm."

"He didn't, huh?" Connie said. "I'll decide who doesn't mean any harm and who does. You just mind your damn business and sing."

"So, where ya from, Archie?" Michael asked.

The short soldier with the curly hair sitting across from him in the mess hall had struck up a conversation with him a few days before at breakfast, and Michael liked his sharp wit. Having arrived at the base two days before, Archie had told Michael that he was involved in infantry training and would be shipping off to Europe soon.

Michael figured him to be about four or five years older than himself.

"Me? Well, originally I'm from Philly, but these days I live in Connecticut."

"No kidding. Where abouts?"

"Just a little town you've never heard of. Derby. I moved to Connecticut because I was finding it harder and harder to find work in Philly. Of course, it was my good luck because I met the cutest little girl you ever did see and married her."

"You're shitting me," Michael said.

His new friend grinned. "I shit you not!"

"Well, you'll find this hard to believe," Michael continued, "but I'm from Derby too. I was born there."

"I'll be damned! Ain't life funny?"

Both men picked up a piece of toast covered with creamed beef, known in the Army, crudely, as "shit on a shingle," bit off a hunk, and began chewing. Food was food.

Michael swallowed hard and said, "So that means, if the Army ever breaks down and gives us a furlough, we'll be headed to the same destination."

"Well, that's terrific news, Michael. We're gonna be great friends."

"So tell me. That cute wife of yours got any sisters?"

"Now that you mention it, she does. Counting my wife, there's five of them altogether, but three of them are married. My wife was the most recent to get hitched after I popped the question only three months after I met her."

"That still leaves two, right?"

Archie grinned at him. "When it comes to arithmetic, I can see you're a regular wiz kid."

"Right. So tell me about the two girls."

"Well, those two are inseparable, two peas in a pod. The older of the two has a thick outer shell, though. Not the romantic type from what I can tell, but the younger one is a real doll."

"And how old would this younger one be, Archie?"

"Seventeen, I think. She's supposed to be a senior in high school, except the little goofball quit school."

"Well, when they spring us from this joint, whattaya say you fix me up with her?"

"I'd be willing to do that if my wife don't have no objections."

"Tell me, Archie. Is she pretty?"

"Well, lemme put it this way. She ain't no Betty Grable, but then again, you ain't no Clark Gable neither." Then Michael's new friend howled like he was the funniest thing since Red Skelton.

"Okay, wise guy. It wasn't that funny."

As his laughter subsided, Archie caught his breath and said, "Got ya good on that one! No, all kidding aside, the kid's a looker. You won't be disappointed, I promise."

At the end of the night, Danny asked Cecelia's sisters if they minded if she went to a local haunt with the band to celebrate. The girls were hesitant, but Danny assured them he would personally drive Cecelia home.

"I promise you, ladies, we'll just get a quick bite, and I'll look after her like she's my own kid sister."

The combination of Cecelia's pleading expression and Danny's maturity and warmth prompted her sisters to allow Cecelia to enjoy her first success.

As the four girls, coats in hand, prepared to walk to the bus stop, Connie whispered to her, "Don't let any of these guys get funny with you, Celia!"

Danny was true to his word and made sure that Cecelia sat with him at the restaurant. After everyone ordered a round of drinks, he tapped a spoon on his glass. "Listen up, boys. Listen up! Let's drink a toast to the new darling nightingale of the All-Stars. She did us all proud tonight, just like we knew she would. Let's hear it for Cecelia Alberino."

The boys clinked their glasses and called out "cheers!" and "here, here!" and "skoal!" and "salud!" Cecelia smiled, clinked glasses with Danny, and sipped her Shirley Temple.

Danny spoke as he watched Cecelia fish a sweet maraschino cherry out of her drink with a toothpick. "So, I don't get it."

"Don't get what?" Cecelia asked, the juice of the cherry squirting into her mouth as she bit into it.

"I don't get how a kid like you can sing like that without ever having any experience."

"Well, I don't have professional experience, but growing up, all I ever did was sing, and all I ever wanted was to be a singer. My big brothers always had me singing at parties they threw. And, uhm, I used to sing at school all the time. Then there were the competitions at the local movie theaters. I never won, but I think that was because I didn't have enough people to applaud for me."

"And didn't anybody ever tell you that you're the real deal?"

"I don't know…maybe my brothers' friends. But they're just local yokels. What did they know? Wait. There was a man once we met after a competition. He said I had what it takes. He told us he was going to give me lessons and train me to be a big star."

"So what happened?" Danny asked, squinting.

"What happened was he took a five-dollar deposit from my sister Valentina and then flew the coop. We never saw him again."

"Get out," Danny said, scowling. "The guy beat your family out of five bucks?"

"Yeah, but it was no big deal," Cecelia replied. "What was five lousy bucks to tycoons like us?"

"You're joking."

Cecelia flashed a winning smile at Danny. "Not one bit. When my dear old dad came to this country, John D. Rockefeller took him on as a partner."

"Okay...okay, I get it. You come from a poor Italian family who didn't have a pot to, well, to you-know-what in, just like me. You don't have to play pretend with me. I know when that hustler took your dough, it must have hurt a lot. That's right, ain't it?"

Cecelia realized Danny wasn't like the average guy she encountered, and she couldn't resist his honesty or compassion any longer. Shrugging, she said, "That's right. I've never forgotten it. I locked myself in my room and sobbed until I didn't have any tears left. But life goes on. It's all water under the bridge now. Or is it *over* the bridge? I'm never quite sure."

Danny couldn't help but marvel at Cecelia's ability to poke fun at her own life. "I get that one mixed up too. Either way, that guy was a bastard, pardon my French. Well, I got a hot flash for you. He may have gotten away with stealing five bucks from a poor family, but he missed a golden opportunity to make a lot more than that. I'm sorry that happened to you."

"Aw, thanks, Danny. I can't tell you how much I appreciate that."

Several days passed, and Michael couldn't stop thinking about how Archie was going to fix him up with his sister-in-law. Not usually that high on blind dates, Michael knew this military life had made him so homesick that he was open to almost anything. He laughed inside. *I just hope she doesn't turn out to be the Bride of Frankenstein.* At this point, actually, that might not be the worst thing that ever happened to him. Anything in Derby had to be better than what he was dealing with in the Army.

Two nights later, as Michael sat in the mess hall, writing letters to his sisters, he asked Archie what his sister-in-law's name was.

Archie was writing a letter too, no doubt to his wife.

"Her name?" he asked, his pen still in motion. "It's Cecelia."

"Cecelia?"

Archie didn't look up from his stationery. "Yeah, that's right. Cecelia. You sound surprised? You don't like the name Cecelia or somethin'?"

"No...noooo! I like it just fine. It's a swell name. Is she from Derby too?"

"Nope, my wife's family is from the other side of the river. Cecelia lives in Shelton."

Could it possibly be the same Cecelia? Michael wondered.

"You said she quit school?"

"Yeah, that's right. It was a stupid thing to do, and she did it without talkin' it over with no one. Of course, all the older brothers and sisters had to quit school. Just like me and just like a lotta people. But they were holding out hope for the youngest."

"How many brothers and sisters does Cecelia have?"

"How many?" Not missing a beat, Archie's fountain pen kept scratching out words. "There's eight of 'em altogether."

"No kidding? And the sister who's still at home with her–what's her name?"

"Connie," Archie answered, absentmindedly.

Now he was certain it was the same girl. *Fate,* Michael mused, *is one helluva beautiful thing.*

"So what's this Cecelia do now that she quit school?"

"She works at the Star Pin Factory in Shelton. One of her brothers got her the job. And now my wife tells me she's singing with a big band. Danny Somebody and the All-Stars. How about that? Just started singin' with 'em from what my wife says. I guess the kid's quite a talent, even though I ain't never heard her sing. But, then again, I been in the picture for less than a year."

"Wow!" Michael heard himself exclaim. "A singer with a band. Is that right? I'm gonna be interested in meeting her. Really, really interested!"

13

Michael – 1932

*I*t is early, and the household is bustling with activity. Vincenza and Josie are in one of the upstairs bedrooms where they are helping their sister into her simple white wedding gown. The younger children are wild Indians, running around the house dressed in their Sunday outfits, playing "tag" while Michael sits at the kitchen table with his nose stuck in a voluminous book called *Oliver Twist*.

Vincenza comes to the top of the staircase, stamps her foot on the hardwood floor, and calls, "Michael! You come to the bottom of the stairs right this minute."

Michael moans, peels himself off of the hard wooden chair, and trudges into the narrow hallway.

"Me and Josie gotta get Lucia ready, and we don' need these kids runnin' around screamin'," she admonishes. "We don' gotta be at St. Mary's until 10:00, so you just take the younger ones outside and play. And be sure they don' make a mess of their clothes."

Like with Lucia, Michael can detect Vincenza's slight Italian accent, even though she's been in the U.S. for ten years. Subtle though it may be, it reminds Michael that English isn't their first language.

Unenthusiastically, Michael shepherds his four younger siblings out the door and takes them up onto the field at the top of the terraces, all of them climbing the series of stone steps in single file as he leads the way, like a general leading his troops into battle.

The summer air is heavy, and Michael can smell the pungent aroma of the chicken coop as he passes it on the third level, only to be soothed on the next level by the fresh, sweet smell of the mulberry trees, speckled with purple and white berries.

When Henry stops to eat some berries, Michael turns to Sofia, commanding, "Don't let him eat those! He'll dribble berry juice all over himself, and then who'll catch hell from Vinny? Me, that's who!"

He understands the natural pecking order in the family. As the first born, Vincenza is the second in command to Mom and Pop and rules with an iron hand or at the very least, with a wooden spoon. The rest of the siblings had better do her bidding if they know what's good for them.

The last thing on earth Michael wants is to be responsible for the four younger ones, never mind play with them. Besides, Sofia and Francesca are just a couple of silly girls, and the two boys are only seven and six years old.

When they arrive at the top level, Michael walks over to the small pond, rips a blade of foxtail grass out of the ground, sucks on the end of it, and lays down in the soft turf and closes his eyes. *I wish Vinny was getting married first*, he thinks to himself. *She's older, and besides, what am I going to do without Lucia living with us?*

"What do you think you're doing?" Francesca asks. "It looks like you're taking a nap."

Michael breathes out in irritation. "Oh yeah? Is that what it looks like?"

"Yes, that's exactly what it looks like," Francesca replies.

"And what are you? My mother? Do us both a favor, Franny, take a powder."

"I'm going to tell Vinny you took a nap instead of playing with us," Francesca nags. "She told you you're supposed to watch Henry and Sonny and make sure they don't get dirty or into any trouble."

"You and Sofia can watch 'em, can't ya?"

Sofia, the innocent bystander, is content to let Francesca argue with Michael.

"We can, but you're the oldest, and Vinny told you to do it."

Michael reluctantly opens one eye, squints, and blinded by the hot sun, abruptly shuts it again more tightly. "Please, Franny, for the love of God, would you leave me alone? Go take a long walk off a short pier, why dontcha?"

"I certainly will not," Francesca says. "What I will do is march myself right back down those steps and tell Vinny that you're not doing what she told you to do, and then you'll see what'll happen to you, Mr. High and Mighty!"

"Over my dead body, you will," Michael complains.

"I'll step right over your dead body if I have to!"

"Oh, Jesus Christ, Franny! You're a royal pain in the ass."

"Ohhhh, you better go to confession with that filthy mouth," Francesca gasps.

Prodded into action, Michael drags himself up from his bed of grass and says, "Okay, everybody, here's what we're gonna do. We're gonna have a race around the pond."

"That's not fair," Francesca says. "You'll win because you're the oldest."

"Don't worry about that, blabbermouth. I'm going to make it fair. I'll give you all a head start. Here's how we'll do it. When I call your name and say 'go,' you can start running. Sonny first because he's the littlest, then Henry, then you, blabbermouth, and then Sofia. After Sofia has had a good enough head start, I'll go. Fair?"

Everyone agrees that it is fair. Henry yells out, "Hooray, let's do it," and Sonny chimes in, "Yeah, come on, let's race."

Michael calls each name in succession as promised. When he calls Sofia, Sonny is halfway around the pond and Henry is gaining ground. When Michael judges Sofia to have a ten yard head start, he takes off. The girls are easy to pass in their Sunday dresses, and by the time he rounds the last curve of the pond, he passes Sonny. Little Henry is quicker than the rest, but Michael effortlessly overtakes him and wins the race.

Huffing and puffing, the four children stand, clutching their knees and catching their breath.

"Let's do it again!" Henry yells. "This time I'll beat ya, Michael."

"I don't want to do it again," Francesca complains.

"Aw, you're just sore because you came in last," Michael says.

"Am not sore," Francesca shoots back.

"Are too!"

"Am not!"

"Are too! Okay, everybody, we'll do it again, and Miss Prissy can race if she wants or not. I don't care. This time, everybody gets an even bigger head start."

Moments later, Michael sounds the call for each of them to start running.

Now a mere spectator, Francesca can see that Michael has presented himself with a bigger challenge as promised. As the group approaches the finish line, Michael pushes himself to overtake little Henry, who is once again in the lead. As he nears the finish line, passing Henry on the inside, Michael's foot slides on a patch of pond mud and he stumbles, reels to his left, and slides into the shallow edge of the pond.

"I won," yells a gleeful Henry. "I won! I won!"

Sofia and Francesca run over to Michael. "Are you alright?" Sofia asks.

"Oh, God," Michael says, "my pants are all muddy, and I think I ripped them in the back."

"Stand up," says Francesca. "Oh gee, yes, they're completely ripped down the back. Your underwear is showing."

This remark sends Henry and Sonny into a fit of laughter, but the girls understand the weightiness of the situation. Suppressing their own urge to giggle, they know Michael is capable of throwing them in the pond if they fail to maintain their composure. The girls know it's a dire situation. Michael can't very well go to the wedding in torn pants, and they are the one decent pair that he owns.

"What am I going to do now?" Michael asks.

"Maybe Vinny...or Josie can sew them before we go to church," Sofia feebly offers.

The five of them head back down the stone steps to the house. While Michael waits in the kitchen, the two girls reluctantly report to Vincenza.

Stomping into the kitchen, she barks, "Let me see those, you!" She grabs Michael by the arm and turns him around.

"What did you do? You made a mess outta your pants. Damn you! Look, they're not even ripped on the seam. And they're filthy dirty. Even if they were ripped on the seam, I wouldn't have time to sew them. We have to go to the church right now. A car is coming to take Lucia any minute. Buzz's friend."

"But I have to see her get married," Michael says.

"Well, you can't! You ruined your good pants, and you can't let everyone see your rear end hangin' out in the church. What kinda thing would that be? You'll just have ta stay home. Sof, you take the kids and walk down ta the church. Get going right now, because the wedding starts in less than a half hour."

Michael hides in the pantry, crying, until everyone is gone. Once alone, he paces back and forth between the kitchen and the living room. He has to see Lucia get married. Reaching around behind himself, he manages to grab the ripped edges of the seat of his pants and hold them together, and he decides to walk to the church.

When he arrives, Lucia and Buzz are already at the altar. Michael creeps up the stairs to the choir loft above and nestles himself into the darkness of the far corner. The only other person there is the church organist, unaware of his presence.

Michael has never before seen a wedding ceremony. He gazes down at Lucia, kneeling in a faded white dress and veil alongside Buzz, who is decked out in a suit and tie. He has never seen either of them so dressed up before. He listens to the organ music and to the parts of the Mass–the priest intermittently chanting in Latin. He watches as Mom and Pop and the rest as his family and their small group of friends receive Holy Communion, feeling he should be in the Communion line with them. *Lucia must be wondering why I'm not there*, he worries.

After Communion, Michael watches as Lucia and Buzz exchange wedding vows. He can hear the booming voice of the priest, echoing throughout the church in a loud monotone, "Do you, Lucia…" and "Do you, Marcello…" Then the much softer responses of the bride and groom, who he assumes have said "I do," but he can't quite hear. Michael can't contain the stream of tears that are rolling down his cheeks.

When the Mass ends and the organist plays the recessional, Michael watches Lucia and Buzz stand up and, holding hands, sweep up the aisle toward the vestibule. As she passes by the small congregation, Lucia looks to her left and right, flashing a demure smile at her family and friends.

Michael has to flee the church. He can't be seen by anyone, given the condition of his pants. He pushes open the heavy oak door and hobbles down the steps, and after zigzagging between neighbors' houses and through back yards, he looks for a place where he can watch the picnic that is to follow the wedding. Climbing the stone steps to the second terrace, he hides among the rows of tomato vines, now bearing plump red fruit. Obscured behind the leafy vines, he won't be detected.

Hidden away, he spends the afternoon smelling the aroma of a small roasted pig cooking on a spit, listening to old Mr. Fernino squeeze the bellows of his cranberry colored accordion with its white and black keys on one side and its many little silver buttons on the other, and watching the family and friends dance to traditional Italian songs, like "Torna A Surriento," "Funiculì, Funiculà," and "Tarantella Napoletana."

As everyone eats and sings and dances below, Michael holds his position, heartbroken. Mainly, his focus is on Lucia. Lucia, who has looked after him in times of trouble. Lucia, who has cared about him more than anyone else. Lucia, whom he loves with his whole heart and soul.

She must see I'm not there, he thinks. *What did Vincenza tell her? Is she worried about me?*

As the afternoon wears on, Michael, sitting in the garden dirt, contemplates his condition. What's the difference now? His pants are ruined. He knows that he won't get to talk to Lucia on this, her wedding day. He also knows that when the picnic ends, Lucia and Buzz will be living in an apartment together for the rest of their lives. After today, she will no longer be nearby on a daily basis looking after him.

With the soiled palms of his hands, Michael wipes away his last tears, smudging dirt across his cheeks and eyes. Laying down in the dirt, exhausted, he wonders how he will explain to Lucia why he let her down on the most important day of her life.

14

*H*e waited until an hour before the date to shave. A smooth chin was what was called for on this night of nights. As Michael lathered his face with the soft bristles of his shaving brush at the bathroom sink, his two kid sisters hovered at the door, giggling.

"Never seen a guy shave before?" he asked the girls with some amusement.

"No, we've seen a guy shave before," Francesca sang. "At least we've seen *you* shave before. But it seems odd that you're shaving so late in the day, doesn't it, Sof?"

Sofia giggled, "Sure does!"

Michael couldn't help but smile. The two closest in age to him had been scorchers ever since they stopped sucking their thumbs and started talking, especially Francesca. The reality of it was that they looked up to him, and he knew it.

"Yeah? Well, let's just say I didn't feel like it until now. Too lazy." Michael swept the sharp blade of the straight razor down the right side of his cheek and swished it into the porcelain sink basin in one glamorously fluid motion.

"I think Michael's in love, don't you, Sof?" Francesca teased.

"Sure do," Sofia repeated.

"How can I be in love, ya dumb asses? It's a blind date. I've probably never even seen her before."

Sofia smirked. "Whattaya mean *probably* never seen her before?"

Sofia, the eternal skeptic, he thought, *and Francesca, the blabbermouth.*

"Yeah," Francesca chimed in. "Whattaya mean?"

"I didn't mean a damn thing by that. But who knows? Maybe I've run into her somewhere or other."

"Ooooh, so it's not a real blind date," Sofia squealed. "What's her name again?"

"Her name, Miss Nosy, is Cecelia." Michael had both cheeks done and was now working on his stubbly chin and neck.

"Better be careful," Francesca offered. "Don't nick yourself. You don't want to bleed all over her, especially since she's somebody you might know."

"Alright, you two. I've had enough, so get lost."

As Michael concentrated on the space above his upper lip, the phone rang, and he heard Francesca's voice answer.

"Yes, Lu, he's here...shaving...he's getting ready for a big date tonight...oh yeah, it's a big secret...well, you know him. He thinks he's hot stuff..."

Before she could continue, Michael appeared next to her, giving her a wry look as he wiped the creamy residue from his face with a hand towel.

"Uh-oh," Francesca said. "Here he is, Lu. I better give the phone to him."

Michael brought the receiver to his ear and spoke into the mouthpiece. "Hello, Lu. Sorry I haven't had a chance to see you yet...of course, I missed you, something awful...don't worry, I'll stop by tomorrow. Promise...yup, that's right. It's a blind date... that's right..."

And now, looking about the kitchen, he realized the girls were no longer in sight. Bringing his face very close to the mouthpiece, he continued in a hushed tone. "Can you still hear me, Lu...I don't want those two busybody sisters of ours listening...but remember that girl I told you about a few weeks before I enlisted...that's right, the one I met at a dance...I think this blind date might be one and the same girl...I'm practically positive...that's right, Lu...well, sure...I know...what a crazy coincidence, right?...okay...okay, right...I'll be by tomorrow and let you know...you bet...I'll see you tomorrow...bye."

Hanging up, he could hear his younger sisters singing in the pantry, echoing each other.

"Michael and Cecelia"..."Michael and Cecelia"

"Sittin' in a tree"... "Sittin' in a tree"

"K-I-S-S"..."K-I-S-S"

"I-N-G"..."I-N-G"

"First comes love"..."First comes love"

"Then comes marriage"..."Then comes marriage"

"Then comes baby"..."Then comes baby"

"In a baby carriage"..."In a baby carriage"

Michael walked over to the pantry and, without warning, grabbed the two girls, hoisting them off the floor, one under each muscular arm.

"You two think you're pretty damn cute, don't ya?"

Francesca, kicking and screaming in a frenzy of laughter, yelled, "No we don't, do we, Sof?"

"Absolutely not!" Sofia cried out hysterically.

"What we think," Francesca howled, "is that *you're* pretty damn cute!"

An hour later, Michael sat on a couch in Archie's living room, waiting for the girls to finish dressing and come downstairs. As Archie finished tinkering with some task in the nearby kitchen, Michael looked down at the perfect, white gardenia he held between his thumb and index finger. If Cecelia Alberino was, in fact, as he had suspected, the same girl he had met, he hoped she would like that he had remembered every detail about her, even the flower in her hair.

While Michael looked dapper in his uniform, Archie wasn't wearing his. They had been home on furlough for three days, and Archie, having had plenty of time to reacquaint himself with his wife, had no need to impress anyone. Michael, on the other hand, wanted to make the best first impression. Or in this case, the best second impression. *Or*, he thought, *my third!* He remembered the awkward meeting at Vonette's.

When he arrived, Archie had remarked, "That's quite a get-up, but you won't need to worry about passing inspection here, soldier."

"I'm just trying to get a passing grade when she sees me."

"At ease, Corporal. She'll like you. I have a sixth sense about these things."

"I hope so. It's been almost eight months since I've had a date with a girl. I'm almost not sure how to act. I know she's not one of those floozies we used to run into in McCook."

Archie grinned at him. "I think you'll figure it out. It's like riding a bike, ain't it?"

Michael, now on the couch, contemplating his gardenia, heard a knock at the door. Archie emerged from the kitchen. "One of my wife's other sisters," he said to Michael without looking at him, "to watch the baby while we're out."

"I didn't know you had a kid," Michael said.

"Yeah...my wife gave birth six weeks ago. It's a boy! Remind me to give you a cigar later."

When Cecelia's sister Connie entered the living room, it clinched it for Michael.

"Connie, this is my army buddy, Michael DeMarco. Michael, meet Cecelia's sister. We like to take advantage of free labor."

Michael stood up and brought the gardenia behind his back. "How do you do?"

"I'm doing good," she replied with hesitation. "You look... terribly familiar for some reason. Have we met before?"

"We may have. You never know. It's a small world."

Michael wasn't going to say he knew who she was. Not yet. First, he wanted to see if Cecelia remembered him. That was what was most important.

"Oh, I just hate blind dates, Val," Cecelia complained while deftly applying a thin, dark line to the upper lid of her right eye at the vanity. "You know how much I hate them."

She set the thin brush down, pulled her head back, and looked at herself in the round mirror, satisfied with her handiwork.

"Cut the crap, you. You'll survive," Valentina called from the bathroom. "Archie says this Michael is a stand-up guy. Besides, the guy's been away from home for three quarters of a year now, and he's lonely. Consider it your contribution to the war effort."

"I'll bet he's got buck teeth and beady eyes," Cecelia whined.

"Will you stop it?" Valentina said, brandishing a hairbrush as she entered the bedroom. "Archie promised he's good looking. We wouldn't fix you up with some goofball."

"Well, I hope I'm not sorry I agreed to this."

"You'll be fine, Celia. Don't be such a brat!"

"I just don't see why you wanted to fix me up."

"We wanted to fix you up because you're almost eighteen years old, and you need to start thinking about getting married and raising a family."

"I can meet boys on my own. I meet plenty."

"You haven't been meeting plenty lately because of this damn war. There are fewer and fewer eligible men around. You must see that when you sing at local dances. And you don't need to get involved with any of those guys in the band. Most of 'em are married, anyways. I'll bet you ten to one that those cads would cheat on their wives if you were willing to give them a whirl."

"Well, I'm not going to give a married man a whirl, so you don't need to worry about that. And besides, I'm too young to think about marriage."

"But who knows when this war will end? What if it lasts for four or five years like the last one? Or even longer? You could be an old maid by the time it's over."

"I hate this war," Cecelia said. "And I hate marriage. And I hate blind dates."

Valentina was the first down the stairs. Archie had been right. She couldn't have been more than five feet tall, and she was as cute as could be. Once again, Michael stood, and as Archie made the obligatory introductions, he continued to hold the gardenia behind his back with one hand as he shook Valentina's hand with the other. Valentina's hand was small, but her grip was firm.

"Skipper's already asleep," she told Connie. "You can listen to the radio all night and not have to worry about him. My hunch is he won't make a peep."

"I hope he does make a peep," Connie replied. "I want to play with the little tiger."

Then, Michael's heartbeat accelerated as he heard Cecelia's feet coming down the steps. She was wearing a black skirt and a cardinal red blouse, a stunning combination.

When she reached the bottom of the stairs, she turned into the room and made eye contact with him.

"You!" she said, her eyes wide with astonishment.

Michael could feel himself blush. "Yes. Me."

Archie squinted, an almost satisfied smile on his face, like he couldn't have planned it better if he had tried. "You two kids already know each other?"

"Yes," Cecelia said. "We met once. Wait, twice, actually. Why didn't you tell my brother-in-law you knew me?"

Connie put the pieces together too. "Oh, now I remember you. You were the guy who walked us home from the dance that night, with that dopey friend of yours in the truck."

Not losing his focus on Cecelia, Michael said, "I wasn't one hundred percent sure it was you. And besides, I thought it might be fun to surprise you."

He brought his arm from behind his back in a sweeping gesture and handed her the gardenia. "I remembered," he said.

Cecelia smiled. "Oh, how thoughtful of you. Thank you." Then she added with a sigh, "Well, I *am* surprised, to say the least."

"But I hope not disappointed."

She twisted her lips into the cutest smirk he'd ever seen. "I'll let you know in a few hours," and she pulled a bobby pin out of her pocketbook and fixed the white flower into her hair. It was perfect.

The two couples headed out the door. Archie suggested they walk since the Commodore Hull Movie Theater was a couple of blocks down the street from their Elizabeth Street apartment. Michael had walked by their house during his life more times than he could count.

As they walked by the Sterling Opera House, Michael remembered sneaking in to see operettas as a younger kid. He told

Cecelia, Valentina, and Archie about Donald O'Connor performing there and how he and some of the neighborhood boys had played catch with him across the street on the Derby Green.

"I also remember seeing Amelia Earhart give a lecture. I was, maybe, twelve. She talked about becoming a pilot just because she wanted to and about flying across the Pacific. Imagine that. A lady pilot. It made me think that maybe we can do anything if we want it badly enough."

Cecelia was moved by his stories and the passion in his voice.

Michael was excited about seeing *Casablanca*, a new film starring Humphrey Bogart and Ingrid Bergman, and he hoped Cecelia shared his enthusiasm. The movie was chock full of romance and suspense and, like a lot of recent movies, had an anti-Nazi message, which wasn't lost on Michael. As far as he was concerned, the Nazis deserved what was coming to them. While the film met his expectations and more, he couldn't help wishing they had done something else on their first date, because it didn't give him much of a chance to talk to Cecelia.

After the movie, the four walked back to Archie and Valentina's where they found Connie asleep on the couch. The four of them sat at the kitchen table and had a quiet conversation over coffee.

As they talked, something fascinated Michael. He noticed that Archie and Valentina called each other "Butch."

"How'd ya like the movie, Butch?" Archie asked her.

"I liked it a lot. How about you, Butch?" she replied.

"Yeah, it was a good one. That Ingrid Bergman is quite a dish."

"Now don't go calling another girl a dish, Butch, if ya know what's good for ya!"

And it went on like that. Michael had heard of couples calling each other lots of pet names. "Baby" and "Honey" and "Sweetie," but never "Butch." It tickled his funny bone.

Feeling it was time to go, Michael asked if anybody minded if he drove Cecelia home. Valentina wasn't too keen on the idea, but Michael assured her that her kid sister was safe with him.

"I don't know about this. What do you think, Butch?" she asked Archie.

"Oh, it's fine," Archie assured her. "I vouch for Mike. There ain't nothin' to worry about, Butch."

"But what about Connie?" Cecelia asked.

Archie chimed in again, "We don't want to wake her up. She can spend the night on our couch."

Michael realized Archie was running interference for him.

After saying their goodbyes, Michael opened the car door for Cecelia and headed for Shelton. Upon reaching her street, the engine grumbled in its attempt to climb the hill.

"Oh, jeepers, this is a pretty steep hill," Michael complained.

"Yes, I'm sorry," Cecelia replied. "It's called Hillside Avenue for good reason. I should have mentioned it."

"No, that's fine. It's just that I think I need a new transmission, and…"

As he downshifted, the car wasn't responding.

"I think that's about as far as she's willing to go."

"What now?" Cecelia asked.

"Now? Now we walk the rest of the way up the hill. I hope you don't mind."

"But how will you get the car home?"

"I'll get her turned around somehow and pop the clutch. That usually works."

Walking up the hill felt like a good opportunity to make his move, but he didn't want her to think he was some kind of big-time operator because that wasn't his style.

"Would you mind if I held your hand, Cecelia?" he asked.

"No, I wouldn't mind."

"Just because…because it's dark."

"Yes," she said with a knowing smile, "just because it's dark."

Upon arriving at her porch, they took a seat on the steps. Michael didn't release her hand. It felt good right where it was. He didn't know it, but it felt good to Cecelia as well.

"So, I hope ya don't mind my bringing up this subject, but Archie tells me you quit high school. How come?"

She looked into his eyes and sighed. "It's a long story."

"It's just that an education is important."

"I know," she agreed. "If I get to know you better, maybe I'll tell you about it someday."

"And he said you're singing in a band."

"Yes, that's right."

"How did you ever end up doing something like that?"

"I just went and auditioned, and the bandleader liked me."

"You like doing that, Cecelia?"

"I sure do. It makes me feel like…like I'm alive. Like I have a purpose."

They sat together, not speaking, her hand in his, as he mulled over what she had shared. Finally, he broke the silence. "I want my life to have purpose too. I'm not sure what I mean by that yet, but I'll figure it out, see. Because, one way or another, my life is going to have purpose. I'm going to be somebody someday. I guarantee it, Cecelia. Or I'll die trying."

"I don't doubt that," she said, and he felt a comforting sensation in his heart, like warm honey pumping through his veins.

She rubbed her thumb across his index finger. "You have quite a bump on your finger."

"Yeah…I guess I do."

"What happened?"

"Oh, it was just a lame-brained thing I did when I was a kid. It's a long story. If I get to know you better, maybe I'll tell you about it."

She smiled and said, "That's fine. When we get to know each other, maybe we'll learn all of each other's deepest secrets."

"I'd like that," he said.

"I better be going in, though, or my mother will wonder what we're doing out here. She never goes to bed until I'm in the house, safe and sound. You know how mothers are."

He got up to walk her to the door.

Summoning all of his courage, he asked, "Is it okay if I ask you a few more quick questions?"

The naked overhead bulb shined down on Cecelia, brilliantly illuminating her face.

"Sure, of course," she replied. "Ask anything you like."

"I've only got a few more days left. Do you mind if I come calling on you again?"

She smiled. "I'd like that."

"And do you mind…what I mean is, would you allow me to write to you while I'm away? A large army base is an awfully lonely place."

"Sure, Michael, you can write to me if you like."

And, finally, he voiced what he had been working up to. "And one last question. It's been ages since I kissed a pretty girl. Would you mind if…if I–"

"I wouldn't mind at all," she said, helping him and flashing a smile that would win any man's heart.

It was the sweetest first kiss he had ever experienced, and he knew at that very moment, it was a kiss that he would take back to Nebraska with him–one that would sustain him no matter where this man's army sent him, even if it was to the front lines.

Dazed, he made his way back down to the car and let the Ford roll backwards, backing it into a nearby driveway. Then, standing outside the driver's side, he gave her a push with all his might, jumped in, let her gain some momentum rolling down the hill, and when he popped the clutch, the engine coughed and came back to life.

Michael drove home feeling renewed. Cecelia Alberino had jump started his heart, and he knew it. Michael had felt down-hearted since enlisting, but now maybe he had something to feel good about, something to look forward to, and someone he could call "my girl."

15

Michael – 1937

$\mathcal{D}$espite now being fifteen years old, Michael awakens on Christmas morning with a glimmer of hope in his heart. Having stopped believing in Santa long ago, he knows it will be a Christmas morning just like every other, but there is something he doesn't know. At first, it appears his hunch is correct. He and his younger brothers and sisters receive the usual stockings filled with a few chunks of coal, topped off with an orange or two and a handful of walnuts. His disappointment is slightly diminished when he finds a fifty-cent piece as well.

But when his older sisters arrive late in the morning for Christmas dinner, Lucia has a special present for him–a small box wrapped in festive red and green paper. In the past, she had given him a pair of knitted mittens or a scarf. But there is something different about this gift, and something different about the glow in her cheeks as she hands it to him.

Trembling, Michael hastily unwraps the small parcel. Taking the cover off the square velvet box, he finds a pocket watch. It isn't twenty-four carat gold like Pop's, only gold-plated, nor does it have a cover that clicks open and shut–but still, it is a real watch, shiny and round with a perfect white face and bold black hands that point to prominent Roman numerals. Best of all, it is his very own.

His eyes sparkling, he looks at Lucia, unable to comprehend the gift. "But how? How did you…"

"I have a job," she replies. "I saved my pennies and nickels and dimes until I had enough to buy it at the jewelry store."

"But I just can't believe th-th-that…" Michael stutters and then runs to her, wrapping his arms around her and squeezing her tightly.

Lucia understands. She has seen how Michael, since he was a toddler, loved to sit in his father's lap and play with his pocket watch and fob chain. On many a late Sunday morning while helping to prepare a meal, Lucia had watched Michael press the button atop the gold crown of the watch, causing the shiny, round door to spring open, repeating the same operation, delighting in the *click, click, click* sound of the opening and closing of the timepiece. Lucia knew. She remembered stirring a stew as Michael studied the black numerals and examined the precise movements of the small and big hands, despite being too young to tell time. Quiet and observant, Lucia watched, time and again, how Michael pulled the watch chain through the buttonhole in Pop's vest, wrapped his fingers around the links, and let the pocket watch swing back and forth, his wondering eyes hypnotized by the pendulum-like movement.

And now, his dream is a reality. Michael is the envy of the younger siblings, who understand that Michael, as the first born in this country, is the crown prince of the family.

Before dinner, they gather around him as he displays his precious trinket to them but won't let them touch it. "See, just like Pop's," he proclaims. Michael can't wait to show the kids in the neighborhood.

The next morning, Michael dangles the glimmering timepiece before the covetous eyes of his friends. After a chorus of "oohs" and "ahs," the children get to the business of sliding down the hill near the woods at the end of Smith Street. With his new treasure tucked securely in his front pants pocket, Michael slides down the hill sitting on the lid of an old trash can. Repeatedly, he trudges up the icy hill and then races down like Flash Gordon flying through space.

When Scooter yells, "Hey, Mikey, give it a try on your belly, like me," Michael goes down the hill, lying face down on the lid, knees bent and pulled toward his backside. When the lid catapults off a ridge of a high snowbank and launches Michael airborne before crashing back on the surface with a thud, he realizes something is wrong. Rolling onto his back, heart pounding, he desperately reaches into his pocket and withdraws the watch, finding its back cover dented and its crystal cracked.

Arriving home, Michael rushes to his bedroom and pries the back cover off with his pocket knife, exposing the detached and damaged wheels, springs, and gears. He knows he wouldn't have the slightest idea how to repair his ruined treasure. Heartbroken, Michael sits on his bed, staring at the shattered remnants of his Christmas hopes and dreams.

Cecelia – 1937

On the morning of her twelfth Christmas, Cecelia has no expectation she'll be receiving anything she's dreamed of. Dreams, she knows, don't come true. So, her eyes light up with surprise when she finds a rectangular box, wrapped in festive paper, under the tree. Kneeling down, she examines it, discovering a little white tag: "To Cecelia, from Santa."

She chuckles and then looks at Connie and Valentina. "Okay, what's going on, you two? Is this some kind of joke?"

"It's not a joke," Valentina replies, giving Connie a conspiratorial glance. "It's just a little something we working girls thought you might like. You can also thank Betty and Phyllis when they get here because they pitched in too."

Cecelia sighs and begins unwrapping the box with care. She will save the ribbon and the gold wrapping paper. Lifting the lid off of the long box, she discovers a celluloid baby doll swaddled in an immaculate white dress. Her heart fills with a mixture of conflicting emotions.

"Oh my," she begins, tears filling her eyes. "Val, Connie…I don't quite know what to say. I've never received a real present before. You shouldn't have. Really! I don't…just…thank you."

Observing her youngest's emotions, Mama smiles, but Valentina and Connie, puzzled by their sister's reaction, give each other a questioning look.

"If all of you don't mind, I think I'll take this upstairs where I can...I'd just like to take it upstairs."

Slipping out of the living room, Cecelia heads up the stairs to her bedroom.

Rivulets of tears stream down her face as she sits on the bed, forlorn and embarrassed. Staring down at the doll, Cecelia contemplates how beautiful it is. But she has an implicit awareness of the changes happening in her own body. On the cusp of adolescence, she thinks, *It's just too late*, feeling ungrateful and guilty. She can't tell her sisters how she feels. She wouldn't even know how to begin.

But Cecelia can't imagine playing with the doll like she might have several years before. In her frustration, she wants to take the doll and smash it against the bedroom bureau, but fortunately she is able to control herself. How would anyone understand? With trembling hands, Cecelia tucks the babydoll back into its box, mourning the end of her childhood, now gone forever. She takes the box and places it on a high closet shelf, never to be opened again.

16

*C*ecelia slept restlessly after her blind date with the ever-interesting Michael DeMarco. When her sister told her his first name, Cecelia hadn't made the connection with the guy she had met at the Lakeview Casino months before. And that was quite a trick he pulled, not telling Archie that he knew her. She didn't mind, though. Michael was charming. And he was also very good looking, which was a nice bonus. And despite not wanting to get serious with anyone, when Michael asked if he could write to her, how could she say no? Like Valentina had said, it would be Cecelia's contribution to the war effort. But wasn't it more than that? When Michael told her he was going to be somebody someday, there was a fire in his eyes that was hard to ignore. She recalled that, once, her brother Ernie had said to her, "Before you get involved with a fellow, make sure he's going somewhere instead of nowhere!" It was good advice, she knew.

So she was pleased when he showed up at her door late the next afternoon. He wasn't wearing his uniform this time, but instead, he was decked out in a pair of gray slacks with a black sport shirt which his muscular frame filled out quite nicely.

The two sat on the porch and drank lemonade, and he told her about military life.

"Basic training was rough," he said. "Of course, it was rigorous, physically, but that part was a cinch. It was rough in other ways.

You have to learn to take orders quickly, and I'm a guy who values his independence. Add to that, I had never been away from home before, so I guess I got pretty homesick. I'm close to my sisters and brothers, ya see, not to mention Mom and Pop."

"That must've been hard," Cecelia replied, giving him her full attention. "But you must have made new friends there."

"Not many. Let's just say the drill sergeants discourage talking to anyone. Meals are silent. They keep you busy from dawn until lights out, and if you talk, there's hell to pay. To make matters worse, I was even there for Christmas, and I have to be honest. I was pretty down in the dumps that day."

"Wasn't there anything special for Christmas?" she asked.

"Not really," he said. "Oh, they gave us the day off, Mass, and for once, a decent meal, but otherwise, Uncle Sam was more like Uncle Scrooge. I spent the day waiting for a phone call to go through to my family, and boy, was I ever depressed when it never happened. The phone lines were twisted into a tangle of granny knots. Making matters worse, we spent Christmas Eve digging ditches and on New Year's Day, we hiked twenty miles with full gear. What a raw deal."

Cecelia didn't know what to say, and she had learned long ago that sometimes silence is the best response when someone shares something personal. She just gazed into Michael's eyes, hoping that he could see she cared.

As he finished his lemonade, he clinked the ice around in the glass and continued, "The thing is, what they're doing is training us to kill. I hope hearing that isn't too much for you. Don't get me wrong. I can be a pretty rough and tumble guy when I need to be, but I don't know. We had drills where we charged stuffed dummies holding our rifles and plunged the bayonets into their chests. It's kind of hard to imagine doing that to another guy. Does that make sense?"

"Yes! It makes perfect sense."

"Well, anyway," he continued, "it's pretty rough when you've led a headstrong, independent life like I have. Usually, when a guy wants to break a habit, he does so in steps so that it can't hurt him. It's different in the Army, though. They force you to change your whole life immediately. They don't allow any mistakes or excuses.

Any that a fellow makes, he pays for dearly. We can't do a single, solitary thing without being given an order first. And a fellow can go to jail for six months just for saying a few words that he shouldn't have said, so you just keep your mouth shut and take it."

"I see," she said.

He let out a deep sigh. "I'll bet you think I'm a big crybaby."

"No...not at all," she said, taking his hand in hers once again.

"It's just that we're not even supposed to think. Sometimes I feel so fed up I think I'm about to burst, but I still hang on. It can't last forever, right?"

She smiled at him. "Right. It can't last forever. It won't."

Then he talked about medic school, his current assignment, and how a few months before, they had failed to save the life of a guy who had been electrocuted working on some electrical wires. The team of medics had taken turns giving the man mouth-to-mouth resuscitation for hours, which was all they could do since there was no way to get him to a hospital, but they couldn't save him.

"Death is something I guess I'll be seeing a lot of down the road."

Cecelia nodded, and they sat for a good spell in silence, listening to the birds sing until Michael finally said, "I hate to say it, but I better go. I promised Mom I'd have dinner with the family, but I'd love to stop by tomorrow."

He couldn't resist kissing Cecelia for the second time–a sweet, short kiss in the broad light of day.

The next day, one of the boys from the band stopped by in the late morning. A trombone player named Augie Norko, one of the few unmarried band members, had called on her several times now. A nice guy, Augie couldn't have been any older than Cecelia.

It was hard to resist Augie's flirtations, but she said playfully, "I keep telling you, Augie, that Danny doesn't allow any of the guys in the band to date me."

"I know that, baby. But what Danny don't know won't hurt Danny. If you don't tell him, neither will I. Deal?"

"No deal," she said, trying to suppress laughter. There was something awfully cute about the way Augie's lips curled when he smiled.

"Well, how's about you and me just being friends then? Friendship's still legal in this country, ain't it?"

"Yes, friendship is still legal," she teased back. "I guess that's fine. But I think it will be best if Danny doesn't know about our friendship."

"Well, you know me, baby. Like I've already said, my lips are sealed."

Cecelia's eyes opened wide as she spotted Michael's Ford coming up the hill. As he approached the house, he slowed down almost to a stop, then with a deafening squeal, he sped away, leaving skid marks on the tarred, black road.

"What the–? Who's that guy?" Augie asked.

Cecelia sighed deeply, and not knowing how to answer, said, "He's just a guy I met recently. He's in the Army, and I don't know… it's just all very confusing."

She felt compelled to get rid of Augie sooner than she would have liked and walked to her sister Valentina's after lunch to tell her about the episode with Michael.

"Would you do me a big favor, Val?" Cecelia asked. "Would you have Archie get in touch with Michael and tell him I'd like to see him today? But, oh God, I think it would be best to meet him somewhere away from the house because I'm not sure what to expect from him. He seems like he can be very hot-headed, so maybe Archie can set up a meeting for tomorrow afternoon on the Derby Green."

"Hot-headed?" Valentina asked. "Are you safe with this guy?"

"Oh God, yes, I'm fine. Maybe hot-headed isn't the right word. I just need to talk to him."

"Okay, Celia. I'll have Archie take care of that, but be careful."

Cecelia arrived punctually at 1:00 on Sunday and waited by the Civil War cannons on the far side of the Green. When she saw Michael pull up and walk up the stone steps and cross the walkway toward her, she wasn't sure what she was going to say.

He sat down on the opposite end of the park bench.

The two of them sat across from each other for a few minutes without speaking, and then finally, she patted her knees and spoke. "What was that all about yesterday?"

Michael shrugged and said, "You told me I could call on you, but I wasn't expecting you to, uhm…to be there with your boyfriend."

"He's not my boyfriend. He's just a friend. His name is Augie, and he's just a nice guy from the band."

"Listen," Michael said, "if you have a boyfriend, you can be straight with me. I'm a big boy."

"Hey! What's the big idea? I told you. He and I are just friends."

Michael pressed his lips together. "Look, you're obviously naive. That's okay. I know some girls can be that way. But let me clue you in. No guy wants to be *just friends*, not with a knockout like you."

"Well, thank you for the compliment, but it doesn't matter what he wants to be because that's all we are, and all we'll ever be, because Danny–he's the bandleader–Danny doesn't allow guys in the band to date me. And even if he did, I'm not so sure I'd be interested in Augie. But, let me ask you something else, Michael DeMarco. What makes you think you have some kind of claim on me?"

Sheepishly, he said, "I just...I just thought, you know, that you let me hold your hand and kiss you goodnight, and...well, you said I could write to you."

She shook her head. "I know. But you're not the first boy that's ever held my hand or kissed me goodnight, you know? And saying you can write to me doesn't mean we're going steady or anything, at least not yet. I'm still too young to get serious with anybody."

Michael was learning that Cecelia was a spirited girl who wasn't afraid to speak her mind. He let out a deep sigh, signaling his discomfort. "Listen, I apologize. I can see you're not interested, so I'll just leave you alone and you won't ever have to worry about hearing from me again."

Cecelia couldn't have been more frustrated. *What is it with this guy? Is he going to walk away, just like that?* she thought. It didn't make sense.

"Please don't be like that," she pleaded. "I have said nothing of the kind. I think you're honest and witty and charming and a lot of other great things. And if the time comes when it feels right to get serious with someone, well, I hope that it's someone like you. When I said I wanted you to write to me, I meant it. I hope you and I can always say what we really mean to each other. So, you go back to your army, and as soon as you get there, you go ahead and write to me. And I promise to write back. I can't make you many promises, but I can make you that one."

Michael made eye contact with her and held her gaze. "Do you really mean that?"

"I would never say anything to you that I didn't mean," she said. "And if you're in the Army when Christmas comes this year, at least you'll have someone back home to write to."

"Whew! That'll sure help." Michael smiled and slid a foot closer to her. "Christmases were never what I would have liked them to be, growing up. It seems funny, doesn't it? And I'm not even sure where I'll be next Christmas."

Cecelia reached out and took his hand in hers. "I know what you mean about Christmases gone by, but I hope your next Christmas, wherever you may be, is a little merrier than the last one."

"If I receive a letter from you, I know it will be."

"I'm glad."

Michael looked to his left and right, and then, after he turned and looked behind him, he slid closer and kissed her. It was a longer kiss than either of the first two had been.

That night, he visited because he would be, as he put it, "shipping out" early the next morning.

When Cecelia saw his car pull up, leaning over the porch railing, she called out, "That old jalopy made it up the hill this time, did it?"

"Hey now, you can make fun of me all you want, but no making fun of my car."

The exchange made them both laugh, lightening the mood. As they once again sat on the steps of the little porch, she noticed his melancholy smile.

"I was thinking," he said. "Spending this time with you, all I've done is talk about myself. I must sound awfully egotistical. But what about you?"

"What about me?"

It occurred to Cecelia that most guys spent their time handing her one line after another, and here was Michael, asking her about herself. "You're not egotistical at all. And what would I tell you about myself? My life is so boring in comparison to yours."

"That can't be true."

"Well, I'm not plunging bayonets into dummies or trying to save lives. Life at the Star Pin Factory is dull in comparison."

He liked her razor sharp sense of humor.

"Being a singer with a band doesn't sound boring to me."

"Yes, well, I suppose that's the one aspect of my life that isn't completely dullsville."

"Getting to do something you've wanted to do since you were a little girl. That sounds just swell."

"Yes, it's a little piece of a dream."

"I guess our dreams are about all we have." Sitting with that thought, she knew he was right.

"Maybe one day, I'll get to hear you sing," he said.

"I'd like that."

Michael gazed up at the starlit sky, deep in thought. Then he surprised her. "How about you sing something for me now?"

"Now?"

"Sure. Right now."

"Here?"

"Well, why not?"

"I'll wake up the whole neighborhood," she said, giggling. If he could have seen her face in the darkness, Michael would have seen embarrassment written in her cheeks.

"Sing something soft then. Something tender."

"Well," she said, blithely, "why don't you tell me what one of your favorite songs is? I do take requests, you know."

He loved how playful she could be.

"Let me see...let me see..."

Egging him on, she said, "You must have a few favorites."

"Well, there is one I'm thinking of..."

"And what is that?"

"It's a little bit of an older song, but it's a beautiful one. 'What'll I Do?' Can you do that one for me?"

Thinking of the lyrics, Cecelia hesitated before smiling a sad smile.

Taking a breath, she closed her eyes and opened her mouth, allowing the song to flow from her heart:

What'll I do
When you are far away

And I am blue?
What'll I do?

What'll I do
When I am wondering who
Is kissing you?
What'll I do?

What'll I do
With just a photograph
To tell my troubles to?

When I'm alone
With only dreams of you
That won't come true
What'll I do?

When she finished holding the last perfect note, their eyes met.

"That was just about the most beautiful sound I've ever heard. Your voice is—I don't even know how to describe it. Magical!"

"Thank you," she said, feeling that they were connected by song now.

They now sat in silence, each wondering what the other was thinking, what the other was feeling.

Michael sighed. "It's a sad song, isn't it?"

"Yes, Michael. I'm afraid it is."

Without another word, Michael kissed her. And then he kissed her again and again. Their lips continued a melody they no longer needed lyrics for. At first Cecelia worried that her mother or her sister were watching from the parlor window, but his kisses somehow made her stop caring.

Finally, he whispered, "Songs are funny things, aren't they? I mean, the way they can make you feel."

"Yes," she said, "I guess they are."

"Starting tomorrow, I'll be far away."

"I know you will, Michael," she said, taking his hand in hers.

"I'm sure gonna miss you, Cecelia."

"I know, I'll miss you too."

Even in the darkness, she could see that his eyes were filled up.

"Maybe you'll send me a photograph that I can tell my troubles to. That probably sounds corny, huh?"

"No, it doesn't, Michael," she said, her voice trembling from the romance and the beauty and the music written in the night sky. "I'd be happy to send you a picture. But it's late, and I should be going inside before Mama sends Connie out here to drag me in by the scruff of the neck."

They both giggled at that remark.

"Right! Well, we wouldn't want that. Expect a letter from me soon. I hope you meant what you said, because, knowing myself like I do, I know I'll write every day."

"Write as often as you like, Mr. Michael DeMarco!"

"Corporal Michael DeMarco."

"All right, then. Write as often as you like, Corporal Michael DeMarco."

He gave her one final kiss goodnight, and then he sighed, stood up, and waded across the shallow lawn to his car. He looked back before driving away, and Cecelia saw the silhouette of a man who didn't appear to have a phony bone in his body. She saw an honest man. She saw a man who wore his heart on his sleeve–a man who cared about life in a different way than other men she had known. Most importantly, she saw a man she wanted to get to know better.

Moments later in her bedroom, now clad in a white nightgown, Cecelia sat at the little secretary desk that Papa had made years before her birth. Accompanied by the gentle rhythm of Mama's snoring, she opened her diary and began to write.

May 13, 1943

Dear Diary,

Remember the boy I wrote about a few nights ago? The soldier? Yes, that's the one. Well, he's gone back to his base in Nebraska, but he's going to be writing to me. I can only wonder what the contents of his letters to me will contain. I can't wait to hear from him, and you know better than anyone that I'll be checking my mailbox daily. Getting letters is such a delight. But let me tell you a little more about Corporal Michael DeMarco...

17

May 15, 1943

Dearest Cecelia,

It's about noon on Saturday, and I'm writing from Union Station in Chicago. You see, I couldn't wait until I got back to the base to write. I tried writing on the long train ride from New York, but my hand shook too much because of the vibration and the motion of the train. Add to that, my fountain pen was running out of ink. Finally, I just said the heck with it. I'm not even going to tell you what they charged me for a package of new ink cartridges at Grand Central Station. Highway robbery!

Now that I have some time to kill, I'm making my second attempt to write. Coincidentally, I ran into a guy, Irwin, from my base. A good thing because saying goodbye to everyone yesterday morning caused me to run late, which didn't work out too well as you'll see in a moment. When I finally rolled into New York, I had just missed the noon train to Chicago and had to wait until 6:00 p.m. So it was nice to have a friend to keep me company. Irwin and I went to see a movie about the military, "Bombardier" with Pat O'Brien. I don't know if the show would be your cup of tea, but you can't see it anyway because only New York has the latest films. You should see the movie theater. Wow! It makes our Valley theaters look like phone booths.

Anyway, let me just tell you—getting from Connecticut to

Nebraska takes an eternity, and it's all very dependent on train schedules and which train a guy ends up on. You see...

The skinny clerk at the ticket window looked at Michael and asked, "What can I do for you, soldier?"

"My buddy and I need a couple of tickets for McCook, Nebraska," Michael replied.

"Let me see...let me see. There's the Number One, the New Denver Zephyr, which leaves this afternoon at 5:00 and gets into McCook early Sunday mornin' at 5:32."

That sounded good to Michael. "Alright. That'll give us the whole day to rest before going back to work on Monday. Let's have two tickets for that train."

"Well now, ya see, ya gotta have a reservation for that one."

"How do we make a reservation?"

"You do that with me, only ya can't seein' there ain't no more available."

Michael looked at the clerk's beady eyes, two small dots behind his round spectacles. "Okay, what else ya got?"

The clerk adjusted his visor and searched his schedule. "The second one I got is the, uhm, the Number Seven. Leaves at 11:55 tonight."

Exasperated, Michael whined, "Not until 11:55? That's almost midnight!"

"That's right."

"Isn't there anything before then?"

"Nope. There ain't," the clerk replied flatly.

"Well, what time does that one get into McCook, mister?"

"The Number Seven? It arrives in McCook depot at, let's see–Sunday night at 10:20."

"You're kidding me," Michael complained. "That doesn't make any sense."

"That's why we call it the 'slow-boat-to-China milk train.' "

Michael studied the clerk's face to see if he was making some kind of bad joke, but the little man's face remained expressionless.

"But we need to be back at the base before bed check. We won't even be close. How can one train take twice as long as the other?"

"Cuz, first of all, that Number Seven runs a different route, and makes thirty stops, while the Number One makes only four stops. Not to mention...the Number One is a Zephyr and the Number Seven ain't."

"Can't ya help us out and get us on the Zephyr, mister?"

"I'll tell ya what I'll do. You boys stay nearby, and if I get any cancellations, I'll give a whistle."

Michael and Irwin dragged themselves to a bench and took a seat.

"So, Mikey, tell me about this new girlfriend of yours," Irwin said, crossing one leg underneath the other like he was in his living room at home.

"Well, it's like this," Michael explained. "I met her on a blind date, see, except it wasn't a true blind date. You should have seen her face when she saw me..."

...So Irwin and I had to hang out close to the ticket booth all after-noon and into the evening waiting for a cancellation. I'm afraid I dozed off for several of those hours because I hadn't been able to get much sleep Friday night sitting up on the train as it rambled and vibrated and bumped along this enormous country of ours. When we weren't sleeping, I told Irwin our whole story, honey, starting with our dance at the Lakeview Casino right up to me kissing you on your porch steps Thursday night. And I didn't pull any punches neither. I hope you don't mind that I opened up to a friend about you. And I hope you don't mind my calling you "honey." Look, I'm going to be straight with you. I'm crazy about you. I hope you feel the same way. Besides, I don't think a nice girl like you would have kissed a fellow like me the way you did if you didn't feel something. I'm usually right about these things. What do you think?

I want to tell you something else. I wasn't looking to get serious with anyone. I'm a guy who likes living life his own selfish way, doing whatever he wants. I'd been out with plenty of girls, but none of them ever unlocked the key to my heart like you did, Cecelia. The fact is, when I first laid eyes on you, I knew you were the one for me. I hope

you don't mind my honesty, but I don't know how else to
communicate...

When the station clerk whistled, it distracted Michael from his letter writing and woke up a dozing Irwin. The two G.I.s ran over to the ticket window.

"Just got a cancellation for that Zephyr, boys. You're in luck!"

"Jeepers, that's fantastic, mister. I can't thank you enough," Michael replied.

"Always happy to do my part for Uncle Sam," the clerk said, sliding the tickets into the slot under the window.

...Honey, it's early Sunday night, and I'm back on the base. I
waited to put the final touches on my letter to you until now. Gosh, I
hope you don't mind, but I miss you already. Who knows when we'll
see each other again? I have something to ask you, though. Remember
when we sat on your porch my last night home when you sang to me
and you said you'd send me a picture? It'd mean the world to me,
honey. I'm so glad I have a girl back home to write to. It means every-
thing to me!

But time for me to hit the hay. I'm shot. Tomorrow, it's back to the
grind for me. Until then, honey, I am...

Your soldier,
Love, xoxo
Michael

A week later, as Michael stood, brushing his boots against the dirt in impatient circles, like a bull preparing to charge a matador, a freckle-faced private shouted out last names at mail call. His cap sitting back on his forehead, the brim folded up, he called out one name after another in a staccato rhythm as each recipient triumphantly broke through the circle of G.I.s to retrieve his prize.

"Sabatino...Foley...Beauchemin...Walsh...Takacs...Pereiras..."

When the carrier's bag appeared empty, Michael approached him. "Hey, buddy, what about me? Ya got anything in that sack for DeMarco?"

"If I did, Corporal, I woulda called your name."

"Nuts," Michael muttered, stomping away from the gathering. Irwin followed close behind him. "Hey, Michael. You okay?"

"Nope! I didn't get any mail. I'm pretty pissed off."

"Nothing from that new girlfriend of yours, huh?"

"That's right, Einstein. You win a fuckin' blue ribbon. Congratulations!"

"Hey now, don't take it out on me."

The bespectacled Irwin was different. He wasn't rough around the edges like most soldiers. He was the more refined, studious type, like a few of the guys Michael had known in high school, even though they weren't his crowd.

"Yeah, you're right, Irwin. Sorry. It's just—I've written every day and not one response yet."

"I get it, Michael. I'd feel the same way if I were in your shoes. Well, maybe you'll hear from her tomorrow. You know how sometimes the mail gets delayed. Why, just last week, I got five letters from my kid sister on the same day. You'll hear, eventually."

Two days later, dirty and dog tired, Michael waited at mail call once more. He hoped today there'd finally be something for him after an interminable drought.

The mail carrier once again yelled out one name after another.

"Anderson...Zuraw...Bryce...D'Angelo...Ahearn..."

As Michael felt the same discouragement that had plagued him all week, the carrier's voice droned on and on. His mind drifted into a murky swamp of negativity, and for all practical purposes, he was no longer listening.

"...Bouteiller...Martin...Ramatowski...Cribbins...DeMarco..."

Lost in a daydream, Michael didn't hear his name called.

"DeMarco? Any-a you bozos named DeMarco?"

"Michael, wake up," Irwin said, with a stiff elbow to his ribs. "He just called your name, for God's sake!"

"Oh, shit, I...I was—"

Michael ran to the carrier. "I'm DeMarco!"

"Where ya been, Corporal? Here ya go. Okay, movin' on, let's see...Keller...Kafargo...Murphy...oh, and you again, DeMarco..."

Michael did an about face and headed back to the carrier. "Let's see, and that's DeMarco...and DeMarco...and another one for

DeMarco...and, uhm, DeMarco. That makes six, Corporal. Ya hit the jackpot, huh?"

The group of men laughed boisterously and slapped Michael on the back as he passed by, "Wow! Nice goin', Corporal"..."Ya lucky bastard"..."Bingo, pal, you win the prize"..."Yer sweetheart put perfume on any of them there letters, Mikey?"

As the crowd dispersed, Irwin approached him. "Your lucky day, huh, pal?"

"Yeah, I guess so...finally."

"All from your girl?"

Shuffling the envelopes, Michael said, "Four from Cecelia, one from her sister, Valentina, and one from my big sis, Josie."

"That's swell."

"Sure is. Cecelia's got four sisters, and I've got five. With all those gabby women, though, you'd think I'd never go a day without hearing from someone."

Irwin chuckled. "Yeah...I hear you. Well, enjoy all those letters."

...After waiting almost a week, today I got four letters from you, honey. I had begun to think that maybe you're a mean kid and that you weren't going to write. You wouldn't do that to a nice guy like me, would you?

I'm glad to hear that you're keeping busy at the factory, even though I wish you had finished high school. And don't be such a lazy-bones and go to church on Sunday. I try to go here on the base every Sunday, if I'm not completely exhausted. Of course, here it's not a real church but just one of the buildings, the same one where we watch movies. But I guess God doesn't care where you go to church, right?

By the way, I'm sorry to hear that there are fewer dances and the band isn't working as much, but I guess that's the reality of war.

Not much is going on around here, except the normal routine, like shooting practice and long hikes. Sometimes, they make us hike in double time and some of the guys faint from exhaustion. For me, as a noncom officer, I have to be tough and grind it out.

Anyway, honey, I don't mean to bore you with talk of army life. I guess I'm procrastinating because I have something more important to say, so here goes. I'm in love with you, Cecelia. I hope that it isn't shocking to hear. You might think that we barely know each other, but

I have to go by my feelings. Remember the night that we met at the dance? For me, it was strictly love at first sight. Honest! A few days later, I even told my pal Scooter that I was going to marry you some-day. On top of that, after you sang "What'll I Do?" for me, if I wasn't already in love with you, it would have been love at first "sound," if that makes any sense. That clinched it for me. What I'm talking about is something a guy just feels in his heart and even in his gut. Do you think you can feel the same way about me? Don't make any rash deci-sions, and don't feel any pressure. It's just, you're all I think about morning, noon, and night, and I just couldn't hold it in any longer.

So that's it for now. It's almost time for lights out. Just remember one thing. There's a soldier in McCook, Nebraska who loves you!

Your soldier,
Love, xoxoxo
Michael

P.S. I'm still waiting for that picture, honey. I hope you'll send it soon!

18

*F*riday arrived at long last. Another work week gone by, thank God. As she finished her cigarette in the stock-yard a few minutes before the break was over, Cecelia heard her name called.

"Hey, Cecelia, wait up a minute. I wanna ask ya somethin'."

It was Tony Vitti, a guy who ran a machine on her floor. Cecelia reluctantly slowed her entrance back into the building. There was something about Tony that rubbed Cecelia the wrong way–a gut feeling. Why couldn't he just leave her alone? Turning to him but not making eye contact, she said, "What is it, Tony?"

Tony took a last drag on his cigarette, tossed it in the dirt, and ground the toe of his boot over it. Stretching his long right arm above her shoulder, he rested his calloused palm on the brick exterior of the building, veritably blocking her way.

"How about going out with me tonight, baby?"

"I'm sorry, Tony," Cecelia said. "But I have plans."

"You always got plans. You should give me a shot, baby."

"Sorry, Tony. Like I said, I can't."

"Well, how about this?" he cajoled. "How about you give me a little kiss right here, baby? We're the only two left out here, ain't we? No one'll see."

With a steely glare, she inhaled deeply. "I need to get back to my machine, Tony, or I'm going to get docked pay."

His lips twisted in a frown, Tony withdrew his arm from the wall.

"Oh, and one more thing, Tony," Cecelia said, her eyes burning. "I'm not your *baby*, so don't ever call me that again. Besides, you might want to know that I have a boyfriend who's in the Army."

When Cecelia burst through the screen door after work, Connie called out to her, "Ya got a letter from that soldier boy of yours, princess!"

"I did?" Cecelia said. "Where is it? I can't wait to read it."

She trotted into the kitchen where her sister was snacking on a rolled up slice of baked ham.

"It's right there on the kitchen table. What's that now, four? Five?"

"Maybe," Cecelia replied. "Maybe four or five. Who's counting?"

"*You* are if I know you," Connie said and popped the rest of the rolled ham into her mouth. "It seems like he writes every day."

"Maybe," Cecelia repeated.

"Bullshit, maybe! A word of advice for you, little sister. Don't let a lonely soldier fill your head with a lot of romantic nonsense."

"Oh, Connie, you're such a killjoy. Don't you ever feel like it'd be nice to have your head filled up with a little romantic nonsense?"

"I don't have time for that noise," Connie mumbled, her mouth now full.

In a sing-song rhythm, Cecelia teased the same way she had done since the two were young girls. "That's because, you haven't, yet met, the guy, who makes the kind of *noise*, that makes your heart go pitter-patter!"

"Oh, and I suppose you think you have, Miss Wise Ass!"

Cecelia skipped back out through the front door and sat on the porch steps, where she read Michael's words. She smiled as she contemplated his honesty. She liked seeing him address her as "honey," but she worried about his future in the Army. Would he be sent overseas soon and would he even come back alive?

Cecelia had a lot to think about. *Michael certainly doesn't give a girl very long to make up her mind,* she thought. She rubbed the soft palms of her hands over the neat script on the page. Finally, letting out a deep sigh, she folded the blue pages which featured a graphic of a military plane across the header, and slipped them back into the envelope with care. Deep in thought, she glanced down at the four letters he had printed on the back of the envelope: SWAK.

After finishing writing back to Michael, she ran over to Stella's. Banging on the screen door at the side of the house, Cecelia yelled, "Stell, it's just me!"

The two sat down on the stoop and Cecelia filled Stella in on how Michael wrote to her from the train station in Chicago and had been writing every day since.

Stella frowned. "I've never been on a train before."

"Only once for me. Last April when Connie and I went to New York with little Connie and her cousin."

"Oh yeah! You went to that nightclub. Which was it?"

"Jack Dempsey's...you know, the boxer. What a night. He had pictures of himself all over the walls with all kinds of celebrities. Frank Sinatra, Mickey Rooney and Ava Gardner, Jack Benny. Even the President. And everything was so fancy. Even monogrammed napkins."

"I wish I coulda been with you girls, living the high life."

"Yeah, it'll probably never happen again."

The two girls laughed.

"So what else did Michael's letter say?" Stella asked.

"Not much. Just about the trains and the stations. Oh, and how he bragged about me to his buddy. And other stories about life on an army base. He wants me to send him a picture."

"Well, that's a good sign. You've been writing back?"

"Sure have–every day."

"What did you tell him?"

"Oh, about how God-awful boring it is to sit at a machine doing the same repetitive task all day. It's not like I have anything interesting happening in my life."

"Get lost. You must be writing about more than the ins and outs of life in a factory. Give me the real lowdown."

"Well, I did tell him about that guy Tony at work."

"You told him about that rat?"

"Well, a little bit. I didn't go into the gruesome details because I have the impression that Michael can be hot-headed, and I don't want to set him off."

Stella stretched. "Well, you must have said something romantic. Don't be so secretive. Tell me the juicy stuff."

"Well, I don't mind telling you that in his letter, he asked if he could call me honey, and I told him he could go right ahead if he likes. I told him it had kind of a nice ring to it."

Stella screamed. "That's my girl! And?"

"And I told him...that I'm a nice girl...and I assured him that I don't kiss just any boy the way I kissed him that night. 'So, there must be something about you that I like,' I wrote, 'mustn't there be?' "

"Holy shit! No kidding? You said all that?"

"I certainly did!"

"Well, I'll be damned. Your letter to him sure sounds steamy to me. I knew you were holding out on me."

...Cecelia, I'm going to get right to the point. If you run into him again, you can tell that louse who's bothering you that when I get a furlough, I'm going to come to his factory and knock his block off. And I'm not kidding neither. I don't know if you think of yourself as my girl, but that's how I think of you now, and I'm not going to put up with some jamoke bothering you.

I have to tell you, Cecelia. I've been feeling pretty low lately. It's hard not knowing my fate. Lots of guys are getting shipped overseas. That might happen to me any time now. If it wasn't for this lousy war and if it wasn't for having met you, I would have taken off for South America a long time ago. I'll bet that sounds pretty funny to you, but I'm not exaggerating. There was nothing for me in Derby. The reason I joined the Army is that I almost beat the h-ll out of a supervisor at the stockyard I was working at. Someday I'll tell you more about that.

Anyway, army life can get pretty lonely. A lot of the fellows feel awfully homesick. A strange thing happened last night. The guy who bunks next to me—his name is Tex, or at least that's what we call him, started singing a song called "The Last Letter." I don't know if you've

ever heard that one. It's just a cowboy song. Anyway, I can tell you
that Tex sure has no voice for singing, but...

"Hey, Mike. Snap out of it, will ya?"

As if being awoken from a deep sleep, Michael looked up and saw a buddy, Jimmy Cohen. "What?"

"I said snap out of it, man. I know that look. You were back home. No sense in going there, Mike."

Now a half hour before lights out, Michael breathed in and out several times, trying to gather himself.

On the bunk to his left, Tex Garvin lay, also staring at the ceiling. Unexpectedly, Tex broke out in full voice, singing a country song.

The chatter in the room died down until the only sound echoing across the open space was Tex's voice. Michael listened thoughtfully to the story of a guy writing a letter to a girl who no longer loves him.

After a verse, Michael abruptly rolled off his bunk and headed for the exit. He needed a smoke like he'd never before needed one. Irwin, seeing him pass by, followed him outside into the brisk Nebraska night.

"What's the matter, man?" Irwin asked. "Tex's singing too hard on the ears?"

Not answering, Michael lit a cigarette.

"Well, the guy sings way the hell off pitch, that's for–"

"Yeah, but that's not it." Michael flicked the cigarette pack. "How about a smoke?"

"No thanks. So, what's got you so spooked then?"

"It's...it's not his singing. He's no Sinatra, but I don't give a rat's ass about that. It's the words to that song, and the emotion in his voice just cut right through me like–like a knife. I had to get outta there. Tex must think I'm a rude son-of-a-bitch for bolting out the door, but shit, man, I just miss home so much...and I miss Cecelia. I can't even explain it..."

...You see, Cecelia, I'm fighting a private war here in McCook. I
could get sent to Europe or to the Pacific any day now, see, and maybe I

won't come back. But, I'm not afraid to die. Seriously. I'm not afraid of
anybody or anything, honey. For me, there's two wars going on—one
against our enemies and another deep inside me. What I mean is that the
d-mned enemy doesn't scare me one tenth as much as my own feelings
do. That's the war I'm fighting. I'm just afraid of breaking down. And, I
don't know how to explain it, darling...I just can't let myself do that...

———————

Sitting next to her on the porch steps, Stella held Cecelia's hand firmly in her soft palms. "Why are you so upset?"

Feeling a burning need to share, Cecelia needed to open up to someone. Stella and she had been inseparable since toddlerhood and shared just about everything.

"I feel so...so rattled by Michael's letters," Cecelia said. "He's just so honest."

"Isn't that a good thing?"

"Yes...but it's...it's...he's very direct about what he thinks and feels. He doesn't pull any punches, and he just wants so much."

"Don't you love him?"

"I don't know. I just don't know. I haven't spent all that much time with him. Only that night when he walked me home from the dance and a few nights when he was home on leave. Do we even know each other? But I can't break his heart. I just can't."

"But I do think you feel something for him, don't you, Celia?"

"Well, sure I do. I've never met a guy who has his combination of strength and sensitivity. The two almost don't go together. I want to know more about him, but I don't know if I'm ready to go steady or if I'm...in love with him. I just–I can't even think. What if he goes overseas? What if I break his heart and he never comes back? Then what? How will I feel then?"

"Easy...easy." Stella now wrapped her arms around Cecelia, pulling her into a safe embrace. "You're letting your emotions run away with you."

A picture of Stella's father suddenly popped in Cecelia's mind. A Ukrainian man of immense stature known in the neighborhood as "Big John," Mr. Kostenko had become like a second father to her.

Sadly, Big John died just a few years after Cecelia's father's death, further bonding the two girls.

"Oh, Stella, I'm so lost. What do you think your father would tell me to do if he was still alive?"

"Oh, you know what he'd say. He'd rub his long index finger across that mustache of his, and he'd say, 'Follow the heart, little one. Always you must follow the heart.' "

Cecelia emitted a rueful laugh, and then, no longer able to contain her emotions, burst into tears. Stella held her friend tightly.

"You go ahead and have a good cry if you need to, Celia. I'll sit here with you as long as you need me to."

19

May 30, 1943

Dearest Darling,

I want to begin by thanking you for the beautiful picture! I lay it down right beside me each night as I write to you. It makes me almost feel like I'm talking to you. But I have to tell you, honey, you've created quite a stir here in the barracks because now all the guys are jealous of me. They all say you look like a movie star. In fact, some say you look just like Hedy Lamarr. They get no argument from me on that one. When you get a bunch of men together like we have in the Army, a lot of horseplay often takes place, though...

It was a half hour before lights out, and Wally and Steever had made a plan. Steever's job was simple. Just distract Michael.

"Hey, Michael," he said. "Do you think you could help me with this thing?"

"What thing?"

"Well, ya see, I was just practicing wrapping a tourniquet around my wrist here. It's just a homemade job, but I don't think I've got it on me the right way."

"Let me see." Michael had been in medic school longer than Steever, and he was all too happy to help out.

As Michael examined Steever's tourniquet, Wally moved into the space alongside Michael's bunk, snatching the picture.

"Hey fellas, look," Wally yelled, holding the picture triumphantly over his head, "I'm going to kiss Michael's girl! I'm going to kiss Hedy Lamarr! Eat your hearts out!"

Michael angrily made eye contact with Steever, and gave him a hard shove, sending him reeling and onto his back over a nearby bunk.

"Okay, the joke's over, Wally. Just give me that picture back," Michael ordered, motioning with his right hand.

"Why, Mike? All's I want is a little kiss. Just cuz I'm real lonely."

"I swear, kiss that picture and your pathetic life is all fuckin' over."

The onlookers unleashed a chorus of "whoas" upon hearing Michael's threat.

Now, predator and prey, Michael stalked Wally, who climbed over one bunk after another, evading Michael. Michael methodically stayed on the trail of his prey across the length and width of the barracks. The men taunted Michael and encouraged Wally. "Awww, poor Michael"..."Go ahead, Wally, give her a big kiss"... "Yeah, give her a smooch"..."Show her how a real man kisses, Wally"...

Trying to remain in control, Michael felt the blood, like boiling lava, rising in his cheeks. "I'm telling you, Wally, your joke was funny for about a half second. If you don't want to get your ass kicked, just hand the picture here, and we'll all forget this ever happened."

Despite the stage he had set for himself, Wally still had his wits about him enough to size up the situation with a modicum of rationality. With fire in his eyes, Michael's seriousness of purpose was unmistakable.

...So you see, honey, it was all in good fun. Or was it??? Let's just say Wally gave me back your photo without kissing it, which I might add was very fortunate for him.

Guess what today is. Pay day! I'm rich! I got my pay envelope with

$50 for the month, except I have to put out $3.25 for insurance, $1.25 for defense bonds, and $1.50 for laundry, not to mention the $.75 a week they milk us to get a haircut. So that leaves me with only $41.00. What a life, huh?

Gee, honey, living in Nebraska sure makes me miss Derby, which is something I never thought I'd hear myself say. There's some pretty country out here, but it's the darndest state. You can drive into a vast nothingness where you don't see a single house or a solitary human for miles and miles. And the weather! Some days it rains on one side of the street while the sun is shining on the other. Have you ever heard of a dust storm? Why, just the other day, on Tuesday, we had one the likes of which you can't imagine. The dust swirling around was so dense you couldn't see two feet in front of you, but we still had to do our normal drills—an hour of calisthenics and then a two-mile run. But that's how it is in the Army. You follow orders, or else!

We were so covered with dust, we had to keep spitting the stuff out of our mouths. The dust even seeps under the doors and through cracks in the windows, and gets all over everything in the barracks, so we had to sweep and wipe the place out three or four times before it ended. I swear I took four showers that day.

Honey, there's something else I want to tell you about. As I've told you, fellows are being shipped out of McCook every day. Mostly over-seas. I want to do my part to end this war, but I have another idea of what my part is. I don't want to be a medic. There's no shame in it, but I've got a new plan. Since I was a kid, I've had this idea in my head that I'd give anything to fly a plane. The only way to do that in the Army is to become an officer, so I recently made an appointment to find out how a guy gets into the Cadet Program. Well, more specifi-cally, it's called the Aviation Cadet Training Program, and it's how a guy becomes an officer and trains to fly...

"Well, first of all, Corporal," the lieutenant began, "you need to be in excellent physical health, which shouldn't be a problem. But let me ask you a few important questions."

Michael couldn't take his eyes off the two silver collar pins and the embroidered sleeve patches the lieutenant wore—his wings.

"Are you married, Corporal?"

"No, sir, I've got a swell girl, though."

The lieutenant leaned back in his oak swivel chair and tapped his pen on the surface of his desk, amused by Michael's enthusiasm. "Good, keep it that way. The Cadet Program doesn't accept married men. Now, do you have at least a high school diploma?"

"Yes, sir, I'm the only one in my family so far."

"Any college?"

"Sir?"

"Did you attend college at all?"

"No, sir. My parents couldn't afford college. They're from the old country, you see."

"The old country. Yes, I understand. That means then, as part of the application process, you'll have to take some tests to see if you have an aptitude for college level academics, which will be required of those who haven't had any college. Twenty-two tests in all, covering a wide range of subjects, from history to physics and everything in between. There's even a battery of psychological tests we put you through."

The lieutenant could see the color fade from Michael's face. "I know it sounds daunting," he continued, "but it's the only gateway into the program for you. An officer is a gentleman, and a college educated one at that. I have to be honest and tell you it's quite competitive, as it damn well should be. Would you still like to apply?"

"Well, gee, I sure would, sir."

"Then, Corporal, you may be in for the adventure of your life. Our nation's future depends upon command of the air! Good luck."

...Honey, I know it's a pipe dream, but I'm going to give it my best shot. If I don't try, I'll wonder for the rest of my life if I would have made it. I know I probably won't, but at least I will have tried. Does that make sense?

The most important thing is that you're my girl. Just keep in mind, darling, that every step I take from now on is about making you proud of me. I want you to see that I'm the kind of person worth loving. Although you haven't agreed to go steady with me or expressed your love for me, I also know that if you didn't care about me, you wouldn't have sent me your picture and you wouldn't write every day like you do. I'm going to have to go to bed now, though. It's

time for lights out. I love you more every day. Until tomorrow,
I am...

Your soldier,
Love, xoxoxo
Michael

Troubled, Cecelia sat at the kitchen table drinking tea with the two Connies. "So you see," she explained. "He has this idea that he's going to be a pilot."

"That sounds exciting to me," little Connie replied. "I'll bet he'll look handsome in one of those leather jackets, a flight helmet, and goggles."

"What good will looking handsome do if his plane gets shot down?" Cecelia complained. "You were with us a while back when we saw *Air Force* at the movies, weren't you?"

"I sure was! I never miss a picture show that John Garfield is in. He's dreamy!"

"Well, maybe you were too infatuated with John Garfield to see what it was about."

"I saw. It was about how that bomber plane, the *Mary-Ann*, flew into Pearl Harbor when the Japanese attacked, and then the crew was ordered to go on fighter missions in the Pacific."

"But did you watch the whole picture?" Cecelia asked. "Did you see how planes shot each other out of the air, how ground forces shot at planes with big machine guns, how the planes went up in flames and crashed? Did you see any of that, Connie, or did you see nothing but John Garfield?"

"Why?" Cecelia's sister said. "Will your boyfriend be safer fighting on the ground?"

"I suppose not," Cecelia said, blowing the steam off the top of her teacup.

"Gee, I hate to say it, Celia, but you sound stuck on this guy," little Connie said, heaping two teaspoons of sugar into her cup.

Cecelia's sister snatched the sugar bowl away from their friend. "Easy on the sugar, Connie, for Christ's sake. We only get so many ration stamps for that stuff each month." Little Connie looked down contritely into her cup.

"I don't know if I'm stuck on him. What I am…is lost!"

"Will you get off it?" her sister continued, now driving the conversation. "He's all you talk or think about."

"Is it a crime that I'm worried about him getting killed?"

"No, it's no crime, but why don't you stop kidding yourself and admit that you're in love with the guy?"

Cecelia hated how direct Connie could be and how she, all too often, cut to the heart of the matter. "But I'm still young."

"You're not that goddamn young," Connie barked. "Lots of girls fall in love at your age. I'm just getting sick and tired of hearing you whine."

Tears welled up in Cecelia's eyes. Staring at her sister in stunned surprise, she got up from the kitchen table.

"And where do you think you're going?" Connie asked, her tone even more imperious.

"I'm going to…to write in my diary."

"Always writing in your diary," Connie ridiculed. "That's you! It's how you escape life. Someday, I'm going to rip that thing open and see what the hell you're always writing."

In tears, Cecelia bolted from the room, passed her mother, who was sitting in the living room reading her Bible, and climbed the narrow staircase.

"Gosh," little Connie interjected. "Can't ya ever go easy on her?"

"Oh, just mind your own damned beeswax, Miss Two Spoonfuls of Sugar!"

Cecelia sulked in her room. Connie was the devil sometimes. But Cecelia also knew that Connie always had her best interest in mind. She remembered when she was about thirteen and Connie was sixteen how Connie would take a half dollar from her hard earned pay and shove it at her. "Here," Connie would say. "Take this. You might need it. But don't go making a regular thing of bumming money off me!" That was Connie.

She lay on her bed, thinking about what she wanted to say in today's letter. She was sure flattered that her picture caused such a stir in the barracks. To think, Hedy Lamarr. Not bad!

She needed to tell Michael how much it worried her that he might become a pilot. She knew how much he loved driving his car at high speeds. What would he be like in the cockpit of a plane? Men and their machines! And he wrote about planes with such passion in his recent letters, she was beginning to feel that he loved planes more than he loved her. Maybe she'd even tell him that.

Of course, Michael had said that the Cadet Program was highly competitive, so maybe she was worrying needlessly. What she had noticed about him was that he was probably the most determined guy she had ever met. It was something she liked about him. If anyone could get into the program, it was Michael.

She rested, taking a deep breath in through her nose. The hardest thing to write about, she knew, was this talk of love. When most guys had talked about love, she knew they were just trying to see how far they could get. She could see through their baloney in an instant. But with Michael, it was different. Hearing him express his love for her made her feel special. She wasn't going to be able to put him off much longer. If she didn't have feelings for him, she wouldn't worry so much about him flying that it brought her to tears.

She slid off the bed and took a seat at the desk. Picking up a fountain pen, she stared down at the worn maple surface as if the wood grain might tell her what to write. She knew, with each letter exchange, she was feeling more overwhelmed and emotional and growing more deeply enmeshed with Michael. For now, she would just ask that he be patient with her. *Will he be able to do that?* she wondered.

Cecelia tapped her pen on the desktop, wondering where to begin.

20

June 7, 1943

Dear Honey,

Gee, I just read your letter. I'm not even sure where to begin. You asked me to be patient, which I'm all too happy to do, but I have a few related thoughts. You said that you feel you're too young to get serious with someone, but to be honest, I don't buy that. While I understand it must be what you believe, my take is that if you don't feel ready to get serious, maybe you haven't met the right guy. Do you hear what I'm saying? Maybe I'm not the right guy. Listen, if that's the case, I hope you'll let me know and I'll just disappear, because truthfully, honey, I can't stand the idea of loving you as much as I do and not having my love returned. I'm just being straight with you. You're almost eighteen, and if I was the right guy, you wouldn't have any qualms about being serious. I want you to think about that because I love you with my whole heart and soul.

Oh, and one other point. I like that you realize you wouldn't be as worried about me flying as you are if you didn't have strong feelings for me. That makes me feel good. You go ahead and keep having those strong feelings and see where they lead.

Speaking of flying, I am being transferred to Keesler Field in Biloxi, Mississippi Monday to be tested for the Cadet Program. I'll have to take a whole slew of academic tests, physical fitness tests, eye *tests, and God knows what else. I know the fitness tests will be a cinch, but I'm not as confident about the academic tests. The lieutenant told me it's competitive, but I'm going to give it my best shot. Wish me luck, honey.*

Gee, Cecelia, it's sure sweet of you to worry about me flying planes, and you're right, it is dangerous. But so is everything in war. Eventually, one way or another, I'm going to get involved in this mess, and no matter where they send me or what my role is, it's going to be dangerous. My goal will be to come back in one piece, because the most important thing in the world to me is coming back to you. The bottom line, honey, is if it wasn't for you, I wouldn't care what happens to me. Believe me!

I'm bushed, so, if you don't mind, I'm going to collapse now. I love you, sweetheart. Until tomorrow, I am...

Your soldier,
Love, xoxoxo
Michael

Cecelia took the bus to Seymour to seek the counsel of the senior member of the Alberino sisters. Phyllis was gentle and kind like their own mother, but having been born in America, she understood modern society better than Mama. She sat at her kitchen table, feeding her new baby while little Diane played with a doll on the floor nearby.

Cecelia remembered how she had cried on her sister's wedding day. Feeling a profound sense of loss, Cecelia couldn't believe that Phyllis was no longer going to live at home, especially since it had been such a short time since Papa had died.

The family had been surprised that Phyllis didn't have children right away, but pregnancy wasn't something you talked about. When Diane was born six years later, Phyllis seemed more happy and fulfilled than ever.

Cecelia needed Phyllis' calm guidance today. Her big sister was honest and direct without the slightest trace of sarcasm or judgment.

"Yeah, so that's the story," Cecelia said, as she bit into a buttered hard roll.

Little Diane climbed into her favorite aunt's lap, continuing to brush her doll's long blonde hair without interruption. It seemed that Cecelia was the favorite of all of her nephews and nieces.

"So lemme see if I've got this straight," Phyllis said. "Michael feels that if you really loved him, it wouldn't matter what age you were. That sound about right?"

Cecelia replied with a deep sigh.

"Thought so," Phyllis said.

Taking a brush from her pocketbook, Cecelia began running it through her niece's silky, dark hair. "See?" Cecelia said, "I'm brushing my little girl's hair just like you're brushing your dolly's hair." Diane smiled contentedly.

"So, exactly how do you feel about the guy?" Phyllis asked.

"I...oh, I don't know. I mean, I care about him a lot, obviously."

"Do you love him or don't ya?"

"Geez, Phil, you sound like him! I need you to help me figure that out."

"Well, here's what I think, baby." Phyllis had called Cecelia *baby* since her birth due to the eleven year age difference between the two of them.

"First, let's talk about what kind of guy he is...because when you pick a guy, it's smart to think about what kind of person he is. Look at me. I thought I picked a good one. I mean, I still love the big lug, but he drinks too much. I suppose it could be worse."

"Yes, Michael's a good guy. He drinks a little, but I don't think it's a problem."

"You know, I've never met Michael, but you've told me a lot about him, and here's what I think. I think ya got a winner here. He's a hard worker, right? And he wants to be a success in life, right? And he's very determined, right?"

"Right!"

"You could do a helluva lot worse. And, besides, from what you say, he's not too bad on the eyes either. How's he as a kisser?"

Cecelia stopped brushing Diane's hair. "Phil, you're awful!"

"No, but I ain't kiddin'. How does he make you feel when he holds you in his arms and kisses you? Does it give you all those butterfly feelings down in the pit of your tummy?"

Embarrassed, Cecelia said, "Well...yes, I suppose so."

"Have you ever felt this way with another fella?"

"No…not exactly."

"And you feel he's a good person, right?"

"Well, yes, of course I do. He's a very good person. I knew that from the moment he first walked me home from the Lakeview Casino."

"Well then, you can call it whatever you want, baby, but I call it love," Phyllis said, punctuating it by patting both of her hands on the kitchen table.

Cecelia had a date the next day to go to the Plumb Library with Stella. Stella was nearing the end of her senior year and would graduate in June, and for that, Cecelia envied her. Hiding that envy, she knew, was important to keep their friendship strong, and besides, it wasn't Stella's fault that she had quit school. It was because of her own damned pride, and she knew it.

In any case, Stella needed to research a topic she was studying in Civics class. Stella had an uncanny ability to read, take notes, and gab at the same time.

"So, yes," Cecelia whispered. "He's headed for Biloxi, Mississippi where he'll test for the Cadet Program. I'm worried he'll make it although Michael himself doubts it, but I'm happy for him because he's excited. And besides, he hates Nebraska."

"That's good, then, right?"

"Yes, I suppose so."

The librarian, Miss Kluck, gave the surface of her desk three sharp raps with the knuckles of her right hand and glared at the girls.

Guiltily, Stella dove back into her books while Cecelia pulled a sheet of paper from Stella's notebook and began a letter to Michael.

The round clock on the wall ticked off ten more minutes, and Stella finally whispered, "What are you writing?"

"I'm telling him how I went to Seymour to ask my sister Phyllis' advice about him, and how she told me if I was really in love, I wouldn't use my age as an excuse."

"Oh my God." Stella glanced at the librarian and then furtively continued the conversation. "Are you telling him you're not in love with him then?"

Looking down at her letter and pretending to write, Cecelia whispered back, "Noooo, silly. What I'm telling him is that I'd like to try love on and see if it fits."

"You said it that way?" Stella asked, and after Cecelia winked and nodded yes, she added, "That is insanely romantic."

Now, speaking from her desk in a full voice for all of the world to hear, Miss Kluck honked, "Girls, this is my last warning. There is no talking in the library. Don't make me tell you again."

Mortified, Cecelia and Stella could have just about crawled under the table.

Stella looked at Cecelia and mouthed, "We better go."

"Are you finished?" Cecelia mouthed back.

"Good enough."

After putting the books back where she had found them, Stella led Cecelia toward the heavy double doors, passing the librarian on the way.

"Good afternoon, Miss Kluck," Stella murmured.

"Good afternoon," Cecelia echoed weakly.

Once out the door, the two girls broke into laughter.

"That old witch probably hates us now," Cecelia exclaimed.

"And where the hell did she get a last name like that? *Kluck!*" Stella chortled.

"Now, Stella, she can't help what her last name is."

"Oh, the hell with her," Stella replied. "She even looks like a chicken. An old worn out chicken. Cluck, cluck, cluck, cluck, cluck!"

"Stop that this very instant! She'll hear us," Cecelia admonished, failing to hold in her laughter.

"Oh, I don't give a good goddamn what she hears!"

Cecelia, grabbing Stella by the arm and pulling her across the street and onto Coram Avenue, confessed, "We're just awful, aren't we? If the priest was hearing confessions right now, I'd go right into the church this very minute."

"Oh bullshit," Stella said, causing both girls to howl once more.

"Will you stop it?" Cecelia said. "The church is right there across the street. We're going to get struck by lightning if you keep letting that filthy mouth of yours run."

As they passed by St. Joseph's, both girls blessed themselves, remained silent and pious for another moment, and then succumbed to laughter once more.

"Oh my goodness," Stella said, "I'm going straight to hell when I die!"

"I'm almost sure of it," Cecelia agreed.

"Anyway, what else did you say in that letter?"

"Well, I tried to open up to him. I even told him that I think my father's death had a deep psychological effect on me. That it made me afraid to trust in love."

"Wow! It's like you're psychoanalyzing yourself."

"Yes, exactly…and then I told him my feelings for him were deeper than I had ever felt for *any* other boy."

"Golly!"

Cecelia drew the letter out of her purse and said, "Wanna hear the last paragraph?"

"Do I wanna hear the last paragraph? Word for word, if you please."

"Okay then, here it is," Cecelia said, unfolding the sheet of paper and turning it to the last page. "So, I'm going to give it a try. I love you, Michael DeMarco! I've taken a few minutes to digest what I just wrote, and you know what? Saying 'I love you' felt pretty good! I'll write again tomorrow…and again the next day…and the next and the next and continue to see how it feels. Love, Cecelia."

Stella feigned stumbling and said, "Sweet Mother of Christ, help me before I faint!"

"Stella! You're awful!"

"Well, if that isn't the most romantic thing I've ever heard, then I don't know what is."

"Shall we stop at Moscardini's for a soda?" Cecelia asked.

"Yes, let's," Stella replied. "We've got something to celebrate. And I'm so goddamned excited, I'll even buy!"

21

---

*M*ichael wiped the last bits of lather from his face and said, "Let's me and you go into town tonight and celebrate, buddy."

"Celebrate what?" Irwin asked.

"Celebrate love!"

"Love?"

"Yes, Irwin, pal of mine. My girl wrote that she loves me, so we're going to celebrate—you and me."

"This'll be a novelty. You never go into town."

It was true. On Friday and Saturday nights, when the guys went into town, Michael stayed behind, sometimes offering to take over someone else's duty or sometimes just enjoying his own solitude and the chance to catch up on some letter writing.

On the bus ride, Irwin had a bushel basket full of questions.

"So, what did she say, Michael?"

"Well...she said she's never been in love before but has strong feelings for me. She said she wants to try love on for size."

"What's that supposed to mean?"

"I don't know, Irwin, but I have confidence in myself. In my case, I didn't need to try anything on. I knew I was going to marry Cecelia Alberino from the minute I laid eyes on her, before I ever spoke to her."

"How could you know?"

"Just a gut feeling. There are some things you just know."

"I wish I had gut feelings like that. And I wish I had a beautiful girl like Cecelia."

"Your time'll come," Michael assured him.

McCook was a two bar town, the Stork Club and the Watering Hole. Michael and Irwin chose the latter because, while neither one had live music, the Watering Hole had a jukebox.

"Look at this beauty." Michael's fingertips caressed the expanses of the machine. "So colorful and sleek, and how about these bubble lights?"

"Don't spend all your money on records, Michael. Save some for booze," Irwin replied.

"Don't worry. It's early, but when the place starts to fill up, we can listen on someone else's nickel. For now, let's see what kind of change I have," Michael said, reaching into his pocket.

When Michael dropped a dime into the slot, it rattled into the mysterious depths, and the jukebox hummed to life. He perused the twenty-four glowing song options before him. "Let's see. I think I'll play...uhm...'Taking a Chance on Love' because that's what my girl's doing, and...and, oh yes, 'Chattanooga Choo Choo,' that's a good one, and...and...oh perfect, 'In the Mood.' Can you believe that, Irwin? That's the song that the Glenn Miller Orchestra was playing when I first laid eyes on Cecelia. Hot stuff, ain't it? It must be some kind of sign."

Michael pressed a round button and waited for the first record to swing into space and land on a turntable that rose like a flying saucer.

"I saved 'In the Mood' for last. Let's get a couple of beers."

The two men ordered at the bar and then made their way to a nearby booth. The table was littered with carvings, primitive etchings of Valentine hearts encapsulating the initials of soldiers and their girls–T.J. and S.A., E.L. and H.G.–or just the first names of girls who may have nuzzled up to a G.I. at one of the booths–Betty or Helen or Dorothy–and more crass carvings like, For a good time call 3931-H.

Wiping the suds from his mouth after a first sip, Irwin said, "It's great to have you here for a change. I can't remember the last time you came into town. I guess you're not much of a drinker."

"Oh, I wouldn't say that." Michael grimaced. "I like to drink a little too much. And sometimes me and booze aren't, well let's just say, the best combination. There's all kinds of trouble a guy can get himself into when he's had a few too many, not the least of which is trouble with women. And, as far as I'm concerned, Cecelia is the only girl for me. I don't wanna be tempted, if you catch my drift."

"Oh, yeah, I hear what you're saying."

As more and more guys drifted into the Watering Hole, Michael and Irwin needed to raise their voices in order to hear each other.

After their third beer, Irwin was already tipsy.

"You know, Michael, if Cecelia saw me, she'd drop you like a hot potato."

Michael smirked. "Get lost."

"I'm serious," Irwin assured his friend.

"Go shit in your hat." Michael picked up the pilsner and downed a half glass of beer in one gulp.

"Oh, you don't believe it?"

"If I believed it, my friend, I'd have to kick your ass."

Irwin slapped his hand down on the table. "Yeah, of course, I'm just kidding you. The truth is, I've never even had a girl."

Michael sighed. "Well, I've had different girlfriends, but never anybody like Cecelia. Speaking of, here's 'In the Mood.' I'll remember seeing her dance to this song until the day I die."

"Yeah?"

"I mean, I've never seen anyone dance like her. Well, not in person. I swear to Christ, she's like a pro...like another Ginger Rogers. So good, I tell ya, that I was intimidated to dance with her."

"But you did, right?"

"Damn right I did. It was the only way to get near her with all those guys swarming around her. And holding her in my arms. Well, you've never experienced anything like it. And to take it a step further, she's now a singer with one of the local bands. Her singing is...I can't even explain."

"Sounds like a talented girl."

"You can say that again, pal!"

The Watering Hole was now more like an overcrowded fish tank, a bubbling pool of shouting and laughter and music. Couples were dancing to the hits spinning in the jukebox. For the men, it was an escape from the tedium and the rigors of military life. As for the girls, they were fishing for husbands.

Two girls approached Michael and Irwin. "Any chance you boys wanna carve our names into the table?" one of the girls asked. The yellow flower in her honey colored hair matched her tight dress.

The other, a skinny brunette with heavy makeup, piped in, "My name is Margaret, and this here is Bonnie, and we got a jackknife if you need it. We'll even spell our names if ya don't spell so good."

"We spell jus' fine." Michael was feeling it now.

"I don't doubt it. Now if you cuties'd buy us a drink, we're a little thirsty and awful lonely, ain't we, Bon?"

"Lonely?" Michael laughed. "With the whole United States Army crammed inta this joint?"

"Yeah...well, so many of these boys are just so *ordinary*," the skinny one explained. "I and my friend Bonnie are lookin' for boys who are exceptional."

Michael had trouble hiding his amusement. "Sorry, uhm... what'd ya say your name was?"

"Margaret, but you can call me Margie."

"Yeah, well, I don' think I'll be calling you anything because I'm spoken for."

"Ooohhh," Bonnie sang out in a jarring, high-pitched screech. "You got a sweetheart back home, do ya?"

"That's about the size of it."

Trying to be helpful, Margie offered, "But what your girl don't know won't kill her, right?"

"It's not about what *she* don't know or what won't kill *her*," Michael said.

"Oh no?" Margie replied.

"It's about what *I* know and what will kill *me*. So, it was nice meeting ya both, but toodle-loo!"

As the girls left in a disgruntled huff, Irwin couldn't help but exclaim, "Wow, Michael. That was some willpower. Those dames weren't half bad looking."

"I'm not about to let two floozies ruin what I've worked so hard for."

When they got back to the base, it was nearly 2:00 a.m., and Michael was feeling no pain. After brushing his teeth and washing his face, he made his way back to his bunk, ready for a good night's sleep.

Drying his face with a towel, he wasn't more than ten feet from his bunk when a stocky G.I. staggered over to Michael's footlocker and picked up the picture of Cecelia.

"Who the hell is this hag?" the guy called out to no one in particular.

Feigning confusion, Michael asked, "You don't know that girl?"

"No, how would I know her?" the G.I. slurred.

"But you think she's a hag?" Michael asked, still playing the innocent.

"Yep, I think they're all hags, and this one's as big a hag as the worst of 'em."

Without warning, Michael caught the guy squarely on the chin with a hard fist. Dropping the photo to the ground, the stocky soldier stumbled backwards and over a nearby bunk.

He pushed himself to his feet, preparing his counter-attack. "So that's how it is, is it?"

"Yeah, that's how it is, asshole."

In the nick of time, a half dozen G.I.s separated the two, grabbing both drunken warriors and pulling them away from each other.

A guy called out, "Are you two nuts? You get caught fighting, they'll throw you in the stockade!"

Michael was now on his knees collecting the framed picture and the broken glass. "I don't give a shit. You ever call my girl a hag or so much as even glance at her picture, you'll see what'll fuckin' happen to you."

When the ruckus was over and the lights were out, Michael turned on his flashlight and began composing a letter to Cecelia.

June 14, 1943

My Dearest Darling,

You'll never believe what I did tonight. I went into town with my pal Irwin and celebrated. That's right, honey, I celebrated the day that my girl told me she loves me, the greatest day of my life! There are no words to explain what those three magic words mean to me. As you know, I don't usually go into town with the boys, but I considered this a special occasion. I know that you said you're trying love on for size, but I feel confident my love will be a good fit. It is a love that's loyal, a love that's true, and a love that you will always be able to count on, for the rest of your life.

By the way, darling, a little while ago, I had an interesting exchange with one of the boys in the barracks here. You see, it's commonplace for one of the guys to refer to a girl as a "hag." A guy doesn't mean anything by it, really. It's just a dumb thing a guy says. Well, let me tell you what happened...

22

Cecelia – 1931

*C*ecelia and Connie are playing jacks on the front porch when Ernie pulls up in his black Plymouth with its sweeping fenders and silver spoked wheels.

Connie races down the walkway, three steps ahead of little Cecelia, yelling, "Can we drive your car, Ernie?"

"Yeah, can we drive your car, Ernie?" Cecelia echoes.

Ernie knows what they mean. "You betcha," he says, allowing the two girls turns sitting in the driver's seat as they turn the ivory colored steering wheel from left to right with their little hands, making the sound of the car's engine with their voices.

"B-r-r-u-u-m, beep, beep!" they call out, because he won't allow them to honk the actual horn and disturb the neighbors.

"Alright…alright…that's enough for this morning. Come up on the porch, girls. I have a surprise for you."

"What surprise?" Connie asks.

"Yeah, what surprise?" Cecelia chimes in. "Did you bring your mandolin? Are we going to sing songs?"

Ernie is handsome, his dark hair combed with a perfect side part. Even the creases in his work clothes are clean and crisp. His wife Alice sees to that.

Taking a seat in a tattered wicker chair, its caning in need of rewrapping and a fresh coat of paint, he says, "No, I didn't bring my mandolin today because I have a different surprise."

He slips a splendid leather volume with gold foil lettering on its spine from a paper bag. "I want to read you a poem. But first, I've got a question. Do you know who the first President of the United States was?"

"Of course," Connie giggles. "Everybody knows that! George Washington."

"Yeah, everybody knows that," Cecelia says, parroting her sister.

"That's right, girls. Well, this poem is a little story about George Washington. It's a legend of when he was a young boy, not much older than you girls. Maybe you've heard it before, but I don't think you've ever heard it told *this* way. It's called 'Leetla Giorgio Washeenton,' and it's by a poet named Thomas Augustine Daly. Here's how it goes:

You know w'at for ees school keep out
Dees holiday, my son?
Wal, den, I gona tal you 'bout
Dees Giorgio Washeenton.

Wal, Giorgio was leetla keed
Ees leeve long time ago,
An' he gon' school for learn to read
An' write hees nam', you know.
He moocha like for gona school
An' learna hard all day,
Baycause he no gat time for fool
Weeth bada keeds an' play.
Wal, wan cold day w'en Giorgio
Ees steel so vera small,
He start from home, but he ees no
Show up een school at all!
Oh, my! hees Pop ees gatta mad
An' so he tal hees wife:
'Som' leetla boy ees gon' feel bad
Today, you bat my life!'
An' den he grab a bigga steeck

An' gon' out een da snow
An' lookin' all aroun' for seek
Da leetla Giorgio.
Ha! w'at you theenk? Firs' theeng he see
Where leetla boy he stan',
All tangla up een cherry tree,
Weeth hatchet een hees han'.
'Ha! w'at you do?' hees Pop he say,
'W'at for you busta rule
An' stay away like dees for play
Eenstead for gon' to school?'
Da boy ees say: 'I no can lie,
An' so I speaka true.
I stay away from school for try
An' gat som' wood for you.
I theenka deesa cherry tree
Ees goodda size for chop,
An' so I cut heem down, you see,
For justa help my Pop.'
Hees Pop he no can gatta mad,
But looka please' an' say:
'My leetla boy, I am so glad
You taka holiday.'

Ees good for leetla boy, you see,
For be so bright an' try
For help hees Pop; so den he be.
A granda man bimeby.

So now you gotta holiday
An' eet ees good, you know,
For you gon' do da sama way
Like leetla Giorgio.
Don't play so mooch, but justa stop,
Eef you want be som' good,
An' try for help your poor old Pop
By carry home som' wood;
An' mebbe so like Giorgio

You grow for be so great
You gona be da Presidant
Of dese Unita State'!"

Having listened in rapt delight, both girls applaud when Ernie is finished.

"Was George Washington Italian like us?" Cecelia asks.

With a chuckle, Ernie replies, "No, he wasn't."

"Then why's he talk like that?"

"It's just how the poet wants him to talk," Ernie explains. "It helps us to imagine that George Washington was just like our parents, just like us. Poetry and stories help us to feel that we're all a part of something bigger than ourselves."

"Oh, I understand," Cecelia says, not sure if she does.

"Now, I'm going to give you girls this book of poems," Ernie explains, handing the volume to Ceceilia. "There's lots of good ones, and now you can read this poem or any of the others whenever you like."

Seeing the Shashinka boys across the street, Connie asks, "Can I go play now, Ernie?"

"Sure you can, sweetheart. You go right ahead and play with the boys."

Cecelia, thumbing through the pages, sits next to Ernie, lost in thought.

"Everything okay, honey?" he asks.

"I s'pose," she replies, "but can you tell me something, Ernie?"

"Sure, I'll tell you anything you want to know."

Cecelia sighs and pauses. Finally, she asks, "Why did Papa die?"

Ernie pulls her up onto his lap. "He had a heart attack, baby. We told you that."

"No, but that's not what I mean."

"What do you mean then? Tell me."

"I mean...what I mean is...why do people have to die?"

The question takes Ernie by surprise. "Oh...let's see. Uhm, I'm not sure I can answer that one, baby."

"But you just said you'd tell me anything I want to know."

"I know I said that, sweetheart. But I don't know the answer to everything."

Cecelia nods, and the two sit in silence. The only sound is Connie and the Shashinkas chasing each other around the neighbors' house.

"Is Mama going to die?"

"I'm afraid so–someday."

"And are you going to die?"

"Yes, sweetheart."

"What about me, Ernie? Am I going to die?"

With a pensive smile, Ernie replies, "Not for a very long time. Listen, sweetie, everybody dies. Everything dies. Little insects and all of the animals. Even all of the plants. Even the leaves on the trees. Every autumn, what do they do? They turn from green to golden colors, and they fall off the trees and die. But then they come back to life in the spring. That's how it is with people, I think. They teach us that in church, right? Papa died, but he's alive again with God. Does that make sense?"

Cecelia nods. "I know. That's what the priest said at the funeral." But she doesn't understand it, and she's not certain she believes it.

"Listen, Celia. I know it's going to be hard for you without Papa, but if you need anything, all you need to do is ask me or Robert or even Dominic. If you need anything, we'll try to help you. Sound okay?"

"Yeah," Cecelia says, and she sighs once more.

Giving her a squeeze, Ernie says, "Okay, baby. I gotta get back to work, but you be a good girl and don't worry about anything."

As he drives away, Cecelia caresses the poetry book as she sees his car disappear around the curve at the bottom of the hill.

23

*L*ike a scribbled note hidden between the yellowing pages of an old book, some things in life are lost or forgotten. Losing her father at a young age was like that for Cecelia. The memory of that day was tucked away in the pages of her mind, although she seldom looked back on it. She'd not only read that book, she'd lived it. Often, it was as if it had never happened at all. Other people had fathers; Cecelia, simply, did not. What was a girl to do? Cry over spilled milk? Papa's death, of course, meant that certain dreams would need to be delayed or even abandoned. *That's how the cookie crumbles*, she would come to feel.

But Cecelia hadn't been sleeping very well since the night she wrote those three fateful words in a letter to Michael. If she wanted to be honest with herself, she would have to admit that she had historically shielded herself from love. She could talk until she was blue in the face about being too young, but from the moment she was old enough to date, she had built a stone barrier between herself and love. If she wanted to be honest with herself, she would have to admit that the foundation of that wall was laid the day her brother Dominic came running from behind the house, yelling that something was wrong with Papa. She hadn't forgotten the vibrations of panic she felt as she ran to fetch the doctor or the confusion she felt when he listened to Papa's heart with his stethoscope and solemnly shook his head. The memory would haunt her for years to come. If she wanted to be truly honest with herself, Cecelia would have to admit it was a loss from which she would never fully recover.

She didn't know a great deal about his past, but she knew that her father, Gennaro Alberino, named for the patron saint of Naples, had landed at Ellis Island in the spring of 1908 with two young sons, a pregnant wife, and hope in his heart. He saw America as a land of opportunity, and he aimed to make good on that opportunity. By the time Cecelia was born in 1925, Gennaro, through sheer determination and dogged hard work, already owned two houses, one of which he rented out. She knew enough about "the Crash," to know that, like a sledgehammer hitting a boulder, it fractured Papa's dreams into a million tiny shards of rock.

Nonetheless, Gennaro was optimistic, and he remained strong in the belief that he might be able to put things back together and send his two youngest daughters to college. "My bambini will-a be college-a graduates," she often heard him boast to family and friends over a glass of his homemade wine. Little did Gennaro know that he wouldn't live to see his two youngest turn eleven and eight years old, respectively.

Before Cecelia turned sixteen, her eldest brother Robert had abruptly and awkwardly informed the family that he was leaving an unhappy marriage and moving to New Jersey. Everyone was stunned. Cecelia had never known anyone who was divorced. And Robert, of all people, was such a steady, conservative guy. Cecelia couldn't quite fathom how he could ever leave his two daughters behind, her cousins, who were only a few years younger than she. Her heart ached for the girls, and she wondered how they would cope.

It seemed as if the water hadn't yet cooled from the Robert divorce when another family scandal boiled over. Cecelia would never forget that day. When she arrived at the plant and sat at her machine, she felt the oppressive eyes of her co-workers staring at her. Scanning the expanse of the shop, she could see them speaking in hushed tones to each other, and then at the sound of the plant whistle, breaking apart from their sticky webs of gossip to head to their machines.

As Genevieve, a co-worker, sat down across from her, Cecelia asked, "Hey, Gen, what gives? Are people talking about me, or is it just my imagination? Is my makeup smudged or something?"

"No, that ain't it. Your makeup's perfect like always. It's somethin' else."

"Are you going to tell me what it is, or am I a contestant on 'Take it or Leave it'? Because if that's the case, I hope you've got sixty-four bucks to pay me when I get the right answer."

"Well, I can't lie to ya, kid."

Staring down her co-worker, Cecelia said, "Good, because I hate liars."

Genevieve proceeded gingerly. "Yeah, kid, I hear ya. I don't like liars neither. Well, I hate to say it, but do you notice who ain't at work this mornin'?"

Cecelia was feeling increasingly irked by the second. "As a matter of fact, no I don't, Gen. There's a lot of people who work on this floor. I don't have a personal list of every one of them."

"Okay, I hate to say it, but do you see your brother?"

Cecelia felt a cold sweat at her temples as she perused the floor. "Well, no. Maybe he's grabbing a smoke before we start our day."

"Did you notice who else ain't here?" Genevieve added.

"For Christ's sake, Gen, just get to the point, will you? Spit it out. Say what you have to say."

"Dolly Davidson, that floozy he's always flirting with."

"I'm afraid I never noticed."

"Well, you're the one person who hasn't, hon. The rumor is that the two of them ran off together last night."

"Get out. Dominic wouldn't do that. He's got a wife and a kid at home."

"Yeah, we know. It was a shitty thing to do."

After trudging through the long workday and feeling like a leper, Cecelia left work utterly bewildered. She couldn't help questioning the point of marriage. She couldn't think of one marriage that was idyllic. Besides the unsuccessful marriage of her brother Robert and now, apparently, Dominic, several co-workers of hers had complained of troubled marriages during coffee breaks. Whose young husband was out all night playing pool? Whose husband was cheating on her? One girlfriend, Marie, had cried to Cecelia that she had lost her virginity to her husband a month before their wedding day, "And now he calls me a puttana–a whore. All I did was show my love for him," Marie had lamented. Cecelia did her best to console her heartbroken friend, while contemplating the high price Italian men placed on virginity and the double standards that existed between men and women of their generation.

And even her married sisters. Cecelia knew they had their share of problems. Her sisters had confided in her. For some reason, everyone liked to tell her their problems. Walking on Howe Avenue, she couldn't think of a single marriage that was anything to write home about.

Cecelia needed to talk to someone. She felt her brother Ernie might offer some perspective on the matter. She walked to his house and luckily found him home. Ernie listened to Cecelia's story, and after mumbling, "Jesus," he packed her into his car and drove her home.

When they got to the house, they found Dominic's wife Catherine crying on Mama's shoulder, her six-year-old son sitting on the floor looking lost and confused. It was another "hard knock," as Cecelia would come to call it, in the school of life.

Mama looked so helpless. What comfort could she give, speaking so little English? Catherine wasn't even Italian. Trying to rescue the situation, Ernie sat down next to Catherine and whispered to her, ostensibly trying to console her.

Emotionally drained, Cecelia escaped to the porch. She had no idea what Ernie might be saying to Catherine, and she wasn't sure she wanted to know.

Moments later, Catherine bolted out of the house, unable to speak or even look at Cecelia, tugging her little boy behind her as she trotted down the hill. Whatever Ernie had said to her clearly hadn't helped.

Ernie, a step behind, called after his brother's wife. "Catherine! Wait! C'mon, let me at least bring you home, for God's sake!" But Catherine didn't break stride.

Throwing up his hands, Ernie let out a long sigh.

"So, it's true," Cecelia said.

"He left her a note and more or less told her the truth."

Ernie could see that Cecelia was now crying.

"Aw, Celia, don't be sad. This isn't your marriage."

"It's just that," she began through her tears, "just that, no one has a good marriage."

"That's not true," he said. "Mine's not too bad. I mean, it's not a storybook marriage, but Alice and I get on alright."

Cecelia shrugged and wiped her tears with the backs of her hands.

"It's just that...just that..."

Ernie sat down beside her. "Just that what, sis?"

"It's just that I wrote to Michael the other day, and I told him I loved him. But what's the point?"

Ernie reached around and put his arm around his youngest sister. "The point is, you got a pretty good guy there who's head over heels for you." Cecelia shrugged again. "Maybe I only met him one time–that time you stopped over when he was on furlough, but it was one of those things."

"One of what things?" she pouted.

"Sometimes in life, ya just get a gut feeling about someone. That ever happen to you? When I met Michael, I thought, 'this is a stand-up guy.' " He squeezed her extra tight. "You know I'd never let my baby sister be involved with him if I didn't feel that way."

Ernie's warmth broke the tension, and Cecelia let out a bubble or two of laughter.

"Yeah, he is a pretty good guy, isn't he?"

"He sure as hell is as far as I can see."

"I just don't know what I should do."

Deep in thought, Ernie stared at the palms of his hands. Cecelia looked at them too. Cracked and calloused, they were hands that said: this is an honest, hard worker who gets up every morning and strives to provide a good living for his family.

Finally, Ernie spoke. "What you should do is let yourself be in love with your soldier. What you should do is not go by what's happening to anyone else. What you should do is live your own life. No marriage is perfect. We have to work at it. Robert and Dominic had their own problems, and I guess they couldn't work them out. It's not our business. It doesn't mean we'll have the same issues, and it doesn't mean that we can't work out our own problems, what-ever they may be. Personally, I don't think it's a good idea to run away from things, but who am I to judge? Maybe Robert and Dominic just had to do what was best for them."

"But...but, I'll also miss them," Cecelia said. "What if we never see them again?"

"We'll see them again. We're family. They won't abandon us. They won't abandon you. You're the baby–too special to any of us to abandon. They'll be in touch. You'll see."

Ernie kissed her on the forehead, wearily stood up, and walked to his car.

Watching him drive down the hill, Cecelia couldn't deny that he had made her feel a little better. She heard his advice in her head: "What you should do is let yourself be in love with your soldier."

Her family's marriage problems aside, she hadn't been planning to fall in love. Until Cecelia had tried on the words "I love you" in a letter to Michael, she had been dating other guys. She had always been a great believer in playing the field and keeping all of her options open.

She had even been occasionally seeing Augie from the All-Stars. While they had agreed that their visits would remain platonic per Danny's rule, they had been enjoying little rendezvous in New Haven after band practice, "just as friends"–a soda on State Street or a walk across the Green before her bus arrived.

Blond-haired Augie was tall and good looking and funny. There was something attractive about a man with a sense of humor, and Cecelia loved the way he made her laugh, imitating some of the characters in the band.

Danny scheduled the next practice in the later afternoon because he had to attend a funeral that Saturday morning. By the time the practice ended, the sun had gone down, and Augie, like usual, said he'd walk Cecelia to the bus stop at the corner of Chapel and Temple Streets.

As they passed College Street, Augie said, "How about ya let me buy you a sandwich? There's a little place, the Anchor Restaurant, right around the corner here. They got good food."

Despite a wave of reluctance, something compelled Cecelia to agree.

A few minutes later, she preceded Augie in sliding into a wrap-around booth with its shiny black upholstery. Cecelia couldn't help wondering if Augie was sitting a little too close. When the waiter arrived, Cecelia glanced up from the menu and ordered a pastrami on toasted rye with melted cheese.

"How about a highball to go with that?" Augie asked. "It'll help wash it down."

"Oh, I don't know about that," Cecelia hesitated. "I shouldn't."

"Don't be silly. Live a little, why don't ya?" and without missing a beat, Augie ordered cocktails for both of them.

Before Cecelia knew it, one drink turned into two, but she fortunately succeeded in dissuading Augie from ordering a third or he would have had to carry her to the bus stop. Still, she was feeling tipsy when Augie ordered a strawberry shortcake for the two of them to share.

When the dessert arrived, Augie was in the middle of a story about one of his former teachers. "So besides his spectacles and the greasy strands of hair combed over the top of his bald head, which was always wet with sweat, he said, 'You see,' every other phrase, talking through his nose with a phony English accent like this: 'Just as we mustn't use the pronoun *me*, you see, when the nominative *I* is called for, so we must also never do the reverse, you see. We use the pronoun *me*, you see, in the objective case, you see, when it is a DI-rect object. Egg-zample: *The teacher reprimanded James and me*. It is incor-RECT, you see, to say: *The teacher reprimanded James and I*. This is, you see, the essent-sial difference between the nominative *I* and the objective *me*.' The guy was a real character."

"Oh my God, Augie. You are such a scream! I'll bet that voice you were doing is exactly what he sounded like too."

"Yeah, I like to think I got 'em down to a T."

"You're so funny," Cecelia said, tasting the whipped cream topping from the shortcake. "If you weren't such a great trombone player, you could have been a comedian."

"Aw, you're so sweet. Why, you're sweeter than this dessert here."

Cecelia felt warm and blushed.

"Do you mind if I give you a little kiss, just to see if you're as sweet as I think you are?"

"I don't...don't really think you should. Because we talked about it and..."

Perhaps it was his smile, or perhaps it was the shared laughter. Perhaps it was the dim lighting in the Anchor, or perhaps it was the sound of Bing Crosby's voice crooning "Moonlight Becomes You" emanating from the jukebox that made her feel warm and weak. But when Augie leaned in and gently kissed her before she finished protesting, Cecelia didn't stop him.

"There, that wasn't so bad, was it?" he whispered.

"No, it wasn't so bad," she said.

"And I was right."

"Right about what?"

And in a nasally voice with a British accent, Augie smiled and said, "Your lips, you see, are essent-sially just as sweet, you see, as I thought they would be," which made Cecelia laugh more and opened the door for Augie to kiss her a few more times. She even allowed him one last long, lingering kiss, as the bus arrived to take her back to Shelton, a bus ride that in many ways felt like the longest she had ever taken. Her head was still spinning. It occurred to her that, highballs aside, letting Augie kiss her was a way of testing herself–testing if she was really in love with Michael. She was going to have to give it some time...to let it settle and steep, like a tea bag in a cup of hot water. But even before the bus arrived in Shelton, the water had turned into a piping hot cup of guilt.

A week later at band practice, still feeling the burden of that guilt, she averted her eyes and looked down at her shoes when Augie attempted to make eye contact.

With a sad smile, Danny addressed the band. "I'm sorry to say I've got some not-so-hot news for you." He took a long drag on his cigarette and blew the smoke out slowly. "We're going to have to put the All-Stars on hold for a while. Maybe until this bloody mess ends, which can't happen too soon. It ain't like it was. You've seen it. The girls at the dance halls outnumber the guys thirty to one. And, worse still, we all know that the war is decimating the band, making us lose players left and right. I have to keep revising the charts, which, quite frankly, is becoming a royal pain in my ass. Pardon my French, Cecelia."

The members murmured in an unhappy chorus of agreement. Cecelia continued to stare down at her shoes.

"And, sure, I could pull some older guys like me in as replacements, but what's the point? We're getting fewer bookings each week."

Silence echoed Danny's words in the Chapel Street studio.

"Look, I'm as heartbroken as all of you are. But for now, let's put everything on hold. Sound okay?"

The All-Stars responded once more in a gloomy fugue of resignation.

"So there's no point in practicing today, if you know what I mean. I'm sorry I made you all come down here, but I wanted to tell you in person."

Sticks McKenna, the drummer, piped in, "But since we're here anyway, Danny, how about we do a few tunes for old time's sake?"

Everyone else responded in assent, and Danny said, "You bet... for old time's sake."

Cecelia had to admit that the boys never sounded better, even with a missing trumpet here and a missing alto sax there. She herself sang two songs before the practice broke up, and as she did, Danny looked up at her from his wheelchair, his red cheeks puffed with admiration, tears welling up in the corners of his eyes.

"That was just swell, sweetie," he said, after her second song. "I'm sorry you got to do only a handful of jobs with us. What could it have been? Eight or nine?" Then Danny let out a sigh. "Well, I think that's gonna have to be it for today, gang. I don't think I can take hearing any more, especially hearing this angel serenade us."

After Cecelia said her goodbyes to the boys, she embraced Danny and thanked him for everything. She didn't linger long for fear of losing her composure, and a moment later, she was running down the marble staircase en route to the street below.

Heartbroken, Cecelia couldn't hold back her tears. What did she have to look forward to now? Without the All-Stars, without dances, and without the man to whom she had recently professed her love, she had nothing except the dull job at the factory. She wished she hadn't quit school. Maybe she could have gone on to secretarial school. Maybe, at least with a high school diploma, she could have found a more interesting line of work.

As she zigzagged inside and outside of shoppers on Chapel Street, she heard a voice behind her. "Hey, Cecelia! Wait up for me! Cecelia, wait, for God's sake!"

Barely breaking stride, Cecelia did a half-turn as she saw Augie running after her while hugging his trombone case. She didn't know what else to do but wait for him.

When he caught up, Augie said, "Cecelia, what's the deal? I was packing up my horn, and when I looked up, you were gone. What's the rush?"

"I just had to...had to go. It's too...too emotional for me."

"Yeah, I hear ya. It's a bum deal. Whatta we gonna do? But how about you and me go get a soda like usual?"

"I think I just need to get the bus and go home."

"Okay...but would you mind if I wait for the bus with you?"

Cecelia would have preferred to be alone, but to be polite, she agreed.

As they sat on the bench at the bus stop with Augie's eyes closed and his chin resting on top of the tattered trombone case, both were at a loss for words.

When he could no longer stifle himself, Augie said, "I know, Cecelia, that this is lousy, stinkin' news for all of us, but maybe it ain't all bad."

"What do you mean?"

Augie spoke slowly and tenderly. "Well, I'm thinkin' about that rule Danny has about nobody dating you. I don't think that rule counts if there's no band."

Cecelia closed her eyes. *I don't need this right now,* she thought to herself.

Augie persisted. "Cecelia?"

"Listen, Augie," she began. "You're a good friend. I mean that. But that's all we agreed to be to each other."

"Yeah," Augie said, "but I just thought, ya know, after last week at the Anchor, that things were maybe–"

"I know...I know. I'm sorry about that, Augie. I shouldn't have let you kiss me. Listen, Augie...I have a fellow in the Army now. He's in Nebraska and soon he's going somewhere else. I don't know how to...how to say this, Augie, but I've pledged my love to him."

"Oh, I...uhm...I see."

"I'm sorry, Augie. I don't mean to hurt your feelings."

"It's okay. He's a lucky guy…this, what'd ya say his name is?"

"His name is Michael. He's a good man, Augie. He's hoping to become a pilot."

"Wow! A pilot. That's a big deal, ain't it?"

"Yes, if he makes it, it is kind of a big deal."

"Yeah, sure it is. Well, good for him."

"Augie, if you don't mind, I'd like to ask you a question about something–something we've never talked about."

"Shoot."

"Augie, why are you not in the Army?"

"Well, that's the next thing I was gonna tell ya after I asked if you'd be my girl now. I'm not even twenty, ya know, so I was trying to wait, hoping this thing'll end soon. Because, who wants to go get their head blown off? I just wanna play my horn and live my life."

"I see."

"I guess you must think I'm pretty yellow."

"No, I don't. I think I understand."

"Yeah, well anyway…ya know those posters of Uncle Sam ya see at the post office and the library and just about everywhere ya look these days–that top hat with stars on it, his long finger pointing at you, the words *I Want You* plastered across the top?"

"Yes," Cecelia said, tentatively.

"Well, Uncle Sam decided he wants me. I got drafted. I got a letter in the mail. I'm one of the reasons for Danny's talk today."

"Oh, I'm sorry to hear that," Cecelia said glumly. "I guess they need every man they can get. It's our duty, though, to do what we can to put an end to this war, isn't it, Augie?"

Before Augie could respond, Cecelia's bus pulled up. Cecelia, her eyes once more welling up with tears, took Augie's face in her hands and placed a tender kiss on his cheek. "Good luck to you, Augie. I'll miss you, and I'll pray for you."

As the bus drove away, Cecelia could see Augie through the back window, still stationary on the park bench, growing smaller and smaller, frozen in time.

24

June 21, 1943

Dearest Cecelia,

That was quite a story about that fellow, Augie. I'm glad you sent him on his way because I don't react too well to other guys horning in on my girl, as you might remember. And you weren't even my girl back then, were you? But you are now, aren't you, darling?

It's nice to know that you're in love with me now and that we're a steady couple. It makes being away from home a lot easier to swallow!

Well, I got my orders to transfer to Mississippi. I leave on July 11th. I'll be among over 200 men applying for the Cadet Program. Rumors are that very few of us will be accepted. That's not very encouraging, is it?

Right now I'm in the dayroom listening to "I Had the Craziest Dream" on the radio. There's a lot of static coming through the speaker, but I'm still enjoying it. I don't think anybody blows the trumpet like Harry James, and Helen Forrest has a great voice, but she can't hold a candle to you. But tell me, darling, are you a crazy dreamer? Do you have the craziest dreams about kissing me like the song says? I hope so! I know I'm a crazy dreamer. I can't wait until our lips meet again.

And that's not the only crazy dream I have. You even told me your-self that I was a pipe dreamer, which is more true now than ever. This idea of flying planes is the biggest pipe dream I've ever had, but I'm not letting it go. Gee, hon, I've got a lump in my throat even writing about it.

This morning we had a parade, and guess who was there to watch us march. The President himself! My right hand to God, honey. As we passed by the grandstand in formation, I could see him out of the corner of my eye, sitting there in a black overcoat, his fedora tilted back on his head, and a cigarette holder jutting upward out of his mouth, just like you see in the newsreels and magazines! To think— here I am, twenty-one and marching in uniform before the President of the United States!

But, even if the President hadn't been present, I'd wager that you'd get a cold chill up your spine if you ever saw about 10,000 of us marching around the parade grounds. Then, when we were marching back to our barracks, about 500 of us in one battalion began singing the Air Corps song—"Off we go into the wild blue yonder..." Gee, it sounded swell, even as tired as we were. It made me feel proud to be among such a grand bunch of soldiers. Maybe we're nothing but a bunch of kids, but I'll bet my right arm that we could kick the hell out of about 50,000 of Hirohito's so-called Imperial soldiers.

You know, darling, even though some days I hate this army, I couldn't think of someone else fighting my war. My place is here, and I know it. I know sometimes I joke that I miss you so much that I'm tempted to go over the wall in order to see you. But that would jeopardize everything, wouldn't it? I'd lose my chance to be a pilot, and well, it would just make everything worse. But, see, there's something else. I know that I can't come home until this crazy war is all over.

I know you're worried I might get killed, but if I do, I won't be the only one. See, if a soldier dies, he doesn't die in vain. He doesn't die for the emperor or the fuhrer. He dies to restore his freedom and the freedom of his family and friends. He dies to make his country a better place to live. What good will freedom do him if he gets killed? No good, personally, but he knows that his folks and friends will benefit. How does he know that we will win? Let me put it this way. A country with a moral to fight for always wins and that is just what the U.S. will do. We have always won, and we will win again and again, if necessary.

Don't worry about me though, hon. I can take care of myself and *with you always in my mind, I will be twice as careful and many more times eager to live to come back to you.*

Oh, one more thing, darling. You remember Scooter from that night we met? Well, he's in the Navy, and he wrote to me and told me he's going to be home on leave...so I was wondering if you wouldn't mind getting together with him. Scooter's like a brother, and I would trust him with my life...so I hope you'll do that for me.

Well, darling, I guess that's just about it. Well, except for HAPPY BIRTHDAY! I'll bet you thought I forgot! Ha-ha-ha! I could never forget your birthday. I love you way too much! How does it feel to be eighteen? Seriously, though, I'm sending a little present with this letter. You'll see what it is when you get it. Until tomorrow, I love you!

> *Your soldier,*
> *Love, xoxoxo*
> *Michael*

*W*hen she heard the rapping at her door on Saturday at noon, Cecelia felt a surge of apprehension because she didn't know what to expect. The night she met Michael, she had barely gotten a glimpse of Scooter as he drove along the shoulder of the road, talking to the two Connies.

When she opened the door, there he stood in his crisp, white uniform, the round cap tilted on his head. Scooter whipped the cap off of his head, revealing a buzz cut, and said, "Hello, Cecelia. Whattaya hear, whattaya say?"

"Scooter O'Brian! I don't hear nothin' and I don't say nothin'!"

Scooter burst into laughter. "Oh, for the love of God, Michael's been talkin' about me."

"He sure has, but all good things," she assured him.

"I hope ya don't mind gettin' a bite wid me. I ain't been near a dame since I joined the Navy."

She climbed into his truck, and on the way to Woolworth's, Scooter explained to her how the Navy was sending him to the Pacific as soon as his furlough ended. He'd be a crew member on a PT boat, he said, although Cecelia didn't know what a PT boat was.

Sitting at a table in Woolworth's, Scooter chattered on about the

Navy. Finally, he said, "I guess I'm borin' ya wid all this talk about Navy life. Let's talk about Michael. That'd be more interestin'."

"Tell me all about Michael," she said playfully.

"Me and him are practically brothers. Well, he got his own brothers, but I don't, see, so he's the closest thing I got."

"Michael feels the same way about you."

Scooter bit into his turkey club, and then talked with his mouth full. "Yeah, we been inseparatable, me and him, since we was little kids. That bum and me got in more trouble growin' up."

"How?"

"Well, like how he put a bullet in his finger."

Puzzled, Cecelia said, "Bullet in his finger?"

"Didn't Mikey never tell you about it?"

"Well, of course, I noticed the bump in his finger, and he once said he'd tell me the story behind it, but every time I've asked him since then, Michael's changed the subject."

A shade of pink rose from Scooter's neck to his forehead. "Oh boy, well if Mikey didn't tell ya, I better keep my trap shut. But listen, if he ever tells ya the story, ya gotta let me know, because I bet you'll roll over laughin'."

"I'll be sure to do that." Cecelia smiled.

As the two ate their lunch, Scooter talked non-stop about how he had moved from Ireland to Derby, about how his family felt that it was more important for him to work than to go to school, about how he had loved working on the New Haven docks with his father, and about how he was born to be close to the ocean.

She liked Scooter. Michael's and Scooter's friendship reminded Cecelia of hers with Stella—the kind of relationship that lasts a lifetime.

When they returned to her house, like a gentleman, Scooter walked Cecelia to the door.

"Well, I guess I talked too much, but I sure as heck appreciate ya spendin' time wid me. Michael's a lucky guy."

Flattered, Cecelia replied, "Well, thank you, Scooter. That's nice of you to say."

"And lemme add, ya picked a real winner too, Cecelia. Mikey's a first rate guy. I've come across lotsa mugs, but nobody like Mikey, right?"

"Yes, right. I'm learning that more and more each day. And I hope you find yourself a nice girl too. Good luck. I'll be praying for you."

When she walked in the door, Connie greeted Cecelia with sarcasm. "Well, here she is, the *princess* herself, finally gracing us with her presence. Where in Christ have you been?"

"I had lunch with Michael's friend Scooter. He's home on leave."

"Oh, I remember that winner," Connie said.

Little Connie smiled. "Oh, how is he?"

"He's a good guy. He's in the Navy now and being sent to fight on some kind of boat. What are you two up to?"

"I thought it was obvious," her sister snapped, "but maybe it's something royalty like you hasn't seen before. It's called *cooking*."

"Cooking? Why?"

"Because I promised Mama. How's that? So put on an apron and pitch in."

"God! After working all week, who feels like cooking in this heat?" Cecelia moaned, tying a floral apron around her waist.

Little Connie sat silently peeling a large carrot at the kitchen table.

"If you don't like your job, stop complaining and quit, and if you don't like the heat, move to Alaska." Connie snapped.

"I'm not moving to Alaska, silly, but I *am* going to quit my job. The government has repurposed another factory on Canal Street to make flying suits for the Air Corps. Since Michael might become a pilot, I'm going to apply there. Besides, that creep Tony Vitti is always making passes at me."

"Have you told Michael about him?" little Connie asked.

"A little bit, but not everything. Michael would blow a gasket if I told him the whole story. There are some things that it's better if Michael doesn't know."

Cecelia was thinking of Augie Norko, not Tony Vitti. While she had told Michael about Augie, she'd given him half the story. She hadn't told anyone about the kissing except the priest in the confessional, but what good did ten *Hail Marys* and ten *Our Fathers* do? She knew she'd eventually have to confess to Michael when the time was right.

Connie grabbed the chicken out of the icebox by one plump leg and plunked it down on the carving board.

"I don't even know if I can eat that," Cecelia complained. "Yesterday, it was hanging upside-down outside with blood dripping from its neck."

"Jesus Christ almighty, when did you become so sensitive and refined? Mama knocks herself out making sure we eat. Yes, even slaughtering a chicken now and then. She cooks every night of the week, and we take advantage of her, which you know as well as I do. She might not complain, but her arthritis is killing her. So just cut the bull and go outside and pump some goddamn water for the broth!"

Glaring at her sister, Cecelia stormed out the back door. Little Connie, trying to make herself as invisible as possible, continued peeling and cutting bright orange carrots, crooked parsnips, and fat turnips into bite-sized chunks.

When Cecelia returned, she grunted and poured the bucket of water into the black pot on the stove.

"There," she said.

"Good," Connie said, still miffed.

Connie swung a meat cleaver, which thudded against the cutting board, dividing the chicken into pieces. Cecelia took a seat next to little Connie and watched her work with sullen eyes.

Attempting to break the tension, little Connie asked, "So, have you heard from Michael lately?"

"Of course, Connie. Don't be such a dip. He writes every day."

"So, what's new with him?"

"Let's see. He recently wrote about a big parade they had on the base. I guess every once in a while thousands of guys march around the base."

"My goodness. Whatever for?"

"I'm sure I don't have any idea, but the President was even there."

"Wow! That's what he wrote about?"

"Not just that." Cecelia seemed to soften a bit. "He wrote about why he is willing to fight and die for his country."

Little Connie set her peeler down on the cream-colored enamel tabletop. "No kidding. He said he's willing to die? How brave! That must have been some letter."

Leaning against the counter, even Connie felt drawn in now.

"It's a funny thing, you know," Cecelia continued, "to see how different guys think. For instance, that guy Augie from the band who likes me."

"Yeah, what about him?" little Connie asked.

"He just got drafted. When I asked him why he hadn't just enlisted, he didn't have much of an answer. Just that he's young and wants to keep playing music and doesn't want to get killed. All that jazz. And here's Michael saying that he's not about to let anyone else fight this war for him, as if he's some kind of, uhm…one-man army." Cecelia became cognizant of the tears seeping into the corners of her eyes.

"Why are you crying?" her sister asked.

"Because…I'm beginning to think he is."

"Is what?"

"A one-man army." Then, as a single teardrop escaped and rolled down her cheek and onto the table, she laughed. "Oh, I know he's not. But I feel safe when I'm with him, and he cares so much about his family and friends that he's willing to die for them. And for me too, while here's Augie, just trying to save himself. It's the craziest thing. I've spent less than a month in Michael's presence, and with every letter, I'm crazier and crazier about the guy. He has such a sense of honor."

"Gee whiz," little Connie muttered.

"Yeah, gee whiz," Cecelia echoed.

"Yeah, *gee whiz*," Connie mimicked. "Now, if you two would kindly drop those vegetables in the pot, I'll do the same with the chicken. Then let's, all three of us, clean up this messy house. And, *gee whiz*, how about we see what sense of honor *we* all have? Maybe we have enough honor to ease some of the workload around here from our little, old Italian mother. Think of yourselves as good soldiers, and think of me as your drill sergeant. Let's move it!"

25

July 13, 1943

Dearest Darling,

Well, it's early Sunday morning, and here I am in Biloxi, Mississippi. On the way, we crossed six states—Kansas, Missouri, Kentucky, Tennessee, Alabama, and finally, Mississippi. Biloxi is just a dull town, duller than Derby. And it's summer all year long. By that I mean it's hotter than h-ll down here. And where there aren't paved roads, it's just mud everywhere.

I don't mean to bore you, honey. Here I am giving you a geography lesson on the deep South when I should be telling you how much I love you. What a dope I am!

Gosh, I'm sure excited because this whole process begins tomorrow. You're going to find out what I'm made of, honey. I hope you won't be disappointed...

espite the best of intentions, Michael didn't always make it to Mass on Sunday mornings, not while he had been in the military and not even before enlisting. Often, he was too tired or simply too lazy to roll out of bed in the morning, but on his first morning in Biloxi, Michael had a gut feeling that offering up a few prayers might be a good idea.

Tired from traveling, Michael felt his heavy eyelids closing as he heard the priest recite, "Confiteor Deo Omnipotenti, beatae Mariae semper Virgini, beato Michaeli Archangelo…"

On the outer edge of his consciousness, he could hear some of the boys whispering the prayer along with the priest, and he tried to move his lips, but he couldn't seem to get any momentum going. Fighting sleep, he soon heard the familiar chanting of the Gloria: "Gloria in excelsis Deo. Et in terra pax hominibus bonae voluntatis…"

In the midst of his somnolence, Michael wrestled with his conscience. *How can I expect God to help me when I can't even stay awake?* By the time the priest finished reading the Gospel and was ready to deliver his sermon, Michael finally shook off the sleepiness enough to sit up and listen. The bulk of the sermon was the standard, boring stuff that he had heard for years, but then the priest got a little more personal.

"Boys, this morning we welcome a new group of candidates for the Cadet Training Program. About two hundred of you, from what I understand. I hope each of you appreciates what an honor it is to be admitted into the program for consideration. But don't be disappointed if you don't make it, boys. In the last group, only seventeen of two hundred made the grade, so it's no shame if you don't. It's God's will for you to serve your country, boys, or you wouldn't be here. But *how* you serve is also a matter of God's will. It may be that our Father in Heaven has another plan for you. As you begin your testing, I hope you all understand that. In the name of the Father and of the Son and of the Holy Ghost. Amen."

The priest launched into the Nicenum: "Credo in unum Deum, Patrem omnipotentem, factorem caeli et terrae…"

It wasn't exactly the message from God that Michael had hoped to hear. As he lit a cigarette outside the chapel after Mass, a fellow cadet-hopeful blurted out, "How do ya like that guy? Talk about letting the air out of a soldier's tire, huh?"

Michael just shrugged it off.

"Name's O'Mara," the soldier continued, offering his hand. He was short, not more than 5′6″, with a ruddy face and red hair.

"DeMarco, here," Michael replied, not particularly interested in making a new friend, but shaking hands anyway.

"You're here from McCook. Is that right?"

"Yeah, that's right."

"I don't think we ever ran into each other there."

Michael took a long drag. "Apparently not."

"Well, we're in this thing together, so we may as well be friends."

"We're in it together, but we're also against each other, right?" Michael asked, forever the realist. "You know, because of how competitive it is. Look at it this way. If you make it, I probably won't, and vice versa."

"Yeah, that makes sense."

But, like a fly who has intruded on the interior of a house, O'Mara continued to buzz around Michael for the next few days.

After shaking O'Mara at breakfast, Michael's next stop was a meeting with the commanding officer, who addressed the new candidates. Colonel Orville McCarver wore sunglasses underneath the chestnut brown visor of his cap. Even obscured by the dark lenses, the colonel's battle-worn face told a story.

Michael heard some rumblings that it was no coincidence that his first name was Orville. "They say he shares the same birthday as Orville Wright–named after him, they say, and they also say that, from the day of his birth on, all he ever wanted to do was fly," one Southern boy said to another. "I even heard tell that he was decorated during the Great War for flying the first bombing missions."

The candidates sat before the colonel in a set of bleachers at the parade field. He paused, and his head appeared to scan the group from left to right and from bottom to top where Michael sat. Colonel McCarver seemed to be sizing them up and evaluating their potential.

Finally, with a confident smile, he projected in a full voice that echoed across the level field. "I hope you are proud of yourselves, boys, for making it into the Cadet Program. We sure as hell are proud of you. Your superiors sent you here because they believe you are good officer material. That should say something to you right there. As soldiers in this man's army, you have already been through more strenuous training than any soldier in the history of the United States military. I can also tell you with certainty that you will be challenged even further as a cadet. For those of you who make the grade, honor is yours. In my humble opinion, there is no greater honor than becoming a pilot in the United States Army Air Corps. I am a pioneer of this outfit, so I know, boys. Of course, most of you will wash out, and even if you make it through the testing and are accepted into the program now, later on, many of you will still wash out or resign. But here's the thing, boys. If it turns out you don't earn your wings, for whatever reason, you shouldn't feel bad. Better men than many of you will ever be have failed to make the grade. It's an honor, truly, just to be chosen as a candidate and a bigger honor to call yourself a cadet, if that should be your fate. Allow me to wish you the best of luck as you move through the next two weeks, boys. You have the opportunity to become an officer and a gentleman in the United States Army. I know that the cream will rise to the top the way it always does."

As the group dispersed back to their barracks, Michael's new friend approached him. "Well, that's twice in one day we've been told we're not going to make it. I don't know how that makes you feel, but it doesn't leave me with much hope."

"I don't know, O'Mara," Michael replied. "On the one hand, I get your point, but on the other, old Orville gave me some hope. Like he said, if our superiors in Nebraska hadn't felt we were good candidates, they wouldn't have sent us here. So why can't you or I be as good a candidate as the next guy? What do these other bastards have that we don't?"

"I guess I see what you're saying," O'Mara conceded. "So, what do you think your chances are?"

"I don't have the slightest idea," Michael said, "but I'm going to do everything in my power to maximize them. I'll step over, smash through, and even crush these other sons-a-bitches to make it if that's what it takes. And that means you too. That's for goddamn sure!"

Not knowing what to say, O'Mara just smiled and grinned, but he understood.

The next day, after the group had finished the cross-country run, O'Mara approached Michael who was still catching his breath. "What'd you come in, DeMarco?"

"Fourth," Michael replied.

"Fourth? You're shitting me! What were you? A track star in high school?"

"Nope. I'm just planning on trying to break into this piloting business."

...You see, honey. I may not be able to control everything, but I'm determined to do good in the things I can control. Can you believe that? Fourth out of two hundred guys. I finished the 2 ½ mile course in 13:28. Pretty good, right? If I pushed a little harder, I could have come in second because two of the guys were only a few steps ahead of me. But I'm happy with fourth...

A day later, Michael came in second on the obstacle course. "How do you do it?" O'Mara asked as he huffed and puffed each word.

"Determination," Michael said.

"No shit. Where can a guy buy some of that? Christ, I came in 57th and even worse than that in the cross-country run yesterday. I guess my goose is pretty well cooked."

"I wouldn't count yourself out this early, O'Mara," Michael replied, puffing air out through his flared nostrils. "You need to have the right mental attitude, and believe me, that ain't it."

"By the way," O'Mara said, "my first name is Mike."

"Is that right?" Michael said, cocking his head. "So is mine."

"Well, doesn't that beat all? Whattaya suppose the chances of that are?"

Michael smiled. He couldn't dislike the guy. Having met enough assholes in the military for one war, he could tell O'Mara wasn't among them. It wouldn't be the worst idea, he realized, to go through this ordeal with an ally.

Following three hours of academic testing the next day, Michael sucked down a cold drink at the water fountain and splashed some coolness on his perspiring face.

O'Mara was just a step behind. "This Mississippi heat is a bitch, ain't it?"

"Soaked right through my shirt," Michael replied.

"Yeah, same for me. Where ya from, Michael?"

"Connecticut. How about you?"

"Maine. So I'm not used to this shit."

"How'd you do on the last one?" Michael asked.

"Oh, you mean the math test? I don't know. Not good."

"Yeah, me neither. A lot of that stuff might as well've been hieroglyphics to me. I knew I should've paid closer attention in school, but I don't think they ever taught us a lotta that stuff in Derby."

"Derby?"

"Yeah, my hometown."

"I wasn't much of a student either," O'Mara said. "I couldn't have known I'd ever need to know advanced math in my future."

"I mean, it's not like I was going to be an architect or an engineer. My folks don't have the money to send me to–"

"That wasn't too bad, was it?" a voice interrupted. Michael turned to see a long, pole-like figure with blond hair and a thin beak of a nose. For as much as Michael towered over O'Mara, this new stranger towered over him doubly so. "That one didn't give me any trouble," the stranger continued with a drawl. "I learned mosta that material last year."

"Last year?" O'Mara asked.

"Yup, in my required math course. Then, during the first term of sophomore year, I took calculus, which makes this stuff look like elementary school arithmetic."

"Oh, you mean college," said O'Mara, catching on.

"Yes siree. I started college at Auburn...Alabama. Basketball scholarship."

"Oh, a basketball player, huh?" O'Mara wasn't surprised.

"Damn straight. Did my first three semesters, but I made a decision to leave school and do my part to stop the Germans and Japs. My daddy fought in the last war, and now it's time for me to do my part in this one."

"What were you studying at Auburn, Mac?" Michael asked.

"The name's Roderick Davidson, but most folks call me Stretch. I was takin' up mechanical engineering. I'm going to finish as soon as this war is over. First, though, I'm going to finish this pilot training program."

"First you gotta get into it, Roderick," Michael pointed out.

"I ain't worried about that," the basketball player said. "It'll be a cinch."

...Honey, I guess I bit off a little more than I can chew this time. What I mean is that I'm almost sure that I won't make the grade for cadets now. The failing average is too great unless I'm strictly lucky or unless God gives me a chance.

You know, darling, I wrote you about this new friend I made, O'Mara. He's such a good kid. I talk quite a good game when he and I are together, but I'm not 1/1000th as confident as I lead him to believe. They told us, for instance, that the last crew that went through had pitiful results. They only passed seventeen out of two hundred. I can't compete against odds like that. Maybe the rumors that buzz around here are just that, rumors. But here's the real truth. I'm not brilliant, but rather of average intelligence. And men that exceed me in intelligence have failed by a mile. After all, honey, what are the chances that an Italian kid from Derby is going to become an officer and a pilot? What bothers me, though, is that I don't know what to do if I wash out. If I do, the Army gives me two choices...

At breakfast, O'Mara asked, "So what are you thinking your chances are at this point, Michael?"

"Honestly? I think–shitty," Michael said, chewing on a mouthful of spam.

O'Mara sighed. "Sounds like you're singing a new song."

Michael shrugged.

"What happened to all of that confidence?"

Michael shrugged again.

"I hear ya, though. I don't know what I'm gonna do when I don't get in."

"Well, we've got two choices, Mike. Gunnery school or getting shipped out overseas right away. I guess gunnery school is better than going to the front. It's not that I even mind going overseas. I almost want to. It's just...my girl. Once I'm shipped overseas, who knows when I'll see her or hear from her again?"

"Oh, got a girl back home, huh?"

"Sure do."

"That's tough. I don't have a girl, but I'd feel the same way if I was in your shoes."

"Yeah, I'm looking forward to seeing her. All I can think about is the next letter, the next phone call, the next furlough."

"Makes sense."

"Listen, if it wasn't for her...well, let's just say–what's my life worth anyway? What I mean is, what was it worth before I met her? So, if I got killed stopping these bastards, then I did something good for my country. But now it's different."

...Yes, honey, we've taken so many tests now that I feel like my brain is mush. Geography, vocabulary, reading comprehension, history, civics, math, physics, logic. Others. I don't know what all these things have to do with flying a plane, but they apparently do. I don't know how I did on them yet, but I do know I excelled on all physical tests. And I know something else in my heart. I was born to fly. That's why it will kill me if I don't get in.

My pal O'Mara and I have met a bunch of the guys at meals, darling, not only the basketball player I told you about, but lots of guys from all over the country, and they are some of the most intelligent boys I've ever met. Oh, and another thing. Yesterday, I didn't quite make the grade on the eye test, but the good news is they let you take it again. That'll be first thing in the morning, and then we find out who made it and who didn't. So wish me luck...

When Michael ran over to the testing center, O'Mara was there to greet him.

"I can tell from that look on your mug that you passed the eye test," O'Mara said.

"It's surprising what a little determination can do," Michael replied, and he grabbed O'Mara by the shoulders and skipped around him, turning him three hundred and sixty degrees as if they were partners in a square dance.

"Okay...okay, calm down, buddy. Now we just have to wait until our names are called to find out our fate."

The hours dragged by slowly. Michael watched as each candidate was called to one of five folding tables spread across the room, where a staff lieutenant came to deliver the verdict.

Michael didn't need to ask the candidates what their results were because their faces told the tale. Some of them stoically hid their disappointment, while others, with burning cheeks, fought back tears. Michael even heard a few bawling as soon as they pushed through the swinging screen door into the thick Mississippi air.

Intermittently, a candidate would walk away from the table with a bounce in his step and a gleam in his eye, and once outside the door, would let out a yelp that echoed across the base. Michael passed the time by counting these rare instances of success. As the afternoon wore on, studying facial expressions, he estimated that, at best, for every twenty who failed, perhaps one made it.

After lunch, O'Mara's name was called. Michael watched as the lieutenant delivered the bad news. O'Mara turned and headed for the door, stopping to make eye contact with Michael and gave a bewildered shrug. Michael hoped his eyes conveyed what was in his heart: *Don't feel too let down, buddy. I know you'll be a pilot someday, one way or another.*

As the clock continued to tick, the suspense was killing Michael. At almost 5:00 p.m. when he heard the name Roderick Davidson called, he watched as Stretch received the same bad news that the majority before him had received. Stretch did an about face and, with five or six long strides, he was out the door. Discouraged, Michael thought, *If studying calculus at Auburn University didn't help him make the grade, what can I expect?*

A lieutenant then announced, "That's it for today, boys. The rest of you will have to wait until tomorrow to find out your results. Sorry about that."

...What a bad break, honey, to sit there all day and not have my name called. I wonder if you can imagine what that was like for me—a grueling day of waiting, and now I have to wait until morning. I doubt if I'll get any sleep tonight. I don't think I've ever hungered more for anything in my life! Well, that is, anything except to hear that you love me, darling. But anything else. I don't know what I'll do if I don't make it. I guess I'll just have to bite the bullet and deal with the disappointment. It won't be the first time, but gee, I've never applied myself quite like this before...

The next morning, it was back to the same waiting game. The number of candidates at the check-in station had dwindled considerably, at least by two-thirds. Michael prayed under his breath as he sat there. If there was a God, he hoped that He was listening. Michael was boiling. His shirt was now sticking to his back. *Is it just me?* he wondered, *or is it hotter today than it usually is in this infernal town?* Finally, his name was called. He popped out of his chair and approached the fifth table.

"DeMarco?" the clerk asked.

"That's right, Sergeant."

Holding a card that had Michael's scores on it, the clerk turned it face down. "It'll just be another few minutes, Corporal."

Wet beads trickled down Michael's face as he awaited his results. Finally, a dark-haired lieutenant approached the table, examined Michael's card, and then looked up at him. "What the hell's the matter with you, Corporal? You look like you're on fire."

Michael shook his head. "I apologize, sir. I guess I'm just hot, and a little anxious, sir."

"Oh, no need to apologize," the lieutenant said. "And, for that matter, no need to feel anxious. Allow me to congratulate you, Corporal DeMarco. You're a cadet."

"I'm a…a…did you just say that I'm a…a…"

"Yes, Corporal, you heard it right. Congratulations! You qualified. You're a cadet. Details about your training will be posted tomorrow."

…Can you believe it, honey? My mind is brimming with thoughts that don't make any sense, even to me. I love you, Cecelia! When he looked at me square in the eye and said, 'You're a cadet,' I couldn't believe it. I almost passed out. Becoming a pilot is my dream, and I think it's all your fault, honey, because I know you were praying for me. Of course, I prayed too. Did I ever pray and pray! But I think it's like the priest said in church—that praying wouldn't do any good because if we weren't cut out to fly, we wouldn't make it. I guess that means that I am meant to fly, just like I always believed. What I plan to do is to go into town tonight and celebrate. I sure wish you were here so that we could celebrate together.

WHAT ARE THE CHANCES?

If everything goes right for me, about this time next year I'll be a second lieutenant with his wings. Imagine that, darling—me an officer!

The most important thing that I want you to know, though, is that I miss you terribly, darling. I miss you so very much, and I love you more than anything in the whole world. I love you with my whole heart and soul!

Your Cadet,
I love you, xxxxx
Michael

26

September 5, 1943

My Darling,

After five weeks of the most rigorous physical training you could ever imagine in Biloxi, mercifully, here I am in Alliance, Ohio on a college campus instead of an army base. I can hardly believe it. It's as if I've been transported to heaven from h-ll!

It took three days to get here. We had to sleep sitting up for two nights, but I guess I'm used to it. The train took us through Mobile, Montgomery, and Birmingham, Alabama, then through Nashville, Tennessee and Louisville, Kentucky, and then Cincinnati, Ohio, and then a number of small towns before finally arriving in Alliance.

There are about 120 of us cadets from all over the country here along with 300 girls, all civilians, and all students. It's the prettiest little campus I've ever seen, not that I have much to compare it to. I'll say this, though. It's a lot nicer than that mud pit known as Biloxi. But just because we're on a college campus, darling, don't think for a minute it's going to be fun and games...

he cadets climbed the stone steps of the brick administrative building, passing the stately Doric columns on their way to the small auditorium off the main rotunda. Female students in skirts, blouses, and saddle shoes crossing the campus smiled at each other as they eyed the boys in their pressed khaki uniforms with their sharp creases and pleats.

The men filed into the hall and took their seats, buzzing with anticipation, wondering what it was going to be like to live in the presence of pretty girls on a daily basis.

When the captain walked into the room, the boys stood up, snapped to attention, and saluted their superior.

"At ease, boys," the captain said, shuffling through his notes. "Please take your seats. I have some things to go over with you. First, boys, let's talk about a subject I have no doubt is on your minds. Namely, the girls on this campus."

At the mention of the word, the cadets erupted in laughter.

"Now, while I appreciate your enthusiasm, boys, I want to warn you that you shouldn't get overly excited. In case you've had a memory lapse, we are here for educational purposes, and if you want to make the grade, you'll be spending every waking moment studying when you're not in class. But to take it one step further, let me add, as a general rule of thumb, under no conditions may you so much as look at one of these girls, never mind speak to one. Let me give you a moment or two to digest that."

The cadets sat in uncomfortable silence before the captain continued. "We are guests of the college, boys, and we can't have any of you embarrassing the United States Army in any manner, shape, or form."

A cushioned murmur of disappointment rippled across the auditorium.

"In fact, just so you get used to the way it's going to be, for the first two weeks, you are confined to your rooms in the dormitory except to go to classes or to the cafeteria, just to make sure you get used to not having contact with these young ladies."

The disappointed ripple now became more of a towering wave.

"But it's not all bad news, boys. Here's the thing. On occasion, as a group, you may be invited to a dance or social event on campus. In this case, not only may you attend, but you are *required* to do so, not that most of you will need any arm-twisting. Very simply, you will still be expected to accept all invitations. As guests on this campus, it would be rude to do otherwise. Rest assured, though, such events will be well chaperoned, both by college officials and by a few of your commanding officers, so there won't be any monkey business. Understand that in your dealings with the girls here and in everything you think, say, or do going forward, the emphasis in your training is on duty and honor, directly drawn from the West Point code of conduct."

The captain squinted, scanned the group, and then continued.

"Now, let me get down to the business of your studies. The first thing you need to know is, if you don't cut the mustard scholastically, you'll wash out of the program. Let that haunt you while you eat, drink, and sleep. Next, because of the urgency created by the war, we will be consolidating six months of college academics into three months, which will make it that much harder on you..."

...Well, here I am in my dorm room. It's a far sight better than a barracks, I can tell you that. We're assigned to a room with one other cadet, in my case, a boy from Florida named Travis Benson. He's a comical sort, and I think we're going to get along swell. I hope so, because we're stuck with each other in this small room for three months. There's a bunk bed and two desks for us to study at, with a small window overlooking a pond outside our building. It's a pretty view. Even though we're mainly restricted to the room for the first two weeks, the girls have invited us to a dance next Tuesday night. We have to go, as I told you, and we have to buy a war stamp for our admission to the dance. And listen to this. For each additional stamp a cadet buys, he receives a kiss from one of the girls. I can assure you, the guys are delirious about that. But don't worry about me, hon. I don't have any money to buy extra stamps, and even if I did, I wouldn't buy any unless you were selling them!

It was weeks in the making, but Cecelia was happy to be starting a new job. She was relieved to be away from the Star Pin Factory, away from the rumors about her brother running away, and away from that rat, Tony Vitti. *But with my luck,* she thought to herself, *there'll be some new Tony Vitti lying in wait for me here too.* She knew how some men were. Most of the employees were, thankfully, women. The new job probably wouldn't be any less tedious than her last one. What factory job was? One assembly line was like another.

She'd be involved in some aspect of making flight suits for the Army Air Corps. The flight coveralls would have wiring sewn into the lining that somehow drew power from the plane's engine and would keep pilots warm at the highest altitudes. It felt like important work, especially now that Michael would be training to be a pilot.

Of course, Cecelia was proud as could be and savored every opportunity to share Michael's accomplishment with friends, but when she slept, she couldn't get the nightmarish images of warplanes being hit and igniting into flaming nose dives before exploding into the ground below out of her mind.

...I have two pieces of exciting news for you, darling. First, you'll never believe what I'm going to be doing tomorrow. Even though our stay here at Mount Union is about academics, they're introducing us to flying this week. All of us new cadets were given pilot books and logs, and tomorrow morning, I'll be going up in a plane for the first time. It's just a small craft called a Taylor Cub. Over the next few weeks, they'll be giving us ten hours of training. I'm bursting with excitement just thinking about it. As soon as I get back from my lesson, I'll write to you and tell you all about it.

But now for the most exciting news of all. I spoke on the phone with my mother yesterday, and she and my sister Josie are planning to come visit me here in Ohio at the end of September. It's not a short trip, but it's not a fraction as far away as some of the other places I've been stationed, and it's a trip that can be done by train in one day. Here's the real icing on the cake, though. I want you to come on the trip with the two of them! What a treat it will be to see the three of you. They're going to plan the trip for a weekend, so maybe you could ask for time off on a Friday to allow for traveling time. You and I, after all, want to have as much time together as possible...

Cecelia sat before the mirror in Stella's bedroom. She picked up a tiny brush and dipped it into a liquid eyeliner bottle. "I've never been to Jocko's before," she said. "Is it fun?"

"It's a gas," Stella replied, standing at her dresser in just a half slip and bra, brushing her teeth in a gold trimmed, rose-patterned basin. "It's just a little place, but they have a four-piece band, and the drinks are free because it's ladies' night."

"Well, that's good, I guess," Cecelia said, now curling her eyelashes, holding the scissor-like device tightly closed on her right lash. Careful not to move her face too much, she muttered, "Men just want to get us girls drunk."

"Isn't it glorious?" Stella laughed. "That way, we never have to pay for drinks!"

"You're the devil," Cecelia scoffed.

"It'll be good for you to get out and have a little fun. You know, dance a little."

As Stella prattled on, Cecelia gazed into the mirror, pensively evaluating her own body.

"Can you imagine what it'll be like when we're married and we're sharing a bedroom with our husbands?"

Cecelia snickered. "Not completely."

Stella put her left foot on the bed and began applying flaming red paint to her toe-nails. "It's all I think about! I imagine being undressed like this in front of Donny all the time. Having him watch me put on my makeup. All that kind of sexy stuff."

Cecelia squeezed the curler onto her left eyelash. "Well, you can't let a man see *everything*. You have to leave a little mystery. There are some things that I simply wouldn't want Michael to see, that's for sure."

"Like what, for instance?"

"For instance, I wouldn't want him to see me brushing my teeth and spitting into a wash basin like you were doing a few minutes ago, and I don't plan on having him see me squeeze this contraption onto my eyelashes. I'm not even sure I want him to watch me putting on any of my makeup. I'd rather he see nothing but the finished product. You can be sure I'll never let him watch me smear my face with cold cream before bedtime and then wipe my makeup off with Kleenex. That's not very romantic."

Now with her lips parted, Cecelia began to apply her lipstick as Stella chuckled. "You won't be able to avoid it. I think once you're married, your husband sees everything. And by everything, I mean *everything!*"

Both girls howled and Cecelia said, "Now you stop that. You almost made me ruin my lipstick. There are just certain things that a man wouldn't like seeing. I'll say this. I'll bet Donny wouldn't like seeing you go dancing at Jocko's, and neither would Michael. When they find out, they're going to think we're a couple of hussies."

"Oh, don't be silly. It's just dancing, Celia. Besides, how are they going to find out? Donny's fighting in Europe, so he'll never know."

"You're not going to tell him when you write to him?"

"Hell, no. You know my motto! What Donny doesn't know won't hurt Donny. You don't tell Michael every goddamn little thing, I hope."

"I suppose not," Cecelia said, thinking of Augie. Perhaps telling him about Jocko's would be a way of testing the waters. What was the worst that could happen? Hopefully, he wouldn't make a big deal out of a few harmless dances. Michael knew how she loved to dance.

"Of course, it's not like I don't miss Donny," Stella said, now switching feet. "You must miss Michael too."

"I sure do. But I guess I'm going to see him soon. He wants me to visit him in Ohio with his mother and his sister, Josie."

Her makeup now done, Cecelia swung sideways in her chair and began rolling a stocking over her left foot and up to her thigh.

"He wants you to do what?"

"You heard me. He wants me to come to see him in Ohio."

"Oh my good God, you must be thrilled about that!"

"Well, that's the thing. I am and I'm not. Sometimes I wonder about myself because it seems like that's how I feel about everything. Happy…but not happy."

"What's the problem?"

"The problem is that I don't know his sister and his mother that well. I mean, they're nice to me and everything. But his mother is so…I don't know, so *something*. So serious. Stella, the woman never smiles."

"Well, I'm sure she's had a hard life, so maybe she's, I don't know, tired."

Suddenly, their conversation was interrupted. Stella's mother knocked at the bedroom door and peaked in. "Stella, ne zalyshaysya nadto pizno s'ohodni vvecheri."

"Okay, Mama, we'll be home before midnight. I promise," Stella called back. "Cecelia is going to sleep over, okay?"

"Dobre," Stella's mother said, followed by a high-pitched song, "Pryvit, Cecelia. Pryyemno vas bachyty!"

"Hello, Mrs. Kostenko, nice to see you too," Cecelia sang back.

"Oh, and you sey hel-lo to you mutter and sesters for me, plees!"

"I will Mrs. Kostenko. I'll tell them you said hi."

"You esk your mutter how es de artritas, plees."

"I will, Mrs. Kostenko. Thank you for asking."

"Laskavo prosymo, Cecelia," Mrs. Kostenko said, pulling the door shut.

Cecelia couldn't speak Ukrainian but, from all the years she had spent at Stella's house, she understood most of what was said to her.

"See, that's another thing," Cecelia continued. "Michael's mother speaks no English at all, or at least I've never heard her speak a single word. And, I've gotta tell you, my Italian is as rusty as old nails because, you know, like you do with your mother, we almost always answer my mother in English even though she might be talking to us in Italian. But the DeMarcos answer their mother in Italian, which may seem nice, but I don't think it's ever encouraged her to learn English. Anyway, the other thing is she speaks so soft and fast that I'm lucky if I can understand anything she says. And then when I do understand and answer her, I always feel like she's judging me. You know what I mean? She gives me that 'What kind of Italian are you?' look. It really makes me feel uncomfortable. Imagine being with her on a train all day. Ten hours of all Italian and no smiling!"

"Oh, wow! Yeah, I see what you mean. And what about Josie?"

"Josie's a sweetheart. All of Michael's sisters are. But Josie is a lot more Italian than I am. I mean, sweet mother of Jesus, she lived the first seven years of her life over there. She's even engaged to a guy who only came here from the old country a few years ago."

"So what are you going to do?"

"What other choice do I have? I'm going to have to go, I guess."

"You guess? Well, forgive me for being so blunt, but if I could see Donny right now, I'd cross the Pacific in a leaky rowboat with Lizzie Borden!"

Stella's remark tickled Cecelia. "Oh, God, Stella, you're such a nut!" Then with a sigh she added, "I'm just being a big goddamn baby, aren't I? I should be grateful for the opportunity. I'll just have to do my best when Lizzie Borden is talking to me in Italian!"

...Honey, the captain wasn't kidding when he said we'd need to be studying every spare minute. I'm doing all right in my studies, better in some than in others. For instance, I have a 92 average in math, but a 78 average in physics. I'm going to have to pick that one up. By the way, darling, you asked me what physics is. It tells us why things happen, like why a light goes on when you throw the switch or why wheels turn. It's interesting, but challenging.

You'll never believe what's going on right now just outside my window, hon. There must be about a hundred girls, and they are throwing certain girls into a pond with their clothes on. I imagine it's a sorority initiation. Right now, four girls have one by her arms and legs and they're swinging her back and forth...and wait. SPLASH! There she goes into the water. All of the others are in absolute stitches. College girls are crazy!

Oh, I don't want to forget. I don't mean to give you a hard time about going to Jocko's with Stella, but I just want to make sure you realize that Jocko's is nothing but a pick-up joint. I understand, of course, that's not the reason you girls were there, but you may want to be careful about where you hang out. What will people think? Remember, honey, it's public opinion that makes or breaks a person.

Anyway, now that it's the end of our second week, we're not quite as restricted as before, so I've gotten to see the town of Alliance. Travis and I went bowling with a few of the guys and we met some high school boys who gave us a tour of some of the local neighborhoods. You wouldn't believe some of the houses. They must cost $20,000. I kid you not. And then they took us to the local Elks Club. I've never seen anything like it. It's pretty much a castle on 50 acres of land. They told us it was shipped in pieces from England. Unbelievable, right?

Of course, everything I've encountered here isn't peaches and cream. Let me tell you about what happened at a local soda fountain the day before yesterday. I came d-mn near getting myself thrown out of the program...

Michael and Travis sat in the Polka Dot, the campus soda fountain, amongst a dozen other cadets. In the midst of the tranquil September afternoon, a group of local boys entered, noisily taking up residence at two vacant tables. A beefy, rosy-faced boy pulled what looked like a flute out of his pocket and brought the mouthpiece to his purple lips. Normally, Michael wouldn't have thought twice about it, but the boy played dissonant runs up and down the flute, while his friends smirked and giggled. Michael could smell trouble a mile away. He counted twelve in the group.

One of the boys, a tall piece of work with a t-shirt that hugged his muscular chest and arms, walked across the room and took a seat at the table next to Michael's and Travis's. He turned the chair backwards, and it scratched against the floor before he straddled it. Another boy, a stocky fellow, followed and took a position behind the tall boy, his arms folded across his chest.

Leaning on the back of the chair, the tall boy addressed one of the cadets. "Tell me, soldier, you got a girlfriend back home? A wife maybe?"

The cadet frowned and answered. "A girlfriend."

"Oh, that's nice," said the boy. "Ain't that sweet, fellas? This one's got a girl back home."

The gang of boys whistled and hooted.

"And what might be her name, soldier?" the tall boy asked. "Is it Mary?"

The soldier averted his eyes as the flute player persevered, continuing his off key serenade.

"Not Mary, huh? Well, is it Charlotte?" And without giving the soldier time to answer, "Or, wait, let's see, is it Rebecca?"

Angry, Michael began to size up the room. He realized his fellow cadet didn't want to get into any trouble by having a row with local teenagers, but Michael himself was losing his patience.

A round of laughter spilled over from the boy's friends as the shrill tones of the flute continued to pierce Michael's ears.

A sloppy looking boy with a grease stained t-shirt called, "How about Marilyn? Ask him if his girl's name is Marilyn."

"Yeah, that's it," said the tall one. "I'll bet it's Marilyn, ain't that right, soldier boy?"

Like a bottle of shaken up soda pop ready to spray, Michael could no longer contain himself. "Okay, funny man," he said. "Your joke stinks, so why don't you just lay off?"

He had always hated bullies and smart alecks.

"Oh, look fellas, this soldier's feeling left out," the tall boy said. "I think he wants to tell us about his girl!"

The ensuing fit of laughter from the group caused the greasy boy to fall out of his chair, which only encouraged more howling.

Michael stood up. "How about just the two of us take a step outside where I'll be happy to tell you all about her?"

Travis was quick to react. Up on his feet in a flash, he wrapped both arms around Michael's torso, murmuring into Michael's red ear, "You're way too hot under the collar, man. Let's get the hell out of here."

The ringleader smirked. "My, oh my. Hey fellas, I don't think either of these soldiers got girlfriends at all. I think we got a couple of queers for ourselves here. Look at 'em, hugging each other in public."

"Listen, you fuckin' asshole," Michael growled, "how about I show you which of us is really a queer? In fact, how about I–"

Interrupting, Travis held on tightly. "No, Michael! Cut it, man!" Although Michael knew Travis was right, he held his position, but Travis pulled him closer and closer to the door, like a tugboat hauling an overweight barge, moving him out onto the street.

The gang of boys called out, "Buck, buck, buck-buck! Buck-buck-buck!"

Travis continued to move Michael down the sidewalk. "Don't do it, Michael, don't," Travis repeated, his jaw clenched. "If you do, you'll never fly!"

A day later after the almost disastrous confrontation with a dozen locals, Michael sat on a repurposed school bus, preoccupied in a new way with the number twelve. *I'll be damned*, he thought to himself. *It's the twelfth of September and I'm about to fly a plane.* The dark green bus transported a dozen cadets and a dozen flight instructors to a privately owned airfield on the outskirts of Alliance where a dozen Taylor Cubs, fueled and ready to fly, awaited them on the tarmac. They weren't military planes, but they would serve the purpose of introducing them to flying.

Michael's heart swelled at the sight of the planes lined up along the runway, their bodies a lustrous mustard yellow under the piercing rays of the morning sun. Squinting at the twelve beauties, it was hard for Michael to believe that his dream was actually materializing.

Their morning started in a training room in the hangar where Lieutenant DeVaney, the chief flight instructor, stood before a replica of the cockpit controls and explained in detail the purpose of each component.

"Boys, you are about to embark on a great adventure. The academics on campus here in Ohio are the beginning of your ground training, but you will also get a taste of piloting a plane while you're here as part of your Basic Flight Training. It'll be just a nibble, but I think you'll enjoy it. Eventually, you'll move on to Primary and Advanced Flight Training, but for now, you need to be patient. I'm going to begin by going over everything, from A to Z, so pay attention. Now, first of all, this stick here, which looks kinda like a car's stick shift, controls a few things. Next, let's talk about pitch. You boys just push it forward when you want to pitch the nose of the ship down, and you pull it backwards when you want the nose to pitch up. Now let's say you want to roll the ship left. You just shift the stick to the left. Simple. Same if you want to roll the ship right, you pull the stick to the right. Got it, boys?"

The group of cadets murmured that they did.

"Here's the thing, though. If you pitch the nose of the ship up too much, your ship will go into a stall. But, boys, this isn't like how a car stalls, but rather it's an aerodynamic stall. Should the nose be up too much, the ship simply can't continue flying because it's not getting enough air over the wings to provide lift. In that case, boys, the ship wants to fail in the sky. If that happens, your craft will stall and go into a tailspin. So, starting today, right from jump street, we're going to be working on what to do if that should happen."

As he listened, Michael could feel his blood warming, thousands of little bubbles forming, like water coming to a boil in a pot on the old stove back home.

In their anticipation, the group of cadets were boys once again back at a hometown carnival in New Jersey or Georgia or Kansas or Oregon, waiting for their first ride on a roller coaster.

Michael continued to listen with fascination as the lieutenant further explained that they didn't need to worry too much about engine failure or running out of fuel because, he said, "The craft then just turns into a glider, and you can fly it just the same as always, except you'll need to find a safe place to land at your earliest convenience." But that was something, he explained, that they would learn in upcoming lessons over the next few weeks.

> ...I can tell you that flying was everything I thought it would be, darling, everything I hoped it would be. We did all kinds of amazing things. First, I had to learn some basics like how to take off and turn in the air. And then we did some tailspins, which were quite exciting. I'm told one of the boys even got sick up there, and I sure feel bad for the poor sap. But, I didn't feel sick at all, just exhilarated! Believe it or not, honey, on just my third time up in the air, I flew to Akron. First, the pilot who is teaching me just let me fly around until I got lost, and then he directed me toward Akron, where I saw a big hangar where the Navy keeps two big dirigibles. It was quite a sight, I can tell you.
>
> I don't mean to bore you with all these details, hon. The main thing is that, if you were ever up in a craft at 5000 feet like I was, you'd know how I feel, floating through layer after fluffy layer of clouds. I tell you, darling, I've never experienced a more peaceful feeling or a better feeling. In fact, I wish I could be up there every time I need to be alone.
>
> The best news of all is that I will be seeing you in less than a week. Can you believe, honey, that the last time we saw each other was nearly four months ago? I've missed you so, and I'm looking forward to Friday when you, Mom, and Josie arrive here. What a treat it will be for me...

27

*C*ecelia left the house at 7:00 a.m. and walked to the train depot in Derby, her small suitcase in hand. As she walked, she contemplated the ten-hour train ride ahead. She felt comfortable enough with Josie. A twig of a girl in her late twenties, Josie was warm and without airs, which Cecelia liked.

Despite being confused, the three women managed to change trains at the Bridgeport station en route to Grand Central, where they would change again before arriving in Columbus and board one final connecting train to Alliance.

Josie had packed sandwiches—salami with homegrown lettuce, tomato, and basil sprinkled with olive oil on Italian bread. Cecelia wondered if the DeMarcos ever ate what Italians called American bread, neat slices of what was more commonly known as white bread with a soft rather than hard crust. Cecelia happened to like Italian bread better, but American bread is what they served at the local lunch counters like Woolworths, and what the kids that her family called "Yankees" had brought for lunch when she was a schoolgirl.

The conversation on the train was, as she had anticipated, in Italian. Cecelia was grateful that Josie recognized when she seemed confused and helpfully translated in a whisper what her mother had said. Mrs. DeMarco herself seemed oblivious to these momentary translations, or, if she noticed, she pretended not to. Cecelia appreciated most the long stretches when Mrs. DeMarco closed her eyes and seemed to fall asleep, intervals where Cecelia could gaze out of the train windows and admire the sights, the towering concrete apartment buildings in metropolitan areas like New York, the smoke-stacked factories that reminded her of the one she worked at, and the vast farms sprawling across the long state of Pennsylvania, sprinkled with rolled hay bales and spotted cows. Those moments of quiet gave her a sense of tranquility, and she enjoyed glimpsing parts of America she had read about but never before seen.

When they reached the depot in Alliance, she saw that it wasn't unlike the Derby station where they had begun their journey. As they stepped off the train, she could see Michael. What a sight he was as he took long, confident strides toward them, almost breaking into a full run, a broad smile on his face.

He approached his mother and sister first with a genuine greeting, "Mom...Josie, buona sera. Mi siete mancati molto entrambi," he said, hugging both of them. Then he turned all of his attention to Cecelia. "And, oh my God! You!" Taking her in his arms, he squeezed and held her for what Cecelia felt was a bit too long a time. Before releasing her, he whispered, "I can't believe it! Are we finally together again?"

Cecelia smiled, still feeling a little uncomfortable with Michael's display of affection in full view of his mother and sister. She hoped he wouldn't kiss her yet.

"Let me take your bags," Michael said. "The hotel is just a short walk from here. You can all freshen up, and then we'll grab a bite. You must all be dying for something to eat." Then, turning to his mother, he repeated himself in Italian.

Main Street in Alliance was a thriving downtown area, which reminded Cecelia of downtown Shelton or Derby, although some of the buildings reached higher into the sky. As they passed by the City Savings Bank & Trust, she noticed that the architecture reflected the same dignity as the Birmingham Bank in Derby or the Connecticut National Bank in Shelton. Similarly, when she saw the sign that read Gray's Drugstore, she thought immediately of the Mahoney Drug Store on the corner of Howe Avenue and White Street, and up ahead she could see the G. C. Murphy Co. 5c and 10c

Store and even a Sears Department Store, with its brightly lit sign. Thinking of the Woolworth and J. C. Penney stores in Derby, it seemed to Cecelia that every small town in America might be interchangeable.

When they arrived at the Gordon Hotel, Cecelia thought of Derby's Clark Hotel, although like everything else in Alliance, the Gordon had several more stories than the Clark. Michael urged the ladies to try to hurry up because the food counter at G. C. Murphy closed at 7:00 and he didn't feel they could afford anything fancier.

Once in the basement of Murphy's, Michael recommended the blue plate special, which included roast fresh ham, applesauce, mashed potatoes, wax beans, and a roll with butter. Everyone agreed that it sounded great for the fifty cent price.

After ordering, Michael launched into a stream of Italian that lasted until they were finished eating. Cecelia remained silent, nervously cutting her piece of ham into dozens of tiny rectangles as she listened. Unconsciously, she pushed her food around the plate. Michael caught up on how all of his brothers and sisters were doing, as well as his little nieces and nephews.

Although she understood most of what was being said now, Cecelia felt certain, now more than ever, that Michael's family seemed more Italian than her own. Her mind wandered, thinking about her brother, Robert, who, despite being born in Italy, had never seemed to embrace his Italian heritage. She couldn't recall the last time she had heard him speak Italian. Robert had even written, recently, that he had legally changed his last name from Alberino to Alber, without further explanation.

The sound of Michael's voice brought her back to reality. "You alright, honey?"

"Oh…me? Yes. I'm fine."

"You seem a million miles away, and you've barely touched your food. Don't you like it?"

"I like it just fine. I guess the long train ride, instead of making me hungry, had the opposite effect."

"That's alright, darling. Whatever you don't eat, I'll take with me. I'm sure Travis will be happy to eat it. He's like a bottomless pit."

When they finished eating, Michael saw his mother and sister back to the hotel. He wanted to have some alone time with Cecelia, although he knew it would be brief or his mother would make a fuss and Josie would have to deal with it.

The two strolled down Main Street, and Cecelia felt unsure of herself and unsteady on her feet. Michael wrapped his arm around her waist and asked again if she was alright.

"Yes," Cecelia replied. "It's just been such a long day."

"I can understand that," he reassured her. "Gee, honey, I can't wait to give you a tour of the campus tomorrow. I know you're going to just love it."

"I'm sure I will," Cecelia said, wondering if her tone of voice gave away her uncertainty.

"Guess what," Michael continued. "I fly for the third time on Monday. Isn't that swell, hon?"

"Yes," Cecelia said. "I...I suppose it is."

A wave of emotion washed over Cecelia, and she couldn't stop tears from spilling from the corners of her dark eyes and rolling down her cheeks as Michael rambled on in the darkness.

"Well gosh, honey, you only suppose? I can assure you that it was swell to be up in the air, flying through the clouds. It's hard to imagine, I know, because you've never had the experience, but I just need you to trust that..."

It was then that he noticed her wiping the tears away with her index fingers.

"See," he said, taking her in his arms, "you *are* upset about something. What is it, darling? You can tell me. You can tell me anything. Honest!"

"It's just that...that..."

"That what, darling?"

"It's just that...that...I don't think I'm...I just don't think I'm the right girl for you."

At the very same time that Cecelia seemed to be losing her senses, Michael exuded patience and calm. "Wait, Cecelia, please. Why don't we take a seat right here?" he said, pointing to a park bench at the corner under an ancient elm.

He wrapped both arms around her and held her as they sat. "Now, just tell me why you'd ever say a thing like that."

"I don't know. It's just that I'm not as...as *something* as you are.

As driven. And I don't speak very good Italian. And your mother must think I'm the worst Italian alive!"

"Your Italian is fine," Michael assured her. "Why, I think your Italian is adorable. And Mom? Mom thinks you're swell, just like I do. My sisters are nuts about you. The whole family loves you, Cecelia. Honest!"

"I don't know," Cecelia replied, still not able to curb the flow of tears. "I'm just all out of sorts today."

He looked into her eyes, now puffy and swollen. "Well, please don't let your imagination run wild with you, hon, because that's all it is."

Cecelia sat in silence, trying with all her might to compose herself.

"Is there anything else that's bothering you?"

She looked down at her glossy red fingernails. "It just seems that sometimes planes mean more to you than...than I do."

"You're kidding me, right, darling? I mean, you can't be serious."

She seemed to have no control over her emotions. "Well, you should read your own letters about flying and examine how you talk about it. It seems like you love flying more than you love me." No sooner had the words escaped her lips that Cecelia regretted having spoken. *I'm such a big baby,* she thought to herself.

Rather than feeling upset, Michael felt like he loved her more than ever. "Now listen, darling. Can you believe that I would ever compare you with a plane? Think about a plane. She's just a ship in the air, isn't she? A sweet ship, yes, but she's cold and strange. Can you picture me putting my arms around her like this and cuddling up and kissing her like this?"

Michael squeezed her and gave her three mini-kisses, one on the lips and one on each cheek. Cecelia couldn't help but smile and giggle at him through her tears.

"No, of course not," he continued tenderly. "I won't say that I don't love flying, but it's a different kind of love. Every love a man has is different, darling. When a man loves a woman, he loves her with his whole heart, with his whole *life*. Please believe that I love you that way. I only love a plane with my mind, don't you see? So from now on, please don't ever compare yourself with an airplane, because one thing is for certain. I couldn't sit in a parlor and neck with an airplane and tell it that I love it and expect a return answer, now could I?"

When she responded to him with laughter for the second time, Michael knew that he had comforted her in her distress, and his heart was full.

"You're my one true love, Cecelia. And I'll let you in on a secret. Once in a while, when I'm feeling lonely, I think about what it would be like if you should change your mind about me. I can't bear to think of it, hon, because you're now a part of me, like a propeller is to an airplane. I couldn't go on without you, just the same as a plane can't fly without a propeller."

The two spent the next twenty minutes kissing, obscured in the shadows of the old elm. Walking back to the hotel, no words were spoken. Michael felt content, and Cecelia settled into a sense of calm for the first time since waking up that morning.

The next day, Michael brought them to campus and showed them around. They walked the quad, and his mother and sister marveled at the historic buildings which, Michael explained, had been built in 1846, nearly forty years before his mother was born. None of them had ever been on a college campus except for Cecelia, who had, months before, walked along the streets of Yale University. Thinking of this all-girls campus, she couldn't help imagining what it must be like to be a college student.

After getting a bite to eat, Michael shepherded them onto a bus for a trip out to the airfield. They were all impressed by the sight of the yellow Taylor Cubs, some preparing for takeoff and others flying above them since Saturday was a training day like any other.

Being something of a photography buff, Michael had brought along his camera. "Josie, do you think you can take a picture of me and my girl over here by this ship?"

"I'll do my best," Josie replied. "Just tell me how to work the thing."

While Michael instructed his sister, Cecelia imagined him in the cockpit, taking off into the blue sky above, as she was seeing his fellow cadets do. It occurred to her that navigating a plane was one thing, and navigating a relationship was quite another. Despite her reservations, she put on her best face for the photos as Michael stood tall and proud in front of a Taylor Cub with his arm around her. They spent another twenty minutes taking pictures in different combinations: Michael and his mother, Michael and Josie, Michael and both of them. Cecelia had had very little experience operating a camera, and she hoped the photographs would develop correctly.

Dinner was less stressful for her that night, as she had calmed down considerably. After dinner, she and Michael found their way back to their bench at the corner under the elm. In the quiet of the night, the two lovers did much less talking than the previous evening.

Michael searched for words to express his deepest feelings. "I'm thrilled that you came, darling, but it almost hurts worse than if I didn't get to see you at all, to have you for such a short time."

With great willpower, the two knew they had to tear themselves away from each other.

At the hotel entrance, Cecelia looked into his eyes and said, "Parting is such sweet sorrow that I shall say goodnight till it be morrow."

Michael was puzzled. "That's beautiful," he said. "What is it? A poem?"

"In a way…it's Shakespeare," she explained. "*Romeo and Juliet.* I read it in school."

"I read *Julius Caesar*, but I didn't understand it."

"That line is from the balcony scene."

"Beautiful, and I understand what it means," he said. "Let me try. Parting is such…"

"…sweet sorrow," Cecelia prompted him.

"Parting is such sweet sorrow, that…that…"

"…that I shall say goodnight till it be morrow."

"That I shall say goodnight till it be morrow."

After another kiss, he watched her walk through the double doors and into the hotel lobby.

Look at me, he thought, *quoting Shakespeare. Go figure!*

As Michael strolled back up the street in solitude, he heard the buzz of a Pabst Blue Ribbon neon sign in the window of a local haunt and saw the bright liquid red, white, and blue drain from the neon tubes. *Ten o'clock,* he realized. *Closing time.* There was something comforting and peaceful about a small town at closing time. He made his way back to the bench where he rested for close to an hour and contemplated the evening. Cecelia and he had met one night by chance, and now she was his girl. It was hard to believe. After a long while, he looked at his wristwatch and knew it was time to get back to his dorm room. With a deep sigh, he patted his hands on the green boards of the park bench. It reminded him of the bench on the Derby Green where, after an uncomfortable conversation, Cecelia had agreed to let him write to her. Looking up at the moon through thousands of cut out leaves decorating the hearty limbs of the elm on the corner of East Main Street and South Freedom Avenue, he reflected, *For some damn reason, things seem to work out for me when I'm sitting with my girl on a park bench.*

March 23, 1944

Dearest Darling,

Guess what today is! It's our six month-anniversary. I'll bet you don't even remember. You see, it's been six months since you visited me in Alliance, six months since we sat on a park bench on East Main Street, and six months since the last time I kissed those perfect lips of yours. Can you believe I keep track of things like that? Well, believe it, darling, because it's true. And because I love you so very much. I hope you love me back the same way!

Other than that, I don't have a lot to write about because it's the same old humdrum routine here, day after day, week after week, and month after month. Today is just another day in Kansas.

By rights, I should be on to the next level of training instead of being stuck here in maintenance. All I do every day is work on planes. Everything from washing them to fixing engine parts. I bet you I can take one of these engines apart and then put it back together blindfolded.

The one thing that gives me any pleasure is starting the ships up in the morning. Which makes me itchy as h-ll to fly again. I may take one of these babies up the air, unauthorized. Of course, if I do, I'll end up getting court-martialed and sent to Leavenworth, so maybe I better not!

*It's not that I'm completely unhappy. The other day, for instance,
while we were washing off the wings of our ships, a full squadron of
P47 Thunderbolts flew over our airfield. You wouldn't know what they
are, but it sure was an inspiring sight to see. I don't even know how to
explain it. Seeing those birds made my hair stand up. When I went to
sleep that night, I closed my eyes and saw myself buzzing through the
clouds all alone and free from any old flying field, the whole sky as my
highway and nothing standing between me and flying.*

*Have I told you about my friend, Stack? He's one of the funniest
guys I've ever known. The other day, for instance, he wrote some girl
back home a letter, but I noticed that he only wrote a single page.
When I asked why, he said, "Because I'm running low on money to
buy stationery. I even have to stretch my soap, so I only wash one hand
now!"*

*Of course, Stack thinks I'm crazy because I write such long letters
to you and because I stay at the barracks rather than going into town
on Saturday nights, but I finally explained it to him a few weeks ago...*

*S*tack came out of the showers, toweling the white dabs of
shaving cream from his earlobes, another towel around
his waist.

"DeMarco," he said, "I hope you're coming into town with me
tonight."

Michael smiled. "Sorry, old pal."

"Get outta town! Because you and that girl of yours back home
have an imaginary date?"

"Well, it's not imaginary to us."

Stack scratched his head. "Man, do you realize what a bunch of
whores some of these Kansas girls are?"

"No, I don't," Michael said. "And I'd rather not know."

"Because of your girl?"

"Well, that's one reason, for starters."

"Look at it this way, buddy, your girlfriend'll never know."

Michael stretched out on his bunk and rested his head contentedly on his pillow. "I suppose you're right, Stack. But that's just not
how I want to live this life."

"Well, tell me this, at least. Please tell me your plan is to try the milk before you buy the cow!"

Michael just chuckled. "You just don't get it, do you?"

"Ab-so-fuckin'-lutely not!"

Michael laughed. "C'mon man, you've got a girl back home, right?"

"I wouldn't call her my girl. She's just someone I like to play around with. She don't mean nothin' to me."

"That's a damned shame," Michael offered, "because there's nothing in the world like having someone who means everything to you!"

"Well, that and a nickel'll get ya a cup of coffee! Me? I'm going into town, like I always go into town, and I'm gonna tie one on, like I always tie one on. And with a little luck, I'll enjoy some love and affection from a real flesh-and-blood dame."

"You do that, Stack. And I hope you have a good time."

...I don't think I've ever told you how Stack got his nickname, have I? His real name, see, is Frank Haller, and it's kind of funny how it happened...

On a crisp Kansas morning, the maintenance crew felt the chill go right through them, even as they hovered in the tent. Like every day, the crew had warmed up the planes for the cadets in Primary Flight Training who were now soaring above the clouds, the lucky stiffs. Waiting for the ships to come in for gas refills or other adjustments, Michael and the crew tried to stay warm.

Michael was glad that the staff sergeant hadn't shown his ugly mug yet. The crew hated Dimik, who suffered from a bad case of "small man complex" and whose officious demeanor really irritated everyone.

"Let's try to get some sleep before Little Jesus bursts in here and starts screaming in that irritating voice of his," Michael commented to the boys.

"I hate that little bastard," Frank Haller remarked. "I'd love to give that asshole a good slap in the fuckin' head."

"I don't like him neither," Michael replied. "The guy thinks he's God."

210

"That's it," Haller said. "We got the name all wrong, guys. He's too big to be called 'Little Jesus.' From now on, let's call him 'God'!"

That gave all of the boys a good laugh before they flopped here and there, as close to the pot-bellied stove as possible, hoping to catch a few winks.

They hadn't been resting for twenty minutes when Sergeant Dimik's voice jolted them from their catnap. "Alright, alright, you slugs. Up on your feet and clean this place up. The base tech is coming to inspect today."

As if they had planned it, not a member of the crew stirred or even opened an eye.

Dimik sang out once again, "Hey! You heard me. Let's go before the base tech gets here."

Frank Haller opened one eye. "Before the *haystack* gets here? Who in the hell is the *haystack*?"

Blowing a fuse, Dimik bellowed, "Goddammit, Haller, I'm really getting sick and tired of you! I didn't say *haystack*, I said *base tech*! Now get off your fuckin' ass and get this place polished up!"

"You heard it, boys," Haller blurted out. "Get on your knees and bow down. God has spoken!"

> *...We still laugh about it whenever anyone brings it up, and now, none of us can look at "God" with a straight face. I guess it's not as funny reading about it in a letter, but at the time, we got the biggest kick out of it, but anyway, that's how Stack got his name. It was one of those things that just stuck. The guy always seems to get himself into one pickle or another...*

As Michael started the engine of an AT-6, he looked over his left shoulder, admiring the big white star imprinted in the blue circle atop the silver wing. He opened the throttle wide and looked at his tachometer. 2000 R.P.M.s. Just the sound of it thrilled him. He pulled the stick all the way back so it pressed against his lap, and he held the brakes tight. As his eyes surveyed the other planes on the runway, he could see that Stack sat in the ship directly in front of him, maybe thirty yards away.

Michael was stunned when Stack's ship suddenly jumped the chocks, nose over, and turned upside down.

Startled, Michael acted quickly, cutting the engine of the plane he was warming up.

He ran to Stack's plane, and as he got to the cabin, he yelled, "Stack, are you okay? Are you okay?"

"Yeah, I didn't hurt myself. I'm okay. But look what I did to the fuckin' plane!"

The damaged prop had stopped spinning.

"But, Stack, what the hell did you do?"

"I let go of the brakes and pushed the stick forward."

"Are you nuts, man? Why would you do a thing like that?"

Later, as Michael waited for Stack to come out of a meeting with the commanding officer, he thought to himself, *Goddamn Stack sure is a crazy bastard. And now it caught up with him.*

When Stack emerged from the building, Michael was there waiting for him. Stack wore a wry smile.

"So what happened, Stack? He chew your ass out?"

Stack smirked. "You might say that. I'm on permanent restriction. Like I give a shit! Like there's anything to do in this hellhole of a town anyway."

"Well, you need to be more careful, Stack. You could end up washing out. Or worse, court-martialed."

"Fuck 'em," Stack muttered. "I'm too smart for these bastards."

...It's hard to believe almost another month has passed. I'm so lonesome and so darned bored, I can't stand it. When am I ever going to get up in the air again? And when am I going to get a furlough? I'd give anything to see you. Are you dying to see me too, honey?

You're right about Stack. He sure is a crazy, reckless fool. But he isn't as smart as he thinks, honey, and neither am I, because guess what. I ended up getting restricted too...

The ships had all been prepped and were off for the morning, and the crew went about the task of washing the planes that didn't go up that day. After having a sleepless night, Michael decided to try his hand at goldbricking and dozed off in the airfield tent.

When the chair came out from underneath him and he crashed to the floor, Michael looked up to see Lieutenant Rogers, one of the flight instructors, hovering over him.

"And what in the name of Christ do you think you're doing, Corporal?"

Michael blinked. "I'm sorry, sir. I must have dozed off, sir. By accident, sir."

"We can't have accidents happening in this outfit, Corporal. At the end of your duty, you are to report to my office and sign the Articles of War. And consider yourself restricted to the base for a month."

...I sure caught h-ll from that lieutenant. But don't worry, signing the Articles of War is just some military red tape meant to govern the conduct of the men. Anytime we get in the slightest bit of trouble, we have to sign it. So, just like Stack, I'm on restriction too, even though it's only a month. And just like Stack, I don't care that much. But I do care some because I can't let anything keep me from becoming a pilot. But I just hate following orders and getting picked on for every little thing. It's like I once told you. It's on account of how independent I was in civilian life. When I get out, I'm going to be twice as independent.

Anyway, I don't know if they'll ever tame the fierceness that burns in my heart. Speaking of fierceness, darling, sometimes I realize that I love you with a fierceness that even I can't understand.

Until tomorrow...
Your soldier,
Love, xxxooo
Michael

he month of April, instead of offering a thawing sense of relief, blasted Shelton and the Valley with an unexpected surge of wintry vengeance. Over the course of a week, successive snowstorms covered the sidewalks and roads with sheets of snow and glazed every vulnerable plate of glass over with ice. Despite the towering snow drifts, Cecelia still had to be at her machine at 9:00 sharp after trudging through the narrowly shoveled pathways. Day after frigid day, she labored in the drafty brick building wearing a heavy sweater and even a scarf. Why was God delaying spring? Uncertain of what she hated more, the glacial weather or the humdrum routine of factory work, Cecelia yearned for solace and relief.

In the midst of her chilled work environs, Cecelia was surprised when three strangers in dark suits, fedoras, and black wool overcoats arrived on the floor one morning. Their demeanor was gray and ominous.

The foreman, Rudy Valillo, nervously announced that the men were on government business and that he would be calling employees one by one for an interview.

The shortest and oldest of the three men interjected, "Let me add that you are not to speak to each other about this matter at all going forward. If you do, it could be bad for you."

Cecelia couldn't imagine what the man meant by "this matter," and making eye contact with her fellow workers, she could see their puzzlement as well.

As the meetings began, the two younger men walked the floor, observing the various workers at their stations with stone-faced expressions.

When Cecelia's name was called, she felt like she was being sent to the principal's office, except she didn't know for what reason. Entering Rudy's office, the first thing she noticed was that the man was sitting at Rudy's desk. Rudy himself, in his mid-sixties, was like a benevolent grandfather. She had never had a nicer boss, and besides, he was the first boss who was a fellow Italian.

Her neck was hot and prickly. She looked at Rudy with imploring eyes. "Have I done something wrong?"

"We sure hope not, sweetheart," Rudy replied. "This is Agent Reynolds from the F.B.I., and he has a few questions for you."

"Sit down, Miss, uhm, Miss Alberino, is it?" Agent Reynolds said, his eyes fixed on a manila file.

Isn't he looking at my employee folder? she wondered.

"Yes, that's correct," Cecelia replied diffidently.

"Yes, Al-ber-i-no," he pronounced while entering it into a black leather-bound notebook. "Let me get right to the point, Miss Alberino. It has come to our attention that some random flying suits leaving this plant are defective."

"How do you mean, defective?" Cecelia asked.

"Someone has cut the wiring."

"Maybe there's been some kind of accident or…mistake. I mean, in assembling them. Accidents can happen, can't they?" Cecelia suggested, trying to be helpful.

"This is no *accident*, Miss Alberino," Reynolds sneered.

Cecelia sat, shivering, not sure whether it was the low temperature or Agent Reynolds' noxious demeanor. His tone of voice made her feel somehow guilty, even though she knew she had done nothing wrong. Cecelia studied Reynolds' face as he held her gaze with a steely look.

Her interrogator continued, "It's bad enough that we're fighting these dirty Japs and Krauts, but now we've got *you* people on our home turf trying to sabotage our efforts. It's sickening, and I'm going to find out who the bastard is if it's the last thing I ever do."

Cecelia finally spoke. "I hope you do. My boyfriend is training to be a pilot, so I don't want to see this kind of thing happening."

Hearing this news, Reynolds softened a bit. "That's nice to hear. You seem like a nice enough girl. If you see anything amiss or hear anything that might give us a clue as to who the culprit is, I trust you'll tell us. There's no use in protecting such a scoundrel. Can I count on you to do that for me?"

"Oh yes," Cecelia replied. "You most certainly can."

After Michael heard from her about the issue, he helped Cecelia to a more complete understanding of the situation.

...That's quite a sour deal that's happening at your plant, honey. I hope they catch the S.O.B. Those wires are meant to keep us pilots warm at high altitudes. If one of them doesn't work, a guy can freeze to death at 40,000 feet. What kind of person would do that? I'd like you to keep me updated, darling...

For the rest of the week, Agent Reynolds' men spent every day at the plant, hovering over the workers. Meanwhile, workers were intermittently required to meet with Reynolds for repeated interrogations.

Cecelia was asked various questions in the interviews, some of which she didn't understand. Did she know what a Marxist was? (She didn't.) Had she ever been asked to join a labor union? (She hadn't.) If she had been approached to join one, would she have done so? (She didn't know enough about unions to answer the question.) Had she voted in the last election, and for whom? (She wasn't old enough to vote, but if she had, she supposed she would have voted for President Roosevelt.) For what reason did she think the United States was at war? (She believed it was because of the attack on Pearl Harbor.) Had she lost any close family members or friends in the war? (She hadn't, thankfully, but she was worried about her boyfriend.)

Cecelia answered each and every question with sincerity, but she wondered if her answers were the right ones. And then there were briefer meetings where she was asked if she had seen anything suspicious lately. She had not, but the question confused her since the two younger agents were on continuous surveillance, watching every move the workers made.

When the weekend arrived, Cecelia, Stella, and the two Connies decided to have some fun. On Saturday afternoons, the dance floor at the Lakeview Casino became a roller skating rink. Its long expanse lent itself beautifully to that purpose, and the owners had acquired assorted pairs of high-top skates, which they rented out for ten cents an hour.

The girls walked past tall, dirty walls of plowed snow on their way to Derby. As she laced the gray suede skates, Cecelia noticed a fellow worker, tall and lean with blond hair and pale skin, who skated beautifully. He was a picture of grace on wheels as he effortlessly turned forwards and backwards, gliding from one end of the floor to the other.

"Girls, do you see that boy?" Cecelia asked.

"What a skater!" little Connie replied.

"He works at the factory on our floor."

"A friend of yours?" Cecelia's sister asked.

"No, I don't know him."

"What's his name?" Stella asked.

"I haven't got a clue," Cecelia replied.

"What? How can you not know his name?"

"Well, he's been with us for maybe a month or so, and he keeps very much to himself. There's something about him, something mysterious."

"I'd love to get my hands on him! He's so good looking," Stella offered with a short laugh.

Cecelia shook her head. "That's all you ever think about! Anyway, there's just something different about him. I don't know, something intangible. He's not like other boys I know."

Connie continued with irony, "He sure as hell doesn't *skate* like other boys I know either. He's a little too graceful for my taste."

"Oh stop it, Connie," Cecelia replied. "Anyway, I'd love to talk to him. Not about skating, but about all of this business with the F.B.I. at the plant. Ask him what he thinks about the whole fiasco. But I've sworn not to talk about it."

"You should try to strike up a conversation with him," Stella said, "because, if you don't, I will."

The girls made their way onto the floor, slowly adjusting to their skating legs. All four could glide competently about the floor, but none had the finesse of the tall boy. The girls alternated between holding hands, making a four-link chain, and skating one behind the other, like the cars of a passenger train.

The boy passed by them, moving at twice their speed. Sometimes he zigzagged in the spaces between them, and several times, while holding hands, they broke their chain and giggled as he zoomed by.

When the boy came to a stop by the makeshift wooden rails to rest, Stella saw her opportunity and moved in.

Slowing to a stop, she greeted the boy. "Hi there! You're quite a skater."

"Oh, thanks. I love skating. It makes me feel free."

"My name's Stella," she said, making eye contact with Cecelia as she skated by, a mortified look on her face. "What's yours?"

"I'm Vincent."

"Nice to meet you, Vincent. My friend says you work with her."

"Oh, yes, the dark-haired one. Yes, I've seen her on the floor. She's very lovely."

"Listen, Vincent, we girls are going to Vonette's for a soda when we leave here. Would you like to join us?"

"I don't think I should," Vincent replied, his face flushed.

Stella persisted. "We'd really like for you to come. It's nice to have a male influence to keep the four of us in line."

Vincent appeared amused by her remark. "Well, maybe, if you'd really like me to."

While the girls were taking off their skates, Cecelia scolded Stella. "You are something. You really are. How could you talk to a stranger just like that?"

"It's easy," Stella said, and stuck her tongue out at Cecelia. "And besides, Vincent said he has a car, so now we don't have to walk."

When they arrived at Vonette's, the five of them squeezed around a small table in the back, and the girls fired question after question at Vincent.

"Where do you live? Do you have brothers and sisters?"

"In Seymour. And, yes, I have four sisters."

"Are your parents immigrants?"

"No, they were both born here. My grandparents were born in Poland."

"What do you like to do besides skate?"

"I like to dance and draw."

"Oh, you're an artist?"

"I wish. No, it's just a hobby."

Finally, Cecelia's sister asked, "Tell me, Vincent, why aren't you in the military?"

Exasperated, Cecelia scolded, "Connie, that's not an appropriate question."

"No," Vincent said. "It's okay, Cecelia. I don't mind. I was in the military, but, uhm, let's just say that I got a certain kind of medical discharge."

Vincent's answer created an awkward lull in the conversation as the girls looked down into their glasses and fiddled with their straws.

Little Connie saved the day when she told the group about a new book she was reading. "Yes, I got it at the library," she explained. "It's called, *What is Hypnosis?* by a psychologist named Andrew Salter. It's very intellectual. I gotta tell you that sometimes I don't know what the hell, oh, pardon my French, Vincent, what the *heck* he's talking about. But still, very fascinating."

"You're always into something weird," Connie remarked.

"It's not weird. There's a lot to these things if you have an open mind..."

Connie smirked and rolled her eyes. As little Connie continued, Cecelia could see that Vincent seemed relieved that the attention had shifted away from him, and she also noticed that he seemed fascinated with little Connie. She couldn't quite discern, in fact, whether his enchantment was with the story or the storyteller. If it was the former, she thought to herself that she couldn't imagine Michael being remotely interested in hypnosis.

When Vincent dropped the girls off at their house, Cecelia lingered for a moment after the others said their goodbyes.

"Listen, Vincent. I just want to thank you for keeping us company and apologize for my sister. She's too blunt sometimes.

We hardly know you, so I'm sorry if it made you feel uncomfortable."

"That's alright," Vincent replied. "Like I said, I get that a lot. Of course, I gave the short answer. The long answer is a lot more complicated. Maybe someday I'll tell you more."

"That's fine, but only if you want to. I'll never ask about it again."

Vincent smiled with appreciative eyes.

"Vincent, I've gotta run, but I'll see you at work on Monday."

"Actually, you won't."

"I…what do you mean, I won't? Is everything okay?"

"I was called in and let go at the end of the day on Friday."

Startled, Cecelia muttered, "Oh my God. But why?"

With downcast eyes, Vincent said, "That's another long story, Cecelia, and kind of related to my military one. I'm afraid I've faced a lifetime of long stories, and I doubt that you have the time to hear them all. And, to be truthful, it might be better if you don't know this one. Or any of them. But thanks for allowing me to join you girls. It was fun. Maybe I'll catch up to you again sometime."

Not knowing quite what to say, Cecelia patted Vincent's hand and said, "I'd like that very much, Vincent. In fact, let's plan on it."

As he drove away, Cecelia contemplated her own motivation in suggesting that she and Vincent stay in touch. It wasn't because she was interested in him romantically. There was just something different about Vincent, something that invited trust and friendship. Her woman's intuition wanted to answer that call.

Her chance meeting with Vincent had left Cecelia brimming with curiosity. After washing the dinner dishes with Connie that night, she took her diary out and allowed her pen to reflect upon her newfound friendship:

April 11, 1944

Dear Diary,

Some things in our lives are written in the stars or left up to chance. I don't know which. Today, I met a most graceful, gentle boy. His name is Vincent, and I think we're going to be great friends…

30

_L_etterless days impelled Michael into a dark place. He had long ago learned that it wasn't Cecelia's fault. She explained that she wrote daily, and she wasn't about to be blamed for glitches in the mail system. Michael didn't know whether to hate the postal service or the military for the apparent inefficiency. Some days, he'd receive no letters at all, and other days, he'd be rewarded with a small stack. He never knew which to expect.

It was on a Saturday afternoon that Michael received a letter with an unexpected return address. It was from Scooter's mother, Mrs. O'Brian. She had never written to him before, and he couldn't imagine what it was about.

Ducking into an alleyway between the mess hall and one of the barracks, he tore open the envelope and began reading.

May 6, 1944

Dear Michael,

Myself and my husband received some bad news about our boy Timothy yesterday, and I thought I should write. You may know that Timothy was assigned to a PT boat in the Pacific about six months ago. We hadn't heard from him since, you see, and yesterday we got a sad telegram from the authorities telling us that our boy is "missing in

*action." I had never heard of that. But the telegram said his boat was
attacked by Japanese aircraft off the coast of Mindoro Island in the
Philippines, and the authorities don't know if Timothy and the other
sixteen crew members are living or dead or what's become of them.*

*Our hearts are broken. Please pray for him, Michael. Our Scooter
has always loved you.*

Yours truly,
Sally O'Brian

Michael's breathing became labored, as if a heavy stone was
pressing against his chest. He felt a watery rage in his eyes, and he
wanted to rip the letter into pieces, to stomp on it, and to crush his
anger into the ground with the heel of his boot. Instead, he folded
the letter up and stuffed it back into its envelope, his hands trembling. Michael couldn't imagine feeling any lower. Of all people.
Scooter.

It was the end of his day, and he continued working on a pen-
dant he was creating for his girl, a remnant of a discarded plane
windshield that he was carving into a heart. It had been an idea he
had hatched after seeing sheets of the stuff collecting dust in the
hangar.

At first he took some ribbing from the guys, but when they saw
how well his piece was coming along, several joined him, Chuck
and Steever and Vogel. Theirs weren't coming out half as good, but
then again, Michael wasn't about to be outdone. Besides, he knew
he had always been better with his hands than just about anyone.

After receiving Mrs. O'Brian's letter, Michael didn't feel like
working on the heart. Instead, he plopped down on his bunk and
tried to catch a few winks. Maybe sleep would make the ugliness of
war go away.

Restless, Michael was still half awake when Stack gave the
underside of his mattress a swift kick and sat down on the bunk
across from him.

Michael opened his eyes and yawned. "Hey, pal, what's the
latest?"

"The latest," Stack said, lighting a cigarette, "is bad news."

"Oh yeah, same for me. What's yours?"

Stack gave his cigarette package a skillful shake, offering Michael one. "They've decided to bounce me outta here."

"What the hell are you talking about?" Michael said, taking a cigarette.

"Just like I said. They're bouncing me the fuck out because of the episode with the plane."

"They can't do that!"

"The hell they can't. You know as well as I do that they got a surplus of cadets and they're just lookin' for reasons to wash guys outta the program. Fuck, man, they not only *can* throw my ass out, but the company commander just *did*. Monday morning, I'm on my way to the infantry. I'll be in Europe or the Pacific fighting on the ground within two weeks."

The two sat smoking in silence. Michael lay back on his pillow, blowing white clouds of emotion into the air.

"And what's your bad news?" Stack finally asked. "It can't be worse than mine."

"I just got a letter from an old friend's mom. He's MIA in the Pacific."

"Or maybe it can be," Stack conceded, taking in a deep drag. "What a tough break. I guess ya gotta just hope for the best." Stack shrugged. It was an old story.

"Yeah, for whatever good that'll do."

"Well, I got a bit of good news too. Since I'm shipping out of this wasteland on Monday, my restriction has been lifted. That means I'm free tonight. Your restriction ended last week, right? Whattaya say you and me go into town and tie one on? Or you gonna sit around this dump pinin' for that pretty girlfriend of yours?"

Michael sighed. "The last time I tied one on, it was a celebration. This time, it'll be the opposite."

"So let's do it…in honor of old times and old friends."

"Yeah, old times and old friends," Michael echoed.

Michael and Stack sat at a corner table in the little bar on Jefferson Street. Michael surveyed the room as they spoke. A musket hung above the stone fireplace to his right. A dozen or so ceramic beer steins with decorative etchings of Bavarian forests or castles with pewter tops lined a nearby shelf. Antiquated pictures of faces, long ago deceased, dangled crooked on the wall to their left. A smoky shroud in the air offered a hazy view of the soldiers and girls jammed into the tight space.

It was hard to hear each other with the shouting and laughter in the room, so the two men had to raise their voices. Within an hour, both men were crocked.

"Scooter was a damned good kid," Michael said. He could hear his speech beginning to slur.

"Not was. *Is*," Stack replied. "Shit, man. He might still be around somewhere. Hidden away, or…or in a prison camp, God forbid. But tha's better than the alternative, ain't it?"

Michael rambled on. "Scooter was–*is* a comical little Irishman, I tell ya, a real quirky bastard right out of the funny pages, but with a heart of gold."

"I'll bet! Le's get us another couple o' beers. You need another drink."

"Maybe we better…slow down."

"Slow down. Bullshit. We're jus' gettin' started!"

"Get the hell outta here, just gettin' started. We musta had a dozen already."

"The night's young," Stack said, raising his glass and holding his free hand up with two outstretched fingers, signaling the bartender to pour two more.

"You know," Stack said. "My ol' lady is Irish, and she used ta say, 'There's an ol' Irish proverb: A best friend is like a…like a four-leaf clover, hard to find and, and, and–lucky to have.' Anyway, tha's what she used ta say!"

It was clear to Michael that Stack was plastered.

"I like that, Stack! And who would've guessed that I would have found a four-leaf clover without looking any further than Smith Street in Derby? A place I thought I'd never miss, and now I'd do anything to get back to."

"Well le's hope I end up better off than your buddy. But with my luck…with my luck…"

"With your luck, what?"

"With my luck, I'll get picked off by some stinkin' Jap sittin' up in a palm tree like a monkey with a…with a machine gun."

"Now don't go sayin' shit like that," Michael complained. "You'll be fine. Just be careful."

"Aw, hell. I don't give a good goddamn anyways. It don't make one bit of fuckin' difference. I mean, a plane can, can get shot outta...outta the air, right? Oh, our beers are ready. This one's on me," Stack said, making his way across the room to the bar.

Michael surveyed the room. At one corner table, he could see a G.I. passionately kissing a dame as if the two of them were the only ones in the joint. Michael knew the guy was barking up the wrong tree. He had written to Cecelia about the girls who frequented these bars and what bad news they were. How they would do anything to ensnare a soldier. They threw themselves at guys, just like this one was doing now.

In the far corner, a soldier banged on the keys of an old upright while a half dozen guys and girls sang "Harrigan," a song that was becoming something of an Irish National Anthem since being sung in the film *Yankee Doodle Dandy* about songwriter George M. Cohan, played by Scooter's favorite actor, James Cagney. Normally, the sprightly tune and the raucous off-pitch singing would have raised his spirits, but it only made Michael feel more blue.

Stack returned and slammed the beer mugs on the table. "Yeah, Mike, so like I was sayin'. A plane can get shot outta the air the same as a guy can get...can get his fuckin' head blown off."

"Yeah, sure," Michael replied, coming back to reality. "But, listen here, Stack. Maybe this war'll end soon."

Stack chugged half of his beer and wiped his mouth with his sleeve. "You fuckin' wish."

"Damn right, I do. I got a girl back home I need to get back to."

"I know ya do. She's all you...you ever talk about, you asshole."

Michael broke into laughter.

"Somethin' funny?"

"You are! Ever been in love, Stack?"

"Hell yeah, ten or twenty times! In fact, I think I'm in love right now."

Stack got up and staggered over to a girl who was surrounded by three G.I.s. Michael could tell that Stack was giving the dame some kind of line or other.

A G.I. gave Stack an angry shove and yelled, "Where the hell do you think you get off talkin' to her like that?"

Michael moved with urgency as he heard Stack yell, "Oh yeah, ya prick? Le's go outside and I'll, I'll kick your fuckin' ass. You and these two losers with ya!" Then, seeing Michael, he continued, "Oh here ya are, Mike. My buddy and me'll take on ten like you, right, Mike?"

"Wrong, Stack," Michael said, attempting to diffuse the situation. "Hey, forgive my pal, guys, he's had a few too many."

"The hell I have–" Stack yelled, but Michael spoke over him.

"And so have I. You know how that is, right? We don't want no trouble. We'll just get outta your way now, so you boys have…have a good night."

With that, he started to maneuver Stack toward the table.

"What the hell are you doin'? I'll fight those three bast–"

But Michael now pressed his palm against Stack's mouth. "Jesus, shut the hell up! You've gotten yourself in enough trouble as it is. You wanna get yourself fuckin' court-martialed?"

"Let 'em court-martial me! What the fuck do I care?"

Luckily, Michael was able to distract Stack by waving a girl over to the table.

"Listen, honey," Michael began, "that's an awful nice dress you got on. Blue's her color, ain't it, Stack? And guess what. My buddy was jus' sayin' to me that you remind him of Ava Gardner."

It was Michael's good fortune that the girl was easily flattered.

"You don't say."

"I *do* say. Stack here just got the bad news that they're sending him to the front. A little female company would sure do him some good."

With Stack and the girl in the blue dress in a lip lock, Michael walked out the door into the freedom of the night with one thing on his mind, getting back to the barracks. He needed to write to Cecelia before he went to bed.

May 7, 1944

My Darling,

It's late, but I wanted to make sure I wrote you before bed. I'm glad

*you liked the ten-page letter I sent, honey. Hearing how much you
enjoy my letters makes me feel like a million bucks.*

*Guess what! I've been working on a present for you. It's a master-
piece! You're probably wondering what I'm talking about. It's a heart
made from an old plexiglass windshield from a BT-13. You don't know
what that is, darling, but that don't matter. I've been working on it for
two weeks. I used a simple pocket knife to shape the plexiglass into a
heart with an arrow through it, and right in the center I carved the
Army Air Corps wings. It's pretty much done. I'll send it to you as soon
as I get through polishing it.*

*It isn't fancy enough to wear in public, honey, but at least you'll
have something I made for you. You can just look at it if you want. But
don't handle it too much, darling, because it gets dull very easily. I
polish it about 100 times a day. And guess what else. A bunch of the
boys saw me making it and started making their own. But theirs aren't
one tenth as good as mine.*

*There's only a few guys in the barracks right now, darling, because
it's late and most of the men are in town carousing. Right now, the
radio's broadcasting Glenn Miller's "When You Wish Upon a Star,"
and there's not another sound in the place. Remember the night we
first met, darling? I don't remember if the Glenn Miller Orchestra
played it that night. Like me, I'll bet you know the words. I've been
singing along, but every time I get to the part that says, "Your dreams
come true," it's making me feel awful blue. A song is a strange thing.*

*If my writing doesn't seem too normal tonight, I got a confession to
make. I went into town with Stack and got pretty tight. You see, Stack
himself got some pretty bad news. He's being bounced out of the Cadet
Program because of that plane stunt. They've assigned him to the
infantry, so before we know it, he'll be on the ground fighting the
enemy. So don't be mad at me for going out drinking with him. I had
to do it for old time's sake. For Stack.*

*You know, honey, my heart is breaking tonight. Sometimes things
build up, and it feels like too much for me. I just wish this d-mned war
would end because all it brings is heartache, heartache, and more
heartache! I'm sorry if this letter isn't making any sense. What I mean
is, I'm just so confused.*

*See, darling, besides Stack's news, I got more bad news today. You
remember Scooter, right? Of course you do! I know you really only*

talked to Scooter once, but you liked him, right? Me and Scooter grew up together, so he's not just some nobody. But you know that too, don't you? And even though I had a lot of problems through the years with the Irish, never with Scooter or his family. His mother treated me just like one of her own. So much so, I used to jokingly call her my "stepmother."

Well, it's hard for me to write about this, but today I got some mail from Scooter's mother. She told me about a letter she received from the military authorities. It's pretty bad news...

31

Cecelia – 1935

*S*itting on the bed in her big sister's room, Cecelia asks Valentina, "But why are they coming here? I thought they were married."

Valentina busily removes her clothes from the dresser and the closet, laying each item, a blouse, a skirt, a slip, on the bed and folding the items in neat, compact piles. "They *are* married, obviously. You saw them get married, didn't you? They're coming here because they need somewhere to live for a while, so Mama told them they could live here."

"But none of the other married ones live here," Cecelia says. "Not Robert or Ernie or Phyllis or even Dominic, and he just got married a year ago."

"I know, honey, but Betty and Johnny are broke and don't have any place decent to live right now."

"Isn't Dominic broke too?"

"I suppose, but he's got a job at least."

"Doesn't Johnny have a job?"

"Apparently not."

"Why not?"

"How on God's green earth am I supposed to know, Celia? I don't know everything!"

"But where are you and Connie going to sleep?"

"We're getting a cot from Mrs. Kostenko and we're going to put it downstairs. I'm going to sleep on the couch and Connie'll sleep on the cot. At least for the time being."

"But that's the living room, not a bedroom."

"It'll have to serve both purposes right now, Celia."

"But I didn't know Stella's mother had a cot."

"Well now you know," Valentina says, now starting to lose her patience.

"Where are you going to put all your clothes?"

Valentina sighs in annoyance. "In cardboard boxes in the living room."

"You're going to clutter up the whole living room."

"Listen, honey. You can see I'm busy. How about if you just stop asking so many damn questions and help me take some of these clothes downstairs?"

"I don't feel like it," Cecelia complains.

Valentina shoves a stack of skirts into Cecelia's small chest. "Just do it!"

"Why are you always bossing me around?" Cecelia asks.

"Because I need your help," Valentina replies.

Carrying the clothes down the narrow stairs, Cecelia whines, "Why is everyone always bossing me around? I feel like I have eight bosses."

"You just feel that way because you're the youngest," Valentina calls after her.

"But it's not fair!"

"So, cry me a river."

Cecelia wonders where Mama is. It's almost noon, and she hasn't seen her since waking up a few hours before. Probably visiting a neighbor, which is good, because if she was home, Mama would make Cecelia walk the goat, which she hates to do, or go to the store to get a pound of lunch meat. The thing is, Cecelia wants to be home when Betty and Johnny arrive.

Of course, Mama doesn't boss her around like everybody else. She just asks nicely, "Tesoro, potresti andare al negozio per la mamma?" Mama's kind requests simply elicit a "Yes, Mama, I'll go to the store for you. What do you need?" So, as far as Cecelia is concerned, Mama might just as well be bossing her.

Following Valentina into the living room, Cecelia continues to badger her sister. "I just think it's too many of us trying to live here at once."

"We've had this many before," Valentina says. "You know that. Remember? Before Phyllis got married?"

Cecelia rolls her eyes. "But this is different, Val. All of us girls squeezed into one bedroom just fine back then. And Johnny is a man. What I think is, it's just not going to work."

"Well, it doesn't matter what you think. It'll just have to do until Johnny can get a job. It's temporary. Now, please Celia. I'm busy. Why don't you go play with Connie? I think she's in the back yard with the Shashinka boys." Valentina pulls the cord on the shade and it snaps open. "Yes, they're up in a tree."

"I don't like climbing trees."

"Jesus Christ," Valentina moans, heading back up the stairs.

Following a step behind, Cecelia asks, "But I can still sleep with Mama, right?"

"Yes, dammit. Of course you can. Why the hell wouldn't you be able to still sleep with Mama?"

"I don't know why you're swearing and being so crabby," Cecelia replies, shrugging her shoulders. "Why are you always in a bad mood?"

Cecelia stands gazing out the window while Valentina continues to evacuate the room, and when she sees a car rolling up the hill, she calls out, "Oh look, here they come!"

Running down the stairs and pushing through the screen door, she calls out, "Hi Betty! Hi Johnny!" In a flash, she runs to Betty who picks her up and spins her around. Then Cecelia returns to the porch and straddles the railing as she watches Betty and Johnny carry boxes and luggage through the screen door and up the narrow center stairs.

When her sister comes back out through the front door a few moments before her new husband, Cecelia calls out, "Betty, if Johnny doesn't have any money, how'd he buy that car?"

"What do you mean, 'doesn't have any money?' " Betty replies.

"Valentina says you guys are going to live with us because Johnny doesn't have any money!" Cecelia yells.

Betty, not breaking stride, shushes her and whispers firmly, "You don't need to broadcast it to the whole neighborhood."

Cecelia can see that the car doesn't have the same polished finish that many of the automobiles she has seen around town have and decides that it must have been inexpensive to buy due to its dull gray exterior. *Ernie's car is a lot shinier than Johnny's*, she thinks to herself. *And so is Robert's.*

A moment later, Johnny bursts through the door. "How was the honeymoon, Johnny?" Cecelia asks, still riding her porch railing.

"It was great, little lady. The best," Johnny replies, giving Betty a little pat on the behind as he reaches the car.

Glaring at him and giving him a knowing smile, Betty shoves a cardboard box against his chest and whispers, "Don't give her any ammunition." Johnny just chuckles.

When they finish bringing all the boxes and suitcases upstairs, Johnny shuffles down the steps and says, "See ya later, little darlin'."

"Where ya going now, Johnny?" Cecelia calls.

"That's for me to know and for you to find out," Johnny answers, and then he starts the car and heads back down the hill.

She goes into the house and calls up the stairs. "Hey, Betty! Where did Johnny go? He just drove away, but he wouldn't tell me. He said it was for him to know and for me to find out."

"Don't worry about it, baby," she hears her older sister call from the bedroom above. "Just go play with Connie and the kids out back."

"I'd rather talk to you two."

"Well, you can't talk to us two," she hears Valentina call out. "We're talking about grown-up things!"

Cecelia covertly tiptoes up the stairs, trying hard not to make any creaking sounds on the worn wooden treads, and sits outside the bedroom door, her arms wrapped around her ankles.

Although they are speaking in low tones, she can make out most of what her sisters are saying behind the closed door. *It's not fair,* Cecelia thinks to herself. *Val's not a grownup. She's barely six years older than me. How come she gets to listen to secrets and I don't?*

Realizing, though, that she can't eavesdrop and fret at the same time, Cecelia concentrates hard on just listening to what her two sisters are saying.

"So then, what happened next?" she hears Valentina say.

"Well, what do you think happened next?" Betty answers. "We went to the hotel room, and he started to take my clothes off."

"Get out," Valentina says. "Every stitch?"

"Every stitch," Betty confirms. "It's legal now. We're married, aren't we?"

"Didn't he even kiss you?"

"Well of course he did, silly. Eventually."

"But what did he do next? Did he take his clothes off?"

"I'm so embarrassed," Betty replies. "I can't even tell you."

Cecelia is now kneeling with her ear pressed against the door. Every now and then, she looks through the keyhole trying to see them.

"Oh, to hell with being embarrassed. You've got to tell me," Valentina pleads. "Just tell me what he did next. I want to know what to expect when my time comes."

"Well, believe it or not, he told me to undress him."

Cecelia hears Valentina gasp. "And did you?"

Suddenly Cecelia can't hear anything for a short while.

"And when all of his clothes were off, did you see his...his..."

"His pecker?" Betty teases, and they both burst into hysterics. "Oh yes, I saw it alright. I did more than see it!" Now the two are in tears laughing.

Outside the door, Cecelia loses her balance and topples over sideways. In a flash, Valentina is at the door. "What in the hell are you doing, you little brat?" Valentina screams, grabbing her little sister by the ear and pulling her into the room. "What did you hear, you devil?"

"Ouch," Cecelia cries out. "That hurts!"

"You're going to find out what hurts! I'll ask again, and if you don't tell me, I'll pull this ear right off of your goddamn head. What did you hear?"

"I heard everything."

"I ought to give you a good beating."

"What's a pecker?"

"Don't say that word."

"But *you* said it."

Valentina gives her a good shake. "Well, it's not a nice word, so just don't say it."

"But why can you two say it if it's not a nice word?"

"Because we're grown-ups."

"Maybe Betty is, but you're not. You're not even seventeen yet!"

"Listen, you little witch. You're gonna get it in about one second."

Betty is at the window, pulling up the sash and calling, "Connie, I need you to come get your sister right now!"

"If you two don't tell me what it is, I'm going to go stand on the porch and start yelling 'pecker...pecker...pecker' at the top of my lungs."

"If you do, I swear, you'll be sorry you were ever born!" Valentina yells.

Trying to be more helpful, Betty explains, "You're too young to know what it means, sweetie."

"Don't call her *sweetie*. There's nothing sweet about her."

"Well, if Val's old enough," Cecelia says, gesturing with her head toward Valentina, "Then so am I."

"That's it," Valentina yells, "now you're really going to get it."

"No I'm not, Valentina. Mama never hit me in my entire life, and she wouldn't like it if anyone else did, so you better not, or I swear I'll tell her."

"Oh you swear, do you?" Valentina snarls.

"Yes, and what's more, I promise if you don't tell me what a pecker is, I'm going to yell it from the porch, just like I said, until someone comes and does tell me."

Valentina grabs her by the arm. "Someday that big mouth of yours is going to get you in trouble, you little b-i-t-c-h!"

Connie, sweaty and flushed, arrives outside the door. "What's the matter? What'd she do now?"

Valentina shakes her head. "Never mind what she did now. Go back out and play with the Shashinkas. Cecelia's going to stay here with us."

Connie shrugs and skips back down the stairs.

Scowling, Valentina says, "Alright, you brat. Sit your ass down on the bed and let's have a long talk!"

---

32

*C*ecelia stood at the counter at Husti's Meat Market on Center Street. After a long, tedious workday, she promised Mama that she would pick up some sausage and a box of macaroni. She remembered how when she was a little girl, Mama had made homemade pasta, but at her advanced age, it was becoming too much work.

Waiting in line for the butcher to get to her, Cecelia was more than a little surprised when she heard a familiar voice.

"Don't we know each other, miss?"

"Oh my goodness," she exclaimed. "You're about the last person I expected to run into today. It's so great to see you again."

"Likewise," said Vincent, who was as happy to see her as she was to see him.

"I thought you said you lived in Seymour. What brings you to a market in Shelton?"

"My Polish grandmother. She won't let me buy kielbasa anywhere else," he explained. "You know how the old timers are."

"Do I ever. My mother's one. In my case, I'm getting sausage for a meat sauce. Luckily, we have a couple of last ration stamps left for the month."

"Yeah, same for us. You come from a big family?"

"Most of them are married and long out of the house. Just

Mama, me, and Connie now. I'm the youngest of eight. Mama was fifty-one when I was born!"

"Wow, those Italians don't fool around, do they?"

"Apparently, they do," Cecelia joked, "but I don't like to think about that."

Her comment gave them both a good laugh, peeling away any shred of tension the two new friends felt.

Walking out of the store together, each clasping a brown paper sack, Cecelia asked, "Will we see you this Saturday? I hope the answer is yes."

"One thing you'll learn about me is that I have to get skating in, so yes. I was hoping to see you anyway, and now I know I will."

"Count on it," Cecelia said.

When Saturday came, however, none of the girls were available. Stella was visiting relatives, Connie, a newly licensed driver, had promised to take Mama shopping, and little Connie wasn't feeling well.

Cecelia, ultimately, was relieved since going by herself offered her the opportunity to speak to Vincent, perhaps, in confidence. She was dying to learn more about him, particularly why he wasn't working at the plant anymore. She didn't want to pry, but she was open to anything he wanted to tell her. There would be no Stella with her impulsive flirtations or Connie with her clumsy questions.

The experience of skating was different this time and felt a bit date-like. Instructing her how to skate backwards, Vincent held Cecelia by both hands as they glided across the oval space. It reminded her of a newsreel she had seen featuring Olympic ice skaters.

"You're so graceful, Cecelia," Vincent commented as he guided her. "You've taken dance lessons, right?"

"I wish," Cecelia responded. "But I do love dancing, and most people say I'm very good at it."

"I'm sure you are."

It felt good to be in the company of a man again. And somehow, Cecelia felt safe with Vincent. Despite having a wonderful time together, even holding hands together, she didn't have any sense that he was interested in her romantically. Or, if so, he was different from the average guy like Augie, who, while nice enough, clearly had designs on her. The same was true even for Michael. She had no way to explain it to herself, but with Vincent, it was just different.

Afterwards, he suggested they go to Shea's Riviera instead of Vonette's.

"It's just a hop, skip, and a jump down the road," he offered, turning the key in the ignition. "Ever been there?"

"Only once," she said.

Vincent's engine turned over but then stalled. "Oops, gonna have to choke it. Hold on."

She didn't know what he meant, but she watched him pull a knob on the dash out and push it back in.

"No kidding. Who with? The girls?"

"No, with my boyfriend, the last time he was home on leave."

Alluding to Michael gave her a sense of relief. Now Vincent knew she was spoken for, just in case her hunch about him only being interested in a platonic friendship was off the mark.

He turned the key once more, and after a couple of grunts, the engine started.

"Oh good. Then you know it's essentially a bar, but they have a menu, which you must also know."

"Perfect," she agreed.

"Yes, it gives us a little more privacy to talk because they have booths there."

When they arrived at Shea's, they passed by the bar on their way to a booth in the rear.

Sitting down, Cecelia asked, "Did you notice that woman at the end of the bar, the one who works at the plant?"

"I didn't." Vincent turned and looked over his shoulder. "Let's see. Oh, yeah, her. I've seen her there, but I don't know her."

The woman, perhaps in her mid-fifties with thinning gray hair and gloomy eyes, sat staring bleakly down into a mixed drink before her.

"Well," Cecelia continued, almost in a whisper, "her name is Barbara, and she's very strange."

"You know her?"

"No, she keeps to herself. I just know her name because the girls gossip about her."

"Well, I can't say anything. I mean, I kept to myself at work. That's how some people are."

"Yeah, but she just seems so, I don't know. Those dark circles under her eyes make her look so sad. Don't you think it's odd that she's here drinking at a bar by herself?"

"After a long week at the plant, she probably needs to drown her sorrows. I guess everyone has their own problems." Then shifting gears, "How about we order us a couple of hamburgers and root beers? On me."

They ordered, and after the waitress left the table, the two seemed at a sudden loss for words.

"So," Vincent finally said.

Cecelia smiled warmly. "So."

"I don't really know what to say."

Cecelia spoke from the heart. "I feel there's something you'd like to tell me."

"Is it that obvious?"

"I'm afraid so. Is it about you getting let go at the plant?"

"Partially," he said. "But maybe it's best if you don't know the details."

"I'm a big girl," she assured him. "And you'll find out that I'm a good listener. Does it have something to do with the cutting of the flight suit wires?"

"Yeah," he said with sheepish eyes. "In a way."

"Please don't tell me you're the person who was cutting them."

"God, no, I would *never* do that."

"But they think it's you?"

"I'm a suspect."

"But why you?"

Vincent took a long pause and appeared to Cecelia to be deep in thought. Finally, he opened up, his voice shaking with emotion. "I was discharged from the military four months ago with...with a Section 8."

Cecelia reached and laid her palm over his trembling hand.

"I don't think I know what that is."

"A Section 8 is given to soldiers the Army deems mentally unfit for service. They send you to a psychiatrist and the whole nine yards."

"But you seem a hundred percent sane to me," Cecelia offered.

"I am. I mean, at least I hope I am."

"What would have made them think otherwise?"

"I don't know if I can tell you this. Or, to put it another way, I don't know *how* to tell you this."

"You can tell me anything."

The waitress arrived with the hamburgers and sodas, and seeing Cecelia's hand covering Vincent's, she teased, "Here ya go, you two lovebirds!"

Her remark made the two new friends smile, lightening the moment.

After she walked away, Vincent continued, but even in a softer voice. "Somebody saw me in town. With another guy. An older guy. He's a civilian, actually. We were in an alley alongside a bar in town, and…and…"

"And…"

"And…" Vincent seemed paralyzed. "I just…I can't…"

"It's alright," she assured him. "I think I understand."

Even without real knowledge of boys like Vincent, Cecelia realized why he wasn't interested in girls the way other boys were.

"But who saw you?"

"One of the guys in the platoon. He ratted me out."

"And then what happened?"

"What happened is the next day the company commander calls me in and starts in on me. Before I know it, I'm sitting with a psychiatrist who's asking me a lot of awkward questions about growing up and showing me these cards with ink blots and asking what I see."

"What kinds of questions did the psychiatrist ask you?"

"I don't know. About why I think I don't like girls and how my mother and big sisters treat me, and what kind of guy my dad is, and if I was ever molested. He was trying to figure out why I am who I am."

Cecelia continued with caution. "And Vincent, why do you feel you are who you are?"

"Because, I don't know. Maybe I was born this way. Just like you were born the way you are. Do you remember the first time you felt attracted to the opposite sex?"

"Well, I don't know about the very first time, but I guess there was some kind of attraction ever since I was a little girl."

"Same for me. Ever since I was a little kid, I felt attracted to other boys. I mean, I didn't admit it to myself, so I pretended to like girls, to ask girls out on dates. Even a few times to kiss a girl, but it never felt right. You want my take? I was born who I am, just like you were born who you are."

While surprised by his answer, Cecelia still felt an overwhelming compulsion to understand him.

"I see. And what about the ink blots? I don't think I've ever heard of that. What did you see in them?"

"I didn't see anything. They looked exactly like what they were. Like big blotches of spilled ink, but I tried to make things up so that they wouldn't think I was crazy."

"But it didn't work." Cecelia realized that it wasn't a question.

"Right, it didn't work. So they bounce guys like me out. They call it a 'blue discharge.' It's not honorable or dishonorable. They just throw you out, with no future G.I. benefits. It's like you were never in, except the record follows you and ruins your life. A guy like me usually can't even get a job."

"But you got a job at the factory."

"Because it's wartime. With so many in the military, they can't afford to be too picky."

Cecelia looked down at their plates and chuckled. "We haven't even touched our food."

Vincent sighed. "We should eat." But after a few bites, he said, "Actually, I don't have much of an appetite, I'm afraid."

"Neither do I," Cecelia agreed.

The two paused, still not touching their food, and finally, with a sad smile, Vincent broke the silence. "It's funny, isn't it?"

"What's funny?"

"When you're someone like me, your whole life is a secret. Until someone finds you out, and then it's not."

"That's funny?"

"Well, you know what I mean."

"I don't think I do, Vincent."

"Now my secret is out, and my life will never be the same."

"You mean…because of how this all played out at the plant?"

"That's just the beginning. Agent Reynolds figures I'm some kind of malcontent, see, because I got booted out of the Army, and that I'm a pervert on top of it. So it stands to reason that I'm the one that's been sabotaging the flight suits. I guess it makes sense."

"Oh, God," Cecelia muttered, "it does *not* make sense! I hate that damned Agent Reynolds. He's such a bastard. Forgive my language."

"I know. But like I said, I would never–"

"But what now?"

"Now, I'm obviously unemployed, and I'm also kind of under house arrest. I am not to leave the Valley for any reason without permission. My take is they're watching me. I bet they're watching us right now. It's why you shouldn't be with me. I'm sorry. I don't want to get you into any trouble."

"Vincent, dear, I think you're getting carried away. I doubt if anyone here is watching us. Unless crazy Barbara at the bar is spying on us."

Vincent snorted and almost spit out a mouthful of root beer.

"Besides," Cecelia continued, "I'm not worried about it. I'm just happy to be someone you can open up to."

On Monday, no sooner had Cecelia arrived at her station that Rudy approached her and told her Agent Reynolds wanted to see her.

Cecelia was overcome with trepidation as she headed to the office. Reynolds was studying a folder as she sat down. Once more, not looking up from his paperwork, he muttered, "We won't be needing you, Mr. Valillo."

Cecelia didn't flinch, but kept her eyes on Reynolds as she heard Rudy close the door behind her.

With his gaze still fixed on the folder, Reynolds began, "Miss Alberino, I understand you are a friend of Vincent Demski."

"I know Vincent," she replied. "He worked here."

"But you *are* good friends, correct?"

That he conversed without making eye contact made Cecelia despise Agent Reynolds even more than she already did.

"Pretty good friends, I suppose."

"Good enough to go skating with him and out to a restaurant?"

Cecelia felt the muscles in her neck constrict. "Excuse me, sir, but are you having me followed?"

Finally, Reynolds looked up. "No, Miss Alberino, we're having *Demski* followed. Did he tell you why he was fired?"

Cecelia's emotions kicked into high gear. "No, he didn't," she lied. "I asked, but he told me it was personal."

"He did, did he? And do you know what kind of personal life he leads? What kind of man Vincent Demski is?" Reynolds asked, his tone acerbic.

"Yes, I believe I do. A very nice man."

"Let's just put it this way, Miss Alberino. If you've got romantic designs on him, you're barking up the wrong tree."

"Are you trying to tell me that–"

"I'm just telling you that you should be careful who you keep company with."

"You're not telling me who I may or may not be friends with, I hope." She could hear the razor sharpness in her own voice and regretted her tone.

"Listen, girlie, don't be stupid your whole life. I'm just giving you some fatherly advice. If you're smart, you'll take it."

"Are you quite finished with me?"

"Yes, for today."

Agent Reynolds buried himself back in the manila folder. As she reached the door, Cecelia needed to offer one more remark.

"By the way, Agent Reynolds. My name is Cecelia, not *girlie*, and my father died when I was seven years old. No man alive has ever been able to replace him, so if you don't mind, please keep your fatherly advice to yourself."

Reynolds made no attempt to disguise his rancor with her. "You better be careful there, Miss Alberino, or someday that big mouth of yours is going to get you into more trouble than you can handle."

Without another word, Cecelia scowled at him and walked out, pulling the door shut with a rude thud. Her cheeks burned as she headed back to her machine, and they were still ablaze when she walked home at the end of the day. She was damned if Agent Reynolds was going to keep her away from Vincent. *America is still a free country, isn't it?* Vincent had a right to live his life his own way.

Cecelia knew she had always been good at reading people, and she had no doubt that Vincent had been truthful with her. Examining her conscience, she felt an unbreakable resolve to continue spending time with Vincent, to support him, and to comfort him. She didn't care if other people judged him because he was different. Her plan was to show him she was a true friend.

33

Cecelia now slept fitfully. She had been seeing Vincent almost daily. She thought of them as needing each other. No matter where they went, Cecelia knew they were being watched, but not knowing who was watching them made her feel all the more paranoid. She had shared a little about Vincent in a recent letter to Michael, but he had reacted negatively.

> ...You need to be careful about this matter, darling. If the FBI pressured the boss into firing your friend, and if they've ordered him not to leave town, they must have good reasons for their suspicions. Those boys don't play around. I know he told you he is innocent and you believe him, but you never know. Sure, I understand. He's a nice guy, or at least you feel he is, but you don't want to jeopardize your job, or even worse, your reputation. What if people at the plant start associating you with the crime? What if the FBI does? That's a hornets' nest you don't want to get yourself tangled in, honey. Besides, you have plenty of girls to spend time with. What do you need with a fairy like this guy? I'll tell you one thing. It's lucky he got a Section 8 because I'd hate to tell you how miserable the boys in the barracks could make his life...

To say that Michael's remarks rankled her would be an understatement. She didn't care for his use of the word *fairy*, and she had a good mind to tell him that sometimes he was too preachy. Who did he think he was, anyway? She had, in fact, let him have it with both barrels when he had told her to quit smoking, scolded her for going dancing at Jocko's, and accused her of not writing every day. In those instances, after she had set him straight, he dropped the matter. But in this case, she felt a reluctance to get into a ballyhoo with him.

To make matters worse, Michael would be home on a much awaited furlough in two weeks. His excitement about the leave jumped off the pages of every letter. Of course, Cecelia was looking forward to it too. She'd just have to avoid talking about Vincent to him.

Keeping secrets was a royal pain in the ass as far as Cecelia was concerned. She already had one big secret she had been carrying for months, the matter of Augie kissing her. That was a long time ago, but it still nagged her. And now it seemed that her friendship with Vincent was a new taboo subject.

In the meantime, she still felt a strong pull to share with someone who would understand. The two Connies and Stella had been in Vincent's presence at Lakeview a few times since they first met him there, and they had been continuously quizzing her about their friendship. Cecelia deflected their questions but sometimes not so successfully, much to her dismay.

"From what I'm seeing, you're spending an awful lot of time with him," Stella recently teased.

"Is that what you're seeing?" Cecelia replied curtly.

"It is!"

"Yeah," little Connie interjected. "She was just out with him on Wednesday afternoon, and they went shopping together yesterday."

"Oh mind your own damned business, nosy," Cecelia snapped.

"Well, he is awfully good looking," Stella said.

"Too good looking," Connie added.

"Now what is that supposed to mean, sis?"

"It means just what I said! Everything about him is perfect. His hair, for instance. Never a hair out of place. And his fingernails. They're almost like a girl's. You know what I think, don't ya?"

Cecelia frowned. "No, I certainly do not. And I'm not interested in–"

"I think he's a mama's boy," Connie interrupted and then sancti-moniously pursed her lips.

"What the hell is a mama's boy?"

"You know exactly what it is."

The blood rushed to Cecelia's face. "Oh, just shove it, will you, Connie? Did you know he was a basketball star at Seymour High School? And that he was a Boy Scout who loved camping and fishing and all those guy things? For Christ's sake, he was in the goddamn Army and did everything that Michael and any other guy had to do in basic training. What in God's name makes him a mama's boy?"

Stella, now interceding as the peacemaker, said, "Please, don't bicker, girls. All I said is that he's very good looking. But the big question is: How does Michael feel about Vincent?"

"Vincent is just a friend. There's nothing more going on between us than that."

Stella persisted, "But how does Michael *feel* about him?"

Cecelia snapped, "Listen, Stella. You've told me you don't tell Donny everything, and I don't report every detail of my life to Michael. Like I said, Vincent is just a friend. If Michael doesn't like it, he can lump it!"

"Oh, Jesus! You really don't need to be so hyper-sensitive. I was just kidding."

Cecelia could see the matter was too sensitive to discuss with them, and she had reservations about Valentina and Betty as well. She didn't know if they would understand.

Instead, she made a decision to confide in her eldest sister once more. When Cecelia had brought her concern about committing to Michael to Phyllis, her sister had listened and given her good common sense advice.

As Cecelia sat at Phyllis' kitchen table, Phyllis was busy cooking, and her children were conveniently napping.

Contemplating the problem, Phyllis said, "And you're being followed by the FBI, you say?"

"Well, it's not that I'm being followed. Vincent is, and I'm with him a lot."

"That sounds pretty serious to me. Hmmm," Phyllis murmured as she sprinkled paprika into the goulash she had bubbling on the stove. Her husband Fred was the son of Hungarian immigrants, which had prompted Phyllis to become quite an expert in his native cuisine, so much so that some people mistook her for Hungarian herself.

"There's just no chance he's guilty, Phil. I would bet my life on it," Cecelia added.

"Well, don't go betting your life just yet, baby." Continuing to stir, Phyllis added, "And you say he is a, uhm, a mama's boy."

"You're the second person who said that in a week! I said nothing of the kind, and I don't think he'd appreciate being called that."

"But you know what I mean, right? That's what got him in trouble in the military, right?"

"I guess, but why should that matter? Isn't that his own private business? Shouldn't a person be able to live his own private life?"

"Yes, that's a good point. But it's gotten him in trouble, hasn't it? Because if he hadn't gotten discharged from the Army for this reason, he wouldn't be a suspect in this flight suit business."

Cecelia felt dejected. "I suppose. But it's not fair."

"Life ain't fair, sweetie. We've experienced our share of that right in our own family, haven't we?"

"Yes."

Phyllis scooped a spoonful of goulash, held it over a bowl, and brought it over to the table. "Here, taste this and tell me what you think."

Cecelia blew on the spoon and then made a dainty slurping sound as she sipped the contents into her mouth.

"Delicious!"

"Too spicy?"

"No, just right…so what do I do now?"

Phyllis turned the blue flame down to low on the burner, letting her stew and her thoughts simmer. "Okay, then. Tell me what you want to do."

"I want to remain friends with Vincent."

"And how will Michael feel about that?"

"Michael, Michael, Michael! All anybody says is *Michael*! I mean, it's not like Vincent is a rival for his love."

"I know that. But what does Michael have to say about it?"

"It's just none of Michael's business."

"You're telling me that you're none of Michael's business?"

Overcome with frustration, Cecelia almost shouted, "No, I *am*. He doesn't like it, okay?"

"Fred wouldn't neither."

"Guys like Michael and Fred simply don't understand guys like Vincent. That's the whole problem."

"Do *you* understand him?"

Phyllis' question gave Cecelia further pause.

Repeating the question, Phyllis gave Cecelia a compassionate smile. "Well, do you?"

Cecelia let out a deep sigh. "Not completely. How could I? But Vincent can't help how he feels, can he? He said he's felt like this for as long as he can remember. What is he supposed to do? Just start pretending he likes girls? He told me some men who are like him play pretend and even get married. Then what? I mean, he can't help being who he is."

"I don't know, baby. Heavens, I don't have any answers. I just think everybody deserves a fair shake. But the world isn't running around giving everyone a fair shake. We both know that. I think you just need to follow your woman's intuition. And your heart. Just be careful. Tell me you'll be careful."

At work, Agent Reynolds had adopted something of a new tack. During their latest meeting, he greeted Cecelia with a broad smile and began their conversation with niceties like, "What's new?" and "How's your family?" and "I hope your boyfriend is doing well." A far cry from their previous meeting.

Cecelia gave polite answers even though she could see through his game.

Soon enough, though, Reynolds needed to get to the matter at hand. "Has your friend revealed anything new lately?"

"Which friend?" Cecelia asked.

"I think you know which friend," Reynolds replied, barely maintaining his composure.

"We've stopped talking about it. He told me that he's innocent, and that's good enough for me."

"Well, it seems coincidental to us that since he was let go, no flight suits have been tampered with."

Cecelia grimaced. "How could they have? With your agents watching us like hawks, the guilty party isn't about to cut any more wires."

Reynolds chuckled. "I gotta tell ya, you're a pretty sharp cookie, Miss Alberino. Anyway, I trust that if your friend does reveal anything, you'll do the right thing."

"I will indeed, sir. I've been doing the right thing my whole life. I don't intend to stop now."

She needed to break the news to Vincent that Michael would be home soon and that she wouldn't be able to get together with him for a while. He'd be disappointed, she knew, but he'd understand. He'd have to.

It was all Michael had written about in his recent letters, and his enthusiasm to see her and to spend time with her was palpable, to say the least.

> *...I hope you are as excited as I am, honey. These last months have been the worst, filled with nothing but routine and tedium. It will do my heart good to see you again, to feel your hands in mine, to kiss your lips. Even just talking to you will lift my spirits. Enjoying the companionship of a woman, and, may I say, a woman who loves me, will be a d-mned sight better than spending time with these mugs here on the base. Tell me your anticipation is as high as mine, honey, because mine is sky high...*

Cecelia was looking forward to Michael's furlough. She hoped that seeing him again would anchor her and hopefully help her to get her bearings. It would be a good diversion from the drama of the flight suits and being spied on by F.B.I agents. In the midst of the anxiety she was feeling, a dose of common sense from Michael might be just what she needed.

34

Cecelia – 1934

*M*iss Hewitt announces to her fifth-grade class that starting in November, on the first Friday of the month, each student will be responsible for making an oral presentation. The assignment elicits a surge of excitement in Cecelia's heart. Although the first Friday of November is three weeks away, Cecelia feels an urgency to choose her poem. When the school bell rings, she drags Stella to the Plumb Memorial Library.

As they walk along Howe Avenue, Stella complains, "But we don't go to the library on Thursdays, we go on Saturdays."

"I can't wait until Saturday, Stell," Cecelia explains.

"But you said the presentation isn't until the first Friday in November. That's three weeks away, isn't it?"

"That's right. But I need to find a poem today."

"But why?" Stella moans.

"Just because."

"But, because *why?*"

"Because it's just how I am, Stell," Cecelia replies. "So just stuff a sock in it, will ya?"

Stella is right. The Plumb has become a refuge for Cecelia where she has spent many a Saturday morning combing the shelves of the spectacular Romanesque-style brick building, named for

D.W. Plumb (who had envisioned it but didn't live long enough to see it come to fruition), completed in 1895, funded by his brother on land donated by his wife.

Of course, young Cecelia knows nothing of the Plumb family or how the library came to be. The Plumb is simply an oasis Cecelia loves visiting. The Plumb is an adventure land where Cecelia has mined for golden poems to fill the treasure chest of her heart. Poems like "The Charge of the Light Brigade" by Alfred Lord Tennyson and "The Children's Hour" by Henry Wadsworth Longfellow and "How Do I Love Thee?" by Elizabeth Barrett Browning. At the Plumb, Cecelia feels safe and calm, wrapped in the comfort of shelves and shelves of books.

When the first Friday of November arrives, Cecelia announces to Miss Hewitt and the class that she will recite the classic poem, "O Captain! My Captain!" by Walt Whitman.

After Cecelia's recitation, Miss Hewitt asks, "And where did you find that poem, Cecelia?"

"At the library," Cecelia replies with pride.

Miss Hewitt is a humorless woman with dark, hollow eyes.

"That's a sophisticated poem for a fifth-grader. Do you know what it's about?"

"Yes, Miss Hewitt. It's about President Abraham Lincoln. The librarian told me," Cecelia says.

Satisfied with her explanation, Miss Hewitt flashes a wry smile and says, "Well, I think the poem is a bit advanced for you, but still, you did a lovely job reciting it."

"Thank you," Cecelia answers proudly.

"Tell me," Miss Hewitt continues, recognizing Cecelia's precociousness, "What would you like to be when you grow up?"

Giving the question a moment of thought, Cecelia replies, "Let's see. I'd like to be a poet and a famous singer."

"A poet and a famous singer," her teacher flatly echoes.

"Yes, I want to write poetry books and sing on the radio."

Her teacher almost laughs. "I'd like to suggest that you don't invest in pipe dreams, my dear."

That evening, as Valentina brushes her hair before bed, Cecelia asks, "What's a pipe dream?" She figures that Valentina, at fifteen years old, knows just about everything.

Valentina pauses before answering. "A pipe dream? Now, let's see how to explain it. A pipe dream is a dream that's, uhm...that's never going to come true."

"Why not?" Cecelia asks.

"Well, because it just isn't realistic to think that such a dream will come true."

"Why?"

"Oh, I don't know," Valentina says, sweeping the brush in a downward motion against the back of Cecelia's head. "Because just any dream can't come true."

"But why not?"

Valentina sighs. "You ask so many questions, Celia!"

"I just want to know. Why not? Give me an example."

"Okay...let me see. Oh yes, here's an example of a pipe dream. Do you know how they tell you in school that anyone can become President of the United States?"

"Yes. My teacher told us that Abraham Lincoln became president even though he was very poor growing up."

"Exactly! Well, that's just a lot of bull! The truth is, we can't become the President of the United States, I assure you."

"Why not?"

"For one thing, we're not men. Has there ever been a president who's a woman?"

"I don't think so."

"You don't think so because there *hasn't* been. And there never will be."

Suddenly, their brother Dominic raps on the door and pokes his head in. "See ya later. I'm off to pick up my girl."

"Okay," Val replies. "Have fun."

"I will! Don't wait up for me," Dominic adds with a laugh and then rambles down the stairs.

"I can't wait for Dom's wedding next month," Cecelia says.

Val frowns. "That's nice."

"You don't like her?"

"She's fine."

"But why don't you like her?"

"Don't worry about it. I said I like her just fine."

Cecelia remains silent for a moment as Val's brush continues to pass through her hair.

"Can Dom become the president?"

"Not a chance."

"But he's a man."

"Celia, Dom didn't even finish the eighth grade."

"But–"

"But nothing! No matter what they tell you, presidents are not usually the children of poor, uneducated people, Abraham Lincoln notwithstanding, and presidents are *never* the children of Italian immigrants."

With each downward stroke, Valentina realizes she is brushing hope from the dark strands of Cecelia's long hair, but at the same time, she feels it's for Cecelia's own good.

"Well, I don't care," Cecelia says, as if she's made an important decision.

"Don't care about what?"

"I don't care if it's a pipe dream. I'm going to be President of the United States when I grow up anyway. And I'm going to be a poet and a famous singer too!"

Valentina shakes her head in bewilderment. "Well, honey. Then you'll be the first."

"The first what?"

"The first poor, Italian-American lady president, who is also a poet and a famous singer." Valentina can't resist laughing at the folly of her own words.

"What's so funny?"

"Nothing. Nothing at all."

Opening the poetry volume Ernie had given her, Cecelia mindlessly flips through the pages to the poem about Leetla Giorgio Washeenton.

"Val?"

"Yes, honey?"

"Is it still a pipe dream if I just wanna become a poet?"

Valentina sighs again. "Well, maybe it's not as big of a pipe dream as thinking you'll be President of the United States, but yes, I'd say even that's a pipe dream."

"But why?" Cecelia protests. "Girls can be poets! There's a poem in this book by a lady named Elizabeth Barrett Browning and two by a lady named Emily Dickinson."

"Okay, you go right ahead and become a poet," Valentina says, shaking her head at her sister's spunkiness.

"Good. I'll be a poet and a singer."

Valentina simply grunts.

"What was that noise for?"

"Nothing, Celia. Absolutely nothing."

Cecelia frowns. "You don't think I can even become a poet and singer, do you?"

When Valentina responds with nothing but a shrug, Cecelia adds, "But, if not those, what's going to happen to me when I grow up?"

Taking Cecelia's hands in her own and caressing them, Valentina says, "Listen, sis. It's hard for people like us to become famous writers or celebrities. But what I do think is that someday you're going to meet a nice guy and marry him, and together you're going to have a beautiful family, and you'll take care of the kids while he earns a living. I think that's what's going to happen to me. In fact, it's what I want. Just like Phyllis and Betty. And I think that's what's going to happen to you when you grow up. How does that sound?"

Cecelia lets out a long breath and concedes, "That's fine."

But in her heart, she hasn't conceded. Admitting to herself that she can't be president is one thing. *Who wants to be a dumb old president anyway?* But lying awake in bed that night and gazing at the crescent moon aglow outside the window, Cecelia hopes Valentina is wrong. Visions of having her own poems published in hardbound anthologies and dreams of singing on the radio swim in her head. *And besides, why can't a poet or singer marry a nice guy?* When she can no longer keep her eyes open, she snuggles close to Mama, hearing the gentle hum of Mama's snoring and thinking, *Oh, please, God, please, let it be!*

*a*s Michael stepped off the train in his uniform, his worn green duffle bag slung over his broad shoulders, he was a sight to behold. Cecelia trotted to him, he caught her in his arms and lifted her into the air, and she thought he'd never let go.

"This is too good to be true," he said. "I just can't believe it!"

"Neither can I," she agreed.

That night, he took her to dinner at Shea's Riviera. The last time she had been there, ironically, was with Vincent.

Michael couldn't stop talking about the military.

"It's been twelve weeks in this preflight stage, but it was only supposed to be six. And there's no telling when that will change. That's the thing. The military can do anything they want, and we are powerless. Anyway, even when there's a little excitement, it's usually of the negative variety. Like the mishap Stack had. You remember that."

She had remembered the letter he had written, half drunk, about Stack and about Scooter. Michael's disappointment and disillusionment had cut right through her.

Then Michael launched into a story about a fellow cadet on the maintenance team who injured his hand when a miscommunication happened on the runway.

"The boy turned the prop with his hands and as the engine started, the prop suddenly spun at full speed and hit him in the hand. It was a gruesome sight, I can tell you. His hand is pretty well smashed, and he may lose it."

"Oh my, that's awful!" Cecelia didn't like hearing about injuries. She even cringed when one of her small nephews or nieces skinned their knee.

"Golly, what a chatterbox I am. I've been monopolizing the whole conversation, haven't I? I'm sorry. Tell me about you and what's been going on lately."

"I don't know what to tell you about. My life is so boring in comparison."

"Well, what's new with the flight suit business?"

Since her last letter, she hadn't shared anything new. "Oh, the same old thing. The agents are watching us as we work. Every once in a great while, that awful Agent Reynolds randomly calls one of us in and questions us."

"And do you still see that boy they fired?"

"Let's not talk about that, Michael."

"No, it's okay. We should tell each other everything, shouldn't we?"

"Yes, I see Vincent occasionally. He's a nice boy, and he's great company."

It wasn't the whole truth, but it wasn't a bold-faced lie either.

"I'm sure he is," Michael replied. "But if I can give you a little advice...I'll bet you a million bucks that the FBI is keeping tabs on this guy. You told me he couldn't leave the Valley, right? You don't want to get caught up in this mess. What if he's guilty?"

"He's not."

"But what if he is?" Michael persisted.

The conversation had been going so well when Michael was talking about the Army, but now Cecelia felt smothered.

"Michael, listen. I said he's *not!*"

"How do you know?"

"Because I *do.* Because I have a sixth sense about these things."

"About what things?"

"About whether someone is being straight with me. I've always had a strong sense of that, ever since my father died. When he died, I lost all sense of, I don't know what to call it, all *naivety.* I can tell when someone is being honest with me, whether it's Vincent or

Agent Reynolds or that creep Tony at my last job, or quite honestly, *you*. It's the main reason I love you, Michael, because I know you've always been honest with me."

Michael felt a warm tingling inside of his chest. There wasn't much he could say in response.

Cecelia reached across the table and took Michael by the hand. "Please listen to me, Michael, and look me in the eye. You're a good man. A good, good man! Please don't be cruel and small-minded like so many people around here are just because someone is different from you. Vincent is a wonderful man, and he's my friend. If I had the slightest inkling that he was guilty, I wouldn't be friends with him. You know that, don't you?"

Michael sheepishly shook his head that he understood.

"Good," Cecelia continued. "So let's not worry about this anymore and let's not talk about it. Having you home gives me an opportunity to put it out of my mind for a while. Is that okay with you?"

Michael smiled warmly. "Yes. You're right. I want to make the best of my twelve days here. I'm sorry. I shouldn't have brought it up."

Cecelia agreed, and Michael was true to his word. He made no further mention of Vincent. And making the best of their time together is what they did. Michael was by her side every minute that Cecelia wasn't working or sleeping. Nightly, they danced into the wee hours at the Open Gate when they were practically out on their feet. On weekends, they enjoyed walks across the Derby Green. On several evenings, they parked alongside the Lakeview Casino and necked under the warm glow of moonlight bouncing off the glassy stillness of the river. They even shopped for a new dress for Cecelia at The Fair Shoppe in Derby. Michael loved to see her dressed up and took a great interest in the styles that she wore.

With each and every visit, Michael gave Cecelia a fresh gardenia from a burgeoning plant in his mother's garden. At the end of each date, Cecelia pressed the flower into the old volume of poetry her brother had once given her and jotted down the date in pencil at the bottom corner of the page.

On the Friday before he would go back to Kansas, the two babysat for Valentina who wanted to go to the movies with a girlfriend. Listening to the radio and watching little Skipper, now a year and a half old, Cecelia dozed off on the couch. As Michael kept the child occupied, he imagined being a father himself. He could picture himself and Cecelia owning a home together–a small bungalow, perhaps. Nothing too extravagant. But it would be theirs. A place to build a life together.

Skipper, after exhausting himself, conked off on the floor at 9:15. Valentina would be home soon, so Michael had to act fast. He sat down next to Cecelia and gently blew on her eyelids. Cecelia stirred and swatted away an imaginary fly. With a little more pressure, Michael blew on her eyelids a second time.

"Hey you," he whispered.

Without opening her eyes, Cecelia smiled. "What happened? I fell asleep."

"You sure did. It's not the first time. You pulled that the other night when we were listening to the radio in your living room. What is this, anyway? Some kind of defense mechanism?"

She smiled again. She liked when Michael teased her. He could be so charming.

"Open your eyes. I have a little surprise."

Cecelia opened her eyes to see his face close to hers. Michael kissed her, a short, gentle kiss on the lips.

Glancing down playfully, he said, "Which hand?"

She saw both of his hands resting in his lap, his fingers curled together into two tight balls. Cecelia pointed to his left hand.

"Wrong," he said. "But I've got some good news for you. You get a second chance."

"A second chance?"

"Shhh," he whispered, "the baby."

He kissed her again, and then very gently whispered, "Yeah, ya better take it, because life doesn't give us many second chances."

"Okay," she whispered back.

When she pointed to his right hand, he opened it to reveal two shining gold wings.

"They're pins," he said. "Army Air Corps pins. I'm hoping maybe you'll wear them on your clothes from now on."

Using both hands, she picked both pins up. "They're beautiful."

"Well, they're nothing real expensive. Just souvenirs from the PX, but it's all I could afford."

"Oh," she replied.

He continued carefully. "Because, see…I couldn't afford an engagement ring just yet, so I thought these might do for now."

"Are you saying what I think you're saying?"

Sliding off the couch and onto one knee, Michael took both of her hands, cupping the pins in his. With little Skipper asleep not a yard away, Michael looked into Cecelia's brown eyes and said, "Yes. I'm asking you to be my wife. As soon as this damned war is over, I want you to marry me. Please tell me that your answer is yes!"

Cecelia surprised herself when she nodded and said, "Yes, Michael, I'll marry you." She had lived her life too carefully. While others had dove into the cool water of the river in one carefree lunge, she had gingerly walked in, letting herself get wet a little at a time. But she knew that, ultimately, a person needed to immerse herself in the water, and she was now ready to do so.

Michael sat back down and kissed her again, a long, passionate kiss. And then he drew her into his arms and held on tightly. "This is the happiest night of my life," he said. "I promise you I'll buy you a proper ring as soon as I have the money. For now, I hope these wings will serve the purpose. There are two, you see. One represents your love and the other mine. Think of our love as wings flying toward each other, their destiny to merge. Maybe you can wear these, maybe on the collar of a shirt or jacket or on the sleeves of a blouse."

Cecelia's cheeks were now wet with tears. "I won't go out without wearing them. Ever!"

Cecelia knew that she and Michael weren't perfect, that they didn't always agree on everything. She had no delusions that their life together would be trouble-free. As she told him, she had lost any sense of idealism long ago. But she believed in Michael and had faith that they'd be able to work out their differences. *Michael is a man I can count on*, she thought to herself as she pinned the wings on the sleeves of her blouse.

The next morning at 7:00, they waited on the platform at the Derby train station. With no words to express his feelings, Michael held still in the silence. The lovers breathed in the fresh, cool morning air. Michael felt sick inside. He didn't want to leave her, ever.

Hearing the shrill whistle blow from around the bend, the two made eye contact.

"Well, this is it, I guess."

"Yes, but we'll be together soon," she said. "Have faith!"

He struggled to hold back the tears. "I'll try. You'll still write every day?"

"Of course I will. You don't even need to ask that, silly."

Michael smiled. "I know. I've been pinching myself to see if I'm dreaming." He pressed his forehead against hers. "I'm an engaged man. I mean, what are the chances? About one in a thousand?"

"At least," Cecelia whispered back with a giggle.

"And who ever said pipe dreams can't come true, right?"

"Right!" Cecelia hugged him and squeezed tightly.

"I want you to promise me you'll never take those pins off."

"Never."

"Not even in the bathtub?"

Playfully, she beat her fists against his chest as the train pulled into the depot. The lovers' lips joined once more in a kiss they would both recall in the months to come. An eternal kiss.

"All aboard," the conductor called.

Ignoring his pronouncement, Michael's and Cecelia's lips remained connected.

"Hey, soldier," the conductor yelled, "all abo-o-o-a-r-d! You don't wanna miss this train!"

"He's right," Michael whispered at last.

After climbing the small staircase, his duffle bag in tow, he rushed to an empty seat and pressed his palms against the window.

Cecelia walked alongside the passenger car, blowing kisses at her fiancé as it began to pull away. The steam engine picked up speed and he looked at her, his face pressed against the window, until the very last second, until he could only see her in his mind.

36

*J*f daydreaming had been an Olympic sport, Michael would have certainly been a medalist, which is to say he was a deep thinker. It wasn't that he daydreamed at the expense of being a hard worker. Whether it was time to work or to daydream, Michael gave it his all. It was his nature, he knew, to think a thing out, though. And he did some of his deepest thinking on long train rides. Something about the motion and the continuous rumbling of a train as it chugged across the country soothed him and created perfect conditions for deep thinking. Let other guys read newspapers or gab with each other. He was content to sit back, close his eyes, and contemplate life.

On the long trip back to Kansas, Michael's thoughts meandered to the events of recent days. Unbelievably, he was an engaged man. Feelings of elation rose up in him. He had come to feel, long ago, that maybe dreams couldn't come true for people like him. Pipe dreams, he had heard adults call unrealistic hopes. A newfound faith now stuck to his ribs like oatmeal on a winter morning. Then, hadn't he also been accepted into the Cadet Program, and wouldn't he soon be a pilot? Better still, now the girl of his dreams had said yes to his marriage proposal. Maybe, after all, dreams could come true.

Relaxing, with eyes closed, Michael designed and built a unique home where he would spend his life with Cecelia. He imagined having two or three children, maybe boys, maybe girls, or a combination. He didn't care. Michael imagined himself and Cecelia visiting relatives and celebrating holidays and taking care of each other. There was so much to look forward to.

What he wasn't looking forward to was returning to his job in Independence. No sooner did he arrive than his optimism suddenly wavered. First, there was the brutal summer heat, causing his work clothes to stick to his skin and making it hard to even breathe. And he had had enough of maintaining and servicing planes, that was for damned sure. Flying was what he wanted to do, and he had waited long enough. The delay was exasperating. How many months had it been? Three? Four? He was starting to lose track of time.

Even before Stack washed out, Michael had heard the rumors, read the magazine articles, and endured the pep talks that there were a surplus number of cadets; that normal schedules should be disregarded; that they shouldn't feel badly if they washed out; that if the war ended by October, the odds of finishing the program were slim.

But while others had indeed washed out, he was, miraculously, still in the program. If only command would move the damned thing along, maybe he could earn his wings.

On his first day back at work, besides his normal routine of prepping planes, Michael was assigned to a ten-hour shift of KP duty. At the end of an interminable eighteen hour day, he wrote:

> ...That's right. A ten-hour shift! You might think KP duty means peeling potatoes, which it sometimes does, but yesterday it meant mopping floors. My back is broken, AND I'm fed up! When we came into the program, we were told we would one day become officers and gentlemen. And here we are, being treated no better than enlisted men. Even worse...

His discouragement continued as more bad news followed. One of his friends was sent to the guardhouse for failing inspection; another two washed out for conduct unbecoming an officer. It was almost as if those in command were purposely trying to break them.

...You remember how a while back I got restricted for a month?
Well, it's getting worse and worse, darling. They throw the book at us
every chance they get. I think I've made my mind up. Trying to become
an officer might not be worth it...

"I'm starting to worry about Michael," Cecelia explained to Stella who sprinkled flour on the tabletop and began rolling out dough for a batch of fresh pierogies she was making.

"Why? What happened?" Stella asked.

"He's just been so down lately. It's not like him."

"But about what?"

"Oh, I don't know. Things that seem trivial. Like how strict the Army is. As if that's a big surprise. It's the Army, after all."

Stella took a knife and ran it across the flattened dough, dividing it in small rectangles. "Of course! Donald's letters are filled with that kind of stuff."

"Yeah, sure they are. I just don't know what to think. Michael is usually so upbeat. I can't help worrying."

Cecelia's worries were well-founded. Suddenly and without warning, Michael stopped writing. He couldn't bring himself to sit down after a long, soul-crushing day to write a letter. What could he say that wasn't negative? He had now sunk into an abyss of downheartedness that was unlike anything he had ever experienced.

A full week passed without a letter, and Cecelia knew that something was radically wrong. In her letters, she pleaded with him to talk to her, to tell her what had happened. Upon her request, he called her on a Sunday afternoon. After waiting for half the day, the operator told him that the call had, at last, connected. Michael rushed to one of the phone stations lined up against the wall.

"Hello, darling. How is my favorite fiancé?"

"Your favorite fiancé is worried. That's how I am! What in Heaven's name is the deal? Don't I rate letters anymore?"

"No, of course you rate letters, honey. No one rates letters more than you. It's just that, that...listen, honey, I can understand why you're so mad at me, but I've just been so exhausted at the end of every day, and I'm feeling so down that I haven't had the energy to write. The physical or emotional energy. I know it's wrong of me, but–"

"But nothing! We've all been worried sick about you. Even your sisters. Francesca called me and told me that you haven't written to any of them either."

"I haven't even read their letters, honey, or yours. They're all sitting in my locker, unopened. I just can't..." He could feel his voice beginning to break. "I'm sorry. I never felt like this before."

"Don't apologize, Michael. You want to know what I think? I think the best thing to do is to get back to writing. Every day. And not only to me. Get those letters out of your locker and write your sisters some kind of response. Don't worry about the length. Even if your letters are short, write something. Even a half page. Do it in small steps, gradually, but write. It'll take your mind off of your troubles."

"Okay, darling. I'll do what you say. Did I ever tell you I love you? Hearing your voice has lifted my spirits."

Cecelia's advice was the perfect remedy. Each letter answered made him feel a little better. He even attempted to improve his spirits by going to church. For a good long while, he had slept in on Sunday mornings, but now he forced himself to get up, shower, get in uniform and go to the base church. Taking it a step further, at night he started listening to a new radio station.

...Guess what I'm listening to on the radio, darling. Church music. It's a strange thing to be doing, I know. I thought it might be a good idea, but I have to say, I'm beginning to hate the darn stuff. You know why? Because it does something strange to me, like someone is reaching into my body and squeezing my heart. It makes me feel all tied up inside. You know what I think, honey? If I should ever do anything wrong and someone tries to make me own up to it, the best way would be to turn on some organ music so that I couldn't turn it off. It seems to bring out the conscience and the goodness in me...

Otherwise, it was the same old humdrum routine: warming up planes, making minor repairs, washing them and tying them down, pushing his way through the heat of the Kansas summer. Doing his darndest to remain hopeful, he used each and every opportunity to write something positive.

> *...I've been feeling better, honey. I guess the best part of my day is when I get to the airfield in the morning and jump into the cockpits to warm up the planes for the lucky so-and-sos who are one step ahead of me. The wind from the prop blowing against my face energizes me like nothing else does. The throaty roar of the engine of a PT-17 is music to my ears. That's because it's a radial engine, not like those "Mickey Mouse" engines on the Taylor Cubs I flew in Ohio. Those pea shooters are only four cylinders and sound as bad as my old Ford back home. But I have a hunch I'm getting too technical for you, aren't I? That's alright, honey. I still love you anyway!*

When he wasn't writing about how much he loved planes, Michael filled his letters to the brim with his love for Cecelia.

One evening, a lieutenant passed by his bunk and said, "This your girl, DeMarco?"

"You betcha she is, sir," Michael replied.

"Well, if you have a brain in that head of yours, you should marry her."

"That's the plan, sir! That's the plan!"

> *...See that, darling? Even the lieutenant thinks I should marry you. Most of the guys have pin-ups next to their bunks. But your picture gets more attention from the guys than Betty Grable or Rita Hayworth. You're my pin-up, honey! (I hope you don't mind). Please keep telling me you love me, honey. Every time I read that you love me, my heart beats a drum solo on my insides that sounds like: I-love-you-rat-a-tat-tat...I-love-you-rat-a-tat-tat...I-love-you-rat-a-tat-tat. Oh yes, and one more thing. Don't ever stop kissing the envelopes after you seal them. I must have worn the lipstick off of every envelope you've sent...*

With the tedium of his work on the airfield, it was a daily challenge to think of something to write about. Often, he'd ask about Cecelia's family:

...How is your mother's arthritis, honey? Please tell her I was asking for her. And, how is little Skipper? He must be getting big. Don't ever forget, darling, Skipper was the only family member present when I proposed to you. Maybe I should ask him to be my best man. What do you think? Ha-ha-ha-ha! Oh, and I mustn't forget. Please thank Valentina for putting our engagement announcement in The Evening Sentinel. My sister Sofia sent it to me. Seeing the clipping did my heart good. It's official now, honey. The whole world knows...

His excitement about the engagement was curtailed when he learned about a brouhaha between Cecelia and her sister Connie, which concerned him, to say the least.

...Now listen to me, darling. I know how you feel about what happened between you and Connie, but you need to open your heart and forgive her. God only gives us one family, and we need to stay close to our brothers and sisters. She shouldn't have done what she did or said what she said, but please, darling, forgive her...

"What in Christ's name do you mean you looked at my diary?" Cecelia yelled, pulling the diary from Connie's hands with such force that it fell to the floor. "How could you do that? How could you?"

"I mean, you left it unlocked and open on Papa's old desk, and curiosity got the better of me. If you don't want anyone looking, then don't leave it open where anyone can see it. You're lucky Mama didn't see it."

Kneeling to pick up the volume, she said, "Go to hell! You know as well as I do that Mama can't read English."

"But what if she could? Then what?" her sister replied.

"But she *can't!*" Cecelia said, her eyes now burning with tears as her acrimony surged.

"You just better be careful. That's my advice!"

"Careful about what?"

"Careful about a lot of things, not the least of which is what you do in the backseat of a car with a certain Michael DeMarco!"

Embracing the diary, Cecelia shook her head in disbelief. "Goddammit! That was private and it's no one's business but ours."

"Then don't go writing about it and leaving your diary where anyone can see it. You want to know what I think?"

"What?"

"I think you wanted to be found out!"

"I can't believe my ears! I can't even believe you're saying these things!"

"And I can't believe you're not worried about getting pregnant!"

"But we didn't go that far!"

"Not this time, but what about next time...or the next? It's a matter of time. And besides, if you ultimately give in, and you probably will, I hope you know how Italian men are!"

"Just...just get out of my room!"

"Mama's room, you mean. How ironic, trying to act so grown up but still sleeping with your mother!"

"GET OUT! RIGHT NOW! Do you hear me? And don't ever speak to me again!"

...I'm glad to hear that you and Connie finally made up, honey. I was worried sick about it because, after all, I'm the major reason for the fight, aren't I? But let me say this, Cecelia. What we did that night had to do with my last night home on furlough and how much we love each other. And let's not forget that we're engaged now. People who love each other need a physical way of expressing that love, so please don't feel guilty. You've committed no sin, unless being in love is a sin, and I think you'll agree with me that it is not...

At long last, Michael had some good news about himself to share. He had written to Cecelia that so many guys had now washed out of the Cadet Program that the original twelve on his crew had been reduced to six. It was a Friday afternoon when these six were ordered to meet with the commanding officer right before dinner.

"I guess it's over for us," one of the boys, Mouse, bemoaned. Michael was mystified where he got that nickname since he stood well over six feet.

"Yup," Russo replied. "I guess we can kiss it all goodbye, just like the others."

Michael remained silent. Maybe he was living in denial, but he didn't want to give in to what might be the truth.

After they cleaned up, the six trudged over to the C.O.'s office. When they walked in, his assistant said, "Right on time! Go right in, boys. Major Donovan is waiting for you."

Michael led the way, followed by the crew. The six stood at attention and saluted.

Donovan, busy with some paperwork, looked up. "At ease, boys. I asked to meet with you because I have some news."

The six men looked at the major, their eyes swimming in a sea of apprehension.

"You don't need to look so damned glum, boys. It's good news. You can start packing your gear. Sunday morning, the six of you are out of here."

Puzzled, the crew gave each other side-eye glances.

"You boys are among the lucky ones. You're moving on to the next phase of your flight training, which I have no doubt you're happy to hear. You'll be on a train to San Antonio first thing Sunday morning. Congratulations!"

Besides the fact that their faces relaxed and they smiled, the six men maintained their composure until they exited the C.O.'s office. Once under the Kansas sky, they threw their hats high in the air, and in unabashed celebration, hooted and hollered and pushed each other. Michael jumped onto Mouse's back and went for a ride across the main road of the base. Russo, Denny, Dutch, and Weber trotted alongside the horse and rider, clapping and yahoo-ing with every ounce of energy they had.

...Darling, I finally have some good news to tell you. Today, the C.O. called our crew into his office, and you're not going to believe what he told us. I can't believe it myself...

37

*C*ecelia understood that Michael was a man, and a man has ambitions and hopes and dreams. Those were qualities she loved about him. He also had a lust for adventure. Piloting a plane at high speeds thousands of feet up in the air excited him beyond her comprehension. Add to that, Michael would be flying a plane in combat situations.

But where did that leave her? Here she was, newly engaged, ready to make the big commitment at last, and now she had to worry about whether her fiancé would return when the war ended. It was enough to make a girl's head spin.

Obviously, she wasn't alone in this worry. Both Stella and Valentina were in the same boat. Their men were fighting on the front in Europe, and Connie had recently met and begun dating a sailor named Pete who was now on a destroyer in the Pacific. A friend of Pete's who knew somebody who knew somebody else who worked with Connie told him about her. Pete just showed up at the gate outside the Sponge Rubber plant, managed to figure out who she was, and introduced himself. Connie's new beau was one of the ship's cooks. Pete cast his line and Connie bit. *Even level-headed Connie,* Cecelia thought to herself.

Cecelia realized a woman's role in the drama of war was to worry about her soldier but not to let him know it. Instead, Cecelia would do her darndest to raise Michael's morale and keep his spirits high while hoping to keep her own head above water at the same time.

On a stifling hot Wednesday morning, as the workers on the floor dragged themselves to their stations, Agent Reynolds and his two assistants burst through the double doors, and with great purpose, traveled the length of the floor. Everyone's eyes followed the trio as they stopped at the station of one of their co-workers. To Cecelia's surprise, it was Barbara, the odd, taciturn woman whom she and Vincent had seen sitting at the bar at Shea's Riviera.

Abruptly, the younger agents grabbed Barbara's fragile, bony arms, perhaps more roughly than they needed to, and locked her wrists in handcuffs. Barbara's black eyes registered panic, and she let out a sharp cry like a wild animal caught in a trap, its eerie sound reverberating across the cavernous factory space.

As they dragged Barbara across the floor toward the double doors, Cecelia felt she had never seen starker despondency written across a person's face.

A step behind his men, Agent Reynolds, his tie loosened and his forehead perspiring, reached the exit and then turned to the employees. "As you have no doubt gathered, the culprit has been apprehended, and after almost three months, our work is done. I thank you for your cooperation in this matter, important not only for you but for the United States of America and, of course, the war effort. Other than that, I can't tell you anything more about the case as it is top secret. Thank you again for your assistance."

As he turned to walk out the door, an uncontrollable urge seized Cecelia's body, mind, and heart, and she ran to the exit doors.

"Agent Reynolds," she called.

Reynolds turned. "Yes, Miss Alberino. What is it?"

"It's just...there's...I assume that...that this means you won't be following my friend and me anymore."

"Mr. Demski?"

His question galled Cecelia. He knew exactly whom she meant.

Still, she persevered. "Yes, Vincent. You were wrong about him," she heard herself say, and she could feel tears in the corners of both eyes.

With a sardonic smirk, Reynolds replied, "I don't know if I was wrong about him, Miss Alberino, but let's just say he's innocent of this particular crime. He's been notified."

The morning continued with each worker busy at her machine, feeling a mixture of relief and confusion. When the clock struck 10:30, they stopped for their first break of the day. Gathered in clusters, the workers gossiped, "I always thought she was strange"... "Never said a word to anybody"..."Why would she do it?"..."I heard her brother was killed in France last winter"..."Never got married"..."What do you suppose'll happen to her now?"..."They'll lock her up and throw away the key"..."It'll serve her right"...

As Cecelia puffed on her cigarette, the gossip was nothing more than an amorphous hum in the outer recesses of her consciousness. Focused on Vincent, she couldn't wait until the end of the workday to see him.

When she arrived home from work, she ran over to Stella's and called Vincent. He agreed to pick her up after she ate dinner.

They decided to take a long drive along the river, cross over the Stevenson Dam, and continue into Newtown. The trip would give them complete privacy and time to talk.

With somber eyes fixed on the faded white line in the middle of the road as dusk segued to nightfall, he listened to her entire account of the events of the morning.

"You don't seem very happy about it," Cecelia complained. "I thought you'd be thrilled. What's the matter?"

Finally, he let out a deep sigh. "No, I suppose I'm happy that I'm not under house arrest anymore and that they're not going to be spying on me. It's just that..."

"Just that what?"

In the semi-darkness of his car, Cecelia spotted a tear from Vincent's right eye trickle down his cheek.

"It's just that I feel like I'll never be left in peace."

"But...but why not? It's over now," she tried to explain.

"Look, you're great, but even you don't get it. It'll never be over for me. I'll never be able to escape the Section 8. I'll never be able to be who I truly am, who I want to be. Not here. Not now."

Cecelia felt lost. She chose silence as the drive continued. Once or twice, she saw Vincent wipe a tear from his cheek with the starched cuff of his shirt. There were things she couldn't fix. The best she could do was to let him know she was in his corner no matter what.

When they arrived back at Cecelia's house, it was almost 10:00. The windows of his Plymouth were rolled down, and the two friends sat in silence, listening to the crickets in the tall grass sing a melancholy song.

Finally, Vincent spoke. "I'm sorry. I don't mean to be so negative and sad. You shouldn't need to hear about my problems. I just–"

"Please don't apologize. Please! I just wish there was a way to help. To make you feel like you fit into this crazy world."

"I'm not sure I want to."

"I understand what you mean. Sometimes, I feel the same way. Well, it's late, and tomorrow's another workday, so I better go in."

"Yeah, listen, just…just thanks for listening and for trying to understand."

When she got into the house, Cecelia began writing a letter to Michael. It was with a sort of involuntary self-righteousness that she told Michael about the day and the fact that Vincent was absolved of the crime. She wanted Michael to know. She wanted the world to know. If Cecelia could have, she would have broadcast it from the crown of the Statue of Liberty.

What she didn't tell Michael about was her late night drive with Vincent and about how down in the dumps Vincent felt because of his station in life. She would have liked to share, but she could find no words to explain the emotion she had heard in Vincent's voice and seen in his face.

A day later, as Valentina stood at the counter of Aconfora's Market on Minerva Street, waiting for the butcher to filet several pieces of chicken breast for her, she was approached by a stranger.

"You're one of the Alberino sisters, ain't ya?"

Valentina turned to see a girl with flaming red hair. Her heavily made-up face masked otherwise unremarkable features.

"Torello," Valentina replied. "I'm married now. Do we know each other?"

"Well, you don't know me, but I know you. And I know your sister. Or at least I know who she is."

Valentina felt an immediate dislike for the redhead.

"I've got four sisters," Valentina replied curtly and without making eye contact.

"I'm talkin' about your kid sister. What's her name? Cecelia?"

Valentina also never liked people who asked a question and then answered it themselves.

"And how do you know Cecelia?"

"Well, I don't exactly *know* Cecelia, but all I'm sayin' is I know her boyfriend, Michael. He lives a few houses down from me over on Smith Street."

"That's nice," Valentina said impatiently.

"Yeah. I even read in the paper that they're engaged now."

"That's right. What's it to you?"

Feigning sadness, the redhead said, "I just feel sorry for her, that's all I'm sayin'."

Though she wished there was a dial, like on the radio at home, she could just switch off, Valentina knew she had to see the scene through to its conclusion.

"I can't imagine why you or anyone would feel sorry for Cecelia. She's got it all."

"Yeah, that's my point, honey. She's got it all, uhm, except for a faithful fiancé."

Valentina couldn't recall ever being more irritated. "And what's that supposed to mean?"

"What it's supposed to mean is that while Michael was home, he and I had a little fling."

The butcher interrupted, "Your chicken filets, Valentina."

As he handed the fat, brown package tied up in twine to Valentina, the redhead persevered. "Look, all I'm sayin' is–"

"Listen you," Valentina almost shouted. "Lemme just tell you something." Then, lowering her voice, "All *I'm* sayin' is I'm going to have to tell my sister about this, and if her heart gets broken over this, and especially if you're lying, which I'm betting you are, I'll find you and you'll be sorry you ever met me. Do you understand?"

"Geez, you don't have to get all huffy. I'm just tryin' to help a nice kid avoid makin' a big mistake."

Valentina smirked. "Yeah, sure you are!"

Cecelia was more than a little alarmed when Valentina shared the news. She certainly wasn't going to remain engaged to a man who would cheat on her, but she had major doubts that the girl's story was true.

The next time she got together with Vincent, she shared the episode with him. More and more, Cecelia had been finding that Vincent brought a fresh perspective to matters that bothered her. Despite what he might have felt about himself or his station in life, Vincent was still a man.

When the two met at Moscardini's, Cecelia unleashed the whole story.

"Have you written to Michael about what she said?"

"Well, no, not yet. I don't want to wrongly accuse him," Cecelia answered and then sipped her vanilla soda through a straw.

"It's not an accusation," he said, "it's just sharing what the girl told Valentina."

"I suppose."

"Do you think she was telling the truth?"

"No, I think she's a liar. That's what. Michael spent just about every waking minute with me when he was home. When would he have fit her in? Besides, he's never given me any reason to believe that he would ever be unfaithful."

"That a girl! Then you've got to give the guy a chance to defend himself."

Vincent's logic put her at ease. She would write to Michael about it that very night.

Cecelia didn't see him, but Tony Vitti walked in the door and spotted her. Vincent, seeing that the stranger was approaching them, motioned with his eyes to Cecelia, who turned and saw her old workmate, now in uniform.

"Tony," she said, "you're in the military?"

"That's right," Tony said, "I joined up. They gave me a leave before they send me overseas...but who the hell is this jamoke?"

"Listen, Tony, I'm sorry, but I'm kind of busy right now and–"

"Busy, huh?" Tony interrupted. "I heard you were engaged to some guy in the Army. What's goin' on here? While the cat's away, the mouse'll play, huh?"

Cecelia closed her eyes and shook her head. Unexpectedly, she heard Vincent's voice.

"Maybe you didn't hear the lady, pal, but she said she'd like to be left alone."

"I ain't your pal, and what are you goin' to do about it anyway?" Tony challenged.

"You're right," Vincent replied, raising his volume to just the right level and rising to his feet. "You aren't my pal!"

As Cecelia looked up at the two boys, she could see that Vincent stood a half head taller than Tony.

"Now if you want," Vincent continued confidently, "we can settle this matter outside."

Sizing up Vincent, Tony smirked and walked away.

When he sat down, Cecelia smiled at him. "Well, chivalry is not dead! I wasn't expecting that."

"Expecting what?"

"I wasn't expecting you to be my champion with that imbecile."

Vincent squinted at her, not quite understanding. "And why not?"

"Well, it's because you're…well–"

With an incredulous look, Vincent interrupted. "Gosh. That's what I was talking about. Even you judge me."

"What? No, I don't judge you–"

"But you do. Don't you see it?"

Cecelia was at a loss for words.

"You realize, I hope, that I'm no different from anyone else, that I was ready, willing, and able to fight the enemy overseas before they bounced me out. I passed all the training with flying colors."

Cecelia felt ashamed. "I'm sorry. You're right. It was wrong of me to think that you're less of a man than Michael or anyone else."

"Apology accepted. But now I have some news for you."

"News?"

"Well, you might not feel it's very good news, but it's something I've been thinking about for weeks."

"Well, what is it?"

"I'm moving to New York."

Stunned, Cecelia gathered herself. "But why would you do that? What's in New York?"

"I need to get away from the small-mindedness of the Valley. I'll always be judged here. New York is a place with millions of people.

Its vastness provides me with a place where I can lose myself if I want, or it's somewhere where I can find lots of other guys like me. Lots!"

"But where will you live? What kind of job will you have there?"

Vincent smiled. "There are answers to those questions. I've already worked the details out. I hope you don't mind, but they're kind of personal."

"But...but what am I going to do without you?"

Vincent took Cecelia's hand in his. "You'll be fine. No one's ever going to pull one over on you. Heck, I've seen you in action. Besides, my mother and father are still here in the Valley, so I'll be visiting. It's not like New York is on another planet."

As Cecelia watched Vincent drive away, she felt like a chapter of her life had come to an end. The thought of Vincent moving to New York saddened her. Sure, like he said, he'd visit when he was home, but somehow she was left with a pervasive sense of uncertainty. She had grown fond of their get-togethers and their close friendship, even dependent on it. Vincent was different from any friend she had ever known, male or female, and she would miss him. Even though they had known each other for only a short time, she knew they had been part of each other's stories, and his departure would leave a void in her life.

38

Michael – 1934

*T*he three boys gallop along, taking the stone steps from one terrace to another two and three at a time. They breeze by the cherry tree and the first vegetable garden, past the chicken coop and the tomato vines, and up to the level where the golden corn stalks grow.

When they arrive at the toolshed, Michael says, "You wait here," and pushes through the old wooden door, kicking up dust from the floor as it creaks open. His father's rifle appears to be missing. *Where could it be?* he wonders. *It's always there in the corner.*

Frowning, Michael frantically ransacks the tumbledown shack, knocking over dirt-encrusted shovels, pitchforks, and hoes in his quest to find the rifle. Pulling rustic wooden drawers open under the tool counter, he is no longer certain what he's looking for.

When he reaches the bottom right drawer, he is surprised to see an old handgun laying there, something he's never noticed. He takes a moment to figure out how to open the chamber and, seeing that it's empty, he tucks the black pistol into the waist of his dungarees. Michael now searches the cluttered drawers for bullets, pulling one and then another open, in frustration, and then slamming it shut. Finally, he finds a few different caliber sizes and stuffs them into his front right pocket. He needs to hurry in case someone happens along.

Flying out the door, he orders, "Let's move it! Hurry!"

Scooter and Arnie follow close behind as he heads for the top level and races up the dirt road, past the little pond until he reaches the woods and all the way to the top of DeMarco Mountain. Once hidden between the trees and the mammoth rock formations, Michael stops and waits for the two laggers to catch up.

Huffing and puffing, Scooter says, "Where's the rifle, Mikey? How ya gonna shoot animals widout a rifle?"

Michael flashes a satisfied smile and reaches into his belt, displaying the black pistol.

"Holy Jesus," Arnie says, "where'd ya get that?"

"Don't worry where I got it. I found it, that's all. This thing'll kill a rabbit or a squirrel just as good as any rifle."

The two boys laugh gleefully. "I guess it will," says Scooter. "I know yer a good shot wid a rifle, but can you hit your target with that thing?"

"What's the difference?" Michael says. "A gun's a gun."

Michael drops to the ground on his backside, reaches into his pocket, and pulls out the handful of bullets.

"Some of these better fit," he says.

As he studies them, he sees that there seem to be three or four different sizes.

He holds one up, showing the boys. "This one's too small, dammit."

Picking up another, he scoffs, "This one won't fit, neither. Both of them guys'll fall right down into the chamber. Shit!"

"How about the other ones?" Arnie asks, fingering a few of the bullets.

"Keep your paws off," Michael orders. "Let me see. Hmmm, yeah, these look more right."

As he attempts to insert one into a hole in the cylinder, Michael tightens his lips.

"Hmmmph! It almost fits. All but the top part."

He pushes his thumb down hard on the top rim of the bullet, putting pressure on it with all of his hand strength.

"*Al-most,*" he repeats.

"If it don't fit, we'll hafta do somethin' else," Scooter remarks. "Maybe make a coupla slingshots."

"We ain't makin' slingshots, Scooter! I'll make it fit. It just needs a little persuadin'. Find a small rock, no bigger than your fist."

Scooter and Arnie scurry about, searching for the right size.

"I got it," Arnie calls, running back to Michael. "Here, Mikey."

"Alright, perfect. I'm just gonna tap it a little. Lightly. That'll do it."

With the bullet three-quarters of the way in, he holds the chamber in his left hand, his index finger on the bottom and his thumb on the top. With his right hand, he begins to tap the top rim of the bullet. *Tap-tap-tap. Tap-tap-tap.*

"Dammit! It's *gotta* go in."

His tapping takes on a bit more force, and suddenly the three boys hear the explosion. The pistol, as if having a mind of its own, jumps out of Michael's hands.

"What the hell happened?" Scooter screeches, staring in amazement at a gray cloud of smoke that now hovers over the three boys.

Michael topples over onto his side, clutching his left hand with his right. He closes his eyes tightly and rolls over once in pain.

"Shit! Oh my God–shit! Oh! God! I think I shot myself!"

"Lemme see," Arnie says, pulling Michael's right hand aside. "Oh, shit! Shit! You did! Your hand is bleedin'. And wait, lemme look better. I think the bullet's in yer finger!"

Michael's eyes open wide at hearing this news; everything looks blurry. "Fellas, help me. I can't see too good. I think I'm gonna...I feel like...I'm gonna–"

Arnie strips his t-shirt off and wraps it around Michael's hand. "Oh shit! I think he passed out."

Scooter cries, "We are so screwed!"

"C'mon, Scooter," Arnie orders, "we gotta get 'em the hell outta here. You get 'em by one arm. I'll get the other."

The two boys lift Michael up and run with him in their grasp. Racing down the hill, the weight of Michael between them, they have trouble staying on the narrow path. The dense woods now a blur, Scooter and Arnie run to either side of a towering white birch, forgetting that Michael is between them. As Michael's eyes open in two small slits, the boys crash him into an impenetrable birch. The boys lose their grip as Michael collapses at the base of the tree.

Scooter, in a panic, cries, "What the hell's a matter with you, Arnie? Ya tryin' ta kill the kid?"

"Fuck you, Scooter! Yer the one who ran to the wrong side of the tree!"

"I did not!"

"Did too, ya fuckin' moron!"

"Screw you, Arnie. Just pick 'im up again, and let's get movin'!"

Out of the woods and down the dirt road past the pond, they make their way back to the old shed and set Michael on the plank floorboards.

"Mikey!" Arnie shouts. "Can ya hear me, Mikey?"

Michael mumbles, "Yeah...yeah...I can hear, can hear..."

"I'm gonna go look for your mother," Arnie says.

The sound of the word rouses Michael. "No, na-no, na-no!" Michael is groggy, his speech listless and slurred. "She'll kill me. I just got a bullet in my finger. Mom'll put a bullet in my-my-my *head*. Ya can't tell her!"

"What do we do then?" Scooter asks.

Wincing in pain, Michael says. "Okay, here's what. Scooter, you stay with me, ya hear? An' Arnie, run down to the back door of the house." Michael is breathing heavily. "Knock. If...if nobody's home, go in the kitchen and call my sister Lucia. Tell 'er what happened. She'll know what to do. If somebody's home, tell 'em that you were just looking for me, but then go to...to your house and call her."

"But..."

"I can' talk no more, man! Jus' do like I tol' ya."

When Arnie knocks at the door and no one answers, he sneaks inside and calls Lucia as instructed. Lucia turns off the burner of the meat sauce and rushes over to help Michael. *It's a good thing Buzz is asleep*, she thinks.

When she arrives, Lucia examines and cleans Michael's wounded finger, takes a plump green aloe vera leaf and squeezes out a large dab of gel, covering most of Michael's index finger, and then she wraps it in gauze.

"You boys go home now," she says. "I gotta take Michael to the doctor."

On the way downtown, Lucia instructs Michael, "It was the best thing that you didn't tell Mama. That wouldn't a' been no good. Now here's what you're gonna do. I'll drop you at Dr. Federico's office, and you go in, tell him that I dropped you off, and show him that finger."

"Aren't you coming in with me?" Michael asks.

"No, I can't. I gotta get home and finish dinner before Buzz wakes up. You just tell the doctor to call me if he has any questions."

"So what do I do after I'm finished at the doctor?"

"Jus' walk home. Tell Mama you hit your finger with a hammer or somethin' and that I came over and bandaged it. Don't tell her what really happened. We don't want no trouble."

Lucia lets Michael out in front of the doctor's office on upper Elizabeth Street near the library.

Feeling alone and confused, Michael sits on the steps of the old Victorian house. He feels that Dr. Federico will almost certainly call his mother. He plays out one scenario after another, envisioning his mother screaming at him, shaking him, hitting him. After angsting for an hour, Michael decides not to see the doctor. Dejectedly, he picks himself up and heads home, the throbbing pain in his finger shooting up into the top of his hand and his wrist.

Upon arriving home, he calls Lucia and tells her he has chickened out.

"But the pain is killing me. What do I do now?"

"You gotta take care of that thing. After you eat dinner, fill a basin with warm water and sprinkle a couple of handfuls of Epsom salts in it. They're in the bathroom closet. Then lock your bedroom door and soak it. Epsom salts will relieve some of the pain. Keep doing that every day now, as much as you need to."

At dinner, when Mama sees his wrapped up finger, she asks about it. "Michael, cos'è successo al tuo dito?"

"Oh, my finger? It's nothin', Mom. I just hit it with a hammer."

"Chi ha messo la benda?"

"Oh, nobody was home. I called Lucia, and she wrapped it up."

"Okay...va bene."

Good for who? Michael thinks. The Epsom salts help a little, but his finger still throbs when he tries to sleep. Over the course of the next few weeks, Lucia visits and continues to apply aloe vera and other home remedies, treating the wound and keeping it wrapped cleanly. It is more than a month before the wound closes up, but the bullet remains lodged in Michael's finger for good.

At first, when people ask why he has a pronounced bump in his index finger, he shrugs and says, "Hmmm...I don't really know." But Scooter and Arnie know. And Lucia knows. And, most of all, Michael knows.

$\mathcal{U}$pon shipping out at 2200 hours, the six men were miffed when they found that they'd be traveling from Independence to San Antonio in a boxcar with nothing but army cots to sit or recline on.

"This is what it means to be an officer and a gentleman," Weber scoffed.

Mouse answered, "Wow! This is going to be the dirtiest train ride any of us has ever been on. Can you fuckin' believe this shit?"

Michael fought to keep his composure. He realized that compared to the conditions of war, riding in a boxcar wasn't the biggest inconvenience they would ever suffer.

It was impossible to get any sleep as the train jostled along the tracks, their unsteady bunks sliding or shaking with each bump and bounce.

When they arrived a grueling ten hours later at the Sunset Station in San Antonio, the glaring Texas sun gleamed off the edifice's Spanish architecture. As the six hoisted their duffle bags onto the olive drab army truck awaiting them, the driver informed them they'd have to wait for a few more hours before heading to the base because other cadets were still to arrive.

While his companions groaned and vented, Michael caught a few winks in the station. He had suffered plenty of discomfort already; he could endure the hard oak surface of the depot bench. He'd just close his eyes and dream of Cecelia.

At noon, when the six cadets walked onto Kelly Field in San Antonio, dusty and wrinkled, they felt newly galvanized, like a half dozen gleaming AT-6s hot off the assembly line. Each one jumped off the truck and strutted onto the hot asphalt pavement, tired and dirty, but with the bravado of a hired gun in the Old West.

After being assigned to a barracks and moving their gear in, the group slept soundly and woke refreshed and renewed. Joined by a couple of dozen other cadets from around the country, Michael and his pals from Independence listened to an orientation by one of the lieutenants.

"I know you hot shots are salivating to get up in the air, but for the first few weeks, you'll be in a classroom, reviewing the ins and outs of navigation, weather, radio, instruments, aircraft identification, and military tactics and science. Some of the stuff you studied in ground school. I know y'all got a few hours up in Taylor Cubs awhile back, learning some basic this and that, some razzle dazzle, but you'll be flying much bigger ships now, as you know, like PT-17 Stearmans and AT-6s. You boys have worked on these babies, taking them apart and putting them back together. With the Stearmans, we'll be working on maneuvers that will prepare you for dogfights in the air against the Japs or Jerries; then when you move onto the more advanced stage of training in AT-6s, we'll be looking at higher speeds and more sophisticated aerobatics, but let's not get too far ahead of ourselves. The point is that y'all need to realize that ya still got a lot to learn, and right at the moment, that learning begins in the classroom."

After going through the better part of the week waiting for Cecelia's letters to be rerouted from Independence to San Antonio, Michael struck pay-dirt when on a Saturday morning he received six.

Michael spent his first day reading and re-reading the treasure trove of letters and then responding. One letter in particular was packed with dynamite. In her perfect script, Cecelia not only gave an account of the flying suit arrest but also told him about her older sister's encounter with a red-headed girl at the market. Michael studied her words, spent several hours contemplating how to reply, and then candidly told her what he felt she needed to know.

...I'm glad the feds solved that one, honey. That's a pretty serious offense, and I hope they throw the book at that woman. Here's something to consider. How would you have felt if I was wearing one of those flight suits? Not very good, I'm sure. Also, I'm happy to hear it wasn't your friend. I'm going to be straight with you and confess that I don't understand guys like him, so I guess I was suspicious. But I was wrong, and you were right. I guess you're just about always right, aren't you? I apologize for any skepticism I may have shown. I mean that. If you think well of him, darling, he must be a pretty good Joe...

The redhead was a different matter completely. Her slanderous accusation got his dander up:

...Listen, honey. I know exactly who the girl is that spoke to your sister Val. Her name is Ellen, but we kids in the neighborhood always called her "Red" growing up. Maybe she didn't like the nickname, so she's spreading rumors about me. I have no idea, but as far as I'm concerned, she can burn in hell for it. That may sound harsh, honey, but it's how I feel. I have never cheated on you, darling, and I never will. Besides, you know I was with you every possible minute. The only time we weren't together was when you were working or when we were sleeping. I promise you that, even in those few hours we were apart, I never went anywhere near Red or any other girl. If we're going to get married, you and I have to trust each other, honey, now and always. If it wasn't my plan to be faithful to you, do you suppose I would have proposed? Of course not...

A day later, he realized he wasn't done with the subjects of marriage and fidelity:

...A few weddings that I've been to in the Army did something to me. They were weddings where you could hear everything the priest was saying. The words a priest uses at a wedding are more than words.

They seem to me like a red hot brand that burns its way into a person's heart. They are words that mean something, darling, especially: "To love and to cherish, for better or for worse, till death do us part." For me, these words sound like a prayer. I plan to speak these words to you someday, Cecelia, and if you're able to look inside of me at the time, you'll be able to read them as they are branded on my heart to last for the rest of our lives together.

When Cecelia responded that she believed him and loved him with all of her heart, Michael felt a great sense of peace deep within.

...You know, hon, I think we're going to be alright, you and I. I have this gut feeling that we were made for each other. Meeting each other was no coincidence. I used to question, when I was a kid, the difference between infatuation and true love. But now I understand. True love makes a man want to do anything for a woman and a woman for a man...

Dying to get up in the air, Michael toughed out the two weeks of classroom training. He felt justified for his impatience. Who could blame a guy? His maintenance duties had dragged on interminably, and flying planes was where his heart was. It was, in fact, who he was.

...Guess what, darling. Tomorrow our classroom work ends and we finally take to the sky. Our last class this week was a refresher on Morse Code. Of course, it's something we learned a long time ago. We have to be real experts in case it's ever the only way to communicate with our squadrons, but I've got to tell you, we've all become "dit happy." That's what we call it, listening to "dit-dit-day-day-dit-day" for hours and hours. Listen, honey, next time I'm home, I'll teach you the Morse Code alphabet and we can write to each other in code, things like "I love you" and "Kiss me" and other secrets just using a series of dots and dashes. You could even use the code in your diary for your most private thoughts. That way, if Connie snoops inside it, she won't know what our biggest secrets are!

Michael lay on his bunk, staring at the ceiling. He'd been in San Antonio for almost a month, and it was another good morning. What else would it be? Any day that he was scheduled to fly was a good one. When the bugler blew Reveille, Michael had already played out ten times over what his day in the air would be like. After getting dressed, gobbling down his breakfast, and cleaning up the barracks, he headed to the airfield for his 8:00 a.m. training meeting. He liked San Antonio. He had already visited the Alamo, the little mission church where heroes like Davy Crockett, Jim Bowie, and William Travis had fought bravely and died. San Antonio, for Michael, held the treasured history of yesterday and the hopeful promise of tomorrow.

Certainly, when he was up in the air, he felt a kind of promise he had never before experienced. He now felt certain that flying was his life, and he was good at it. No one knew that better than Michael himself, and while his training officers didn't go around throwing bouquets at the cadets, a simple look from one of them said, "DeMarco, you've got all the right instincts!"

He had certainly learned his lessons well. In his mind, like grooves in a record, he played acronyms like TMPFF for "trim, mixture, propeller, fuel, and flaps" before takeoff and UMPFF for "undercarriage, mixture, propeller, fuel, and flaps" before landing. They had become his mantras.

Altogether, he'd need to log two hundred hours in the air before he earned his wings and was ready for combat. Even though at this point, he had tallied a little more than three dozen hours, he knew he was on his way.

Every hour in the air was another day in paradise. The weather and atmospheric conditions were optimal, and he'd be going up with a favorite instructor, Captain Emil Griffith, who had returned from a tour of duty in Europe where he flew a P51 Mustang while serving with the 2nd Air Division's 65th Fighter Wing. Griffith himself had earned a Medal of Honor fighting in the air against the Luftwaffe.

Michael couldn't have admired a man more than Griffith with his square jaw, his yellow hair and eyebrows, his handsome weather-beaten face, and his perpetual stoicism. He was what an officer could be, what an officer should be.

Michael had already graduated to flying an AT-6. Once up in the air, Griffith directed Michael through maneuvers they had been working on, rolls and loops and inversions, all of which Michael had mastered, even at this early stage of the game. When Michael executed each one perfectly, it came as no surprise to Captain Griffith.

"Okay, Corporal, let's move on to a little cross-country navigation now."

As Michael increased the ship's altitude, he enjoyed the climb.

After a half hour or so, Griffith, who liked Michael's confidence, grinned and spoke again. "Okay, hotshot, how about we try somethin' a little different today? You with me, Corporal?"

"Roger, sir." Michael was stoked. He could feel the electric current flow between his trainer and himself and he loved a new challenge.

"We're gonna do a little 'engine out' drill this mornin'. Here's how it works. Right here and now, I'm gonna pull the throttle. The deal is, your engine has failed. In fact, right at this very moment, ya got no engine, so what are ya gonna do, Corporal?"

Michael could feel his heart race, but it was nothing he couldn't handle or control. He knew the engine hadn't really failed, but it was a simulation of a failed engine. "I'm going to find a place to land, sir, while establishing the best glide speed."

"Bingo! So, let's consider your glide ratio. What is it?"

"Yes, Captain, this craft has an 8:1 ratio."

"So that means what for you?"

"That means for every eight miles I glide, sir, I lose one mile of altitude."

"Very good. What else it means is, 'there's no time like the present.' Ya better start lookin' for a good place to land this baby, and I mean quick."

Michael concentrated as the craft gradually lost altitude. At four thousand feet, he spotted an open field on the outskirts of a sprawling Texas farm.

"Looks like I've spotted a suitable landing space, Captain."

"I'd say so," Griffith agreed.

Michael examined his altimeter as he circled the plane around his target area while continuing to lose altitude. At two thousand feet, at fifteen hundred, and even at a thousand feet, it looked good. But at five hundred feet, Michael was now low enough to see that the field was fraught with furrows, rocks, and boulders. It was a terrible place to land, as it turned out. Griffith, of course, knew it as well.

With precious little time left, Griffith commanded, "Okay, Corporal, this isn't a place to bring her down. Just give it throttle and let's get the hell outta here."

Michael's eyes were fixed on the altimeter, showing he was two hundred feet from the ground. Preoccupied with having zeroed in on a bad place to land, he was disappointed in himself. In the outer recesses of his mind, though, he had heard the Captain's order. Michael advanced the throttle too quickly while pulling the nose of the plane up too much, causing the engine to abruptly quit. What had been no more than a routine operation had morphed into a major emergency.

Griffith knew it, and yelled, "My plane! You stalled the craft!"

Michael knew the command "my plane" meant the instructor was taking over. And he also knew he had bungled the operation.

As Griffith attempted to find the least treacherous area to land, he called out once again, "Brace yourself, we're about to hit the ground hard!"

With force, Michael pressed his palms against the dashboard as the craft pancaked to a jarring stop.

"Are you alright, DeMarco?"

Stunned, Michael cried out in harrowing pain, "No, sir. I think I may have broken my, my...arms." He winced again, moaning a throaty, "I'm injured, sir."

"I'll radio for an ambulance team, soldier," Griffith said. "Sit tight."

Hours later, Michael lay in a hospital bed, plaster casts hardening on both arms after an emergency surgery to reset the bones in his left wrist. Defeated and despondent, he saw that the hands on the round wall clock read 9:57 p.m. He hadn't yet written to Cecelia, and he had promised that he would never miss writing to her again. But how would he tell her this?

A nurse came into the room. "Hello, Corporal DeMarco, I'm Nurse Jennings. Can I get you anything?"

"No, ma'am," Michael replied. "I guess I'm all set."

"Don't look so glum, soldier. Accidents happen. And besides, this might keep you out of the war if it ends soon enough."

Michael struggled to fight back the tears. "I wasn't trying to get out of the war, ma'am, if it's all the same to you."

"I understand, soldier. Well, if there's anything at all I can do, you just let me know."

"Well, ma'am, now that I'm thinking of it, maybe you'd do me a little favor."

"You bet. Just name it, handsome."

"You see, I write to my girl back home every night. I never miss. But my hands and arms aren't in any shape to write tonight, obviously. Do you think you'd be my hands tonight if I dictate a letter to you?"

Nurse Jennings smiled warmly. "I'd be more than happy to do that. Let me get some paper and a pen."

When she returned moments later, Michael had a confession to make. "Ma'am, I have to tell you something. I hope this won't change your mind about writing this letter for me, but I feel I need to tell a little fib in it."

"Oh?"

"Yes, ma'am. You see, I can't tell my sweetheart the truth about today. It's just, I've built myself up to her, and...it's just that I've never felt more embarrassed in my life."

"You have nothing to be embarrassed about," Nurse Jennings replied. "I've been working in this hospital for a good long while now, and we've had a lot of guys come in for treatment after flying mistakes. It happens."

"Understood, ma'am, but...but, I just can't tell her right now. I promise I'll tell her the truth eventually, but...not tonight. Please understand."

"It's your letter, Corporal, fire away. I'll write down whatever you say."

Nurse Jennings honored Michael's wishes, perhaps against her better judgment, and began to write as Michael dictated the letter.

WHAT ARE THE CHANCES?

September 8, 1944

My Dearest Cecelia,

The first thing you'll notice is that this isn't my handwriting. I'm afraid I had a little bit of an accident today, and I'm in the hospital. Nothing too serious, honey, so don't worry, but I can't write, so I'm dictating this letter to the night nurse, a swell gal who agreed to write it for me.

You'll never believe what happened to me today, darling. After our training day was over, a few of the boys and I went to a public pool for a swim. This isn't like home where the only place to swim is in the river or at Lake Zoar. You'd be surprised how many public pools there are here in San Antonio.

Anyway, darling, it's hard for me to tell you this, but I was running alongside of the pool, and I slipped on a wet spot and fell. As you might expect, I instinctively braced my fall with my hands, and when I hit the deck, I broke both arms. The pain was something awful. The doctor even had to operate on my left wrist this afternoon to set the bones, and now I have casts on both arms.

I'm pretty devastated, honey, because this sets my flight training back weeks, maybe even months. And I've waited so long!

I can't say any more right now because I'm feeling too emotional and because Nurse Jennings has other patients to attend to, but I hope to write again tomorrow if one of the nurses will help me out. Most of all, I want you to know that I love you and miss you a million times more than I have ever loved or missed anyone!

Your soldier,
Love, xoxo
Michael

Setting her pen down on top of the stationery, Nurse Jennings contemplated Michael.

"You're a good man, Corporal, but I'm not sure if this was the best idea you've ever had. Forgive me for throwing in my two cents."

Michael tried in vain to control his tears as they trickled from the corners of his eyes.

"Are you alright, Corporal?"

He had no words. Michael just nodded and squeezed his eyes shut.

"Maybe you'd like to be alone."

He nodded once more.

"If you need anything, and I mean *anything* at all," Nurse Jennings said, "you ring for me. That's an order, Corporal, and as I think you know, I outrank you," she added, trying to break the tension. "Do you understand?"

Michael tried his best to smile, but could manage only a subtle nod.

Nurse Jennings flipped off the light on her way out of the room, leaving Michael alone to sort through his thoughts and feelings.

40

*A*s she lay reading in bed, Cecelia heard Mama calling to her from the bottom of the stairs. "Cecelia, c'è un uomo alla porta che vuole vederti."

Rolling out of bed, Cecelia yawned, opened the bedroom door, and looked down the staircase at her diminutive mother. "What do you mean, a man at the door, Mama? What man?"

"Lui è un soldato. Non lo conosco."

"A soldier? What soldier? God, it's Saturday morning. It's not even 9:00, and I'm not dressed, Mama!"

"Non lo so. Cecelia, figlia mia, vieni alla porta a vedere."

A bit miffed, Cecelia muttered, "All right, Mama. Tell him I will be right down. I need a minute."

After pulling a pair of dungarees on and a button down blouse, Cecelia quickly wrapped a scarf around her head and ran down the stairs barefoot.

Opening the screen door, she saw it was indeed a soldier, standing with his back to her, looking over the railing at the houses lining Hillside Avenue.

"Yes, may I help you?" she asked.

When the G.I. turned, she saw a familiar face.

"Oh my God, Augie! What a surprise. I wasn't expecting to see you. It's been since forever."

"More than a year!"

"I don't quite know what to say or where to begin."

"Well," Augie said, "how about beginning by hugging an old friend?"

Standing on tip-toe to embrace Augie, Cecelia heard herself rambling, "I'm afraid I hardly look presentable. I wasn't expecting any callers this morning. I was just lounging in bed, reading. My goodness, Augie, don't look at me. I'm a horrid mess."

"I disagree. You're beautiful even in blue jeans," Augie argued. "You'd look beautiful if you were wearing an old burlap sack."

Flattered, Cecelia blushed. "And look at you. The uniform becomes you."

"Thanks. Nobody knows better than you that I was trying to avoid this mess. I'm home on leave for two weeks, and then I'm being sent to the front in Europe."

"Oh, I'm sorry to hear that. I hope you'll stay safe."

Something in Augie's tone now changed. "I've never forgotten you."

"Oh, Augie, please, I don't think we should talk about–"

"It's just that…going where I'm going, it would be nice to have someone back home to write to, and I just thought I'd ask if that special someone could be…well…"

"Augie, you know I'm spoken for," Cecelia gently offered.

"That same guy?"

"Yes, the very same one. Only now, Augie, we're engaged. Our plan is to be married as soon as he returns after the war ends."

"I was afraid of that…"

"But you're a good friend, Augie. I'd be happy to write to you now and then to keep your spirits up and for old time's sake. And you're welcome to write to me any time, but with the understanding that we are no more than good friends, that we will never be more than that."

With a grin, Augie said, "Well, I'm gonna swallow my pride and accept your offer. I'm afraid it's the best one I got on the table right now, and I'm gonna be a long way from home. It's just the way the cards played out. How about your fella? Is he over there?"

"He's in Texas, Augie. In the Cadet Program where he's training to be a pilot, or maybe I should say *was*. He slipped and broke both arms, so everything is delayed."

Augie shook his head. "Lucky stiff. Slipping might've been the best thing that ever happened to him."

"He doesn't see it that way, Augie."

"I'm sorry. I shouldn't've said that. Sometimes the wrong thing slips out of my big mouth."

"Listen, Augie. I'll be praying for you every day. I'll even light a candle in church on Sundays."

With a disappointed smile, Augie said, "Thanks, Cecelia. I'm not gonna lie. If you follow through and write, it'll be hard not to wish you were my girl instead of that other fella's. But I get it, and when I write back to you, I'll be on my best behavior. Promise!"

"It's a deal then. Here's to hoping that we see each other again soon and that we'll both be back with the All-Stars."

After church on Sunday, Cecelia sat with Connie and Stella in Moscardini's.

"I can't believe he just dropped in like that," Stella said.

"Life's crazy, isn't it?" Cecelia replied, sipping through the straw and then biting it.

"Don't bite the straw, Celia," Connie scolded, "or it won't work and you'll have to ask Mr. Moscardini for another. He won't like it."

"You're not my mother, Connie. And besides, they might be rationing a lot of things, but the last I heard, there wasn't a straw shortage."

Stella interrupted. "Did you ever tell Michael about that time you kissed Augie, Celia?"

"I told him in a letter."

"And how did that go?"

"Well, of course he wasn't happy, but I explained that it wouldn't happen again and even told him how I resisted Augie's advances a week later, so he got over it…kind of."

"Then you're not going to tell him about Augie's visit and about writing to him, right?"

"Of course I'm going to tell him, silly. I'm not going to lie or withhold the truth ever again."

"Well, from what you've told us about Michael, he'll probably kill the two of you."

"He will not, Stella. Michael can be very reasonable."

"Oh, *sure* he can! Anyway, how about if we compare notes? I heard from Donny the other day."

"Oh? And what does he say?" Connie asked.

"Not much. Mostly it's, 'I love you, I miss you, I love you, I miss you,' which, quite honestly, I never tire of."

"The same with Michael," Cecelia said.

"And the same with Pete," Connie echoed.

"Donny says almost nothing about the war, though. He doesn't like to talk about it. He says I wouldn't like it if he did. But at least I know that he's, thankfully, in one piece."

"The same with Pete," Connie repeated.

"Well, in fairness, Connie, Pete isn't exactly on the front line. I mean, being a cook on a ship isn't the same as–"

Cutting her off, Connie argued, "A ship could be attacked by all kinds of things at any moment, Stella, by airplanes, submarines…"

"Yes," Cecelia chimed in, "just think about what happened to Scooter's PT boat."

"Well, all I mean is that Donny was there on D-Day when the Allies stormed the beaches at Normandy, and I just feel that–"

"I'm warning you, Stella. If you piss me off, I'll pour the rest of this soda right on top of your goddamn head."

"She'll do it," Cecelia cautioned.

Stella switched gears. "And what's the latest on Michael?"

"Status quo. Still at the hospital, and bored to tears. The good news is that the casts were recently removed after eight long weeks."

"So will he be back in action soon?"

"Not very soon. He says next is several weeks of rehabilitation. He doesn't know how many. But he wrote the oddest thing recently."

"What's that?" asked Stella.

"He said falling at the pool wasn't really the way he broke his arms. He confessed that he hadn't told me the truth because, he said, the truth is too embarrassing."

Connie smirked. "What in hell is that supposed to mean?"

"I have no idea, but I'm dying to know. Why would he lie or withhold the truth?"

"Two things, by the way, you just said *you* would never do," Stella offered.

"Alright, smart ass, point well taken."

"Hmmm...well, he and Pete have been writing to each other. Maybe he'll tell Pete."

"Now, Connie, let's not have our guys spying on each other."

"They probably tell each other things about us that we don't know about."

Stirring the long straw in her egg cream, Stella laughed. "Oh, Connie, you're such a cynic. I think it's nice that the two guys write to each other even though they've never met in real life."

"Nice?" Connie replied. "I'll give ya *nice*! Like I'm saying, now these two palookas have something in common, and for all we know they're comparing notes on what it's like to be engaged to the infamous Alberino sisters."

All three girls giggled, and then Stella added, "But Celia, you realize his two broken arms, however it happened, might save him from fighting. Some reports suggest that the Allies are nearing victory. Maybe he'll never go."

"If you're right," Cecelia replied, "it certainly won't be because of cowardice, because Michael is as brave as any guy on the planet. It'll simply be because of his circumstances, his fate. That said, if it works out that way, I'll go to church every day for a year and thank God, and you can quote me on that."

Walking home, Cecelia contemplated something Michael had written about, a rumor that 36,000 cadets were going to be removed from the Cadet Program. He had managed to beat all the odds by getting in and not washing out, but wouldn't this injury make him susceptible to being among the 36,000? Cecelia knew how devastated he would be if he didn't finish his flight training, but she hoped he wouldn't. Despite his dreams, she wanted him to return home alive and in one piece.

As the girls crossed Kneen Street, Connie quipped, "Hello, Lady Daydream? You're uncharacteristically quiet."

"Oh, sorry. I was just thinking."

"Thinking about?"

"Oh, just this and that."

"Well, aren't you an open book!"

"Not to change the subject," Stella said, "but have either of you heard from Connie Radecki?"

"Yes, I just got a letter from her," Cecelia replied. "She and her mother are living in a cold-water flat in Newark, New Jersey."

"That was crazy how the two of them just took off without a word."

"Well, we forgive Connie," Cecelia explained. "In her letter, she talked about how her mother didn't feel safe around her father anymore. The guy is a violent drunk. Connie said he would go into fits of rage and take a meat cleaver to the furniture. They had to run away."

"Some people's lives are so hard," Connie said.

"Yeah," Stella added, "and Connie is such a good kid. I miss her."

Later that afternoon, Cecelia sat at the kitchen table helping Mama jar peppers and eggplant. After mincing the juicy garlic cloves and chopping the fresh dill, Cecelia picked up an eggplant, peeling thick sheets of purple skin off the plump vegetable.

"Come stai Michael?" Mama asked.

"Better, Mama. The doctor took the casts off his arms."

"È un buon uomo," Mama said, standing near the stove and preparing the brine water.

Cecelia couldn't help but smile. "Well, I'm *glad* you like him, Mama. I wouldn't want to marry anyone you didn't like."

Mama just nodded. As she continued her tasks, Cecelia looked at her mother. Mama had aged a lot, her hair now silver, her short legs bowed, the skin around her eyes and lips coarsely wrinkled with the passage of time. Her mother had been fifty-one when she was born, and here she was twenty years later, still watching over Cecelia and loving her. There was nothing like a mother's love, and no one Cecelia cared about and respected more. Mama was many things to her, not the least of which was a font of old world wisdom.

"But tell me, Mama, what it is about Michael that you think is so great?"

"Non capisco."

"Uhm, why do you feel, uhm, perché credi che Michael, uhm, sia un brav'uomo," Cecelia said.

Now scrubbing the mason jars, Mama shook her head. "Becawz-a becawz-a, when I look-a in his eyes, aah, vedo onestà e verità."

"You do?" Cecelia's eyes welled up with tears. "That warms my heart, because when I look into his eyes, Mama, I see the same thing."

"Nice-a, nice," Mama smiled. "My bambina she gawn-a marry a nice-a boy."

"Thank you, Mama. I want you to know I would never marry him or anyone without your approval."

Later that night, after Mama had drifted off to sleep, Cecelia sat up in bed, having just written to Michael. To the rhythm of Mama's gentle snoring, Cecelia reached over and took her precious diary from the nightstand. Unlocking the cover, she opened to a new blank page.

October 8, 1944

Dear Diary,

Today, Mama told me that Michael is a good man, that when she looks into Michael's eyes, she sees honesty and truth. Hearing her say that meant the world to me. Not that she ever gave me any other impression, but to have her speak those very words, well, it just gives me great confidence that I am making the right decision to marry him, God willing. Did I tell you it's Michael's plan to ask Mama for permission to marry me? He didn't have the time to ask her when he was home and gave me the wings. I explained it to Mama at the time, and she seemed fine with that plan, although she hadn't said much. But today, what she said meant everything. As far as I'm concerned, Diary, getting Mama's stamp of approval seals the deal for me.

Cecelia closed the volume and nestled in the bed next to Mama. She lay awake for more than an hour studying her mother's wrinkled face, age lines that told the story of a woman who had faced hardships and heartbreaks but kept going for the love of her family. Cecelia smiled at the peaceful, ancient face before her, gently rubbed her palm against Mama's weathered forehead, and whispered, "Ti voglio bene, Mama."

41

Michael – 1931

Scooter tags after Michael as he makes his way to the summit of DeMarco Mountain. It is more a hill than a mountain, Michael knows, but that's what everyone calls it. Still, the elevation is high enough to overlook the better part of Derby. For both boys on this day, it is Mount Everest, a place of adventure and exploration. It doesn't hurt that the highest level of the landscape is covered with mammoth rock formations that provide crannies that, for adventurous boys, become dark and mysterious caverns.

Michael squats on top of the biggest rock and peruses the landscape below. His flat hand becomes a visor to protect his eyes from the blinding sun. He can see the steeple of St. Mary's off in the distance.

Scooter, a few steps behind, climbs up onto the rock, and breathing heavily, says, "What now, Mikey?"

Michael gives Scooter an arrogant look and then reaches deep into the pockets of his worn overalls, spilling the contents onto the stone surface.

"Whattaya got there?" Scooter asks. "Empty spools and rubber bands and tape and what? Stick matches?"

Michael has indeed raided his mother's sewing box and taken

the two largest spools he could find, now devoid of the thread his mother had used to mend clothes and darn socks. In the pantry, he had also pilfered two wide, oversized rubber bands, some cloth tape, and a box of stick matches.

Michael frowns and scoffs, "Not empty spools and rubber bands and tape and matches," and then he says in a loud, dramatic whisper, "Injun flamethrowers!"

"Whattaya mean, Injun flamethrowers?"

"You'll see," Michael assures his friend.

Pulling out his pocket knife, Michael deftly saws the rubber bands in half. Then, holding a rubber band over one hole of the spool, he wraps the sticky tape around the wooden area where thread had once resided.

"Now watch this," Michael exclaims. He loads a wooden matchstick into the other end of the cylinder and then strikes the tip of the match against the surface of the rock. Scooter's gray eyes light up as the red tip of the match ignites into a hot blue and yellow flame. Holding the spool up in the air with two fingers, Michael pulls the bottom end of the stick into the thick rubber band at the bottom, draws it back, and lets it fly high into the air.

"Wow!" Scooter yells.

"See, just like I said. An Injun flamethrower! Of course, what I'm goin' for is to have it be like a bow and arrow, but I know a spool doesn't look like a bow, so I call it an Injun flamethrower. Kinda like in the last war when those dirty Germans started using flamethrowers. It didn't matter because we whooped 'em anyway. The Germans must've studied the way Injuns used flaming arrows over here. That's my hunch. These ones that I'm making are just more primitive, more like real Injuns used."

"Wow!" Scooter repeats.

As Michael begins to affix a rubber band over one of the holes of the other spool, he mutters, "This one's for you, Scoot."

"Are we gonna play Cowboys and Injuns?" Scooter asks. "Because, if we are, I'm gonna be Gary Cooper. He's the most dapper cowboy I ever seen."

"You ain't gonna be Gary Cooper, Scooter."

"Aw, shucks. It ain't fair that you get ta be him. We should at least flip for it."

"We ain't gonna flip for it neither. First of all, I ain't got a penny, and second of all, *neither* of us is gonna be Gary Cooper."

"Well, whattaya mean? One of us has gotta be a good guy. Dontcha remember when we snuck into the movies and saw him in that show a few months back, *Fighting Caravans,* and he helped that wagon train get across the country and he hadda fight Injuns ta get 'em there? He plays, what's-his-name, Clint somebody, and he beat the Injuns and got the girl and everything."

"A-course I remember, ya dope. It was my idea to sneak in."

"How come we ain't snuck in since?"

"We ain't snuck in since because Nicky Garufi says he's not openin' the side door for us again unless I pay him three cents, and where am I supposed to get three cents? Besides, ya gotta kind of spread it out a little, or the owners'll get wise to us."

Scooter persists, "Well, if nobody's gonna be Gary Cooper, what cowboy is one of us gonna be?"

"No cowboy, ya knucklehead. First of all, a cowboy would have a rifle, and we don't have one. That should be obvious! The only rifle we got is a real one with real bullets, and if I take that without permission, Mom'll give me a beating like she ain't ever given me. But that ain't why."

"Why then?"

"Cuz we're gonna play a game about Injun wars."

"Whattaya mean? The Injuns had wars against each other?"

"A-course they did, Scoot. Don't be ignorant your whole life. Just like we had the Civil War, the Injuns had their own wars. Don't you know anything? Human beings, even the same kind, can't agree on everything, and whenever they can't, they have a war. That's why we had the Civil War over here in this country, and that's why they fought the Great War in Europe. Because all the presidents of all the countries couldn't agree on stuff."

"How do you know so much about wars?"

"Because I read books, which if you have any brains, you'll start doing. I just finished a book I got from the library about Injun wars. It had pictures and everything. When I took it to the desk to check it out, the librarian, old Miss Wilkins, told me I was too young for it, but I said, 'If it's all the same to you, ma'am, I'm interested in everything about Injuns, and I'd like to give it a whirl.' She was partly right, but lookin' at the pictures, I got the gist of it. Anyways, today we're gonna make believe we're on the prairies way back in the early 1800s, and I'm gonna be a Comanche warrior, and you're gonna be an Apache warrior. Those two were natural born enemies. From what I understand, they couldn't agree on anything, not even what kinds of teepees to build. Let's see now, I got about thirty matchsticks here, so we both get half, and then we'll stalk each other and shoot flaming arrows at each other. How's that sound?"

"Sounds great! Let's do it!" Scooter yells and then runs to the edge of the giant boulder and leaps high into the air, landing triumphantly, all the while yelping like he had seen Indians in the movies do.

Hiding behind round tree trunks and silver-gray boulders, the two boys strategically look for opportunities to get a clear shot at each other. Every now and again, a "flaming arrow" flies through the air trying to hit its target.

Each warrior now maneuvers toward or away from the other, at one moment behind a giant oak, the next sliding into a dark cave. It is Scooter who is firing the greatest number of arrows.

Hiding behind a fertile green bush, Michael moans loudly, "Scooter, if you use up all your damn arrows, the war's gonna be over in fifteen minutes. These are the only matchsticks I got. How many you got left?"

"I ain't tellin' the enemy how much ammo I got left," Scooter complains, his voice echoing across the landscape.

But sounds emanating from the street below distract Michael. He runs out from cover and onto the edge of the highest rock. As he does, a flaming arrow flies over his head.

"Dammit, Scooter, did I tell you to cut it out or didn't I?"

Now at a clear vantage point, Michael surveys the scene below. At the bottom of the hill, he sees a half dozen boys and girls racing down the sidewalk on roller skates, creating a unique cacophony of sound, dozens of metal wheels spinning on asphalt. While perhaps a harsh noise to some, it is music to Michael's ears.

Scooter runs over to his preoccupied friend.

"So that's what I heard," Michael says, his eyes cast downward. "I thought so."

"Lucky dogs," mutters Scooter.

"Yeah, they think they're so great!"

"Yeah, they think they're so great," Scooter repeats.

Deep in thought, Michael remains silent.

Finally, Scooter speaks. "You all right, Mikey?"

"Yeah, I'm all right, I guess. Maybe I'm better than all right."

"Uh-oh," says Scooter. "You're cookin' up some kinda scheme."

"You might say that. In fact, I think I got a pretty good one."

"Oh no! What is it?"

Lost in a world of his own making, Michael utters, "I've wanted a pair of roller skates my whole life, and now I'm gonna get 'em."

"Whattaya mean, Mikey?"

"Well pal, here's what I'm thinkin'. If me and you climb down this hill about half way, we can take a match or two, and start the dead leaves and the dry grass on fire. Those kids down there'll get so excited they'll take off their skates and climb up here to see the fire. Meanwhile, me and you, we'll just sneak down around the edge of the hill and swipe a couple pairs of skates, whichever ones we think'll fit us."

"But, Mikey, that's stealin'."

"And don't ya think I know that? Big goddamn deal! Ain't ya never stole nothin' before?"

"No, I didn't."

"Sure ya did. When we snuck into the movies, you basically stole the movie ticket since ya didn't pay for it. Ain't that right?"

"I guess," a puzzled Scooter replies.

"Right. So ya just go to confession and you're done with it!"

"Yeah…but what if they can't put out the fire?"

With the same expression and a subtle nod of his head, Michael almost sings, "I don't care if we burn down the whole damn mountain, just so long as I get me a pair of them skates. Let's go!"

Once the children spy the fire on the hill, a chaotic scene ensues with boys and girls kicking off their skates and running up the hill, screaming "Fire! Fire! Fire!" at the top of their lungs. Responsible adults rush to the rescue, lugging metal pails of water to douse the flames.

Moments later, when Michael and Scooter contentedly impel

themselves down Smith Street, each one in his new skates, Scooter says, "Hey, Mikey, can I ask a question?"

"Don't be a knucklehead. Of course, you can."

"We're best pals, ain't we?"

"Of course we're best pals."

"Can I ask another question?"

"Ask anything you like."

"If our mothers ask us where we got these, what do we tell 'em? And what if we're skatin' tomorrow and one of those kids sees us and tattles on us?"

"Don't you worry. Our mothers ain't gonna know, cuz number one, we're too smart to tell 'em, and number two, I'm gonna hide 'em. There's some loose floorboards in the tool shed where I can stick 'em. And as for them kids...when we feel like skatin', we'll just get lost and skate. We'll go somewhere–down to the Green, maybe, or better yet, we'll sneak behind the stores on Main Street where trucks make deliveries. Nobody'll ever find us there. Then we can skate all's we want, and nobody can tell us otherwise. We can skate for the rest of our damn lives!"

42

*A*fter eight interminable weeks, Michael was relieved to finally have his casts removed even though his spirits remained low. After the maintenance phase of his training had dragged on for such a long time, what had he done to deserve this? Compounding matters, his lie to Cecelia about the way it happened was a piercing thorn in his heart. He strove to stay upbeat in his letters even though he was dying inside.

> *...I know you like to tease me about all the pretty young nurses, honey, but the only girls I see are the four nurses on our floor–Trixie (the horse), Bessy Lou (the cow), Geraldine (the deer), and Emma (the fox). Oh, and I almost forgot one. The Major's wife, an old goat who likes to visit us boys here in the hospital...*

Of course, except for the Major's wife, the aforementioned nurses were strictly fictional characters. Michael had also written about the most real person in his life, Nurse Jennings, but hadn't mentioned that she was an Indian with skin the color of a ripe acorn. The first Native American he had ever met in real life, Nurse Jennings touched Michael with her warmth and her wit. She, in fact, shined a little brightness on every soldier's convalescence, making her so popular that the men called her "Sunshine."

Since day one, when she had penned his letter to Cecelia,

Michael felt a deep connection to her and she to him. Nurse Jennings had continued to transcribe his daily letters to Cecelia for a good three weeks until Michael got some range of motion back in the fingers of his right hand.

Every day, their letter writing session would begin in the very same way.

"All right, big shot, are we finally going to tell your girl the truth today?"

Michael would shrug and say, "I don't know, Sunshine. We'll see."

But at the end of their time together, Nurse Jennings would fold up the letter for him and sigh. "Hmm, another great work of fiction."

A few days after Michael's casts came off, he received a letter from Cecelia that hit him hard. While doing her rounds, Nurse Jennings saw Michael vacantly staring out the window, an open book in his lap.

"You're gonna have to pick that book up, Corporal," she said, waking Michael from his daydream. "It's not gonna read itself."

"Oh, this? I...I, uh, I don't feel much like reading."

"I noticed! You seem preoccupied, but not in a good way. Are you okay?"

"I've been better," he replied, rubbing his thumbs up and down on the pages of his book.

"You wanna talk about it?"

"Uhm...gee, I don't know."

"How about this, then? How about I give you a direct order to spill?"

Kidding about outranking him had become their little game.

Nurse Jennings parked herself on the crisp sheets that lay atop Michael's mattress and folded her hands in her lap.

"Okay, let's have it."

Michael began slowly. "Well, I guess I'm just feeling bad because of something my girl wrote to me."

"Which was?"

"She told me how her mother thinks a lot of me."

"And that makes you feel bad? Well, I'll say this. You're a real pip."

"No, her mother said when she looks into my eyes, she sees onestà e verità."

"I'm afraid I'm only fluent in English and I can get by in the Caddo language of my grandparents."

"Oh, sorry," Michael apologized. "Onestà e verità is Italian for honesty and truth."

"Sounds like an insightful lady, your girl's mother."

Michael loved Cecelia's mother and proceeded to describe her as well as his own mother, how they came to this country not speaking a word of English, how they made a life for their families, how they lived close to the soil, how they were infused with the wisdom of the old world.

"Sounds a lot like my own grandmother who is connected to the earth. And every wrinkle on her face exudes an ancient wisdom."

"Except that Cecelia's mom isn't right about me. I *haven't* been honest or truthful. Nobody knows that better than you."

"Oh, I get it. You're feeling guilty."

Michael hung his head in dejection. "Yeah, and to make matters worse, I've kept it from my mother. I wrote to my kid sisters and told them not to mention it to Mom. It's just that I didn't want her to worry. I remember passing by her bedroom when she was worried about one thing or another and hearing her crying. I just can't bear the thought of it. Mom's already got too much on her plate."

"Sounds like *you've* got too much on your plate, cowboy. But the good news is it's fixable. Here's the deal. It's time to swallow that pride of yours. You made a mistake while training. It happens. Start with your girl. Tell her you were embarrassed at the time and let her know the truth about what happened. Then tell your mother. You'll feel a lot better."

"I guess you're right, Sunshine. I should have listened to you weeks ago."

After Nurse Jennings left him, Michael smoothed out a sheet of stationery on a small desk against the wall and set out to confess the real truth of his injury.

...So you see, honey, I wasn't honest about it. The reason the accident happened was because I was overconfident. Since the day I set my

*feet down on the ground here in San Antonio, I had it in my head that
I was going to be the best, and I don't think that anyone had any doubt
it was true, until I blew it. I felt embarrassed, not to mention the fact
that I could have gotten both Captain Griffith and myself killed. He
saved us both, and afterwards, he was really decent about it. Anyway, I
hope you can understand how it made me feel, and I'm praying you'll
forgive me...*

After writing that letter and calling Mom, Michael felt like the
weight of the world had been lifted from his shoulders, or at least
some of it. Other matters still nagged him. It was on a Friday afternoon that Sunshine delivered a new curve ball.

"Well, Michael, Monday morning, you and I part company. It
was nice knowin' ya, pal!"

"They're sending me back to training?" Michael asked, his heart
racing in anticipation.

"You wish! We got orders that a few of you are moving on to
Camp Mystic for further rehabilitation."

"Camp what?"

"Mystic. It's not far from here. Maybe twenty minutes."

"Whattaya mean, a camp, Sunshine? What kind of camp? For
mental cases?"

"Get outta town, Michael. There's nothin' mental about you. It
used to be a girls' camp, but now the Army uses it for rehab."

"Okay," Michael said with a smile. "This is some kind of joke,
right? You're putting me on."

"I wish I was, but those are the latest orders. It sounds like it'll
be another month, at least."

Michael could see that Sunshine's eyes lacked their usual playful
sparkle.

Trying to comfort him, she continued. "There's all kinds of
activities to do there. You'll feel like a kid again at Boy Scout camp."

Michael smirked. "I never got to be a Boy Scout."

"Well, I'll tell you what, Michael. As far as I'm concerned, you're
a good scout, and I'm sure gonna miss you."

*...It's unbelievable, honey. The federal government leased the place
as a rehabilitation and recovery camp for members of the Army, guys*

like me, apparently. But get a load of this. Guess what it used to be. A camp for girls! That's right, darling, it turns out that I've gone from being a fighter pilot in training to nothing but a girl scout...

Michael found it difficult to grasp life at Camp Mystic. Besides physical therapy, the Red Cross came in twice a week and did arts and crafts with the boys, and Michael, along with those of his fellow inmates in the best shape, spent afternoons at croquet, archery, and horseback riding.

...You're right, darling, it's like a country club. I know what they're doing. They don't want to let us go prematurely before we're 100%. If they do, after we're discharged, they might have to pay out on veterans' benefits for the rest of our lives, God forbid. Anyway, I always thought that I'd like a cushy life, but it's not the case. I just got here, and I'm going batty already. It's not the way things were supposed to turn out. I'm meant to be defending our country in the air and trying to make this a better world for you and your family, for mine, and for everyone. And what am I doing? Hitting striped balls through wickets with a wooden mallet. I hope you can see why I don't feel good about it.

All I know is this sitting around sweating out the war is just h-ll. Accidents like this happen from sitting around taking disappointment after disappointment! All foolishness that could have been avoided. I wish that I could explain better what I mean. Anything could happen in the next six months. The war might end. If it does, I'll have spent all this time in the military without fighting a single battle, except the ones in my heart, but at least I'll be able to come home and marry you. I long for that most, darling. There's nothing more important to me...

But the days dragged on, and before Michael knew it, it was December 1st. He sat in the dayroom, on the verge of winning a chess match against a friend he had made at the base hospital. Jimbo was a big-boned man, standing at a good six foot five, a gentle, amiable giant. Just as Jimbo's fat, clumsy fingers moved his queen out of danger, one of the nurses, Nellie, walked into the room.

She dropped an envelope in Michael's lap. "For you, handsome."

As she made her way down the hallway, Michael yelled, "Hey!

You interrupted our game, but I'm gonna forgive you this time because you brought me mail."

Hardly acknowledging Michael's remark, Nellie lifted her arms out and shrugged without losing a step.

Michael's initial excitement was eclipsed when he saw the return address on the letter.

"Everything alright, partner?" Jimbo asked.

"I have a hunch it's not," Michael replied, tearing the sealed envelope.

"Who's it from?"

"My best pal's mom. He's been MIA in the Pacific for months. I'm afraid to read this."

Jimbo studied Michael's face as he read. Michael's head shook as his eyes scanned the page.

Finally, he dropped the letter on the chess board and muttered, "Oh God, this can't be. Please, say it isn't so."

"Hey listen, pal," Jimbo said, but Michael was out of his chair before his friend could utter another word, reeling like a drunkard toward the double doors that led to the courtyard.

Unable to resist the temptation, Jimbo picked up the letter and read it.

December 5, 1944

Dear Michael,

I'm afraid we got more bad news yesterday. Our hearts are broken. A very official looking letter from the War Department arrived in the mail from someone by the name of Lieutenant Emmett Davies. The letter said that he is the commanding officer of Squadron 3 for the U.S. Navy. Sadly, Michael, he informed us that the Navy has now determined that none of the seventeen members of PT-300 survived the attack last May.

The letter said that Timothy would have a Catholic burial in a cemetery on the island of Manila, which will be his permanent resting place. Lieutenant Davies explained that the Navy assigns their most heroic men to PT boats, and he said they will be conferring a Purple Heart and perhaps other medals on Timothy and the crew for their valor. That's a nice thing, but truly, we'd rather have our boy back.

Our dear Scooter! Myself and my family are stricken with grief as you might expect. I don't quite know what else to say. Scooter loved you, Michael, so I just thought you should know.

Sincerely,
Sally O'Brian

Carefully, Jimbo folded up the letter and hurried to the window where he saw Michael laying in the grass, one arm wrapped like a blindfold over his eyes. Jimbo knew he wasn't any good at these things, and he wished that Sunshine was there. He remembered how close she and Michael had become at the base hospital. Recovering himself from a broken leg, Jimbo limped down the hall with his cane, searching for someone to help. He hoped that the young nurse who manned the front desk would be there, but it was unoccupied.

Holding the envelope limply in his left hand, he lumbered back to the window and pulled the curtain aside. There lay Michael, his position unchanged. Despite his level of discomfort, he realized what he needed to do.

When he reached the spot where Michael lay, Jimbo murmured, "Hey, brother, I can't kneel down with this bum leg, but if you'll give me your hand, I'll help you up. I know how you feel, but you can't lay here like this. Let me help get you to your room. Maybe you can write a letter to your girl...tell her how it is. It'll help a little."

Michael moved his arm off of his face, which was awash with tears.

"Just let me sit down for a minute," Michael whispered, his voice throaty and listless.

Once in a chair, Michael sat hunched over, his face buried in both hands. Jimbo didn't say another word. Silence seemed to be the antidote that this wound called for. He stood by his friend, gently rubbing his back, until Michael was ready to walk to his room.

43

*L*ying in bed next to Mama, Cecelia drifted into that nebu-
lous state when one doesn't know whether she is awake or
asleep. In her outer consciousness, she heard the percus-
sive hammering of sleet pelting the windows and the house. When
the bell of the alarm clock clanged at 7:00, she groaned. Fumbling
for the button, she silenced the obnoxious ringing, and then,
looking at the window, saw it was still dark outside. She lay in bed
thinking she would rather have gone to work. Rudy had given her
the day off to attend Scooter's funeral Mass at St. Mary's, and like it
or not, Cecelia needed to drag herself out of bed and get ready.
Knowing she'd have to walk there didn't help. She hated that the
weather was so awful.

What a day! And with the holiday only nine days away, what a
Christmas it would be for the O'Brians. Her heart hurt thinking of
them.

When she got down to the kitchen, Connie was about to leave
for work. Cecelia tore off a piece of bread from a fresh loaf Mama
had baked.

"Coffee's on the stove," Connie said. "You should have some. It'll
warm you up."

"Thanks," Cecelia muttered, spreading butter on the bread. She
wasn't a good morning person even on the best of days.

"You're walking there?"

The pelting sleet was louder now.

Cecelia frowned and shrugged. "How else?"

"Be careful. It's slippery and sloppy as hell out there."

"That's why God created umbrellas and boots," Cecelia said, chewing.

"I know you don't want to go," Connie said. "Why do it? You hardly knew the guy. How many times were you in his company? Two, maybe three times?"

Nibbling a golden brown piece of crust, Cecelia frowned again. "Twice."

"See? Twice, and one of the two times, you were walking with Michael and ya didn't even talk to the guy."

"Right."

"So?"

"So, I promised Michael I'd go. He was Michael's best friend. And besides, I feel bad for Scooter's family."

Connie poured a mug of hot coffee and delivered it to the table. "You'll probably be invited to the house after."

"I know," Cecelia groaned, and then repeated, "I know. I don't want to be." Hearing her words, she felt guilty at the thought. "It's just that…"

"Just that what?"

"I'm lousy in these kinds of social situations where I don't know anybody."

"Won't Michael's family be there?"

"I suppose. I meant the O'Brians."

"I know, little sister. Well, don't fret. Just do your best. I have to run."

Walking down Howe Avenue, the umbrella did little more than keep her hair and upper body dry as the sleet came down in a cruel, diagonal trajectory, soaking the bottom of her dress and her stockings. Worse still, she had to walk in small steps so as not to fall. When she reached the Shelton-Derby Bridge, fighting to keep her umbrella from blowing inside out, she held one hand on the lower shaft and, with the other, grasped the spring at the top.

At St. Mary's, the heavy church door closed behind Cecelia,

shutting out the unfriendly storm. The plaintive strains of the pipe organ greeted her as she collected herself in the shelter of the vestibule. Still dripping, she creeped down the center aisle a half dozen rows, genuflected, slid into the pew, and knelt to say a prayer. After she blessed herself and sat down, she spotted Josie waving at her to come sit with the DeMarcos who were closer to the front of the church. Arriving at their row, she genuflected and squeezed between Josie and her sister Sofia. Cecelia knelt and said a prayer once again, which seemed like the thing to do. Upon finishing, she sat on the oak pew between Michael's two sisters. It occurred to her that Josie was the next oldest after Michael and Sofia, the next youngest. The two sisters, almost as if they had it planned, took one of Cecelia's hands in theirs and held on tightly. Their gesture made her feel connected to them and melted the chill from her insides. Cecelia leaned forward, looking beyond Sofia, and smiled at Francesca and Michael's mother. Michael's father, his two eldest sisters, and two younger brothers didn't appear to be present. Perhaps they weren't able to take a day off from work or school.

Cecelia sat and contemplated the similarities between their two families. It wasn't uncommon for the old timers she knew to say that marrying your own nationality was the wisest thing to do. Italian to Italian, Irish to Irish, Polish to Polish. Perhaps they were right.

Five rows ahead, Cecelia spotted a man, a woman, and a teenage girl, whom she presumed to be Scooter's parents and younger sister. *Connie...right,* she remembered with a sad smile. Otherwise, there were another two or three dozen people of various ages scattered about the church.

It was a High Mass with organ music and sung Latin chants and responses echoing back and forth from the priest on the altar to the organist in the distant choir loft. "Dominus vobiscum," the priest chanted and the congregation timidly sang back, "et cum spiritu tuo."

The one thing conspicuously missing from the funeral service, she noticed, was the casket. Michael had explained. The military didn't have the means to ship the bodies of the many dead back home. It was a disquieting thought that Scooter's body would forever rest in another country. It felt wrong. She couldn't help wondering if his body had actually been found.

As the Mass proceeded, she gazed up to her right and left, noticing that with an absence of sunshine, the stained glass windows were muted instead of a vibrant myriad of colors.

She felt distracted as the priest in his black chasuble, a gold cross embroidered across the front, moved from one part of the Mass to another. Cecelia felt herself responding robotically along with the somber congregation: "Kyrie Eleison...Christe Eleison... Kyrie Eleison..." and then, moments later: "Sanctus, Sanctus, Sanctus. Dóminus Deus Sábaoth..."

All the while, she held her missal open, but she drifted into a dreamlike state. She was painfully aware she should be more focused, but she felt numb.

When the priest moved to the pulpit for the Gospel and the small congregation stood, Cecelia was still lost in thought. Josie and Sofia looked back at her, puzzled. She stood up, and Sofia mouthed, "Are you alright?"

Cecelia nodded that she was, but she wasn't quite sure.

At the homily, Cecelia finally seemed to be drawn in. The priest talked of the eternal soul of man, and how Scooter, though young, had been baptized in the Holy Ghost and so possessed that very spirit. He further explained that the O'Brians could take comfort in the fact that Scooter was now with God.

So it surprised Cecelia when the priest segued into thoughts about the war in general.

"This loss of life, sadly," he continued, "is something I'm afraid we've all become too accustomed to over the last few years. Personally, though, I'm not sure I'll ever get used to the loss of young life. War is an ugly business. We should remember that our Father in Heaven, when he created the earth with its vast oceans and expansive continents, did not delineate any geographic lines. It was *man* who did that. Over time immemorial, world leaders have sought to conquer other lands, other peoples. Such is man's unquenchable thirst for power and conquest. Since before the birth of Our Lord, from Darius to Alexander to Hannibal, and in these many centuries of anno domini, so many. Attila and Charlemagne and Napoleon and, yes, Adolf Hitler and Hirohito today. But, my brothers and sisters, it has always been honest young men like Timothy who have paid the price. Yes, Timothy died standing up for what he felt, in his heart, was right. In that respect, he is a hero to all of us, as he should be. Timothy served because he cared. Timothy fought because he was brave. Timothy gave his life because he wanted us to be safe from tyranny and conquest. We must never forget his sacrifice. His loss is, to say the least, profound for his parents and his sister, and all of us who knew him. In nomine Patris, et Filii, et Spiritus Sancti. Amen."

These last points from the priest made Cecelia feel confused and dizzy, even. He seemed to have suggested, perhaps, that war was the result of sin and that boys like Scooter were merely pawns. Boys like Scooter...and Michael, Cecelia realized. At least that was how she interpreted his words.

Upon walking out of the church, Cecelia was relieved to see that the precipitation had mercifully ended, and the sun was peeking through the silver edges of the lingering clouds. She walked to the O'Brians' with Michael's mother and sisters, taking some comfort in the fact that at least they would be with her at the gathering. She had known Josie well since they had traveled to Ohio together to visit Michael. But in recent months, since the engagement, she was also getting to know the other siblings better, especially Sofia and Francesca, who were both closer in age to her.

The O'Brian home was cluttered with at least a few dozen people, Cecelia estimated. Josie pulled Cecelia over to Mrs. O'Brian and introduced her, but Scooter's mother was surrounded by people offering their condolences. Cecelia had not yet attended very many wakes and funerals in her lifetime, but she had heard about "Irish wakes" that they were often boisterous affairs that included a good deal of drinking and singing and storytelling. Here at the O'Brians', the songs and storytelling had already commenced. And, of course, the drinking. Uncles and cousins toasted the life of Scooter O'Brian. How different it was from her memory of the wake for her father some thirteen years before, the most grim day of her young life.

After having had a bite to eat, Cecelia was approached by Scooter's mother who asked if they could talk in a nearby room where there was, as Mrs. O'Brian put it, "a bit of privacy."

"I'm so very delighted to finally meet Michael's girl," Mrs. O'Brian began.

"I'm happy to be here, but sad to meet you under these circumstances," Cecelia replied. "Michael wanted me to tell you that he wished he could be here himself."

"He's a good lad, that one," Mrs. O'Brian said. "Will ya be writin' to him soon?"

Cecelia liked the rhythm of her Irish brogue.

"Yes, I write every night."

"Well, please tell him we O'Brians thank him for his recent letter, and say that we send our regards. He's trainin' to be a pilot, is he?"

"He was," Cecelia clarified. "He had a little accident and broke his arms, so that got delayed."

"May it be delayed until after this war is over, God willing. A plane is a dangerous place to be. Did ya know it was planes that was our Tim's undoing?"

"Yes, Michael told me."

"Well, I will say this to you. You are one lucky girl, you are. Michael DeMarco is a great catch, so be thankful for that."

"Oh, I am," Cecelia agreed.

"Although I've no doubt that Michael is lucky to get a girl like you. You've got a warm way about you that tells me your heart is kind and pure."

Cecelia, not quite knowing how to respond, blushed.

"Well, it was so nice to meet you, Cecelia. I hope after you and Michael are married you won't be strangers. A visit from Michael now and again will bring back a good many happy memories of our boy. They were good boys, the two of 'em, except for the times when they raised a bit of hell."

Laughing, Cecelia loved that Mrs. O'Brian could find some levity amidst her grief.

"But the memories are a treasure to us. I'm afraid that's all we've got left."

Cecelia, again, just listened and smiled.

With a pat on the hand, Mrs. O'Brian said, "Thank you again for comin' today, my dear. It's appreciated by my family and myself.

And please tell Michael that he is in our prayers. May he come back to you, and to all of us, safe and sound."

The walk home was far more pleasant than her morning struggle in the ice storm had been. The tamed clouds were now a translucent white, and the sun was shining. The temperature felt like it was now in the forties. At the corner of Elizabeth and Main, Cecelia crossed the street and turned right, making her way to the intersection which led to the bridge, the spot where she had left Michael that fateful night he had walked with her from the dance, his friend close by in his clunker. And now Scooter was gone, a loss of life that struck her as senseless.

At 4:00, Cecelia arrived home. Alone in the quiet house, she seized the opportunity to write to Michael, filling him in on the events of the day. She felt it crucial to communicate in such a way that lifted his spirits. It took her a long time to complete the letter as she painstakingly chose each and every word, phrase, sentence, and paragraph.

She was in the process of sealing the letter when Connie arrived home at 5:30. Sizing her up, Connie asked, "You survived?"

"Yes, I'm fine," Cecelia said, sheepishly.

"Tell me about it."

Cecelia breathed in deeply and let out a long sigh. "Another time, if you don't mind. I just rehashed the whole day to Michael." She waved the letter in the air. "I'm not up to going into it again. Maybe tomorrow."

"I understand."

"The priest said something, though, that got me thinking."

"Oh? What, pray tell?"

"He said that God created the earth but that He didn't create countries. At least that's what I think he meant."

"I don't follow."

"Let's see. He said that God didn't *delineate*, yes, that's the word he used, any geographic lines across the continents…that man did that."

"Man?"

"Yes, as in *mankind*. I never thought about that before, did you?"

"No, I suppose not."

"It makes sense, doesn't it?"

"I suppose."

"So, in a way," Cecelia continued slowly, "if God didn't create countries, then it's wrong to fight wars."

"But what are we supposed to do," Connie replied, "let tyrants like Hitler or Hirohito conquer the world? If they do, there won't be any more geographic lines. The whole world will be Germany. Or Japan. Are we supposed to let that happen?"

"No, you're right. It's just all so complicated and confusing."

At bedtime, Cecelia removed her makeup with cold cream and washed her face. Thoughts of the day weighed heavily on her mind. While Michael was disappointed that his flight training was postponed, she was glad. While he longed for adventure and felt a strong sense of duty to fight in the war, as far as she was concerned, she hoped he never saw a day of action. The plane accident and the broken arms were a blessing in disguise. She didn't give a hoot how it happened or whether he told the truth about it or not. To hell with men and their pride. He was safe, and that was good enough. She hoped that Michael would never be called on to make the sacrifice that Scooter had made. She hoped the war would end before he was fully recuperated. More than anything, she wanted an end to this ugly business of war. That's what the priest had called it–a business! More than anything, she wanted Michael home and ready to recite marriage vows with her.

44

*J*t was on a balmy April day in Mystic that Michael and a handful of men sat in the dayroom, huddled around a radio. Three or four nurses and a few male staff members hovered behind the group of G.I.s. Word had spread across the country like wildfire, draping the nation in a smothering pall. When the news report began, the soldiers hushed each other. The buzzing and whistling and whirring of the radio speaker made it hard to hear the report, but the group, transfixed, listened intently.

Good evening, Ladies and Gentlemen, this is Fulton Lewis Jr. speaking to you from the Mutual Studios in New York City. This nation has suffered, this day, a staggering loss. At this moment, at Warm Springs, Georgia, President Franklin D. Roosevelt lies with the problems of the nation finally lifted from his shoulders, stricken late this afternoon with a cerebral hemorrhage. He passed away before his physicians could be of any assistance, if assistance in such a case is possible at all. Vice President Harry Truman, who from here on will be President Truman, went immediately to the White House. A special cabinet meeting was called, and we should know more about what is going to happen in Washington as the evening wears on. But Franklin D. Roosevelt, the first president to be elected for four terms to the White House, has passed away. And that is the overshadowing of all news events that have happened or can happen for quite a while.

When the radio station announced that it was returning to normal programming, Michael wondered what normal was. Was it normal that a president should die in the midst of war? Was it normal that it had been seven months since he broke his arms? Was it normal to sit around a camp week after week? Was it normal to sign up to fight for your country and then not get to do so?

The group broke out in twos and threes by the coffee table, in a corner, near the hallway. Fears were whispered and concerns were expressed in solemn tones: "What'll this mean now?"..."Christ, Roosevelt's been president for as long as I can remember"..."Can Truman do the job?"..."We're sunk without FDR"..."I knew he was in poor health, but–"..."He didn't want the country to know"... "They say they've developed a new bomb"...

Lost, Michael wandered to his room, asking himself, *How much more bad news can I take?* Cecelia had written that she had visited Mrs. O'Brian twice since Scooter's funeral. He was glad Cecelia had taken the initiative to stay in touch with his lost pal's mom. With a sad smile, he thought, *Mrs. O. sure is a swell lady.* But as his smile faded, he knew Scooter was gone. And now the President was gone as well. Michael needed to connect with Cecelia.

April 12, 1945

Dearest Cecelia,

> *By the time you receive this letter, you will undoubtedly have heard the heartbreaking news of the death of our president. I can't quite fathom that he's gone. I just came from the dayroom where we all heard the radio report. What occurred to me, darling, is that President Roosevelt has been in office since I was just a snot-nosed eleven-year-old. It seemed like he would never die.*

> *I don't know what to think about Truman. It feels like a stranger is moving into the White House.*

> *Honey, I don't know if Roosevelt's death means the end of the war will be hastened or postponed. The word around here is that the Allies were on the verge of victory. But now I don't know what to think. You may have heard that they've developed a new bomb. All I've heard is that it's too hot to handle. I don't think Truman will have the nerve to use it, do you?*

This will be the shortest letter I've ever written to you, darling, but I'm going to have to sign off. My mind is numb! Maybe I'll just lie down and try to sleep. I'll try to dream of a world where everything isn't falling apart. Pray for our country, honey!

Your soldier,
Love, xoxoxo
Michael

Long after the sun had gone down, Michael and a half dozen of his friends sat around a campfire, now just a cluster of red-hot coals, encircled by gray stones. Anything they had needed to say about the death of the President had been said, and as the night burned away, the conversation turned to other matters. Baseball, fishing, family, and eventually, the definition of what they spoke of as "the perfect man."

Jimbo seemed to have strong opinions on the subject. "For me, the perfect man is someone who provides for his family. In my case, when I get married, I don't expect my wife to work. I'll make sure the bills are paid, and she'll take care of the kids and the house."

"That makes sense to me," Michael agreed. "I don't think I'd want my wife working, either, if I can earn enough money so she doesn't need to."

"What if your wife wants ta work? What then?" a short G.I. named Wiggins asked.

Jimbo answered, "The perfect man would explain to her why it's best for the family if she doesn't."

"But what if she don't listen to you?" Wiggins fired back.

"The perfect man is a guy who won't take any guff from anybody, especially his wife," said Enzo, a scruffy, dark-haired Italian. Unlike on the base, a soldier could get away with not shaving at Camp Mystic.

"Yeah," a big-eared private with an eye patch piped in. "What if she got a mind of her own?"

"Then she'll get a fuckin' earful from me, that's what," Enzo scoffed.

When the group laughed at Enzo's remark, he shot back, "Aw, bullshit. Screw you, assholes."

Michael interrupted. "Okay…okay, hold on, you guys. Any of you experts married?" When no one spoke, he continued. "That's what I figured. Sounds like none of us has any experience with marriage. So perfect man or not, we'll all have to cross that bridge when we come to it. I know one thing. I got a girl waiting for me, and once I get discharged and marry her, I'll find out how perfect I am. And not a day sooner. My girl and I will work out life together. It won't always be a piece of cake, I know, but I'm looking forward to it."

The debaters continued on and on until Michael grew tired of their babble. His mood darkened, and he found himself troubled. He remembered how Cecelia had been singing with the All-Stars before they temporarily disbanded. But the war wasn't far from over, and what then? Would she go back to singing with the band? After they were married, would she be out singing every weekend? If so, how would that impact the raising of children? It was a sticky wicket because she loved to sing. How would he even broach the subject? Being the perfect man seemed a daunting challenge.

...Darling, you should have heard the conversation around the campfire tonight. What a bunch of know-it-alls! The guys were talking about what "the perfect man" is. Everybody had their opinions. And there was a lot of razzing and joking. You know how guys are, honey, right? But here's my conclusion. I feel that there is no such thing as a perfect man, but I know, with you, I can be a better man. Hearing these dopes carry on tonight, I realized I need you to complete me! I know that when we're married, we won't agree on every little thing. But I hope we can both compromise and work together to iron out our differences and to become better people in the process...

A week later, Michael received news that his recuperation was complete and he could return to duty. He felt like he had been sprung from prison. He looked forward to reuniting with Russo, Denny, Dutch, Weber, and Mouse, the gang he had transferred from Independence to San Antonio with. What he didn't realize was that while he was living the easy life in Mystic, his pals had moved on to the next levels of training and were no longer in San Antonio.

Michael didn't know anyone in San Antonio when he arrived, except for the instructors.

Was he ever happy to see Captain Griffith who got him up in the air again in a jiffy. Michael didn't seem to lose much, and Captain Griffith never brought up the accident.

At the end of April, the airwaves were filled with one drama after another. Talk of the death of the President still lingered on the lips of Americans in every barbershop, tavern, and luncheonette across the country when the news reported the shocking death of Benito Mussolini who had been shot and then hung upside down on a meat girder in Milan alongside his mistress, Claretta Petacci. Despite the macabre nature of the deaths, most Americans, in their vitriol, felt, "It served 'em right!"

Two days later, the alleged suicide of Hitler hit the airwaves, and the end of the war seemed imminent. Michael had no idea where that left him.

April turned the corner into May, and rumors flew across army bases suggesting who would be discharged first. Michael had explained to Cecelia that the Army would be using a point system based on factors like how much time a soldier had put in, how many medals he had earned, and how many dependent children he had. It would be months before Michael would be discharged. In the meantime, he remained very focused on his passion, flying.

On May 7th, Michael and all of the cadets in San Antonio and across the country received an official letter from Lieutenant General B. K. Yount. With trembling hands, Michael unsealed his letter and, with sober eyes, began to read typewritten text. The opening paragraph of the letter spoke of the "magnificent successes of the Armed Forces in the European Theater" and "the great contribution to the destruction of the Nazi military forces due to the aggressive and heroic warfare waged by the Army Air Forces."

The second paragraph explained the necessity of deploying vast numbers of men to "Asiatic and Pacific combat zones." General Yount further explained that there were a sufficient number of pilots and cadets at the very end of their training to supply the necessary requirement. And then came the words Michael dreaded:

WHAT ARE THE CHANCES?

IT IS DEEPLY REGRETTABLE, BUT INEVITABLE, THEREFORE, THAT YOU MUST BE WITHDRAWN FROM THE AIRCREW TRAINING PROGRAM AND DIVERTED TO OTHER ASSIGNMENTS WHERE YOU MAY CONTRIBUTE IN THE MAXIMUM DEGREE TO THE DEFEAT OF JAPAN. I SHALL NOT ATTEMPT TO MINIMIZE THE KEEN DISAPPOINTMENT I KNOW YOU WILL SUFFER AT BEING WITHDRAWN FROM THE AIRCREW TRAINING THROUGH NO FAULT OF YOUR OWN—BUT YOU MUST CONSIDER THESE MEASURES IN A PRACTICAL MANNER. WE ALL AGREE THAT IT IS FORTUNATE THIS FAVORABLE TURN OF EVENTS HAS MADE THIS ENTRENCHMENT PROGRAM POSSIBLE. WE HAVE A BIG JOB FOR YOU IN THE BATTLES YET TO BE FOUGHT.

Michael's eyes scanned the last three paragraphs of General Yount's justification for terminating thousands of cadets and reassigning them to other combat duties before reading the last few sentences.

WE ARE INDEED FORTUNATE TO HAVE YOUR YOUTH, YOUR INTELLIGENCE, YOUR COURAGE, AND YOUR ENTHUSIASM TO DO A JOB FOR THE ARMY AIR FORCES AND YOUR COUNTRY. WE EXPECT YOU WILL DO THE JOB WHEREVER IT MAY BE YOUR PRIVILEGE TO SERVE.

A group of the guys decided to meet after dinner behind the PX, their best bet for privacy. They hoped not to be discovered.

Four cadets showed up, and at first, no one had anything to say. Each of the men lit up a cigarette and smoked under a starless Texas sky.

Finally, one of the guys broke the silence, a tall beanpole with a dry brush of red hair that the guys called K.C., short for Kansas City. "Well, I think we should all start with a swig a' this." He slipped a pint bottle with the label half ripped off from his back pocket.

"What the fuck is that?" asked Grabowski, his Brooklyn accent unmistakable.

"Just somethin' to wash our troubles away," K.C. answered.

"Geez," Michael chimed in. "If we're caught drinking this stuff on the base, they'll throw the book at us."

K.C. took the first swig. "Let 'em throw the book at us. What've we got ta lose now?"

"He's right," Whitey, a California blond, jumped in. "We don't don't got squat to lose. Hand that over here." After taking a gulp, Whitey coughed, "Ouch! What the fuck, K.C.? You tryin' to poison us? What is this shit?"

"Don't worry about it! It's some home brew I got from, let's just say, a friend. It might not taste good, but it'll do the job."

Whitey passed it to Grabowski, who swished the tonic around like mouthwash, swallowed, and passed it to Michael.

After taking a slug, Michael grimaced and wiped his mouth on his sleeve. "Christ!"

The conversation turned to General Yount's letter.

"How about that part where he said how disappointed we must be?" Grabowski scoffed.

"And all that malarkey about our youth and intelligence and courage," Whitey added.

"Yeah! All that build-up for the bigger let down ta come," K.C. complained.

The bottle was on its second pass around the circle. Each took a bigger swallow and made less of a face this time.

Michael rapped his knuckles on the bottle. "So where do you suppose that leaves us?"

"Where else?" Grabowski answered. "Crawling across some God forsaken island in the Pacific with a rifle in our hands and a cluster of leaves stuck to our helmets, right Whitey?"

"Yup! Where that leaves us is as sitting ducks for the Japs."

Michael, still having some clarity, said, "Well, it's not like we would have been any safer in the cockpit of a plane. The odds were just as bad up there."

"True, my friend from the East Coast," K.C. said. "I don't know about you, but if I'm gonna die for my country, I'd've rather it all ended in the air."

"That makes two of us," Whitey agreed.

The other two muttered in assent as the bottle went around the circle a third time. When it came to Michael, K.C. said, "Finish it up, Michael. There ain't enough to pass it again."

His third swallow was the largest yet, and he didn't wince even though it burned his throat.

Michael let out a deep breath. "What goddamn gets to me is how hard I worked to get into this program. And how I worked even harder to stay in it. Shit, man, I never worked as hard for anything in my life. I mean, I was mostly a fuck-up in high school, because, well, what was the point in being anything else? And now it's over."

The men concurred. Each had come from a very humble background. Each had striven mightily to be a cadet. Each had dreamed of flying.

"Well boys," K.C. said. "There ain't jack-shit we can do about it now. But if you'll just excusez-moi for a few minutes, I'll run back to the barracks where I might have another pint bottle stowed away."

They stayed put for another two hours, drinking and talking about a grab bag of subjects from baseball to religion and from fishing to women. Finally, K.C. spoke. "Listen, boys, I'm just about all talked out. Shit, it's almost midnight. I'm going to bed."

Unsteady on his feet, Michael headed for the barracks. K.C.'s brew had hit him hard, whatever the hell it was! He would like to have collapsed in a heap when he got to his bunk, but knew he couldn't. He hadn't yet written to Cecelia. Picking up a pen, he tried to keep his hand steady as he wrote.

May 7, 1945

My Darling,

> *It's pretty late now, honey. Yeah, it's late. I guess just about every-thing I've ever done in my life was too late. We fellows spent most of the night behind the PX discussing our sorrows while drinking some rot gut that one of the guys had stowed away. Lemme tell you, honey. You never tasted anything like his stuff.*

> *You'll find the reason for our sorrows in the words of the enclosed letter, just the way it was given to me...to all of us. I want you to keep this letter for me if you would, hon. I'm afraid if I keep it, I'll just take a match to it.*

> *Right now, darling, I got an ice-cold feeling in the pit of my*

stomach and an empty feeling in my chest. After sweating out just about nineteen months in the program, you can see for yourself that, once again, I've fallen flat on my face. This was something we'd all been expecting for a long time, but it still was a kick in the teeth. I don't know, honey, what to think or what to do neither.

It isn't just that I wanted to fly so much. It's that I wanted to make something of myself. I wanted to be somebody that you would be proud of. What a flop I turned out to be, huh?

I guess the main thing that stumps me, I mean that stumps all of us, is that we're left out on a limb. We don't know what they'll do with us or where the hell they'll send us...or when.

You know, darling, when we worried about washing out, it wasn't half bad, but when they gave us each an individual letter, it sort of hit low. I guess the main thing that kept me from losing complete control was that I received two letters from you today. It always takes you to lift me out of the dust of discouragement.

I think I'll just break it off there, honey, because I'd rather not talk about it anymore tonight. Not until I cool off. It looks like I'll just go back to living a regular G.I. life again.

I suppose it doesn't matter anyway. All that matters, darling, is that we love each other. In the end, all I have are my memories of being with you. Those memories keep me going. I wouldn't trade them for anything.

Last week you wrote that you'll never fade from me. God, if you ever did, I don't think there would be anything left of me. Without you, my life wouldn't have any purpose at all, believe me!

It's awful late, darling, and I'm not feeling so good. My eyes just won't stay open any longer. I love you with all my heart...and even with all my life, and I will forever and ever! It's the truth!

Your soldier,
Love, xoxoxo
Michael

45

Upon hearing of the alleged suicide of Adolf Hitler, it was as if the country, as one giant organism, breathed a sigh of relief. The death of Hitler prophesied the end of the war in Europe, and President Harry S. Truman's radio broadcast a week later made it official on what would become known as "Victory in Europe Day" across the country and the world.

Like all Americans, Cecelia and Connie tuned into the President's radio address. Stella and her mother joined them, and the three girls pulled kitchen chairs close to the radio and sat at the edge of their seats, with Mama holding her Bible and Mrs. Kostenko clutching a black rosary nearby on the sofa.

The broadcast began with President Truman emphasizing the gravity of the moment:

> *This is a solemn but glorious hour. General Eisenhower informs me that the forces of Germany have surrendered to the United Nations. The flags of reason fly over all of Europe. I only wish that Franklin D. Roosevelt had lived to witness this day...*

Cecelia recalled how she had been unable to curb the flow of tears upon hearing of the tragic loss of President Roosevelt, sitting in front of the same radio not even two months before. Reeling herself in, she forced herself to focus on Truman's continuing message to America:

Our rejoicing is sobered and subdued by a supreme consciousness of the terrible price we have paid to rid the world of Hitler and his evil band. Let us not forget, my fellow Americans, the sorrow and heartbreak which today abide in the homes of so many of our neighbors, neighbors whose most priceless possession has been rendered as a sacrifice to redeem our liberty...

Cecelia pictured the grief-stricken faces of the O'Brians at the loss of their son. A priceless possession indeed. How could such a loss be measured or repaid? It could not. She breathed in and released a deep sigh.

As the President continued, explaining that the war was "half-won" but that it wouldn't be over until "the last Japanese division has surrendered, unconditionally," Cecelia wondered if that day would ever come. Was surrender even possible? She worried that she wouldn't see Michael again, ever.

While the President made his final remarks, talking about building "an abiding peace, a peace rooted in justice and in law," Cecelia contemplated what kind of law could extend across the globe to stop other despots from wreaking havoc in the future.

The President ended with a call for the nation, no matter what their faith, "to offer a moment of joyful prayer to God for this victory we have won," as well as "to dedicate this day of prayer to those who have given their lives to make possible our victory."

Solemnly, Connie reached and turned off the radio dial. The five women sat in silence for a good while. Cecelia could hear Mama whispering prayers in Italian and the click-click of Mrs. Kostenko's beads. She guessed that Connie and Stella were praying as well.

She found herself questioning rather than praying, though. Was it a day of prayer for most people? She was well aware that, in anticipation of the news, celebrating had begun in bigger cities like New York, Chicago, and Los Angeles. Even in Shelton and Derby, people were gathering at local taverns. She herself didn't have a stomach for it. Were the O'Brian's celebrating? Not likely. So, how could she?

Four days later, she received a letter from a disappointed Michael about how the news had impacted his life. The envelope contained a very official looking letter from a Lieutenant General B.K. Yount. Slowly, she read the general's words, and then she reread them. Michael's handwritten message, uncharacteristically sloppy, oozed disappointment at not being able to finish the Cadet Program. She would save General Yount's letter, placing it in the bottom drawer of Mama's old dresser with all of Michael's letters, tidy packets of envelopes, wrapped in lavender ribbon by month.

In her response to Michael, she would encourage him as she had whenever he felt downtrodden. Writing about her anticipation of their upcoming marriage always seemed to lift his spirits. That might be the poultice to soothe his emotional wounds. She was learning more and more how sensitive he was, but she knew he was a man, that he had a mechanism inside of him that caused him to huff and puff, to plan and to strive.

The first day of summer arrived. Cecelia always liked that her birthday ushered in the new season. In a year, she would be of legal drinking age, which she got a kick out of since she had been served at local establishments for at least two years. No one in the spirits business seemed concerned about the matter.

On the day of her birthday, she not only received Michael's daily letter but also a small package.

> *...It's not much of a gift, honey, I know, but I'm afraid they don't have much of a selection for ladies at the PX here. Let's just say it isn't Howard and Barber's. I'll admit I got a couple of strange looks buying lacy pink hankies, but I had to get you something, and they were about the prettiest thing in the PX, but the truth is, nothing can match your prettiness...*

His letter also expressed his ongoing confusion with his possible reassignment.

...I have no idea what's going to happen to me, darling. The strangest thing, though, is that my crew and I are still being given hours up in the air. We're not complaining, though. We're afraid to even ask, so we just keep our traps shut. But if we're not going to finish the Cadet Program, then why are we still flying? Personally, I think it's because they don't know what else to do with us...

Two days later, a silver Buick pulled up outside of Cecelia's house at 11:00 a.m. with the horn honking.

When she and Connie went outside to see who it was and little Connie jumped out of the car, it was a joyful reunion. All three girls screamed and ran to each other, jumping up and down and embracing. After they finished squeezing the life out of each other, the Alberino sisters noticed a man standing outside of the driver's side of the car. He was tall and stout and balding, perhaps in his mid-forties.

"Girls," little Connie said, her face all aglow, "I'd like you to meet my new husband, John Thomas Rafferty."

"Husband?" Cecelia exclaimed as if she wasn't sure she heard correctly.

"Yes, I am now Mrs. Rafferty," Connie boasted.

Cecelia hoped her face didn't give away her utter disbelief at the startling news. Connie invited the newlyweds inside while Cecelia ran next door to get Stella. When they all sat down in the parlor, little Connie explained that she and her new husband had eloped. Cecelia, who was heating up water for tea in the kitchen, had a hunch that little Connie spoke with an inflated volume for her benefit.

"We just up and took off and got hitched three days ago. A JP in Delaware did the honors. Then a very brief honeymoon," Connie tittered, "but I said, 'Oh, John Thomas, how about we drive to Connecticut and wish my girlfriend a happy birthday?' I wish we could have made it here on the day of, but, well, we were busy."

Little Connie had a million questions about the fiancés of her friends. Where were they now stationed? When did they hope to be discharged? What were their respective marriage plans?

John Thomas interjected his own remarks into the conversation a little more liberally than Cecelia thought appropriate. "Yup, I wish I could've fought in this one. I would've shown them rotten Jerries and Japs a thing or two! I keep missing these things, dang it! I was just a boy for the first one, and this time, too old!"

What a blowhard, Cecelia thought. *What would have ever possessed little Connie to run off and marry a man so much older–and one as unattractive in personality as in appearance?*

When Connie mentioned that she hoped that the war in Japan would end soon so that Pete could come home, John Thomas interjected, "You don't gotta worry about your boyfriend. This thing's gonna be over before you can spell Mississippi!"

Puzzled, the girls just looked at him.

"Haven't you girls heard about the bomb Truman's talkin' about droppin'?"

Cecelia spoke. "Michael's mentioned it in a few letters. He said something like, 'it's too hot to handle,' but I wasn't sure what he meant."

"What he meant, dolly, is that when Truman drops them bad boys–*wherever* he drops 'em–they're gonna incinerate every Jap for miles and miles. Do you know how many tons of TNT those things got in 'em? They say *thousands* of tons. Those dirty Japs'll really find out what's good for 'em."

Being addressed as "dolly" irked Cecelia, and while she had heard people use the word "Jap," she feared she would scream if John Thomas spewed the three letter slur one more time.

"But if the bomb impacts its target for miles, won't innocent people be killed?" Stella asked.

Already too loud, John Thomas now raised his volume another notch. "None of 'em are innocent, girlie. And what's the difference, anyway, how many Japs get killed? The more the better, as far as I'm concerned."

Cecelia felt like she was suffocating. Abruptly excusing herself, she walked through the kitchen, pushed the screen door open, and escaped into the back yard. Unable to think, she broke into a trot on the grass alongside Mama's vegetable garden. At the end of a row of bean plants, she grabbed a pod off of its vine, ripped it in half, and threw it to the ground in frustration.

A few moments later, she saw Stella approaching. "Celia!" she called. "What the heck? You okay?"

"No, I'm not okay. I couldn't sit there any longer and listen to that bag of hot air! How could Connie have married such a jerk? For Christ's sake, he's old enough to be her father."

"Who knows?" Stella replied. "She must like him, I guess."

"Like him? How? I can't stand him."

"Wow, you're worked up," Stella said.

"You bet I am. What kind of remark was that, anyway? Saying the more that get killed the better?"

"Well, they are the enemy, aren't th–"

"Hold on now. Are they any different from Michael or Donny or Pete? Aren't they people who left their families…their moms and dads and brothers and sisters and girlfriends to fight this war? Aren't they following orders just like our guys? And what about their families? You yourself asked the question. You heard what Mr. Blowhard said, 'it's going to incinerate everything for miles around.' What if the enemy dropped a bomb over the U.S. and it incinerated everything for miles around?"

Stella didn't know how to reply to Cecelia's barrage of questions. Helplessly, she said, "We better go back in, though, Celia. I left Connie holding the bag."

"Well, if anyone can hold the bag, it's my sister. Look, I can't go back in. I can't deal with spending another minute in that jerk's presence. I'm going to take a walk. Tell them—just make something up. Tell little Connie I'll catch up to her. Tell her to leave her address so I can write to her."

The end of June melted into a sweltering month of July as Cecelia went about the humdrum routine of her life, going to work at the plant every day, coming home, her free time spent with Connie and Stella as they wondered when their beaus would finally be discharged. The highlight of Cecelia's day was reading and responding to letters from Michael.

Listening to the news each day, the girls kept abreast of the greater war effort. In late July when they heard the news of the Potsdam Declaration, a statement issued from President Truman, Prime Minister Winston Churchill, and Chairman Chiang Kai-shek, calling for the surrender of all Japanese armed forces, Cecelia and the girls hoped that the war would come to an end without further bloodshed and death.

Still, news reports had also indicated that the people of Japan were fighting for the emperor, and Hirohito had convinced them it was better to die than surrender. Horrifying reports of kamikaze pilots who often turned their planes into guided missiles, sacrificing themselves in the process, were a clear indication of the fanatical loyalty to the emperor.

The three girls and their mothers found themselves, once again, in front of the radio on August 6th, listening to an explanation of Japan's forced surrender from the President.

Sixteen hours ago, an American airplane dropped one bomb on Hiroshima, an important Japanese army base. That bomb had more power than 20,000 tons of T.N.T. It had more than two thousand times the blast power of the British "Grand Slam" which is the largest bomb ever yet used in the history of warfare. The Japanese began the war from the air at Pearl Harbor. They have been repaid many fold. And the end is not yet. With this bomb we have now added a new and revolutionary increase in destruction to supplement the growing power of our armed forces. In their present form, these bombs are now in production and even more powerful forms are in development. It is an atomic bomb. It is a harnessing of the basic power of the universe. The force from which the sun draws its power has been loosed against those who brought war to the Far East...

Cecelia's mind, as it had on VE Day, once more shifted into high gear. She found it nearly impossible to comprehend the President's description—a bomb that harnessed *the basic power of the universe—the force from which the sun draws its power...*

How could that be? she pondered. She didn't yet know the specifics—that the bomb ironically known as "Little Boy," dropped from the Enola Gay would be responsible for approximately 80,000 deaths—or that a second atomic bomb, more appropriately named "Fat Man," dropped three days later, would kill in the vicinity of another 40,000 men, women, and children, not to mention how many these bombs would injure and maim.

Trying to focus, she listened as the President continued:

We have spent two billion dollars on the greatest scientific gamble in history and won. But the greatest marvel is not the size of the enterprise, its secrecy, nor its cost, but the achievement of scientific brains in putting together infinitely complex pieces of knowledge held by many men in different fields of science into a workable plan...

But when President Truman went on to laud the efforts of American and British scientists who collaborated along with the United States Army on this achievement, and to explain "the unique success in managing so diverse a problem in the advancement of knowledge in an amazingly short time," Cecelia could no longer listen to the broadcast. Everyone in the room was stunned when, without warning, she bolted out of the living room, escaping to the front hall stairs and running up to her bedroom.

She was beginning to feel she couldn't handle anything. With her temples throbbing, she thought, *I just want to be left alone!*

She kicked off her shoes and reached into the drawer of her night table, extracting a few sheets of stationery, her diary, and a fountain pen. Knowing the remedy for her troubled soul would be to get her feelings down on paper in a letter to Michael or in her private journal, she wasn't sure which to begin first. After a long pause and a series of deep breaths, she decided to write to Michael first. As therapeutic as writing in her diary was for her, Cecelia knew a diary couldn't respond with a helpful word of advice. She hoped Michael could. She understood that, in one sense, he was appropriately patriotic, while in another sense, he wasn't blind to the tragic nature of war and to the shortcomings of the military. Spreading the paper before her, she prepared herself to pour her heart out to perhaps the one person who might understand how she felt.

$\mathcal{M}$ichael wanted to be careful in his response to Cecelia's letter about the victory over Japan. It was a complicated subject, and he felt he needed to choose his words wisely.

...I understand what you mean, darling. The dropping of the bombs was as startling to us men in the service as it was to all of you back home. I sure don't understand it, but it appears it was what the President felt he needed to do to put an end to this nightmare. There's never been anything like these atomic bombs. Shocking, I know. I suspect it will be at least another generation before anyone can understand the impact of such a decision. This may not be the best advice, but I think we have to put it out of our minds. Look at it this way: we can't let something we can't comprehend or control destroy us, can we? Let's just try to understand our little corner of the world and do our best to find happiness there...

Once President Truman's historic announcements that the Germans and, soon after, the Japanese had been brought to their knees, Michael wrote to Cecelia expressing his concern that he would be assigned to the Army of Occupation. In his neat script, he explained:

...What that means is that the Army goes into the defeated coun-
tries to enforce the peace terms, to keep order, etc. Such an assignment
is about the last thing I would want. You see, darling, there is no crea-
ture on earth more lonesome and inconsolable than a soldier wishing
he could be with his girl back home. The war is over, and through no
real fault of my own, I haven't seen any front line action. It was just
my fate! Now I just want to come home. You must know by now that
all I've ever wanted was to get discharged and come home to marry my
girl. That's not too much to ask, is it?

As the fall months crept in, Michael didn't see much difference
from the sweltering temperatures of summer. He and his group
found themselves stuck in limbo, although for Michael it might as
well have been hell. He didn't like living in Texas where the seasons
hardly changed, and he liked not knowing what his fate would be
even less. What else could he do but sweat it out? Stuck with irrele-
vant inspections and mundane tasks, he trudged from one day to
the next in a meaningless cycle of smothering monotony.

So, it happened on a hot morning in late October that Michael
was called into a meeting with the battalion commander, Colonel
Lionel J. Cooper. Previously, Michael had only been addressed by
the colonel in platoon or company assemblies. To what he owed the
honor of a private meeting, he hadn't a clue.

Stepping into Colonel Cooper's office, Michael came to attention and saluted his commanding officer, fixing his gaze on a large
map of Europe against the wall.

"At ease, soldier," Colonel Cooper said. "Take a seat."

"Thank you, sir," Michael replied.

"You're no doubt wondering why I've asked to meet with you."

"Yes, sir, I guess I am."

"Well, Corporal, I have two pieces of news for you. Both good."

"That's nice to hear, Colonel. I could use some good news."

"But, upon hearing the news, you'll have a big decision to make."

Michael remained silent and apprehensive, wondering what the
colonel could mean.

"The first news is that you are scheduled to be discharged as of
January 1st."

Shifting in his chair, Michael struggled to contain his excitement. "And the other good news, sir?" he asked, not believing it could be any better than what he had just been told.

"The other news, Corporal DeMarco, is that a good many of our current pilots are battle weary and need to be discharged as well. As you no doubt know, we don't need as many pilots as we did in wartime, but some of those boys do need to be replaced. We're looking for the best candidates we have to fill in the gap. One of your flight instructors, Captain Griffith, has submitted your name, Corporal. He says you have all the makings of a crackerjack pilot."

Michael squinted and tilted his head. "I'm not sure I understand what you're saying to me, sir."

"What I'm saying, Corporal, is that we'd like to offer you the opportunity to finish your flight training and earn your commission and your wings. But here's the hitch. It would mean re-upping for another two years. It was a sense of duty that motivated you to enlist, originally, and we're hoping you're still feeling the same sense of duty."

This news was the last thing that Michael had expected to hear.

"Of course, you don't have to give me your answer right now, Corporal. Take some time to think it over. Talk to your folks."

"With all due respect, sir, I feel I can give you my answer right here and now. I appreciate the offer, sir, I really do, and I hope you won't hear this the wrong way. My sense of duty hasn't changed a bit. But I feel I have to decline. You know, flying was something I wanted more than anything I've ever wished for. But fate–or some inexplicable force–kept getting in the way. Now, I'm feeling it's too late for me. Besides, sir, the main thing is I've got a girl waiting for me back home, and my desire to go home and marry her is greater than my desire to fly. That must sound pretty sappy! I'm almost surprised to hear myself say it, sir, but if you saw her, if you knew her, you'd understand."

Michael's monologue caused Colonel Cooper to crack a half smile. "I think I might understand, Corporal. If memory serves, I was young and in love once upon a time myself. Well, here's the long and short of it. You have until December 1st to change your mind. That's about five weeks away. If, after you've given it some thought, you want to accept our offer, it'll still stand."

Michael floated out of the Colonel's office. While he hadn't accepted it, the offer to finish the Cadet Program felt great. He decided not to tell the others–not K.C. or Grabowski or Whitey. As far as he knew, none of them had received the same offer, so he wasn't about to gloat, and he certainly wasn't about to be pressured or razzed about it either.

Michael had a very few people he wanted to tell about the offer, and one in particular.

...And that's what Colonel Cooper said to me, darling. I couldn't believe it. I thought that my opportunity to fly had come and gone. In fact, I'd resigned myself to that idea. As much as I loved flying and as much as I wanted to become a pilot, you can multiply that by a thousand in comparison to how much I want to come home and marry you.

The way I see it, honey, as we go through life, we have different wants and desires, but some are more important than others–much more important! In life, we need to prioritize those things. Maybe we'll always need to make sacrifices, although I've got to tell you, darling, this doesn't feel like much of a sacrifice. For me, it's a no brainer!

Can you imagine? I'll be home in ten short weeks. On this end, it will still feel like an eternity, but I've just got to put it in perspective and realize that it's right around the corner.

I think we should shoot for a September wedding, darling, don't you? That'll give me enough time to get a job and save up a few bucks for us to get a start. It'll be a pretty modest wedding and a pretty meager start in life, for sure, but it'll be all ours! What do you say?

Cecelia sat on the bus, headed for New Haven. With Christmas just around the corner, she realized it had been more than two years, unbelievably, since the last time she had made this journey. Deep in thought, she replayed a recent phone call from Danny about him sharing the good news that the All-Stars were about to get back on their feet. With the war over, soldiers were returning home, he told her, something that would just accelerate in the weeks and months to come. The dance hall owners were anxious to crank up business, and so was Danny.

Upon hearing the news, she asked him if he would meet her privately. The Anchor seemed like a good spot to talk. She hadn't forgotten the last time she'd been there. It had been a turning point in her life, making her realize beyond a shadow of a doubt that she needed to commit herself to Michael. This meeting would be a second turning point.

When Danny rolled into the Anchor in his wheelchair, he couldn't have been happier to see her. Having arrived fifteen minutes early, Cecelia stood when she saw him enter and met him halfway.

"It's so wonderful to see you," she said, embracing him.

"Likewise, sweetheart, likewise!"

Once at the table, the two caught up and shared what was happening in their lives. Lighting a cigarette, Danny explained that, while he was still waiting for a few of the boys to return, he couldn't wait too long because the band needed to get rolling. Music and dancing were paramount to the morale of the country.

Cecelia explained that Michael would be home in the beginning of January and made a special point to explain how he had passed up the opportunity to become a pilot because it meant reenlisting. She even told Danny about their impending September wedding.

"The poor sap must be head over heels for you," Danny teased, and then getting more serious, "not that I blame him one damned bit."

"Oh stop! You're making me blush."

"It's true, though. What guy wouldn't want to marry you?"

Cecelia sighed. "Well, that's what I wanted to talk about."

"Uh-oh, this sounds like bad news."

Cecelia felt her throat constrict as tears escaped both eyes.

"You're not going to come back to the All-Stars, are ya?"

She was unable to utter a reply.

"I kinda knew that's what this meeting was gonna be about."

"It's just that," she began, "just that…I don't see how I can marry Michael and sing with the band every weekend. You see, we've exchanged a lot of letters about how it will be. We've written to each other about how we want to start a family, and well, I've always felt that when I became a mother, I'd want to be home with my children. You, being Italian, can understand that, right?"

"Yeah, sure, I get it. Just like my mother and probably yours too."

"Yes, exactly. And Michael talks about one day building a house for us. Even designing it. We just have so many hopes and dreams."

"Yeah," Danny said. "I think I get the picture."

Relieved, Cecelia smiled, teary-eyed. "I'm glad you understand."

Danny couldn't hide his disappointment. "Well, I'm not gonna lie and say I'm not heartbroken. Anyway, it's an ongoing problem. We lost Claire Fontaine when she had her baby, and she wasn't the first singer I ever lost. I've been at this game a long time!"

"And Danny, Michael said something that hit home for me. He said sometimes in life we need to prioritize our wants and desires and sometimes make sacrifices. I know in my heart that, as much as I've loved singing with the All-Stars, a life with Michael is my priority."

"Whoosh," Danny exclaimed. "He must be quite a guy."

"He is. He's honest and steadfast and determined, but he still wears his heart on his sleeve. I've never met a guy like him."

"Well, you can tell that bum for me that I don't like guys who steal my singers!"

Cecelia laughed, reached over, and put her hand over Danny's. "Well, you'll meet him before long. When he gets home, we'll be sure to come to one of the dances you're playing at."

"I don't suppose you'd mind singing a song or two with the boys in such a case. We've still got all the charts in your keys, you know."

"I'd love that, Danny! I really would!"

On the bus ride home, the events of the last three years played back in Cecelia's mind, like a movie reel. She remembered dancing with Michael at the Lakeview Casino, and how he stubbornly refused to let a sailor cut in. How brash he was. She remembered the walk back to the center of Derby and how he charmed her while his friend Scooter ran interference for him with the two Connies. And then there was the so-called blind date and the subsequent first kiss. She would forever remember his vulnerability when he asked if he could write to her. When she had wanted to go slow, Michael had a sense of urgency. When she had held back, he had expressed his feelings with eloquence and without apology. When she had felt uncertain, he had forged ahead with confidence. It was impossible to put into words how she felt about each handwritten expression of his love. There must have been over a thousand letters, and she would save them forever.

Upon arriving home, she found Connie swishing a tea bag in a cup of steaming water.

"Where ya been all morning?" Connie asked.

"I went into New Haven to see Danny," Cecelia explained.

"Oh, about the band, huh?"

"That's right."

"Did you tell him what I think you told him?"

Cecelia let out a deep sigh. "Yup. It sure was fun while it lasted."

"Have a seat and let me make you a cup of tea," Connie offered. "Maybe you'd like to talk about it. Or, if not, you and I can talk about our wedding plans. That'd be nice."

"If it's all the same to you, Connie, I think I'll just go upstairs, maybe write in my diary. It's been a long day. But I promise to talk to you about our weddings later on."

"Good, because you and I are going to have beautiful weddings. We have better days to look forward to."

"I know, sis. Thanks for reminding me. Love you!"

"And I love you right back!"

When Cecelia flopped on her bed, she opened her diary.

December 14th, 1945

Dear Diary,

I've spent my life not getting the gifts I dreamed of on Christmas. This Christmas, though, will be different. The gift will be delayed a week or two, but I don't mind. I know it's still going to be the best Christmas ever...

47

Gabriel – 2005

*I*t was a month after Christmas. Gabriel grabbed his over-coat and slipped out the back door of the house. He trudged across the snow covered back yard and up the bank to the frozen garden. The large plot of land, perhaps half an acre, had been rendered fallow for nearly a decade, ever since his father had grown too old to tend to it. It wasn't exactly a farm, but it was the biggest garden he'd ever seen an individual have, except for his grandparents, but in their case, the terraced gardens had been more out of need than anything else, hadn't they?

Dad was sure a chip off the old block. Or maybe *blocks,* because he was a product of both parents. And like his parents, Dad had kept chickens and jarred eggplant and tapped the maple trees for syrup, and…oh yes, kept a vegetable garden.

Gabriel stood staring at the hardened ground, the freezing air numbing his face. He pondered the electric fence that wrapped around its perimeter, covered now by a thin frosting of snow and ice. His father had installed it decades before to keep deer out of the garden. "The bastards eat all my crops," Dad had complained.

The garden had become Dad's escape once they moved into the new house when Gabriel was seventeen. Coming home after a long day at work, Dad would eat dinner and spend a few hours in the garden before nightfall. It was nice when he retired at sixty-five and could devote all of his time to his passion.

Gabriel remembered walking out of the house after Sunday visits with enough vegetables to sink a ship, to use a cliche–more than he, Nan, and the girls could hope to eat in a week. Unable to keep pace with Dad's overabundant harvest, Gabriel sometimes had to throw food away, unfortunately. One thing was for certain. Dad always made sure that his children and grandchildren had plenty to eat. It was the reason Mom, in an ironic tone, referred to him as "Mother Earth."

Squinting, he saw his nephew leave the house and follow him up to the garden, stepping into the imprints in the snow that Gabriel had already made. He tried to recall Joseph's age. *Let's see, he must be about thirty...no thirty one,* he thought as Joseph approached. It was hard to believe, the first-born grandchild now in his thirties.

"Hey, Uncle Gabe, what are you up to?" Joseph called out as he approached. "I hope I'm not bothering you. I saw you through the glass doors and just thought I'd check up on you."

"No, you're not bothering me," Gabriel replied. "I just wanted to come up here and think. What's your dad doing?"

"Oh, he conked out on the couch. You know him. My mom and Auntie Nan and the girls are talking to Gram, trying to keep her mind occupied."

"Well, it's been a rough few days. That was a nice eulogy you gave in church. Good going."

"Oh thanks. I was honored to give it."

"It makes sense. You were his first grandchild. He loved you so much."

Gabriel watched as Joseph made a circle in the snow with the toe of his shoe.

"Anyway, hard as it is to believe, he's gone now."

"We're going to miss him," Joseph replied sullenly.

"For sure."

"The stories. So many stories."

Gabriel sighed and shrugged. His father had been telling the stories to him since he was a small child, and then in turn, to Gabriel's two daughters and to Joseph and his sister. And now

Gabriel himself had begun telling boyhood stories, his father's and his own, to his young grandson.

Continuing, Joseph said, "I mean...the bullet in the finger."

"Crazy, right?"

"And to think it stayed lodged there for all those years until his body expelled it just a few years ago."

"It boggles the mind."

"Yup." Joseph emitted a chuckle. "He lived quite a life, didn't he?"

"True. I don't know if it was always what he wanted, but he did things his way. A fiercely independent man. Think of the house. Designed it himself. Unlike any I've ever seen."

"True."

"And he pretty much built it himself. Besides the plumbing work, he did a lot of the rest–most of the electrical, sheet rocking, laying down the plywood floors. When I was a teenager, he used to make me come here with him after we had supper. What a pathetic helper I was. And how I used to hate to come. I regret that now."

Joseph remained quiet, just holding the space for his uncle's grief.

The two men gazed down at the house, a large square ranch, all of the rooms wrapped around a central atrium with a glass ceiling at least twenty feet from the floor, dark rich paneling, and immense plants with lush tropical leaves sprouting from handmade planters.

"He sure had a green thumb, didn't he?"

"Sure did, Joe. He could do anything with those hands."

"Everything he did had to be bigger and better than anyone else's," Joseph added, "the house, the Lincoln Town Car, the diamonds and furs he bought Gramma, the vacations to Europe. Even the garden. Everything."

"Yup."

"Why do you think that was?"

"I don't know. He had a drive like nobody I've ever known, that's for damn sure."

"You know, Uncle Gabe, it occurred to me back when I was still in college that Grampa achieved the American Dream in a big way. Wouldn't you say?"

"It was important to him, his way of proving himself. After the poverty and prejudice he had faced growing up, he needed to validate himself as a real American."

Staring down at the big house below, the snow now melting off the glass above the atrium, Gabriel recalled Christmases gone by, the fifteen foot tree towering above the blood red carpet, impeccably decorated by his father, and the absurd number of gifts laid out under the tree when they arrived on Christmas morning. It brought back wonderful memories. But he also recalled that each Christmas—in fact, just about every Sunday for that matter—his father got good and drunk.

In the freezing cold of the January afternoon, Joseph seemed to read his mind. "Did it bother you that he drank like he did?"

"Yes, I suppose it did," Gabriel answered.

"I hope you don't mind my asking. My dad doesn't like to talk about these things. Did Gramp always drink like that?"

Gabriel sighed. "When your dad and I were kids, no. Only on Saturday nights when he and Gramma went out to dances and balls. They loved dancing, those two. When they'd arrive home, I could hear that they were tipsy, our bedroom being right off the kitchen in the old Maltby Street apartment. It was so small. But after he built this house...from then on, he started drinking just about every night."

"Why do you suppose that was?"

"I wish I knew. Why does anyone develop a drinking problem? Pressure. Stress. Missed opportunities. Broken dreams. Could be any...or all of those."

Gabriel's response took Joseph a bit by surprise. "Missed opportunities? Broken dreams?"

"Yup. I don't think he wanted to be a plumbing contractor. I mean, he made a lot of money at it, but I wouldn't call it his passion. But you know him. He always said, 'If it was supposed to be fun, they wouldn't call it *work!*' "

"Did Grampa have a passion?"

"Hmm, he was an anomaly because, in one sense, he was the most passionate person I've ever known, but, in another sense, I don't know if he believed in passion. Whenever your dad or I seemed to be discovering a passion, he tended to squelch it, calling it a pipe dream. But..."

"But what?" Joseph asked.

"I think maybe he did once. Flying."

"Oooh! Ri-i-i-ght!" The lightbulb switched on brightly in Joseph's mind. "That didn't occur to me, but you could be very right. He used to light up whenever he mentioned it to me."

"The way I see it," Gabriel continued, "is that he always discouraged what he called *pipe dreams* because, well, because his own didn't work out."

"I see what you mean."

Gabriel's mind went back in time. "Yeah, when I was a kid, maybe nine or ten, Grampa got me going building model airplanes, World War I models like, let's see, the Sopwith Camel."

Joseph chuckled. "Ah, Snoopy and the Red Baron!"

"Yes," Gabriel continued, "it was a British plane. Then I remember making a Fokker biplane, which was, of course, a German plane, but a famous one–and World War II models, like Corsairs and B-52 Bombers. There were others. I've forgotten. I must have built about a dozen of them."

"Oh, wow. I didn't know about that."

"Yup! He had me thinking I was going to go to the Air Force Academy."

"No kidding. I never knew that. So, what happened?"

"I guess I lost interest. The war in Vietnam and all. And he didn't push it. And your grandmother's influence was stronger on us, anyway. So your dad and I both ended up following the career path she would have loved. Teaching. It's all good because we were both born to be teachers."

"As it turned out, he didn't talk about the military and flight training much, at least not to me. How about you?"

"Not much. Through the years, I asked questions and learned he got into and then didn't finish the Cadet Program. When I asked him why, he said it was because the war ended, but I don't know. I think there was more to it than that."

Squinting, Joseph said, "Yeah, he told me that too, but I never knew the real reason either. He also told me that he broke both of his arms, so I always thought that might have been the reason."

"Yeah, I have no idea how he broke them. That was one of his big secrets. How does someone break both arms in one shot?"

"You know what I think, Uncle Gabe? It's just a theory, but I think he tied one on and went up in a plane without permission, somehow had a mishap, and broke both arms inside the cockpit of a plane."

"I don't know about that one, Joe," Gabriel said skeptically. "He would have been court-martialed for a crazy stunt like that."

"Yeah, I guess so. Well, if he never told you or me, I guess we'll never know."

"Not unless we read the letters."

"The letters?"

"All of his love letters to Gramma. They're in a box in a closet in the basement. I noticed them after he built the house."

"How many are there?"

"I don't know. A million!"

Joseph laughed. "Get out."

"There are *a lot* of them. He must have written every day."

"And you never read them?"

"It wasn't long after we moved in that I noticed them in an old box all tied up in purple ribbon. I read one, but it had all this lovey-dovey stuff. You know, when you're a kid, you don't want to think of your parents as being in love. I'll get around to reading them eventually. "

"But they were, weren't they?"

"Were?"

"In love."

"I suppose so. I mean, their relationship was often contentious, but they worked it out somehow. I've learned in marriage that you either work things out or you don't, which is why God invented divorce."

Joseph laughed again.

Gabriel shrugged. "But look at them–married for almost sixty years. I don't think anyone can accuse them of not having worked things out. You know what I think, though?"

"What's that?"

"I think Grampa loved Gram more than she loved him."

"What makes you say that?"

"It's hard to say. A gut feeling. He was just someone who loved with his whole being. Even when he was hard on us, your dad and I still somehow knew he loved us. His love was fierce that way. She's more guarded."

"Did she guard her love with you and Dad?"

"No, not at all. She loved us and accepted us completely. But it was different with him. She took no bull from him, nor did he take any from her. They were an interesting pair."

The two rested in solitude for a few moments, gazing at the frozen garden, digesting the life of a man they had both loved deeply.

Finally, Joseph spoke. "Well, maybe we should go inside and get out of the cold."

"Why don't you go ahead in, Joe? I think I'll stay out here for a few more minutes, if you don't mind."

"Okay, but don't overdo it. You'll get frostbite!"

"You sound like your mother," Gabriel said, and both men laughed once more.

Watching Joseph take small, careful steps down the icy bank toward the house, Gabriel's mind drifted back to the recent week. He remembered Dad's last day at Griffin Hospital. The doctor had scheduled him to go to a local nursing home for rehab. Gabriel remembered that he had to leave the room to take a phone call, and when he returned to Dad's room to say goodbye, everyone was gone.

Lying in his hospital bed like an Egyptian king on a golden palanquin, Dad said, "Hey Gabe, I don't think I'm going to go to that nursing home."

"What are you talking about, Dad?"

Dad just frowned. "Yeah, I'm not going."

"Dad, listen. Doctor Rinaldi said you need rehab. Mom is incapable of taking care of you. You've got to go."

Then Dad smirked and said the last thing of consequence Gabriel remembered him ever saying: "Gabe, don't you know me yet?"

In his heart, Gabe felt that he knew his father better than anyone, that his father and he were cut from the same cloth.

But his father did go, and two days later, unbelievably, his father couldn't speak at all. Five days later, Gabe and his brother Michael got the phone calls at their respective schools. Dad was dead.

Gabriel would never forget speeding to the convalescent home and entering the hospital room. It was the first time he had been in the presence of death outside of a funeral home or church. This viewing of his father's lifeless body was more unsettling–no embalming or suit and tie to dress the pale corpse. *So this is what death looks like*, he had thought to himself. As the raging wind screamed and whistled outside the window, he marveled at how appropriate it was that the gods had whipped up a storm to usher his father into the next world.

And then, an hour later, he and Michael had arrived at the house at the same time, as if planned, to deliver the sad news to Mom. How she had cried. A series of loud throaty sobs that came from a place deep within, a place where we are both human and animal, as he and Michael sat by helplessly listening to their mother's primal lament.

The couple had lived a long life together. Even at fifty-three years old, Gabriel understood a little of what his parents had gone through together. Some of it, he would never know or understand because there are dynamics that can only be experienced directly between two people who live their life together. Gabriel knew that from his own marriage. One thing was certain–his parents had left an indelible imprint on him and his brother.

He spent a few more moments gazing across the expanse of the garden. It would remain permanently unplanted now, he knew, and it made him sad.

Looking down, he spotted some small rocks amidst the snow and dirt. Reaching down with his ungloved hand, Gabriel pried a stone, round like a smooth walnut, out of the crystalline whiteness. He brushed it off with his cold fingers and dried it on his overcoat. He would put it on Dad's gravestone. Tossing the stone in the air and catching it, he decided to go back inside and spend some time with his mother. She would need him now, and he would need her. Gabriel wrapped his fingers around the small stone and slid his hand into the warmth of his pocket. With a sad smile, he headed back toward the house that his father had designed and built.

ACKNOWLEDGMENTS

Writing *What are the Chances?* took nearly two years, which was longer than I had anticipated ("writer's block" is a malady I haven't yet experienced). The writing, though, was informed by the reading of over a thousand letters my father wrote to my mother while in the army during World War II, which took time. Dad's letters are, in my mind, a true family treasure. What happened to Mom's letters is a mystery.

Sometimes reading those letters was exciting and enlightening; other times it was tedious and dull–all depending on what Dad wrote to Mom on a given day. What surprised me was how eloquent and romantic he was, so much so that I sometimes used passages from his letters, word for word.

I spun this work of fiction from these daily letters as well as from stories my parents had told me about their lives when I was growing up. There were, of course, holes in the stories–things I never thought to ask and needed to fill in using my imagination. While some of the stories in *What are the Chances?* could be considered true, there are also a great many characters and situations that are strictly fictional as well.

Overall, creating the story of Michael and Cecelia was a labor of love, and it will live on for the Scarpas as a family legacy. I want to thank a few people. First and foremost, *What are the Chances?* wouldn't exist without the dedication, diligence, skill, and keen eye of my "Girl Friday," Mia Scarpa, who works in partnership with me as my editor. Mia has been by my side throughout the entire process, either in-person or through numerous Zoom calls. Mia's daily involvement along with the support of my wife Francesca, who is my main beta reader, and my daughter Gina and grandson Michael, both of whom will be advising me going forward with marketing the book, make it impossible for me to refer to *What are the Chances?* as *my* book, but instead as *our* book. As it was in the world of theater, so it is in the world of writing and publishing: we Scarpas are a team! No matter what level of success our book ends up having, as we did in our work in theater, we have paid a tremendous amount of attention to detail, and we never had a "good enough" attitude.

Since an important component of the novel is about airplanes and flying, my good friend (and licensed pilot) Mike O'Mara was an invaluable help to me. Over many breakfasts and through numerous emails, text messages, and phone calls, Mike advised me on all things aeronautical, even assisting me in creating an important plot twist in the book. In fact, so helpful was Mike that I named a character after him!

The main means of transportation across the country for a soldier during World War II were trains, and I am fortunate to have a friend and supporter, Steve Gould, who is extremely knowledgeable about the history of train transportation and who is also a veteran of the United States Army. Many thanks to Steve for his valuable input on these subjects.

A million thanks to our team of beta readers, who volunteered to read the manuscript of *What are the Chances?* and to give their feedback. Linda Welch, Sharon Lauretti, Sandy Morrill, Mike O'Mara, and Nick Picknally–each of you gave us valuable feedback, resulting in important edits which improved our manuscript tremendously. Thank you!

I am grateful to have found a talented cover designer in Mario Lampic from Belgrade, Serbia. As one of our beta readers recently remarked upon seeing our cover reveal, "The cover design captures the essence of the story told between the covers." So true! Mario was responsive, creative, and professional in designing our cover, and I hope to work with him again and again.

Finally, many thanks to other friends and supporters who contributed to the authenticity of our story: Ellen Rollinson Kolesk (librarian/archivist for the Shelton Historical Society), Christian Cardozo, Irina Medved, Sarah Bellantoni, and Carolyn Ivanoff.

To contact **Gary Scarpa** *for speaking engagements on podcasts, at book clubs, and more, please email inquiries to ScarpaAuthor@gmail.com*

For information on upcoming books by Gary, visit his website: garyscarpa.com and follow him on social media:

Facebook: @ScarpaAuthor
Instagram: @garyscarpa

Made in United States
North Haven, CT
21 September 2023